Uttarmarga

Pratibha Ray is an author from Odisha, reputed for her short stories and novels. She holds a Ph.D. in educational psychology and has taught in reputed government colleges. She also served as a member of the Public Service Commission, Odisha. A recipient of the Jnanpith Award and several other literary recognitions, she has also been honoured with Padma Shri and Padma Bhushan by the Government of India for her contribution to literature and education. Nearly all her books have been translated into multiple languages.

Kanak Hota holds a Ph.D. in English literature and taught extensively in colleges of Odisha before migrating to the USA. She is currently a full-time writer and researcher. Hota writes in both English and Odia and has staged numerous plays on the immigrant experience and the identity issue. She also writes poems in English.

Uttarmarga
Where Freedom Reigns

Pratibha Ray
Translated by Kanak Hota

Published by
Rupa Publications India Pvt. Ltd 2025
7/16, Ansari Road, Daryaganj
New Delhi 110002

Sales centres:
Bengaluru Chennai
Hyderabad Jaipur Kathmandu
Kolkata Mumbai Prayagraj

Copyright © Pratibha Ray 2025
Translation copyright © Kanak Hota 2025
Originally written and published in Odia in 1988

This is a work of fiction. All situations, incidents, dialogue and characters, with the exception of some well-known historical and public figures mentioned in this novel, are products of the author's imagination and are not to be construed as real. They are not intended to depict actual events or people or to change the entirely fictional nature of the work. In all other respects, any resemblance to persons living or dead is entirely coincidental.

All rights reserved.
No part of this publication may be reproduced, transmitted or stored in a retrieval system, in any form or by any means, electronic, mechanical, photocopying, recording or otherwise, without the prior permission of the publisher.

P-ISBN: 978-93-6156-427-7
E-ISBN: 978-93-6156-286-0

First impression 2025

10 9 8 7 6 5 4 3 2 1

The moral right of the author has been asserted.

Printed in India

This book is sold subject to the condition that it shall not, by way of trade or otherwise, be lent, resold, hired out or otherwise circulated, without the publisher's prior consent, in any form of binding or cover other than that in which it is published.

Translator's Note

During the pandemic, I finished translating Dr Pratibha Ray's well-known historical novel *Uttarmarga* (1988) from Odia to English, and named it *Where Freedom Reigns*. Uttarmarga, as postulated in the Upanishads, is the lighted path of eternal freedom towards nirvana, which the soul takes after its release from the unspeakable misery of hell. The concept is akin to the soul's journey through hell and purgatory and its final arrival in Dante's *Divine Comedy*.

Ray has used *Uttarmarga* as a secular metaphor that stands for India's struggle for freedom from British colonialism, and also the perils of upholding democracy when people do not realize the sacrosanct nature of political freedom.

It is the story of India's freedom movement as it unfolds in a cluster of villages in the Balikuda (formerly Baligada) area of Odisha (formerly Orissa), where Ray grew up in the formative years of her life. Following Gandhi's call, the people at the grassroots there have sustained the freedom movement with absolute dedication and faith. The hope of freedom paints delusions of grandeur for the poor. They believe that a free India would bring respite from oppression, hunger and inequality, but are soon disillusioned, as the end of colonial rule and the oppressive zamindari system hardly changes anything in their lives.

The novel's timeline stretches a few decades into postcolonial India. It shows the lingering effects of the old and corrupt behemoth as the nascent democratic nation strives to navigate the modern world. Should Ray's protagonist Diganta Keshari take arms against what is wrong and fight for justice for the common man? This is the question raised in *Where Freedom Reigns*. The prophetic reiteration that 'eternal vigilance is the price of liberty' makes this historical novel with a political overtone a timely read. It holds the mirror to the perils to individual freedom when democracy is under threat in many parts of the world. Like Gandhi, Ray believes that India's soul resides in her villages, and real change would not happen if the villages are not salvaged from the shackles of poverty, exploitation and ignorance. She belongs to the league of prominent Odia writers like Gopinath Mohanty and Sachidananda Routray, and like them, is a spokesperson for the voiceless and disenfranchised.

Most of Pratibha Ray's books in Odia have already been translated into English and many other languages. She is best known to me for her 1984 magnum opus *Yagnaseni: The Story of Draupadi*, which brought her to national prominence as an Odia novelist. Draupadi's tender but poignant voice in the missive she writes to Sri Krishna is permanently etched in my memory. She remains the universal symbol of a woman's quest for identity and opposition to the binds that patriarchy imposes on her. I love her incisive reinterpretation of the mystique of love and transgression in her 1998 book *Mahamoha* (*Ahalya: A Woman's Eternal Quest for Love*). Both books examine the place of women in the epics Mahabharata and Ramayana. In her 1983 book *Silapadma* (*The Citadel of Love*), Ray delves into the minds of the artists and sculptors who sacrificed their personal lives, family, love and freedom, to build the magnificent Sun Temple of Konark.

Uttarmarga marks a watershed moment in Ray's oeuvre. Its novelty attracted me to translate the book into English. In this book, she does not look into the mythical past but walks the reader through the birth of a nation on 15 August 1947 and beyond. She seamlessly mingles autobiographical elements and historical facts such as marches, meetings, promulgations and agreements during the freedom struggle and the Second World War with her fictional narrative. The ideal schoolteacher Parshurama Das, who galvanizes the freedom movement in the villages, is drawn after her father with the same name. Rama Devi, a freedom fighter from Odisha, leads the Salt March in real time and talks to Ray's fictional characters like Sama Puhana and Sebati. These hypertexts, thus, provide new contexts for the reader to understand the time and events that her book depicts.

I would love to place this novel with her 1993 book *Adibhumi* (*The Primal Land*) and 2004 book *Magnamati* (*After the Deluge*), and state that the realities depicted in these three novels are historical and not removed in time to a far-off point. *The Primal Land* is a story based on the lives of the Bonda people, one of the oldest human communities living in Koraput, Odisha. *After the Deluge* talks about the resilience of the fishing community who clung to the soil in the aftermath of the devastating cyclone of Odisha in 1999. It is a story of the triumph of the human spirit over harsh, unforgiving Nature. Regeneration and continuity of life are the predominant messages of these three books. The sublime humanism of man in the face of unparalleled cruelty makes *Where Freedom Reigns* a great novel, and that made a massive impression on me.

The novel emerged in eighteenth-century English literature

as a form depicting day-to-day life in prose. But storytelling is as old as humanity. Ray has modified the techniques of fiction writing; I call her a *kathakar*, a storyteller in the oral tradition of Odisha. As the narrator, she invites the audience to sit and listen—she digresses, pauses, introduces new threads, binds everything together, and moves ahead with the story. Characters thickly populate her world, the reader gradually finds their interrelationship and relevance to the plot. She challenges Eurocentric narratology and positions indigenous storytelling as a valid alternative. Her craft is eclectic, combining the timelessness of the folktale with psychoanalysis, intertextuality, hypertexts, and subversive parody. The prose shifts from the visceral to the poetic, as it paints an array of human moods. Impassioned and reflective, Pratibha Ray writes here with a profound sense of history and time. The formal ingenuity fascinated me! Hope the reader too is delighted to read her book.

I talked to Ray extensively during the translation of *Where Freedom Reigns*, and tried to understand her extraordinary mind and scholarship. As a native speaker of Odia, it was not hard for me to grasp the soul of the text, but there were moments when I was not sure if I had captured the essence of her thoughts and ideas in English. I was careful that the beauty of the original Odia text was not lost in translation. Language and literature are culture-specific; phrases and idioms might lose their grandeur while rendering them in another language. *Uttarmarga*—replete with puns, allusions and similes—is an excellent reservoir of the rich Odia language. I have tried to hold on to their meanings in English. Often, the reader, critic and translator in me disagreed and debated until I was satisfied with what I wrote.

Novels written in the regional languages of India have not received the critical attention they deserve. I hope the translation of more and more of the 'bhasa' literature into English—the most used lingua franca of the world—will bring them the attention they deserve. It is time to familiarize unaccustomed readers with our stories.

I left Odisha almost 25 years ago, but this translation invited me to revisit the great literature produced in Odia and other Indian languages. The journey was a humbling experience. I'm grateful to Pratibha Ray for giving me the opportunity to translate *Uttarmarga*. It was a wonderful experience working with Dibakar Ghosh of Rupa Publications. I'm thankful to him for accepting my work for publication.

Chapter I

'If killed at all in the battle,
Heaven is your abode!
The winner you be, the empire is yours.
O Kounteya! War is in the offing.
So, rise and be ready for the inevitable!'

These grandiose lines from the Bhagavad Gita, inspiring man to fight for a just cause, flashed through young Acharya Digdarshi's mind on a middling, sleepy night. He felt a tremor within. Sri Krishna kept two choices before a flagging, indecisive Arjuna for joining the inexorable war: if he took up arms against the opponent Kauravas and was killed in the great battle, he would be salvaged as a warrior in heaven; if he won, he would be the absolute ruler of the earth.

Could Digdarshi win the hearts of the poor, illiterate peasants by telling the story of Arjuna? Could he inspire them to rise against the oppressive zamindar and join the freedom movement? He didn't want to speak from the pedestal of the elite to the masses who didn't differentiate between just and unjust causes, hope to ascend to heaven after death, or dream that the gate of an empire would open for them after winning an epic battle. Stuck at the grassroots for generations, mundane struggles crushed them, and they never made a leap of faith. Digdarshi mused that such a banal life impervious to challenges was as good as a lifeless doll. But he believed that the latent spark to rise pulsates in a few and waits for someone to harness that energy.

We can call the freedom movement the elusive spark that nudged its head everywhere, and its impact was like the ripples of a simmering treble. Digdarshi's advent at that moment in that nondescript village in Cuttack district was a godsend. He was ordained to replicate the effectual role of Mahatma Gandhi in the lives of countless rural folks who were repressed and exploited for generations by the zamindars and their intermediaries. He united with people magically; he denied identifying his caste, sect and faith, or remembering the names of his natal place and parents. He blended seamlessly with the commoners and announced that he was one among them, and not an outsider oblivious to their lives. Except Zamindar Graharaj Chaudhury, everyone—young, old, men, women and children—shared a deep sense of belongingness to him. Digdarshi aimed to write history anew and rejected conformity to old biases and practices.

Graharaj Chaudhury was a dreaded monster for the toiling landless poor, not just of that ramshackle village but also in the adjoining cluster of some ten or more. The saying is that the advent of a mighty king forced even an expectant cow to cower in fear. Graharaj's insufferable regime bade a more chilling comparison. People said that if he stared at a lump of rushing cloud, it drained out in fear; if he roved his eyes at the dark sky, lightning hid behind clouds, and thunder crashed and fused in panic.

It's better if we don't give out the name of his village. Let it be anonymous. As you know, Graharaj's grandchildren, great-grandchildren and close relatives are still around; for that matter, they are living in this state, in this town. Gone are those days of glory, but remnants of that time aren't erased from their minds. The people carrying his bloodline know that the country is free from British colonial rule but are nostalgic about that glorious bygone era.

Livid and rude, the zamindar was an enemy of the people and the freedom movement. He stood with the infamous British and was an inseparable part of that machine. He epitomized the idea of a narrow self-serving zamindar who was focused on perpetrating his rule and ensuring that his children retained the legacy after him. He never wished to hear about freedom in his fiefdom.

In contrast, the saintly and irreproachable Digdarshi won the hearts of millions. The wandering mendicant was neither the zamindar's subject nor his subordinate to oblige him. He roamed the length and breadth of the country, from Kashmir to Kanyakumari, and the revolutionary waged war against the status quo—the British Raj and its overlaid system. A devout follower of Mahatma Gandhi's non-violent movement, he was a foot soldier in the freedom struggle. He sang the ode to freedom using the lines from the Gita and speeches of Gandhi, Vivekananda and Sri Aravinda. He believed that because of years of subjugation, the people had lost their sense of self and were resigned to fate; their will to oppose was paralyzed. The listeners were unsure if he was a saint, a soldier, a devout believer, or a passionate patriot. He beamed as he reiterated his philosophy that God and the motherland were one, and that one couldn't simultaneously be an atheist and a patriot. He simplified that God created all lives, and the motherland sustained all in her lap. According to him, if someone equated the motherland with the Almighty, he was the greatest patriot.

While narrating the tales of Rama, Krishna, the battles between Rama and Ravana, and the Kauravas and the Pandavas, Digdarshi stealthily introduced modern reformists and revolutionary thinkers like Aravinda, Vivekananda, Gandhi, Sister Nivedita, Raja Ram Mohan Roy and Lokamanya Tilak into the orbit of his narration. He yoked myth and reality and charmed the masses. Gradually, awareness seeped into dormant minds, and hope and courage suffused their consciousness. Two magical words—revolution and freedom—resonated with their thought, and they cried out against the prevailing system.

The zamindar got regular information on Digdarshi's activities in the village. He certainly didn't welcome someone who ruffled the minds of the timid and voiceless with ideas of change. He seethed in anger but couldn't get hold of the elusive enemy. When his moles informed, and the police reached the meeting to arrest Digdarshi, the scene resembled a religious gathering, and the young, handsome *sanyasi*—his head covered with a huge pile of tangled hair—was seen passionately explaining the intricate lines from the Gita to his audience. Even the police got carried away by his discourse on Karma Yoga.

Digdarshi would abruptly stop every activity and set out on an undisclosed mission when he sensed any danger. The villagers were dependable. Graharaj pounced upon them like a vengeful mad dog for information and banned the people from taking the name 'Digdarshi'—the vagrant revolutionary.

The folks loved the way Digdarshi simplified the story of human civilization. For example, he would say that freedom is a middle path—a concession between slavery and monarchy. Man is born free like the sky and wind; man reigned supreme in the hierarchy of God's creation, and because of his intelligence, he devised the social system and made rules to bring order, but he became a poor slave instead to the rules he created. He also said that man initially lived in the wilderness, then learned farming and living in settlements. Gradually he amassed more, leading to greed, competition, intrusion and violent conflicts. Not God but man created labels like haves and have-nots; might became a right, and wealth determined the position of a master and a labourer.

The *acharya* said that trade and commerce gained the upper hand in the second phase of civilization; man sailed to the farthest corners and made enormous profits from trade. He said that hunger for wealth brought the Mughals, Portuguese and many others to the country, and the English were the last to reach the Indian shores. But by force and treason, those skilled traders built their empire, and plundered and subjugated the people. The country came under the regime of a bunch of shrewd merchants who didn't hesitate to enslave the natives on their soil through brutal force and calculated maneuvering. The consequence of the surrender was layered for the people—the common man lost his voice for survival, some became slaves to their petty ambitions and twisted misgivings.

Digdarshi denounced slavery—the absolute control of one man over other human beings—as the most abominable practice. In the case of India, the outside force repressed the people, took away their right to freedom, and killed their will to protest. The local rulers who worked for the occupiers changed dramatically. The title 'zamindar' morphed them into hardened perpetrators of misery over their people. Long story short, the zamindari system was the offshoot of colonial British rule. History thus simplified wasn't hard for the people to follow.

∞

Zamindar Graharaj Chaudhury's clan was well known for five generations in that area. Their title changed from Khandapati to Chaudhury a few generations ago, but Graharaj didn't care much about genealogy. He knew that the British created the zamindari system under special circumstances. As a worthy heir, he must retain the title and be obliged to the British to continue in that position. He used his power imprecisely, continued the saga of senseless exploitation, and used repression as a necessary instrument of control. One can turn a few pages of history to know that during the Mughal era, people with titles like Chaudhury and Kanungo were given ownership over vast tracts of land. During the Maratha rule, the village heads got ownership over the land surrounding their villages and were known as zamindars. Since then, Graharaj's forefathers were anointed with the prestigious zamindar title; they didn't rise from the rank and file.

When Odisha came under British rule, they went for a permanent settlement with those long-time zamindars who had good credentials since the Mughal times. There were twenty-four such zamindars in the state, and Graharaj was one of them. Zamindars led a decadent life, never collected taxes directly from the people and sublet the tax-collection task to the village head or some petty middlemen. The village washermen, barbers or the priestly class acted as middlemen. As authority changed many hands, those go-betweens did an unimaginable disservice to the masses. It was a vicious cycle; each layer of power tried to maximize benefit, and the victims didn't dare to raise their voices against them or resist unjust exploitation.

On top of this, the British took away the roles of the police and law and justice from the native zamindars. The collectors and the magistrates were Englishmen, completely disconnected from the soil, and the court they established was a sleazy behemoth. Instead of granting a voice to the voiceless, it choked their urge to speak and protest. Justice became a far cry.

Human beings, we can say, are like dormant volcanoes. Violence, anger, jealousy, hatred, greed and lust sit inside them like lumps of brewing lava in a dark pit. People are conditioned to hide those darker emotions behind the mask of conscience and morality. But at times the volcano becomes uncontrollably active, and the vices flare up like hot molten lava and consume not just their lives but also the lives of the people around them. Graharaj Chaudhury was a volcano spewing hot molten lava all his life. His anger never dissipated; his persona seemed to frighten even the sun, moon and stars, and sent out huge shock waves like an irate earthquake. The haughty aristocrat felt that the entitlement came to him owing to his immaculate track record, merit and efficiency, and not as a token of pittance from Mr Bawdy sahib in Calcutta. Pride in legacy inflated his ego. Everything combined to create his vignette and reinforce his irreverent attitude and machismo. He was quite edgy over the presence of the illegitimate children his father begot with other women. He banished those stepsiblings—the assumed claimants to his vast inheritance—especially the bastard males from his fiefdom. All the illegitimate females were systematically cleansed through merciless poisoning. He didn't oppose his father's debauchery, or carry any grudge against his mistresses.

He was proud of his pure breeding and wanted to remain the master of what he surveyed.

Zamindari meant collecting revenue through taxation over a vast tract of land belonging to different people. The collection from taxation was hefty; it might even be in lakhs. Some said that Graharaj yearly collected over three lakh rupees from his people. Blessed was he with everything, proverbially speaking—wealth, women, children, land and livestock. On top of that, he owned three hundred acres of fertile land in his name. His family had been amassing wealth for generations, and he grudgingly sat over the fortune.

Graharaj went to college for some years in Calcutta. He knew that without an English education, he wouldn't be able to have a better relationship with his masters. The bottom line in those days was, 'You better speak the King's language or get kicked out of the frame.' He never wanted communication to get lost in translation with the people at the helm, nor did he want a crook like Mahapatra to spoil the delicate relationship by acting as a go-between for him and the masters. He often hosted parties honouring the visiting British officials where feasting was followed by songs, dances and other amusements. This was a rare honour that very few zamindars of that area enjoyed.

The sun never set on the British Empire. It was a huge distinction that those men accepted the invitation of a mofussil zamindar like Chaudhury and shook hands with warm gestures like 'glad to meet you', which was unprecedented. He also knew how to slump in submission before them if there were lapses in his hospitality. He quickly said 'sorry, excuse me, please!' He hunted, enjoyed drinks and played chess with the sahibs.

We can say he was not just a sahib in the making but almost one. His dress and etiquette never betrayed those signs. He wasn't comfortable talking to dumb, stinking, poor peasants who neither spoke nor wrote in English. His intermediaries were his eyes, ears, nose, feet and hands to manage every transaction with the people. Those notorious bootlickers made the lives of the commoners miserable.

The white masters who shared the revenue and maintained law and order in Graharaj's area demanded special care. Those were tough creatures. Graharaj submitted to their whims and often went out of his way to please them. He agreed that the master was never wrong. But the more submissive he posed before the authorities, the more aggressive he became towards his own people. After each visit of the white officials, his anger spewed, and the rage swept people off their feet like dead leaves in a bellowing storm. His conduct was promptly emulated by those who worked for him, and the unsuspecting poor at the lowest rung became soft targets for those fawning yes-men.

People's bottled-up emotions might erupt in some awkward moments. In one such bizarre instance during a celebration at his place, Graharaj's typical sardonic humour flared up from nowhere. He ordered his official Prapancha Mohanty to cross-dress in a sari and dance in front of guests that included women and children of the palace. Mohanty promptly wrapped a sari and danced with all the titillating gestures of a eunuch. Mohanty's wife in the audience watched the lurid show in shock and couldn't handle the shame. Coming back home, she ended her life. After the mishap, however, the mulish zamindar loved and cared for Mohanty more and threw a great party when Mohanty married for the second time.

The palace where the zamindar lived wasn't huge per se. Still, it was a lone two-storeyed building, and being the only grand building in the area, when lights simmered on the upper floor of the house, the poor gaped at its look and imagined the grandeur of heaven. There were exactly five other regular concrete homes in that cluster of villages, and those belonged to some officials like the *Karan* and *Makadam*. Graharaj had renovated his ancestral home and added some Western architectural modifications. People had heard that he used Italian marble in his bath and toilet but couldn't understand what Italian or marble could be. Their heads reeled as they gazed at the huge outer spiralling staircase that rose like a curling bug and touched the rooftop. They failed to imagine how his people manoeuvred those magical steps daily and thought that since the zamindar's people ate all good stuff like milk and butter, they were strong enough to scuttle easily.

The interior of the palace was tastefully decorated. Select exquisite paintings adorned the walls. Artists worked for months to create the feel and mood of each room. The maids gossiped that his bedroom had the most evocative images of men and women in love; their vivid details of lovemaking in the portraits embarrassed the listener. His family used a beautiful staircase covered in shiny velvet carpet leading to the upper floor, and a regular one was for the use of the servants. Huge oil paintings of his forefathers adorned the drawing room. The trailing glory of five generations was kept alive in the adjacent room displaying family heirlooms, mementos and memorabilia gathered from visits to different places. A sprawling open yard on the ground floor and, beyond that, a high boundary wall surrounded the palace. Four water foyers stood on four corners of the lush green lawn, and beneath the cascading fountains of those foyers, four lusty but graceful maidens in marble chiselled by Italian artists frolicked dreamily. Viewers couldn't avert their eyes off the young sensuous bodies that looked so real, but no one dared to linger over them for fear of the zamindar.

∞

Invisible winds of change were pushing through unsuspecting corners, and India was on the cusp of a massive revolution. It was a complicated time in history. While people were galvanized to fight for freedom from the British, the so-called zamindars—the feudal lords—didn't feel the pulse of the moment; there was a huge disconnect. They were unaware of the mood of the masses and were not ready for that tectonic shift in the system.

Misogyny was deeply entrenched in the feudal system. Despite being married, most zamindars for generations, including the ones in Graharaj's clan, were used to having *dasi*s. A dasi was a fuzzy mix of a handmaid, slave, mistress and concubine. Dasi is a complex tag; she is a woman sans her will, sense of self, voice, identity and rights. She served the master and his family unconditionally. Being the other woman, she bore the brunt of predatorial sexual abuse of the master, and the shame and burden of rearing the children he fathered without social approval. Her children were bastards who didn't carry the father's last name. A male child neither carried forward his father's lineage, nor was he an heir to his property; he was known as *golam, poili pua* or *antara karana*. The golams were casteless, like sticky catfish without scales. It was a popular insult hurled at them in playgrounds. Like the shadow of the zamindar's huge palace, the golams were a shadowy extension of the upper-caste people of power and privilege—the zamindars, nobles and their officials—in every area.

Zamindars threw a little money, a small patch of land, or a modest home as gestures of kindness at the dasis. Everyone knew who the fathers of those children were, but didn't speak out; their mother knew they had nothing to their names except stigma and scorn. The children born of the unfair relationship grew like a parallel tangle of noxious creepers from the gutter, and continued to thrive despite the scuff and derision of society. Like the shadow of a banyan tree, the zamindars had their shadowy lineage in society. The shameful arrangement was tacit. Call it an abuse of power or a privilege sanctioned to them, no one opposed the practice.

A hoard of such maids served in Graharaj's palace, but none of the women in the quarter were worthy of being his mistress. Besides, he never wanted to look cheap and vulgar before his wife, children and the people he ruled. He married to perpetuate his clan, and the wife—the sole female in his life—had no distinct self or identity; her worth and honour were related to her capacity to deliver a male child. Birthing a son gave her the right to speak up to the husband. For him, she was just a beautiful body, an instrument of pleasure with a womb for childbearing. Thoughts and feelings were not ascribed to her. Also, his relationship with his wife lacked romance and tender care. He viewed romantic longing as the staple of imagination. Graharaj had adopted the teachings of saints and scholars like Manu, Parasara, Moses, St Paul, sage Shankaracharya and St Augustin, who had studied the enigma called woman. He agreed with the Bible that woman is the root of evil and followed St Augustin's warning that man should be careful of an 'Eve' hiding in every woman. He guarded himself against the temptation of the flesh and, like Shankaracharya, declared that woman was the doorway to hell.

It was commonly understood that a woman was but a commodity in man's possession. Figuratively called a gem—valuable and rare—finding a desirable woman wasn't hard. A man of means could easily find a beautiful woman anytime he needed. Graharaj could have found a number of wives, but he understood that only one wife was needed to continue his bloodline, and more wives meant more children, leading to the mincing of wealth and resources.

Dear reader, why should someone be burdened with so many wives? When bored with the one at home, he could go out and enjoy the companionship of a beautiful woman. Isn't that right?

Graharaj inherited his deep-seated convictions about women from his forefathers. But while it was normative for those men to have multiple dasis, he had none of that baggage; all the dasis in his palace were old and ugly. His official, Prapancha Mohanty, complained that one might get a severe headache by continuously looking at those ugly and crumpled faces in the palace. Other zamindars with dasis were constantly reminded of their transgressions. The wives harped on their excessive involvement with women and neglect of family and fortune; they made them guilty and timid, and bought their loyalty. He had seen the machismo of his father and grandfather pale into insignificance before their wives as the women harped on their adultery and the other women and children in their lives.

That didn't mean that Graharaj was a devout husband. He had secret relationships and sought pleasure in brothels in distant cities without anyone's knowledge. His poor wife was too young to judge him or understand his emotions. She found nothing objectionable in his dealings with her but wondered what made him so stern and detached. She felt inferior and inadequate and bore his indifference. Some said that she wasn't from pure nobility and carried dasi blood from her mother's side. Luckily, none of his wives ever had to endure Graharaj's abuse for long. Something might have been wrong with the position of the planets in his horoscope that three of his wives passed away one after another in two–three years. It took him a while to find a suitable fourth wife. By his fourth marriage, he was thirty-eight; his only son from his first wife was eighteen, and the new bride was seventeen.

His fourth bride was the daughter of Garbaganjan Dakhinray, another well-known zamindar of the area, but someone who didn't exactly match Graharaj's status. Dakhinray's forefathers reportedly carried lamps over their heads for British officials and received some land as succour. Dakhinray fought hard to fight that rumour. He ordered his bruisers to slam the heavy brass doors at the entrance to his palace several times in the dead of the night to announce his presence to the people near and far, and especially to haughty Graharaj who looked down upon him. Four pairs of heavily built musclemen used to pull forward the huge brass doors to close them at night.

No veneer ever covered up Dakhinray's character. He was fond of women; they were all over the palace—his wife, mistresses, dasis and their daughters. It was no secret that Dakhinray, the patriarch, was the saviour of beautiful girls, young brides and widows. Like some kings, he thought that beautiful women belonged to the palace. His wife didn't take offence to his sensual exploits. She argued that if not the kings and zamindars, who else would have lovers and mistresses? She was fine as long as her husband came home and didn't end up in a brothel or stayed back in big cities like Calcutta and Cuttack. In her view, those escapades were not just a waste of money on women, but his long absence from the headquarters also adversely affected the zamindari.

A wife made a home, preserved her husband's fortune, and reared the children he fathered. Dakhinray's wife was so saddled with her chores and responsibilities that she didn't have even a few moments to spare for him; she had no worries if the maids and mistresses kept him happy and homebound. She had a great life; her only job had been to get pregnant and birth children, and then leave them to the care of the maids. Zamindar households often hired wet nurses from good families to breastfeed their newborns.

One such beautiful wet nurse was Sadhabi who belonged to a poor upper-caste family. She came to nurse Dakhinray's newborn infant when she was the mother of a four-month-old baby boy. The zamindar was so impressed with her looks that she was held up in the palace, first as a dasi, and then as a mistress for the rest of her life. Sadhabi's husband remarried. The poor boy she left behind was abused by the stepmother. He was not welcome at home and hence often roamed around.

Sadhabi gave birth to her daughter Chakori there; her baby boy was killed. Sadhabi sometimes secretly offered food to that poor boy she left behind, and repeatedly reminded Chakori to care for her brother after her death.

The girl never understood how one of her brothers could be so poor. She had seen the 'other father' working as a free labourer in Dakhinray's palace and Sadhabi secretly offering him food with tearful eyes, talking to him in whispers. Chakori heard the man often reassuring her mother that she shouldn't regret being owned by the zamindar; he seemed happy that the zamindar had saved his family from hunger and misery, and didn't mind someone keeping her forcefully for pleasure. But there were times when he choked after talking to his wife. Chakori nagged Sadhabi to know about her relationship with that man, but Sadhabi carefully hid her feelings. Her voice would change and become firm, and she would make her daughter understand that the zamindar was solely in charge of everyone's lives; he was the only father, and he fed and saved all lives.

Sense caught up fast with Chakori. The ten-year-old understood that her mother, Sadhabi, was a dasi and would remain a dasi for the rest of her life, and she being her daughter, would be a dasi too and be stuck in the palace. She started as a handmaid attending to Dakhinray's daughter Devaki, was fed well, dressed well, and remained at her beck and call. Chakori was five years junior to her and virtually shadowed her everywhere, including when the teacher came home to teach her reading-writing or when the music teacher came to train her. Chakori learned reading, writing and singing. She practically did the reading of the epics and scriptures for Devaki while the latter went to deep sleep in her soft bed.

Devaki often wished that after marriage, Chakori should run her household with the same efficiency with which Sadhabi helped her mother run the show in the palace. Sadhabi was the most sensible person in Dakhinray's household. She raised all the kids Devaki's mother gave birth to and managed her father well—weathered his rage, brutal bouts of violence and drunken brawls quietly. Devaki felt that without Sadhabi, her mother would've failed to manage her father and might've ended her life. Her father's first wife committed suicide. Sadhabi was the sacrificial goat but was forbearing and stoical. Devaki's mother often said that Sadhabi was a sorceress; she knew black magic and enchanted the zamindar. Whatever might be the blame, she could hold the family together peacefully, so it didn't bother the daughter at all.

Every woman under the sun needs a tiny private place to unburden her feelings and cry to her heart's content. Sadhabi was caught in such awkward moments of grief, and strangely, Devaki's mother, too, was seen sobbing uncontrollably on some days while rocking alone leisurely in her swing. The rest of the dasis in the palace were somehow pretty and witty, but none was as devout as Sadhabi. Loyalty kept her close to Dakhinray; the rest of the women had secret affairs with other men in the palace. The zamindar used to punish the transgressors brutally if they were caught.

Despite her devotion to the zamindar, Sadhabi, in a secret corner of her heart, cherished tender feelings for her first husband though they weren't a couple anymore. At times, Sadhabi handed out some money to him secretly, saying, 'Don't touch me. I'm a sinner.' While feeding the poor and homeless, she would feed enough to her son and wipe off large tears from her eyes. Some days, she would sneak out through the back door and grab her son and cry, and if some notorious maids informed Dakhinray, he beat her mercilessly.

Growing up, Chakori found the palace unsafe; the employees threw hungry, obscene glances and made her uneasy with sexual advances. She wanted to run away but didn't know where she should go. Her mother considered giving her away in marriage to a golam's son, provided he was good enough to care for her daughter. Sadhabi also dreaded that her beautiful daughter might be a mistress or a wet nurse like her. She wished for the girl to live a humble, dignified life, but not as a kept woman held eternally against her will in the palace. The zamindar's wife killed her newborn son, and denied Narmada dasi's son's request to marry the girl he loved, which forced him to end his life. Sadhabi realized that fate had pinned dasis to situations of no escape.

Dasis-mistresses-handmaids-concubines weren't a uniform class of women. If she were a spinster or a child widow, she reconciled to the fact that she would be a kept woman for the rest of her life, but the one who was uprooted from her home and husband, and held in the palace against her will like Sadhabi, was eternally torn between two worlds. She lived in comfort but constantly worried for her husband and son who were living in abject poverty. Sadhabi glorified the priorities governing a dasi's life, saying that dasis were born to serve others, and she must be brave and stoic. But she warned her daughter Chakori that life in the palace was sinful and unforgiving. Even the zamindar's wife cried enclosed within its four walls, and though the palace offered trappings of a great life, its walls and beams seemed to weep too. Sadhabi often gave up, saying that life couldn't be charted according to one's wishes; fate was all-powerful, and its dictums couldn't be changed.

After the death of Graharaj's third wife, Prapancha Mohanty found a suitable match for him in Dakhinray's third daughter Devaki. He thought the marriage offered widower Graharaj a pretty wife and would stop Devaki's father from upsetting the son-in-law with the loud slamming of the brass doors at midnight. The two rival families would unite to resist the emergent freedom movement enveloping the area. Mohanty further made Dakhinray understand that it would be an honour for Devaki to be Graharaj's proud 'only' wife as he had no mistresses or whores in his life.

The marriage was negotiated, and Sadhabi was chosen as Devaki's chaperon to see the bride's transition in her new home. Families chose maids judiciously, for they were the ones who had access to the close details of the lives of the people of the two families and could easily taint their reputation via unfounded gossip. Not greedy, mean or irritable, Sadhabi stood out with her neat credentials; Dakhinray's family found that she never spread baseless rumours or craved good food, money or unnecessary male attention. A maid from Graharaj's side came to Dakhinray's palace to understand the bride-to-be's life and prepare the home to accommodate her lifestyle. It was a very interesting time for the maids of each side to meet and nitpick; they determined that Dakhinray's palace was traditional and Graharaj's palace was modern and Anglicized. Graharaj's fury was compared to thunder, Dakhinray's to the burst of a firecracker. Devaki feared living with a man with such a fiery temper and had nightmarish visions of her future. She was told that all three of Graharaj's previous wives died because of the doomed planetary position in his horoscope. Though her horoscope matched very well with the zamindar's, she doubted she would survive long with him.

During the time of her send-off, Devaki fainted several times. As the family lifted her to the palanquin, she grasped Chakori tightly and collapsed again. She cried out Chakori's name as she opened her eyes, and insisted that the girl accompany her. Chakori sobbed and mumbled awkwardly that she couldn't part with her sister. In reality, that smart eleven-year-old wanted to escape. She knew that the palace wouldn't be a safe place for her after Devaki was gone. She dreaded the lewd young officials who came to the palace and stealthily solicited her love. Dakhinray didn't oppose her journey and said that once the bride felt comfortable in her new place, Chakori could return with her mother, Sadhabi. His words sealed the deal. Both the mother and daughter plucked the poles of the palanquin and began the journey.

The palanquin holders stopped and rested from time to time. Sadhabi and Chakori followed them and stopped during the breaks. Chakori had never walked for long hours; she was tired and sought her mother's permission to sit inside the palanquin with Devaki. Sadhabi rolled her eyes in disapproval, saying, 'A dasi is supposed to walk behind the carriage; she can't sit inside with the bride.' Until then, Chakori was used to being called a dasi's daughter, but at that very moment, it etched on her mind that her fate was permanently sealed as a paltry dasi. The realization soaked her being, and she became quiet for the rest of the journey.

Sani or Saturn was hailed as the most handsome of all the planets in the zodiac; hence he was the Graharaj—the king of the planetary system. Sani's namesake—Zamindar Graharaj Chaudhury was no less impressive in his striking masculinity. Tall, fair and robust, he was quite manly. His large, intense eyes, and sharp, perfect nose never betrayed his regal lineage. He was deceptively young; at thirty-eight, he easily passed for a twenty-five-year-old man. Chaudhury took great care of his health and looks.

Devaki seemed happy. 'A zamindar better be stern and authoritative, and that's what the role demands,' was the impression implanted in her mind by her parents. Overnight, she became the woman of the house and a mirror image of her mother. She learned to tolerate Graharaj's behaviour and withstand his brutal rage. She had no choice but to accept the role imposed on her.

A dasi could often sense the wealth and class of a groom by looking at the bed he has consummated with his wife the previous night. The dasi usually picked up gold, silver or cash from the bed saved for her beneath the pillow or under the bed. The groom didn't care to pick up valuables sliding from his pocket during lovemaking. The lesser zamindars cared to pick up, but the generous aristocrats never looked back to recount those spoils. As long as the new bride's accompanying dasi stayed in the groom's place, it was her privilege to collect those gifts while arranging the couple's bed every morning. Sadhabi had joined Dakhinray's two elder daughters and nieces; she remembered being treated well and gifted with clothes, jewellery and other valuables while parting from their places.

Sadhabi entered to make the bed in the morning following the first day of Devaki's marriage and found two gold coins, some twenty-five silver coins strewn all over the bed, and a bunch of notes stuck under the pillow. She also found the groom's paan-holder made from ivory with gold carvings, left there. She surveyed the aristocratic decor of the bedroom with amazement. She went on comparing the wealth of the other two zamindars from Kantapari and Balikuda, where she had gone with the brides. Those grooms, she remembered, threw just a couple of silver coins and behaved as if they had rewarded the maid with a fortune. Sadhabi compared the three sons-in-law of Dakhinray and felt that Graharaj was the richest and could easily pass for a king. She sensed that the competition between Dakhinray and his son-in-law was unwarranted. If Graharaj was the sun, Dakhinray was a mere flickering glow-worm. She kept the gifts she had collected from the bed and went to the zamindar to hand over his precious ivory paan-holder. Graharaj didn't show interest in the object and instead flashed a sparkling gold paan-holder, quipping, 'What's that? I've mine.'

He told her to save the paan-holder as a gift and remember Devaki each time she grabbed a paan from it. Sadhabi was dazzled and couldn't blink for a while. She had seen tastefully carved gold-plated silver paan-holders in Dakhinray's palace, but had never seen such wealth and grandeur in any other zamindar's place before. Graharaj, she felt, was wealthy enough to have five more zamindars to work under him, and thought that one should be lucky to serve in his palace as a maid or be his mistress.

Sadhabi advised her daughter that she shouldn't just be a handmaid to Devaki but should rather learn to address her as *santani*—the esteemed lady of the house. Initially, Chakori was a little awkward calling Devaki 'santani', but Devaki loved it. The title was not just ornamental, it gave her power and honour. Their close bond slowly waned, and in no time, the distance between the lady of the house and a dasi as seen between Dakhinray's wife and Sadhabi, emerged in their case.

Girls are pliable—like air, water or mist. They assume the shape of the container that holds them. So, the maid and the wife adjusted to their respective spaces; Devaki adapted to her husband's whims and Chakori became a compliant handmaid.

Devaki took charge of the entire household, except that of her husband and stepson. Mukti, the old dasi who attended to the zamindar, was no more efficient.

Graharaj treated women as trash and wasn't polite to them. He often flung things at them when upset and smashed many valuable objects in the palace; he didn't spare even his wife. The maids came forward like sacrificial goats and hens to shield Devaki from the brunt of his rage. Devaki had learned from her mother to use a dasi as a barrier to shield herself from the outbursts of an enraged Graharaj. But when he calmed down, she hovered around him like a doting wife. Chakori was the buffer when Graharaj was livid and uncontrollably violent. Sadhabi, too, winked at her daughter to manage the situation.

Chakori was very young; her thinly built stature, soft-brown skin and sharp features were remarkably distinct. Her face was passable, but when watched carefully, the appeal of her helpless, frightened eyes soaked with tender innocence made her more attractive. The charm of her comely fragility seemed effectual to stop even a rushing thunder.

Cruel, arrogant and violent men often find the magic of such beauty irresistible. It is seen that radical innocence always triumphs over arrogant brute force. Chakori had seen her mother standing up to the rage of Dakhinray, so she was hardened to face such violence with toughness. She almost fainted when Graharaj shouted at her but didn't run away. The zamindar hurled things at her arbitrarily, but she showed no signs of panic or fear. The idea that a dasi was just a pawn for the oversights of others had soaked inside and overtaken her mind completely. Thus, there were several instances when the little girl hung like a sheet of cloud over a scorching sun and quickly relieved an edgy scene. The zamindar looked awkward in those moments, and his outburst seemed to wane. He realized that Chakori was the new handmaid who accompanied his wife, and her mother, Sadhabi, was around. During one such heated moment, her innocence and humility deterred the brazen rage of the zamindar; he calmed down, shouting, 'Why are you here?'

Chakori didn't cry; she held back her tears forcefully. Graharaj hated tears, especially in the corners of a woman's eyes, which made him weak. She prodded him not to refuse to take dinner. Her lips shook in fear, but she didn't raise her voice. Through the corner of his eyes, he could see that the eleven-year-old girl still stood there; her forehead might be bleeding, or a wound on her leg might be fresh from a flower vase he flung at her, but she didn't seem to care for the pain. She didn't seem like a young girl of flesh and blood. He calmed down and repeated, 'Never show me your face. Ask Devaki santani to serve me dinner.' Chakori fell at his feet with absolute submissiveness as the storm seemed to pass over the household.

When the whimsical zamindar's mood cooled down, Devaki ambled nonchalantly and gave orders to servants. Chakori couldn't understand the changes in her behaviour. Sadhabi saw Chakori endure some tough times but didn't protect her daughter. She hoped that the zamindar might give away the girl in marriage, or in the worst case, she would end up as his mistress or that of his son.

∞

The zamindar's son, Diganta Keshari, was eighteen. He was at his uncle's place for the winter break from college and didn't attend his father's wedding. His mother died when he was seven, and the impression of her face that he carried was mostly from the oil paintings he saw hanging on the walls. Growing up, he heard she disliked her husband's overbearing nature and, in opposition, refused to take any medicine during her illness and died. The other two of his stepmothers died of complications from childbirth—one couldn't deliver her baby and the other died of heavy bleeding after the delivery.

Diganta Keshari was the only surviving child of his father—the scion of the clan. He was very lonely in that huge palace and kept himself busy with studies in his room. He hardly joined the humdrum in the palace. The noise of people—servants, attendants, officials, friends and relatives coming and going—didn't bother him. He was ambitious, passionate and curious, and was aware of the things happening around him. He was critical of the zamindari system and never accepted the status quo. He had his finger on the pulse of his time, and the two revolutionary ideas—freedom and change—preoccupied the young man's mind. He was very different from the sons of the other zamindars.

Graharaj wanted to send his son to Calcutta to pursue a career in law after completing his studies at Ravenshaw College, Cuttack. He thought of the scores of litigations that the abolition of the zamindari system was likely to bring; therefore, he wanted his son to be a lawyer. He further planned for his son to sail to London and become a barrister. A law degree from London was invaluable during British rule, and even after the country's freedom. Diganta Keshari, too, believed that knowledge of law was extremely important for self-governance and overthrowing the British. He stayed away from the fawning people close to his father—those who tried to impress him as the heir apparent.

He disdained the zamindari system perpetuated through land tax, indentured labour, bribes and gifts. He couldn't accept that a zamindar was entitled to have fruits, flowers, fish, fowl, milk or milking cows—whatever his folks had—for free. Kings used to chop people's heads but the zamindars stifled people's necks with their hands. Graharaj felt that whatever he had amassed in his brief life was for his son's inheritance and his progenies in line of succession. Diganta Keshari never rebuffed his father, but mighty time, sitting with its defiant heart, sniggered hard and discredited the logic behind the zamindar's argument.

Chapter II

In 1920, the Congress Party in its Nagpur session declared the non-cooperation movement as the single mode of opposition to British rule. Soon, Pandit Gopabandhu Das in Orissa explained the movement's basic tenets to the people in a huge meeting on the sands of Kathajodi River in Cuttack, urging the youth to give up their studies and join the freedom struggle. Diganta Keshari attended that meeting and heard that electrifying speech while returning from his uncle's village after the winter holidays. He was moved but still undecided whether to abandon college and join the freedom struggle.

The dilemma was, if he stayed away from the massive surge and chose to side with the likes of his father—the zamindars and rulers loyal to the British, he would align with them to oppose and crush the national movement. He knew that the kings, nawabs and zamindars were the facilitators of the English, and those confidantes held secret meetings in the palace to safeguard their power and position. The freedom movement that swept the nation demanded him to abandon the principles upon which the very zamindari system stood. Longing for freedom wasn't new for the people; the Paika Rebellion—one of Odisha's legendary mass movements—was already led by warrior Baksi Jagabandhu and King Mukunda Deva in the state.

Bagha Jatin's death from gunshots in a bloody encounter with the white police in Chasakhanda village was still fresh in his mind. It was 9 September 1915; twelve-year-old Diganta Keshari had gone to his aunt's home in Balasore during the Dussehra holidays. He went out with his relative Naren to meet some young men at the Emporium—the place for young men to socialize in the evening. The town was under military rule for two months. On that fateful night, the police stormed into the scene from nowhere and cracked down on the youth, ending the meeting abruptly. The police didn't spare innocent Diganta Keshari either; he never forgot the sharp lashes on his back. The Emporium, of course, was the site where anti-British sentiments incubated. The police brutalities sent shock waves, and the budding rebellion against foreign rule died immediately. Most revolutionaries were from zamindar families, and their parents threatened to disown them if they didn't avoid subversive activities.

Diganta Keshari was a brave lion's cub in his heart of hearts. Gopabandhu's speech rekindled the spirit of rebellion in him. He was sure that Graharaj would oppose sternly if he joined the freedom struggle. The chasm in their worldviews was huge. Diganta hardly spoke openly with him; the young man opposed his father through dogged silence. He knew his father was cruel and self-serving. But he appreciated that he wasn't debauched like other zamindars who maintained a hoard of dasis and let their illegitimate children roam around. The young man was compassionate towards women. Though he didn't remember his mother dying from lack of care from his father, he was clearly moved seeing the death of his two stepmothers through his father's criminal negligence. When Diganta Keshari met his third stepmother, Devaki, who was close to his age, he silently prayed for her long life—asking God to bless her to thrive well in her new home with sons and daughters. He knew he wasn't the ideal son his father hoped for; never did he feel entitled to his father's vast fortune which he had amassed wrongfully from others.

※

It was time for Sadhabi now to take leave from Devaki's home. But, to her good luck, before she even asked for the family to keep Chakori as a dasi, Devaki asked her to leave the girl with her and promised to take good care of her. Sadhabi agreed immediately and requested her to see to it that Chakori was well-settled. Sadhabi saw her young daughter blossoming as a beautiful girl and didn't want to risk her safety by taking her back to Dakhinray's palace. Before leaving, she asked Chakori to serve the master and his son well. She knew that stepmother Devaki might neglect the son, who was not demanding and sought no special attention. Sadhabi also requested Chakori to never forget her responsibility towards her half-brother Dukhia, who was poor and neglected all his life. Tears rolled down her eyes silently as she said goodbye to her daughter and left. Chakori stayed back in the zamindar's place as a dasi for good.

Strangely, there are no reasonable explanations for many human actions. For instance, nobody ever saw any obvious signs of jealousy in Devaki towards Chakori. Though their age difference was some six years, both bonded quite well. Chakori obeyed Devaki's orders without hesitation, pressed her legs and made her hair. She did everything to pamper Devaki and never felt insecure like a typical maid. But once her mother left, Chakori felt that her place in the palace was clearly marked, and she worked there as nothing but a maid—needless to say, Graharaj's place was safer than Dakhinray's. Promiscuity and unsolicited sexual advances were unacceptable in Graharaj's palace. Dakhinray, on the other, was a rank womanizer and a man of loose morals; his employees and attendants, too, were louts who treated women as sheer objects of enjoyment.

After her mother left, a sense of emptiness—a feeling of not belonging to the place or having someone dear—gripped Chakori. She never felt abandoned in Dakhinray's palace. She might not have any claim over his wealth or the rights of a legitimate child, but she felt secure that she lived under her father's roof. With her mother gone, the emotional emptiness of an orphan overtook her being. Chakori also felt that Devaki had changed very fast; she became very rude, hateful and intolerant, and the dormant notorious mind of a stepsister slowly began to appear in her. It's not just society that never accepts the children of a dasi with dignity. The children of the zamindars, too, were in denial of their presence. They instinctively sensed that the children of the dasis were the morbid images of their father's unbounded lust, and ignored them disdainfully.

Devaki got pregnant immediately. She would scream at Chakori at the slightest provocation. Chakori felt that the pregnancy might have given Devaki terrible mood swings, but observed that Devaki never lost her temper while talking to others and was vile only while dealing with her. She used Chakori as a tool to bear the brunt of Graharaj's terrible wrath. She got used to Devaki's misdemeanor, but at times it was too much. She sincerely longed to return to her mother but her wishes hardly mattered. She knew for sure that if she ran away against Devaki's wishes, the doors of the palace would be closed for her forever. Still she wished to go and meet her mother at least once and complain that if she knew of the miseries and pitfalls destined for a dasi, how could she put her daughter through that same ordeal? It would have been better if she had strangled Chakori to death at birth.

Graharaj was gentle towards his pregnant wife. He knew that Devaki's father, Dakhinray, was a zamindar of standing. If he neglected his daughter, that would affect their relationship, and he might distance himself in other critical situations. Graharaj wasn't sure of Diganta Keshari's loyalty and sincerely desired a son who would expand the lineage and enjoy his vast fortune. He didn't want his zamindari to go to the dogs.

While Chakori desperately longed to meet her mother, a message came that Sadhabi was removed from Dakhinray's palace for her promiscuous conduct; she lost her mind and roamed the streets begging from door to door till the zamindar's men threw her outside his area for good. Chakori then realized that the last door of reprieve had closed on her face permanently; her fate was sealed and the shackles of enslavement bound her irrevocably. She realized that if she ever tried to cross the threshold of Graharaj's palace, she would meet her mother's fate.

Sadhabi's scandalous conduct and removal from her father's palace made Devaki more ruthless towards Chakori. She found every opportunity to humiliate her with swift, sarcastic reminders of her mother's dubious reputation. Chakori couldn't understand how her mother, at an older age, got into sexual misadventures. She was devoted to Dakhinray and never looked at any other man. The daughter found no answer to the shameful conduct and endured Devaki's caustic comments without protest. A dasi never spoke back to the people who owned her. A few of them retorted, but Chakori wasn't that kind of a dasi. Her mother moulded Chakori to be forbearing and calm.

Once the dust over Sadhabi's tragic end settled, Chakori waited to discover the genuineness of the demeaning narrative surrounding it. She cried in hiding and wished to hear from a reliable source about her mother's demise. As chance would have it, Moti dasi visited from Dakhinray's palace to look after Devaki when she neared her day of delivery. Moti was close to Sadhabi. In Dakhinray's palace, she came after Sadhabi in order of standing. Dasis had their rooms at the farthest corner of the palace. When Chakori met Moti, she held her tight and cried to her heart's content.

Moti gave Chakori the details leading to Sadhabi's death. She said that Sadhabi used to go out at night and return to the palace before daybreak. She would gently touch up her face with turmeric and oil, plant a big vermilion dot on her forehead, and slide a paan into her mouth; then, covering the head with the end of her sari, she would step out carefully through the back gate. Without Sadhabi's gentle foot massage, Dakhinray never had a sound sleep; therefore, she would take care to induce him to sleep and then stealthily go out. She would return hurriedly in the morning to take care of him. The routine went on well for quite some time. Her adventure in the darkness created no stir in the palace, for she never missed meeting Dakhinray at night and invariably stood at his foot in the morning. But this risqué behaviour had a nasty rival in Mukti dasi, who had been vying for Dakhinray's love all her life. She kept an eye on Sadhabi's nightly adventures and informed him of the escapades.

One day, Dakhinray pretended to be asleep as Sadhabi prepared to leave at midnight. Two servants were secretly asked to keep a strict eye over her movement. As soon as she set out, they caught her red-handed. The two strong men with truncheons and kerosene lanterns in hand, followed by a triumphant Mukti, dragged her to Dakhinray.

'Where have you been?' Dakhinray hollered at her impatiently.

'To relieve outside,' Sadhabi said, looking down.

'Faithless bitch! Liar! With make-up and a good sari, you went out to poo? Who do you try to fool? I'm not a foolish hay-cutter,' cried out Dakhinray.

She floundered completely and said nothing. But Mukti pulled out a bundle hidden beneath Sadhabi's arm and declared, 'She didn't just go out to meet her lover! She's stealing stuff from this place. Be aware! She might slash your throat someday and run away.'

Dakhinray pushed her hard to the ground and shouted at the highest pitch, 'Tell me! Who's that secret paramour you have been meeting? Wretched bitch! I'll kill you and smudge my forehead with your blood! Speak up!'

He repeatedly screamed at her to reveal the name. Sadhabi stood like a stone. The zamindar's men slapped her mercilessly. She knew that if the zamindar got the name, he would kill him. The uproar attracted other servants to the scene. Someone took pity on her and said that she might've gone out to meet her husband, who had been sick for quite some time.

'Husband? Whose husband? Which of these women in this palace have a husband? All are dasis! My slaves, concubines! Garbaganjan Dakhinray can have all the women of this land as his dasis! You bitch! Just watch what I will do with your so-called husband tomorrow morning! I'll take care of your scoundrel husband,' Dakhinray screamed.

Sadhabi recoiled and knelt on the ground. She held his feet

tight and stroked her head against them in surrender, saying that the information was wrong; she didn't go to meet her husband. She declared that she wouldn't even go to spit on that sick man's face, and growled to throw up a mouthful of spit on the ground. She said she met an unknown mendicant dressed like a sadhu in a saffron robe under the banyan tree outside the village. He offered her a paan, and she put that into her mouth in good faith. But since then, she has been magically drawn to meet him every night.

The zamindar shouted at the top of his voice, asking his men to get hold of that coward who dared to trespass on his territory. Thirty-five-year-old Sadhabi implored for mercy; her voice trembled like a sacrificial lamb dragged to the altar. Dakhinray pulled back his legs and forsook her at that moment. She was forced out of the palace in the dead of night, and the doors closed behind her.

Leaning against Moti with tearful eyes, Chakori heard the dramatic episode and wasn't sure if her mother was under the spell of black magic. But Moti clarified that whatever Sadhabi told Dakhinray was pure lies. Chakori was more confused; her mouth dried off in disbelief.

'The life of a dasi is a bundle of lies—she survives in a web of lies and pretensions. Your mother was a genuine person. Night after night, she went out to see her sick husband who she wasn't supposed to see. She was out to feed him snacks, cakes, rice and curries stolen from the zamindar's kitchen to help him recover fast. I knew she spent countless nights worrying over that man's sickness,' said Moti.

Chakori was in shock. She couldn't understand why her mother hesitated to tell the truth and made up the story of the mendicant, inviting the unnecessary wrath of Dakhinray. Moti helped her understand that Sadhabi was married to the sick man who she risked seeing at night; she was the mother of his son. Years ago, as a young girl, she took the vow before the sacred fire to stay married to him till death separated them. If she had disclosed his name, the zamindar would have killed him.

Chakori listened to the narrative in shock. Moti reiterated that Sadhabi, the pathetic loser, was tossed between the two men. Banished from the palace, she went to her husband and surrendered at his feet; large drops of warm tears flooded the sick man's feet. He rose in shock with a jerk from his bed. The bones beneath his sagging skin rattled with manly pride.

'What did you just say? You've come back? But why? Who's going to let you in? You're barred from our caste. The zamindar has violated you, you're his kept woman, a dasi, a fallen woman,' he screamed.

He didn't want to be ostracized from the village. Everybody he knew—the washerman, the barber, the priest—would have shunned him. He didn't want to take her back and invite the zamindar's wrath—the latter might drive him out of the village. He asked her sternly to leave his place and dissolve into the darkness before anyone came to know about anything at daybreak.

Sadhabi reminded him of the money she gave him to run his household and feed the five children he fathered. The other woman—his wife—stormed into the scene, screaming. She pulled Sadhabi's hair hard and dragged her out, calling her a shameless bitch. She had no qualms about saying that whatever the zamindar had amassed was the sweat and blood of the people. She asked Sadhabi to get out of her place and jumped at her husband, in readiness to tear his flesh and bones apart.

'A fallen woman brings nothing but misfortune to a home. Mind it, tomorrow the zamindar's people will be here to drag you all for back-breaking free labour in the fields. The whole family would face his angry whips,' she warned sternly.

The man's old parents entered the scene, claiming that for a decent family it was impossible to take back a daughter-in-law who had been the zamindar's mistress for so many years. They questioned Sadhabi, 'Tell us frankly, is there anyone in the village who would let you into their home with open arms?'

The family thus ganged up to drive away Sadhabi. She returned to the zamindar's palace, sat at the back door without food and water for days, and mumbled that she couldn't find the mendicant who charmed her. The zamindar pardoned her and let Sadhabi re-enter the palace. Sadhabi's husband's condition worsened from hunger, and lack of medicine and care from his wife. He died at fifty. Sadhabi banged her head countless times against the wall that day, washed her hair, removed the bangles from her hands, and wiped off the vermilion from her forehead. The widow stood before the zamindar in a simple white sari without any gilding. He was shocked to see her in that avatar and screamed as if he had seen a witch or a ghost. Notorious dasi Mukti came forward, twisting her lips; she declared disdainfully that the peasant Sadhabi was married to was dead, and she was a widow who could not dress up anymore like a married woman.

'There're no widows in my palace. Whoever enters here, must dress up like a wife. She has to wear bangles and a red dot on the forehead. I can't stand this pale lifeless look of a widow.

Take her out of my sight. Give her a full bridal makeup…I shouldn't see this widow again…' shouted Zamindar Dakhinray.

Sadhabi slumped, crying, and pleaded with folded hands, 'Ask me to pick up and eat bugs from shit. I'm ready, but don't ask me to dress up like a married woman!'

Those words of a mere dasi were a clear affront to Dakhinray's pride. He couldn't accept that a lowly dasi would dare to renounce the offers of a zamindar to remain adorned in colourful bangles and vermilion, and prefer to remain the widow of a bonded labourer. He ordered for Sadhabi to be dressed by force, decked with bangles and vermilion in his presence. She resisted hard, biting and scratching people around her with her nails. She wiped the red dot off her forehead and smashed the bangles. She tousled her bun and threw her hair open, looking at everyone like a devious witch. She rolled her eyes and warned that if anybody forced her to wear make-up, she would strangle their necks and drink their blood.

The zamindar began to fear Sadhabi as if she were a man-eating witch. Her ghost-like appearance scared him; he asked for her to be removed from the palace immediately. Thereafter, Sadhabi stood silently in front of the zamindar's palace, spreading her hands for alms. Within days, she looked worn out and haggard like an old woman in her sixties; the beautiful woman turned frighteningly shrunken and ugly in no time. People were scared to death if they accidentally encountered her in the darkness. The zamindar, too, found it a bad omen to begin his day with her sight. Finally, to put the ordeals to rest, his men dragged Sadhabi out and banished her from the zamindar's area. After that day, nobody ever saw her shadow; nobody in the nearby villages knew about her whereabouts. It was rumoured that Sadhabi was murdered. On nights, Dakhinray was mortally scared about seeing a ghost-like chimera of Sadhabi standing before him.

It was not Sadhabi's ghost that frightened the zamindar; rather, it was the sin deep inside his mind that scared him. Chakori vowed that she would scare the zamindar as a ghost after her death, sit on his chest and drink his blood. With this tall, false promise to herself, Chakori tried to get over the bleak episode of her mother's death. Sadhabi was dead, but Chakori, her daughter, must continue to live. Amidst all the meaningless absurdities surrounding life, the urge to stand up against every odd and survive was the most powerful. Chakori was tightly tethered to that urge and decided to continue living in Graharaj's palace.

∽

Chastity and motherhood are understood as the two core principles that define womanhood. Motherhood is an innate instinct. But chastity—faithfulness to the man someone marries—is a discipline, a control largely imposed on the female psyche through social conditioning. The definition of a *sati*—the faithful—changes according to time, people and place. But motherhood is universal. Its meaning stays the same in every culture; it's an eternal truth. If society and situation demand, a woman having relationships with multiple men might also be hailed as a sati and worshipped. But there are instances where a woman completely devout in a monogamous relationship and not even contaminated by the desire for another man physically or in her thoughts is denounced as an adulteress. Our scriptures permitted situational consummation. If a married man couldn't produce an heir to continue his lineage, he often let his wife go to another man; the act was not infidelity. As per this canon, the great sati Kunti gave birth to her five sons and Ambika and Ambalika to Dhritarashtra and Pandu, respectively. Ironically, the joy of womanhood lies in being a mother, not in remaining a sati or eternally faithful to a single man.

Graharaj's wives were extremely devoted to him, but unfortunately, motherhood was cursed there. His first wife died from some obscure illness while she was pregnant with her second child, his second wife died during childbirth, and the third wife ended her life. The palace did not celebrate a newborn's arrival after his first wife's death. So far, the only birthday celebrated in the palace was the birth of Diganta Keshari. The three women who married Graharaj thereafter became mothers to Diganta Keshari. A man can have multiple wives and sisters but has only one mother. As per that rule, those women couldn't be the mother of Diganta Keshari; he didn't entertain that thought. On her death bed, his mother held the hands of the seven-year-old son and gave him a last piece of advice: 'A stepmother is a venomous cobra. Pretty soon, you will have a stepmother here. Remember to stay away from the cobra.'

At that point in his life, Diganta Keshari couldn't make out the meaning of her warning, but he was careful to stay away from all the wives his father brought home. Even the stepmothers did not try to be close to him. He was raised by Suhagi dasi, his grandfather's concubine. Some four months back, when Suhagi passed away, no one was around to attend to Diganta Keshari. He spent hours in his study. Some dasi used to serve him dinner late every night and leave. Nobody was there to prod him to finish the dinner or to serve some additional dishes. He never complained but often felt like not having a bite. Graharaj would be in deep sleep in his chamber. He was pleased that his son studied for long hours every night. Diganta Keshari hardly met his new stepmother; they almost never talked. Late into her pregnancy, Devaki was preoccupied with herself, but once in a while, she asked Chakori to look after the young man so that he would not feel ignored by his stepmother.

Gradually, Devaki handed over every charge of her husband and son to Chakori, eventually allowing herself to take a back seat. It was a good chance for other dasis to avoid attending to the father and son. They asked Chakori to wait on the young master; she sat dozing in the kitchen. She warmed the food when Diganta Keshari finished his studies and came out for supper. She served with great care and waited behind the door until the end. The very first day, he was surprised looking at the hot meal served to him. But when he found hot food served to him continuously for a while, he assumed that the special care came from his stepmother and became quite grateful for her kind gesture.

On one of those days, he wasn't mindful of his dinner and rose without finishing the food from the plate. He suddenly heard a soft female voice behind the doors, imploring him not to leave food and eat a little more, particularly asking him to finish the bowl of *khiri*. It was an unfamiliar voice. He was curious and looked back; he saw at the door the new dasi who accompanied his stepmother from her paternal home. He had seen Chakori and knew that Devaki used her regularly to face his father's rage; the zamindar kicked, slapped and threw blunt objects at her. He was sorry for the young girl and annoyed with the mother who unwittingly left the poor girl in the palace. As he considered asking the mother to take back the girl, someone told him that she had lost her mind and had been missing for a while. He knew what a mother was and the pain of losing her. Nobody knew it better than him that the wealth of a rich father couldn't fill the void in the heart that came from the death of a poor mother. He saw the rest of the servants taking advantage of her situation and piling up more work on her plate, with full knowledge of Devaki, his new stepmother. It was a mess.

The following night, Diganta Keshari ignored Chakori's request to finish his meal; it wasn't typical of the men of his clan to listen to women. On top of that, he wasn't ready to pay attention to whatever that young girl said.

'Who ordered you to wait here for me? Don't attend to me from tomorrow. You can keep the dinner at the study table in my room, and I'll eat when I'm done with my studies,' he took some water and said after a pause.

Chakori was overwhelmed with joy as the younger zamindar addressed her with politeness. Tears came to her eyes. She had been treated with disdain every moment of her life till that moment. For the first time, she realized that there was something—a hidden self—inside her that needed to be treated with dignity. She wanted to fathom 'dignity' and try to make sense of the 'self'. She wondered, 'Is it possible that Sadhabi dasi's daughter is treated courteously like a human?' She had never heard anyone talking to her mother with any regard. She went on foraging the shafts of her inner being but couldn't locate that tiny iota of her 'self' that deserved to be treated with dignity.

The following day, Chakori got ready for work. The young zamindar might've declined any special care, but she wasn't supposed to go by his words. She sought Devaki's advice, who reinforced the idea of special care for the stepson. Chakori talked to other dasis, who asked her to follow Devaki's order and do a good job. It became her sole responsibility thereafter to wait upon Diganta Keshari till his dinner was over. The old dasis gave the novice some useful tips in a cautionary tone. They asked her to learn to cope with the zamindars who easily lost their temper. They advised her to manage every situation, good or bad, and try hard to retain the job.

'You're lucky that the zamindar's wife had taken pity on you and let you stay in this palace. Use her favour to your advantage,' said an old maid.

Chakori was scared of the young zamindar who talked less and never paid attention when she talked. But someone in the group assured her that since she was good at handling the stern old master, she needn't worry about the son, who they reported was very kind towards the poor. The old maid confided that as per the horoscope, the young zamindar wouldn't enjoy life in the palace, wouldn't care for wealth and luxury, and instead chase spiritual knowledge, a prediction that worried his father a lot.

Chakori went to the kitchen and sat leaning against the wall. She couldn't even imagine eating before the master was done. Her stomach churned in hunger but she couldn't go inside and ask the master to wrap up his studies and come for dinner. She waited, hoping to warm up the food and serve Diganta Keshari when he came out from his study. But he didn't come; he looked for his food, locked his bedroom door from the inside, and went to bed. A door separated the bedroom and the study. Chakori waited long for the master, then saw that his door was locked from the inside. Fear and misery gripped her heart. She was very guilty and felt that the young man went to bed hungry because she didn't care to keep his dinner in the study. She worried about the furor that might arise in the morning; the maids in the palace and Devaki might find her irresponsible, and the zamindar would punish her severely for keeping Diganta Keshari hungry.

She stood there like a piece of log and worried about the young man's misery who went to sleep on that long, cold night without food. The chill in the late December wind slowly caressed her, removing all her fears and worries; she couldn't withstand the cold and shivered miserably. She didn't know if tapping on the door and reminding him about dinner would be right. The dilemma undermined her confidence. Her tired legs weren't ready to support her any further; she slumped to the floor, and slowly, her eyes closed. Diganta Keshari was upset that a young girl defied his order and didn't keep the dinner in his study. He wanted to summon her in the morning and warn her to pay attention to his words.

Diganta Keshari was an early riser; the sky wasn't clear when he woke up. He went out routinely and visited areas where the common people lived. He often changed the route, walked through different lanes and by-lanes, and saw the dire condition of the masses. He understood first-hand the extreme neglect and callous exploitation of the zamindar's officials, moneylenders and middlemen. He feared that if people lived in that kind of terrible condition for long, their frustration might explode as a revolt against the zamindar. He sensed that it would be hard to contain their anger once things reached a breaking point. As he opened the door that day, he was stunned by what he witnessed at the threshold; Chakori remained asleep and shivered in the cold. The faint moonlight of the winter night washed her pristine, innocent face. The nascent feelings of tenderness buried beneath his cold heart began to well up. He couldn't understand why she laid down there so precariously.

'Who asked you to keep a vigil at my door? Hey, do you hear me?' he shouted.

Chakori woke up in shock. She covered her head quickly and stood up in attention. 'I'm so sorry, master! You went without food because of me last night,' she said, trembling.

Diganta Keshari wasn't amused by her apologies. He repeated that the dinner be kept in the study table in his room and nowhere else. As he walked out, he asked her not to address him as master or his highness. Chakori didn't expect such kind words from Diganta Keshari. She was very thankful to him for treating a mere dasi with such respect. He knew that Chakori's gratitude wasn't a lone voice; she spoke on behalf of the entire dasi community, who wanted the wall of exclusion separating them from the feudal class to break down. She asked for dignity—the dignity that every woman deserved, and vented the ire of that entire segment of mankind wronged for generations. He felt that her voice covered up the sparks of a rebellion against injustice, dominance and repression. The note of opposition that singed the girl within found an outlet. Diganta Keshari turned to her and said that there was no real difference between the two of them. If he was the son of Zamindar Graharaj, she was the daughter of Zamindar Dakhinray—the difference being that his mother was legally married to Graharaj while Chakori's mother never married Dakhinray.

'You're no less human. I respect you as much as I respect my stepmother Devaki,' he said.

'Please hold back your words! If your stepmother hears,

she'll be very upset. After all, I'm a dasi and she's my mistress. It's the dictum of fate,' Chakori answered humbly.

'Man has devised this system, not God; therefore, man alone will abolish this. Wait, the day of freedom isn't far,' Diganta Keshari reiterated his firm convictions and left for his morning walk.

The twelve-year-old girl was overjoyed. In her heart, she knew that Garbaganjan Dakhinray was her father, but the world never declared the truth; even her mother didn't dare to take his name. She was thrilled that the young zamindar affirmed the truth right to her face and gave legitimacy to her birth. It was the most memorable day in her life. She knew that if the matter was reported to Devaki, she would be banished immediately; the certificate from the young zamindar wouldn't change her fate in Dakhinray's palace. The human spirit that rose inside her sunk momentarily in the thick cover of fear, inferiority complex and helplessness induced for years. Dasi Chakori took the upper hand now. She reasoned that she would have to face death if she were swayed by the enlightened young zamindar's words. The sense of security that came with the bargain for the life of a dasi, she felt, was enough for her survival. Human beings often fear uncertainty, and Chakori was no exception. She got ready for her morning chores.

Chapter III

A small table, adequate for a single person to dine at, sat in Diganta Keshari's study. He read till late at night. A servant kept his dinner and a jug of water for his use; someone routinely cleaned the table in the morning. That night he sat thoughtfully after dinner. His vacation was almost over, and classes would start soon at Ravenshaw College. The zamindar took every care that Diganta Keshari lived comfortably in Cuttack in the Graharaj Bhavan, known to many as the Raj Bhavan. He had attendants, and a horse-drawn carriage took him to the college. The young man enjoyed the company of great friends and loved participating in meaningful conversations with them. The city, he felt, offered space for free thinking, and new thoughts and ideas naturally flowed to the mind. The laidback village life and the boundaries Graharaj set around him in the palace suffocated his spirit.

Diganta Keshari wasn't sure whether to return to Ravenshaw College or follow Pandit Gopabandhu Das's call to leave studies and join the non-cooperation movement. The zamindar would never approve of his idea to drop out. He was still young and too frail to stand his ground or oppose the wishes of his powerful father. He agreed that the zamindar was shrewd, wielded enormous influence over the colonial officials, and the freedom movement was an anathema for the supporters of the Raj. He respected the patriarch's unblemished character. So, he was afraid to make an impulsive move and challenge his authority. Conversely, the call to join the freedom movement was no less enticing.

The young man was undecided. Diganta Keshari left his room and stepped out unmindfully. He was surprised to see Chakori standing at the door. Devaki had ordered her to wait until the young zamindar finished his supper. Only then she could eat and go to bed. The servile attitude of the dasi made him uncomfortable, but he understood the girl's dilemma; she couldn't say no to his stepmother's order. He quickly thought of changing his dinner time to early hours so she wouldn't have to attend to him late every night. Graharaj and his son never had their dinner together. Diganta Keshari wasn't fussy about food, while the zamindar was. Devaki was getting close to her delivery and couldn't look after her husband or stepson. So Chakori attended to both. Though the father and son had distinct personalities, both were very similar in their looks, tenacity and level of knowledge. Chakori loved, feared, admired and respected both men. Both were her masters; she owed them her livelihood and entire existence. She felt that the younger zamindar, being immature, talked of strange things like freedom of the people and country, and the end of the dasi system—ideas she hardly understood. She didn't want to clutter her small mind with those complex words of the learned and tried to be a perfect dasi—a peerless maid.

∞

Traditionally, women assumed a respectable position in a family after giving birth to a son. Devaki's claim to esteem stemmed from her role as the carrier of a man's lineage, perpetuating his bloodline by reproducing sons. Once Devaki gave birth to a son, she attained that status. She began to exact power and authority, and became the ruthless mistress of the palace. She wasn't the demure voiceless wife anymore and dared to speak back to the zamindar upfront. All the male servants and the dasis were nervous in her presence. Chakori suffered the most; she was given the role of taking care of the newborn master Darpa Ganjan, while also looking after Devaki's post-delivery health, wellness and looks. She already had the responsibility of attending to Graharaj and Diganta Keshari. But she especially enjoyed caring for the newborn; when she held the baby in her lap, she was overjoyed and momentarily forgot all the hardships and miseries in her life.

In the meantime, the zamindar and Diganta Keshari argued over the latter's refusal to go back to college in Cuttack. Both were in a terrible mood. The zamindar was surprised and worried to see that the young man hadn't moved out when the classes started. Diganta Keshari averted looking at his father, and said he would rather study independently and take the tests. The announcement from the son shocked Graharaj Chaudhury. He was furious and warned that he would not allow him to join Gandhi's non-cooperation movement if he planned to be a part of it. Diganta Keshari collected himself and explained that the college was going through a turbulent phase of protest supporting the students because the police arrested and penalized them heavily for joining the freedom movement. He promised his father to return to Cuttack when the situation became normal.

Graharaj didn't buy his son's explanations and advised like a father counselling a stubborn, wayward young son. He ordered him to pack up and leave for Cuttack immediately. He argued that if he attended classes in turbulent times, the administration would take notice of him, and he would be the much sought-after young man for coveted jobs under the British. He knew how Gopabandhu's speech had inspired a cohort of students like Harekrushna Mahatab, Jadumani Mangaraj, Nabakrushna Chaudhury, Rajakrushna Bose and Narayan Birbar Samanta to abandon college. He warned that the drop-outs had no future, but those who remained in the classes and completed their degrees would be the valuable seeds. He repeated that opposing the powerful British was bound to put him in bigger trouble. He explained that the enormous army of the empire, with its unfathomable stock of guns, bullets and cannons, versus the National Congress and poor Gandhi's strategies of non-violence, were not comparable matches. He repeatedly asked his son to stay grounded and not jeopardize a bright future. 'Sons of kings and zamindars aren't supposed to join such movements,' was the last line of his long diatribe.

The son heard his father patiently but voiced his reservations. He complained that the police harassed many innocent people who were not part of the freedom movement. He also reminded Graharaj of the brutalities meted out to him in Balasore years back. The zamindar assured his son that he would be safe and no police would ever arrest and put him behind bars.

Diganta Keshari set out for Cuttack. Chakori was free of one responsibility and devoted herself fully to taking care of the newborn. Her tender spirit sang joyous notes like the ringing of freedom in the dark cell on Krishna's arrival.

∞

Many of Diganta Keshari's friends had already boycotted college. None of them came from rich zamindar families. Diganta's strategy was to support the non-cooperation movement tacitly without being caught by the police. On the surface, he stayed loyal to his father and devised ways to get money from him to sustain the movement. All the four women his father married, namely his four mothers, came from rich families. Each had a box of dowry full of gold and valuable jewellery. He had seen his father swiftly plucking a gold chain from his neck and gifting a handful to entourages from his new stepmother's place. At his home, gold was as banal as soil and stone. He had no qualms about taking away the wealth that the zamindar amassed from his poor subjects and stockpiled in his coffer. The new wave of awakening that had gripped the urban areas stirred him deeply. It was hard for him to be a silent spectator. He attended no classes in the college.

In a few days, Diganta Keshari returned home in the carriage sick with a fever, and told his father that he had returned since there was no one to take care of him in Cuttack. The zamindar later discovered that he was one of the many students rusticated from the college for picketing against the British. Graharaj was extremely upset with his son. Diganta Keshari created a web of lies and said that he tried to convince his friends to call off the strike, and the police wrongfully implicated him on picketing charges. He claimed he was innocent and unknowingly got caught in the turmoil, and he didn't know he was expelled from the college. The event undermined the zamindar's confidence in his eldest son. He was also scared that the British might be more vigilant over his conduct. He went out of his way to prove to the government that his son was innocent. If needed, he knew how to impose new taxes on his people and replenish the amount lost to please the masters. But he was extremely worried that his son's anti-establishment moves, like the blemishes on the face of the moon, stained his clean image before the masters. He was desperate to know the young man's moves. He urged him to help him in the administration and promised to talk to authorities to expunge the rustication charges so that he could study in another college in Calcutta. Diganta Keshari knew very well about all the serious charges against him and the one unlawful activity that forced the authorities to remove him from the college. He ignored the prospect of resuming studies in Calcutta. He asked the zamindar's permission to open a small school for children in the village.

Diganta Keshari had already undermined his father's confidence in him. The zamindar didn't trust everything the son said but still felt that staying away from the city where the anti-government sentiments ran high might keep his son away from the freedom movement. Diganta Keshari started his ideal school, Vidya Mandir, close to the zamindar's palace. A few like-minded friends flocked to the place; he often returned late from those scholarly engagements.

Prapancha Mohanty, the zamindar's reliable ally, informed him that Diganta Keshari had urged people to unite and not pay the new land tax. The news shook Graharaj; his people were never disloyal to him. He called his son a betrayer and cursed his late wife—Diganta Keshari's mother—for passing on the aberrant bloodline of a bastard clan to her son. The egotist didn't forget to cherish his aristocratic heritage of a *pakki mahal* zamindar, who owned the authority over the land for generations, a position no less important than that of the kings and nobles in the Gadajat states. He imposed fifty-four types of taxes on his people besides the customary land revenue and indentured labour. His subjects had never opposed; they gifted him fruits and vegetables from their gardens, even their milking cows. The zamindar piled taxes one after another to fill his coffer.

The strange new laws imposed were aimed at terrorizing the people. No man in his area was permitted to have a mustache; if someone grew one, he was dragged to a public place and each strand of hair was plucked out carefully. The man was then flogged openly depending on the number of hairs removed. Women were barred from wearing beautiful jewellery; if someone coveted one and was caught wearing it, that piece went to the zamindar's possession, and the woman was taken to his palace to serve as a dasi. If a woman died without a male heir, the zamindar confiscated her property, offering some paltry sum for her maintenance. If a man had no male child, his landed property went to the zamindar. Whenever the zamindar came out on a visit, the villagers lay in prostration till the zamindar's palanquin passed and was no more within their view. Women ululated, blew conch shells, and threw petals and leaves at his carriage in absolute devotion. It was customary for the zamindar's land to be cultivated first at the beginning of the farming season every year; each family member joined the fields with their tilling tools and bullocks to get the job done for free. Diganta Keshari got a clear picture of the vicious system as he stayed for a prolonged period in the village.

One day, following a tip from Prapancha Mohanty, the zamindar stormed into the Vidya Mandir and caught Diganta Keshari advising a group of farmers and day labourers about their rights. He had asked them not to pay the new taxes imposed by the zamindar. The sudden visit made the audience go pale with fear as if they were in the presence of Yama. All of them fell at his feet, pledging their allegiance to him. They prayed to him to excuse the young zamindar, a novice.

The attendant who followed the zamindar recorded the names of the villagers present in the meeting and filed cases against them under various rules; they were also harassed in many other ways. Thus, the raid on the Vidya Mandir ended Diganta Keshari's attempt to bring awareness to his people. The zamindar summoned him privately and warned that galvanizing the farmers against the system was a revolt against the British, and he might be booked for treason. Diganta Keshari denied inciting any revolt and argued that bringing awareness among the masses couldn't be sedition against British rule.

The zamindar was convinced that his son was smart and a staunch supporter of the non-cooperation movement. He threatened to disown him, calling him a shame on the prestige of the powerful zamindars. He asked him to imagine the family's dire position after independence when the subjects wouldn't treat them as their masters, and the government confiscated their land. He urged the young man to understand that the British were their saviours, safeguarding their power, position and comfort. Graharaj had an entrenched conviction that in his next birth he would be a zamindar again. But his son believed that birth is accidental, and nobody had control over that phenomenon; one might very well be a layman, the son of a dasi, or an untouchable in their next birth.

Diganta Keshari's primary initiative to lead an uprising failed, so people were scared to associate with him. Graharaj was worried too. Devaki advised him not to worry if Diganta Keshari ignored his warnings. She explained that if the young man wasn't besotted with the pomp and power of zamindari, he probably carried that typical inferior trait from the dasi blood running in his mother's clan. She called him a betrayer. In the four years of her marriage, she got three sons and was pregnant again, showing all the signs of bearing a son. She was ordained to give birth to sons only and didn't bother if Diganta Keshari joined the freedom struggle, ended up in jail, or if she was disowned by her husband. She wanted that her sons alone should inherit the zamindari. Devaki was the daughter of Zamindar Garbaganjan Dakhinray, who never allocated land or built homes for the sons he begot through the dasis. He instead wished that all his dasis should birth just daughters. He gave away those girls in marriage to Golam families—the mishmash segment having no name of the father for their origin. Dakhinray, some say, ordered the murder of all male children born to the dasis. A twenty-two-year-old young son he had through a dasi died in suspicious circumstances after he claimed inheritance right over his wealth.

Graharaj was often hurt hearing Devaki deprecating her stepson. He was the zamindar's firstborn, the beacon of hope for his clan for eighteen years, and held a special place in his heart. He knew that Diganta Keshari loved the people and was extremely kind towards them. Graharaj often feared that the son might not give him a chance to disown him but abandon his claim over the estate and leave him on his own will. Graharaj was hurt that the boy ruined all his dreams of a bright future and feared that he might cut off all the fetters of worldly life and be like the Buddha.

∽

In just five years, Chakori's body and mind changed dramatically. She was almost sixteen, a blossoming young woman. She was awkward too, thinking how a dasi like her grew up to be a charming young woman. She faced many challenges—the servants in the palace and the zamindar's officials made unwanted advances at her. If Graharaj hosted some English officials at his place, she was asked to attend to them. Devaki offered her nice saris and jewellery on those special days to dress up well. The intoxicated white men often muttered something that she didn't understand, but she knew from their gestures that those men were vulgar.

Chakori had another set of roles—she was supposed to dress well and look good, so that the zamindar was implicitly tempted to stay home and remain calm. The zamindar personally took care that Chakori remained close to Diganta Keshari and took good care of his son. He was planning to solemnize the young zamindar's marriage. A wife, he believed, would keep the young man homebound. Proposals for marriage came from many well-known families; some even sent photographs. But the young man was not ready to marry. Diganta Keshari was born to Graharaj when he was twenty. But no one knew why the son was unwilling to marry even at twenty-two. The young men of the time, touched by the unique phenomenon of freedom, had vowed to see their motherland freed from the British before they married. Graharaj found this funny as, according to him, freedom of the country and marriage were unlikely ideas to yoke together. He ignored these lofty ideals of the young and continued looking for a suitable bride for his son. But there were three big hurdles that many of the prospective brides' families worried about. First, his bloodline from the maternal side wasn't from the nobility; second, he had a young stepmother who might live long with four half-brothers, plus few possible siblings, as future liabilities; third, and the biggest drawback, was that he was a staunch supporter of the non-cooperation movement and was thoroughly opposed to the zamindars.

Besides taking care of Graharaj, Chakori had to look after the four tiny kids of Devaki. Saddled with household chores, she didn't find time to oil or comb her hair. After giving turmeric massages to the young ones, she would touch the palms over her face. After she made Devaki's hair with scented oil, she might run her hands over her thick hair that she tied into a bun. But even with the least makeup, the bright brown beauty stood out amidst the old ugly maids in the palace. Perhaps without her knowledge, the season of youth wrought its magic over her body, making her adorably beautiful. While she stood near the huge mirror and made Devaki's hair, her eyes automatically stopped over the reflection of her unkempt image. Devaki's yellow face, beautiful like that of goddess Lakshmi, beamed like a full moon. No less attractive was Chakori's face, pale but mystique like the slender crescent moon emerging on the second day. Prapancha Mohanty rushed to find a suitable groom for her from the Golam community. But Devaki ignored it. She needed Chakori by her side to run the household. Loyal, caring and devoted to her four little boys and the overbearing husband, Chakori made her life easier. An orphan, she had no strings attached; she was honest and upright. Devaki had no issue if she stayed with the family for the rest of her life.

Despite having these thoughts for Chakori, jealousy seethed deep in Devaki's heart. Fear lurked within; the more charming she found her, the more insecure she became. At times, things flung from her hand impulsively and wounded Chakori. Encouraged by their mother's actions, Devaki's children bit and scratched the poor maid unprovoked. Graharaj also never talked to her gently. But Diganta Keshari seemed like someone from a different planet. Chakori never felt the young zamindar ever look at her changing body.

Devaki sat at the dresser with Chakori to get her hair done; their faces reflected in the large mirror in front of them. Devaki's face looked pale and haggard beside the dasi's youthful, plum one. Repeated childbirths had taken the charm off her face; deep dark circles beneath the eyes and a pallid and lifeless set of lips made her look pitiable. She had no respite from a goading unknown fear. She was uncomfortable watching from the corner of her eyes that Chakori stealthily gloated over her face several times while doing her hair. Blinded with unfathomable envy, she screamed, 'Do you think yourself a prettier woman? Ugly dasi, don't be so vain! Mind the job you're doing.'

Chakori slumped submissively. Devaki quickly tousled her already-made braid and snatched the comb from Chakori's hand, screaming, 'You aren't mindful of your work. Leave this place and go wherever you want. Not surprised! You've taken after your mother.'

The comb flew so hard from her hand that it cracked the mirror. Devaki's face looked creepy, while Chakori's sad but radiant face reflected perfectly on the opposite corner of the broken glass.

'I ask you to get out of my home,' she cried out, seething in anger, and went on kicking Chakori.

∞

Needless to say, the guilty pleasure of secret love and conflicts within impact the human body. The silent tension between the father and son was taking its toll on the usual calmness of the home. While Graharaj was riled up completely, Diganta Keshari maintained the calmness of a stone. He stayed home without any sign of protest—he didn't care what he ate and remained completely engrossed in his thoughts. On one particular day, Graharaj had a bitter confrontation with his son. Devaki often preferred to stay away from such difficult situations. Chakori came with a cup of tea and stood before Graharaj. His eyes glistened like burning charcoal.

'Get lost! Leave me alone,' he roared.

She didn't move. Agitated, he sprang from his seat, snatched the cup from her hand and smashed it on the ground. He slapped her hard on her cheek, roaring, 'Incorrigible bitch! How dare you defy me? A single stroke can finish you. Don't you know that?'

Chakori had been bearing countless abuses from the zamindar for seven long years in the palace, but she was extremely hurt that day. The dasi in her had winced in pain so far, but that day, the human in her crumbled irretrievably. She stood still, her cheeks red like blood from the blow. The intrepid stoic posture seemed unforgiving to her challenger; the zamindar's iron-strong pair of arms fell hard on her shoulders. He shook her hard, shouting, 'How dare you? Don't you know I can throw you to the street tomorrow morning? I can't bear with such arrogance of a mere dasi.'

Chakori couldn't control her tears; her lips quivered as she pleaded softly, 'Master, you can kill me if you wish but don't throw me to the streets. I've nowhere to go in the universe except this palace! You are my father, mother...you provide for me. My saviour.'

The gush of tears from her eyes calmed down the surging temper of the zamindar momentarily. He evinced sympathy; his tight, clenched fist loosened as if he became the saviour of a forlorn creeper in a perilous storm. He didn't know what power pulled him back from within. Chakori, to her surprise, realized that her tears had drenched the zamindar's heart. The cruel man touched the bruises his slaps left on her cheeks.

'I shouldn't have hurt you so hard! Diganta Keshari drives me crazy these days… Please take care of him, he's very sick… no one's here to take care of him,' saying this, he stormed out

Chakori wiped her eyes and walked away. She finished the chores and carried the dinner for Diganta Keshari. He had not left his room that day; the zamindar's informers would follow him everywhere. He was asleep when Chakori entered his room. She kept the food on the table and stood at his feet. Twenty years younger than the father, he almost matched the zamindar physically. The pair looked like brothers, with the major difference being that while the son was full of love and compassion, the father was bitter and full of disdain for the entire world. Admiration for the young man overtook her heart. She prayed that if there were some movement in the country, that shouldn't affect the relationship between the father and son.

She touched his feet humbly and realized that he had a high fever. Chakori hadn't ever dared to touch him; she was awkward. She slowly stroked his feet; touching that wonderful human being convinced her of the love the zamindar felt for his son. Diganta Keshari never encouraged anyone to massage him. He opened his eyes and withdrew. Chakori was still holding his warm feet and replied, 'Master! I'm not your family! At least think of me as a dasi, and let me do my duty. The zamindar is very worried about your sickness. He ordered me to take care of you.'

'You can't understand his mind. Of course, after my mother's death he worries if I become sick...' Diganta Keshari replied sarcastically.

Chakori's hands still pressed his feet gently. After his mother passed away, no woman had ever touched him caringly. Dina the servant's rugged hands weren't meant for caregiving. He thought God created woman to remove every sickness from the face of the earth. He felt better from the gentle touch of Chakori's hand.

'Where do you go stealthily every night and return before daybreak? You might catch a cold and fever from the damp air outside. It won't be good if the zamindar finds out,' she asked as she pressed his feet gently.

Diganta Keshari was startled. He feared that all his hard work would be wasted if the young woman spilled the information. He warned her promptly not to make his nightly visits known to anyone. He also knew that Chakori met a young man secretly every night and threatened to expose her. She began to worry that her clandestine meetings also had a witness. She cast her eyes down and continued her work silently.

'Who's that guy?' he asked.

'He's someone I know from our village,' replied Chakori, uninhibited.

He asked if she was in love and willing to marry the man. He was ready to talk to his father and arrange everything. He felt that marriage would free her from the demeaning life of a dasi. Chakori denied being in any relationship and asked him not to tell his father about the man, especially to his stepmother. He was confused; he disapproved of men who kept such clandestine relationships with women. He demanded to know his name. With tearful eyes, Chakori finally identified him as her half-brother Dukhia, her mother Sadhabi's son from her previous marriage. Diganta Keshari then discovered that Dukhabandhu, his follower, was Chakori's half-brother. Chakori further disclosed that her mother came to Zamindar Dakhinray's place as a wet nurse when Dukhia was one year old, and never got a chance to return home. He was banished from Dakhinray's area after their mother's death and lived in extreme poverty, fighting a false case brought against him. Chakori confessed tearfully to giving him some food secretly on some nights.

'You're lucky that freedom fighter Dukhabandhu is your brother. I'm so jealous of him for having such a kind-hearted sister like you!' Diganta Keshari was sorry to have misread their relationship.

Chakori was overtaken with emotions but was very calm. She said dispassionately that brother Dukhia came to her in his bad days, but she was sure he wouldn't take her into the fold of his family if she were ever thrown out of the palace. Dukhia, in her eyes, belonged to a society that didn't accept her mother. But she was confident that the zamindar and the little master wouldn't throw her to the streets, come what may. That night, Diganta Keshari choked listening to her words and the faith she reposed in his family.

'One day, the fetters of slavery will be gone. The rule of the rich and the privileged will be history. All will be equal in free India. There will be no zamindar, no dasi or golam…

I promise to see you first and wipe the tears off your face that day. Be patient!' He assured her like a seer.

Tears knew no bounds as the deeply empathetic voice stirred the finer chords of Chakori's soul. She was caught in the spell of that rare, exalted moment, and held his feet tight in total surrender as if they were the feet of God. She wanted her entire body to dissolve into a stream of tears and be salvaged from the curse of being a dasi and redeemed forever from the bondage of slavery. Diganta Keshari, for the first time, lifted that tender liana of tears from the ground and comforted her, saying, 'Be patient, freedom is sure to come. Its march is unstoppable; after relentless darkness, the night fizzles out. Be patient. It's going to end.'

They heard footsteps outside. A dasi informed from outside that the zamindar had summoned Chakori. He was anxious to know about his son's health. Chakori told Diganta Keshari to eat something and left his room. Despite all their differences, Diganta Keshari's eyes turned wet in love and respect for his father. He felt much better with Chakori's care; she had brought calmness and filled his troubled heart with peace.

Chapter IV

It wasn't a secret that during the time of the British, the lane of the prostitutes, Darisahi, thrived well in villages. Like the neighbourhoods for the upper-caste Brahmins, Karans or the lower-caste people, Darisahi was a regular feature of a village's making. But people were still ashamed and awkward in taking the name of that lane. In his childhood, Diganta Keshari knew that the people living there were better off than the rest of the commoners; they had good homes, the women dressed up well and decorated their dwellings impressively. People knew that the English officials who came to the village on duty were their guests. Diganta Keshari believed that the villages regularly visited by the white officials had those lanes. Those women were accomplished and beautiful, especially excelling in singing and dancing. He never understood why those women had only girls in their homes and no boys were born to them. As a kid, he was eager to go to those homes and watch them sing and dance. Graharaj disapproved of those requests as bad ideas and even smacked him hard for asking permission to visit.

'Your father had never stepped into those places! How dare you insist on going there? I can't understand how the idea came to you at this tender age! Never think of going there,' Graharaj warned him sternly.

In time, Diganta Keshari understood the profession and appreciated his father's disapproval of going to those homes.

He assumed that perhaps his father was the only honourable person among the zamindars who never got fascinated with those amoral creatures. Diganta Keshari wanted the abolition of prostitution to become a part of the freedom movement that aimed to fight some of the old social evils. He was prepared to talk to some of those women in person.

Graharaj was out of the village for four days. The neighbourhood of the prostitutes was a little far; it sat at the village end and came after a cluster of some small villages. One of those days, Diganta Keshari secretly set out on his mission with a reliable follower very early in the morning. He didn't want to get noticed, so he didn't use the palanquin and instead got into a bullock cart.

He stopped his cart a little farther from the red-light area, and sat hiding inside; his face was covered so no one could recognize him. From the place of his hiding, Diganta Keshari could recognize his father's palanquin resting at the doorstep of the most famous *veshya*—whore—of the area. Soon he saw Graharaj coming out of the house, smiling. While parting, the pretty woman offered him a paan with an endearing smile and implored with her usual coquettish sweetness. 'When're you going to come back? You don't even visit me once a month these days!'

'My son is grown now. He's very watchful of all my moves. I must be very careful,' Graharaj pushed the paan into his mouth and smirked.

'Hi, hi,' she laughed.

'After Diganta leaves home, I'll come to you regularly. First, I need to finalize something for him. I am trying to send my boy to Calcutta for higher studies.'

The scene seemed nothing but surreal, and it stunned the young man. The death of his mother hadn't made him an orphan; he held on to the pillar called father. But at that moment, he had become fatherless and an orphan instantaneously. The face-off shattered the image of the ultimate ideal man, one who had always epitomized perfection of character and virtue for him. The disintegration had seismic effects; the breach of trust shook his faith in the irrefutable distinction between right and wrong. Nothing seemed real; the ground beneath his feet, the sky over his head, and the sun and moon above—all seemed completely unreal, like the mask over his father's face. His young heart sunk deep under the burden of an irreconcilable turmoil. Before the bearers took out his father's palanquin, he asked his cart puller to hurry up; lashes fell sharp on the back of the animals, and he rushed out.

∞

Graharaj had ordered the villagers to work for free to dig a huge pond named Chandan Pokhari. Diganta Keshari secretly asked his follower Dukhabandhu to unite everyone and ask them to defy the order. The zamindar had no control over his son, but he could punish the people. Once the work stopped, the village guard implicated many in false cases, arresting and torturing them. Graharaj didn't want to lose his grip over the matter and confronted his son, saying, 'I'll be lucky if I don't have to look at the face of a useless son like you.'

The statement was almost an order for Diganta Keshari to leave the palace. The promise of freedom to Chakori and the poor villagers held him back in his native place. He was determined to fulfil his goal and listened to the patriarch without protest. He returned from the pond site in the evening. By the time he reached home, another storm had already roiled the palace. The servants told Diganta Keshari that Devaki had locked Chakori in a room, beating her brutally while other maids joined hands with her.

'Leave me, mistress, I might die. I can't give out the name of the man responsible for this! You chop my head but I won't say!' he heard Chakori begging his stepmother.

'Tell the name! Who is he?' Devaki didn't listen and continued asking.

The beating continued, followed by more painful wailing. Diganta Keshari was numb upon stepping inside the palace. He couldn't understand the nature of Chakori's crime and the brutal punishment meted out to her. It was hard for him to witness the torture and remain silent. Zamindar Graharaj was home; he sat stoically in his room. He didn't even try to stop the inhuman abuse. Diganta Keshari rushed angrily and kicked the door hard; the door opened. He found Chakori sitting in a corner, bruised all over. She leaned against the wall and sobbed uncontrollably. When she saw the young zamindar, she covered her face and broke down.

'What's going on here? Do you want to kill this girl? What did she do to upset you?' He screamed out.

'Oh, now I got you. No need to explain. I can tell why you're so lenient towards Chakori!' Devaki retorted.

Chakori banged her head against the wall like a mad woman and cried, 'For God's sake, don't take the young zamindar's name. He's like God in human form; someone even thinking anything vulgar about him will rot in hell,' she implored.

'Shut up! Stop all your excuses! Don't try to convince me! Who else is there in the palace except him? Shame! Shame!' Devaki screamed again.

'This is a lie! In the name of God, this is a lie!' repeated Chakori once more.

'What's the issue?' Diganta Keshari asked in shock.

The zamindar appeared and asked Diganta Keshari to mind his business and not put his head into everything. The young man worried that Chakori might die from the beating. Devaki was sarcastic about his concerns for the life of a mere dasi, saying, 'How does her death matter to you?'

Her spate of angry reproach continued. A dasi clarified to the young man that Chakori was a debauchee like her mother. She carried the fruit of her sin in her womb but didn't say her partner's name. She tacitly targeted the zamindar or his son as the perpetrator. The zamindar's wife was probing to find out the truth. The woman said that God would punish Chakori for the awful offence, and she would rot in hell like her mother, Sadhabi.

The finest chords of Diganta Keshari's heart tore silently. He lowered his head in shame and went back to his room. He was confused, thinking whether Dukhabandhu was Chakori's half-brother or lover. Zamindar Graharaj worried that there was no guarantee that a dasi could be devoted to a single man, and she might be seeing his son or having multiple lovers. Devaki got more impatient with each passing moment and asked her to speak up. She wanted to be sure that the father of the unborn wasn't Diganta Keshari or her husband, Zamindar Graharaj. Chakori, under the trial, sat silently, staring at the floor. Tears gushed from her eyes and blended with the blood oozing from the cut in her lip. She knew it didn't matter if she declared the name of the man who raped her, nor would it change the identity of the life growing inside her.

Devaki got impatient; vengeance overtook her impulses. She pounced upon Chakori with all her might and stood atop her belly like a terrifying demon. Chakori gave a sharp cry and lost consciousness. A splurge of fresh blood spilled from her womb and stained the floor. Ranting at the top of her voice, Devaki declared insanely that she, the proud daughter of Zamindar Garbaganjan Dakhinray, would never allow another claimant to the estate that legitimately belonged to her four sons.

Devaki's last few words were flung at Diganta Keshari discreetly. She assumed that her stepson was the partner in the crime. The young man stood still like a stone facing his room but imploding inside. Chakori's painful wailing stopped, but Devaki continued to revile him with abuses during that interim silence. He thought that if Chakori died, she would be free from the misery of being a dasi. But ironically, she didn't seek liberation through death; rather, remaining alive held the promise of nirvana for her. Her transgression baffled him; the pregnancy outside wedlock was condemnable and not an act of freedom in his eyes.

Zamindar Graharaj finally declared that the sinner could not remain in his palace; she needed to be shifted to another place. Chakori was still unable to hold herself together; her condition was critical. Diganta Keshari was terrified to see how some dasis dragged and dumped her semi-conscious, cold body into the cart with utter disregard. She was removed to the outhouse some four miles away from the palace. Nobody precisely knew about Graharaj's punishment for the culprits in the outhouse.

But Diganta Keshari knew that the physical punishments in that torture chamber were cruel and gut-wrenching, which might result in the victim's death.

The silence of a burial ground filled the palace that night. Everybody speculated over the trial and punishment awaiting Chakori. The very mention of the outhouse made people nervous; they preferred silence and never raised their voice against injustice. The palace hid tales of unspeakable misery and chilling methods of punishment that gratified the zamindar. The dasis in the palace worried about Chakori's fate and shunned eating anything that night. They weren't able to understand her foolish permissiveness and misadventure. They knew that lust, like hunger, was natural but failed to understand how the girl, at such a tender age, dared to violate the sanctity of Graharaj's palace. Many whispered that she should've taken the advice of the midwife Ranidhai and undergone an abortion. Women in the village reached out to the midwife to save their honour, and very few unlucky ones ever died in her hands. Chakori's death would be disgraceful, creating an uproar and publicizing her sin.

In that village, midwife Ranidhai was a familiar face. Like the undisputable presence of God in the lives of the rich and poor, she was a fixture in the lives of all. No one could ever deliver a baby and become a mother without her help. If a virgin ever became pregnant before marriage, Ranidhai was the saviour of the so-called adulteress. Ranidhai effortlessly released babies from mothers' wombs and removed unwanted pregnancies with equal proficiency. She knew the remedies to help women who couldn't conceive as well as to stop women from getting pregnant in the first place. Everyone liked and feared her. Even the zamindar, his revenue officials, police and clerks dreaded her and talked to her with an awkward grin. She came to the rescue of respectable families in the village; they sent her gifts and shawls. In the long end of her sari, she was the one who carefully knotted the secrets of every daughter and daughter-in-law of the village. She was needed most in Darisahi—the lane of the prostitutes. She was their family who loved and treated her as one of their own.

Ranidhai had a great life. She had good food on her plate, wore nice saris, and lived in a decent home, as did some respectable officials of the zamindar. Carefree and upbeat, like someone with a good income and some spare money in their pocket, she was someone to be seen. Plump like her fat income, the midwife covered her body so well with her sari that one couldn't miss the flowers, patterns, design and the folds on it. She wore silver jewellery on her fingers and toes, and gold on her neck, nose and ears. The dark, red juice from the paan with *ketaki khira** in her mouth covered her lips impressively. Her skin was shiny. The adornments, combined with the typical smell of scented oil from Calcutta on her hair, made her presence felt from a distance. A hint of a sweet, mysterious smile always lingered on her lips. People were often intimidated if she brushed past them. They feared that Ranidhai might make their most sensitive secrets public and spill the beans they didn't want anyone else ever to know. But, no. Ranidhai wasn't that type of a character. She was like a secret box that was closed tight, but some might feel that it was open to peep inside. Her eyes, face and look seemed to chase people, but she spared them;

---

*Ketaki khira is a type of paan masala. Khir leaves a deep-red colour and the masala is sweet-smelling and strong.

she followed them close but didn't kill them. She saved women who were cursed as barren and others from the shame of being denounced as an adultresses.

Diganta Keshari wasn't allowed to go out. Graharaj sat tensed like the loaded dark sky before the storm. Devaki had been spewing demeaning words against her stepson's corrupt maternal lineage. Nothing was heard of Chakori for two days. Most of the incidents from the outhouse were never made public. Diganta Keshari was lost in deep thought. He wanted to meet Dukhabandhu desperately. If it could be determined that he wasn't Chakori's half-brother and that she was in a secret relationship with him, her death wouldn't affect him much. But to his biggest disappointment, Dukhabandhu was missing from the village. The village guard searched for him desperately. The zamindar's trusted official, Prapancha Mohanty, wanted to arrest and put him behind bars.

Clueless, Diganta Keshari presumed that Dukhabandhu, Chakori and Prapancha Mohanty were part of a love triangle. Per the narrative in his mind, Dukhabandhu was Chakori's paramour and vanished when Chakori was found pregnant. Prapancha Mohanty wanted to avenge his competitor. But it was not as simple as that; there was a separate story. He learned that some Vira Swain, a young man from the village, went to Rangoon and made some money. He returned after ten years, overhauled his crumbling home and replaced the shoddy, bug-eaten bamboo front door with a solid, wooden double door. Prapancha Mohanty came to Vira's place and asked him to remove the new installation as a mark of respect for the zamindar, and send the door to Prapancha Mohanty's home. Vira didn't want to give up his right over his door.

Vira's other offence was that he dared to walk in front of the zamindar wearing the boots he got from Rangoon, and he didn't touch the ground as a mark of respect to the zamindar, and bowed instead. Prapancha Mohanty flogged Vira hard for his irreverence to authority, in the presence of scores of villagers; out of fear, no one came to his rescue. Gasping in pain, poor Vira agreed to part with the door. Dukhabandhu, at that moment, pushed through the crowd and gave a hard blow to Mohanty, who fell to the ground. He hit again on his back several times and warned that he might piss on his face and drink his blood someday. Dukhabandhu thrust past the melee before the zamindar's people could catch him.

The new narrative about Dukhabandhu's heroic rescue of Vira made Diganta Keshari very proud. He worried about Chakori's vulnerability, the scandalous accusations, and the brutal beatings she got from his stepmother. There was nobody he might've turned to, to find out about her; no one was willing to speak. In that strange land, birds and animals screamed against the outrageous, unjust and oppressive things, but people didn't stir; they were dumb and deaf. It was hard to stimulate them or get any response from them.

Ripping through the darkness of that nameless night, Diganta Keshari emerged as a shadowy figure at the steps of the outhouse and carefully peered through the slightly-opened door. A kerosene lamp flickered inside; it gave him a little hope. He believed that Chakori wasn't dead; the place didn't seem ghostly, dark and frightening. He pitied that the naive young woman didn't know her rights or demands, and took abuse for granted. He simply wished for her to survive the ordeal and be forthcoming in giving out the name of the perpetrator to him. He wanted that whoever that man might be, must be brought to justice. A resolve slowly overtook his senses; his mind was possessed by the goal of freeing Chakori from misery. He didn't care if, in that process, he killed someone or got himself killed. He stood there to push open the door and step inside. His eyes then caught something unusual. He was puzzled to see his father's pair of shoes sitting at the entrance. He withheld his steps momentarily and paid attention to the conversation inside. He heard the zamindar blame Chakori for being a fool who couldn't avert the shameful situation by going to Ranidhai to clean her womb.

'Devaki would've had no hint of your pregnancy if there were no trace. You went through this unnecessary hassle because of your foolishness. I've no idea that Sadhabi's daughter could be such a damn fool!' he said.

'I know nothing about this, master! My mother asked me to obey your orders. You're my saviour; I submit to your wishes. But I didn't know this was in store for me.' Diganta Keshari heard servile Chakori pleading before his father.

Zamindar Graharaj was negotiating with dasi Chakori. He reassured her that Ranidhai, the midwife, had washed every trace of the life growing inside her. He promised her permanent shelter in the outhouse and a livelihood till death. He warned her to take Ranidhai's potion and never to conceive and birth another golam. He announced arrogantly that he didn't care for his wife, and planned to visit her regularly. But he declared his love for Diganta Keshari and warned her that she shouldn't ever let his dear son get any hint of the things going on in her life. The very name of the son shook Chakori completely; her soul was crushed under the weight of her unbearable misery. She cried inconsolably.

'Why do you cry?' screamed the zamindar reproachfully. Signs of misgiving clouded his face. Masculine rivalry, jealousy and hatred buried inside for a competing male over a desired mate seemed to vitiate his thinking.

'Yes! The young zamindar will know nothing,' promised Chakori as she rose with difficulty to lock the door. Graharaj threw open the door and came out. He sensed that someone stood in the haze of the night.

'Who is there?' he stopped quickly and asked.

A shadowy figure emerged from the darkness. The zamindar could make out the face of the strong, bright and handsome male in the thin ray of light from the kerosene lamp leaping beyond the door. He was dismayed to meet his son.

'Lord! *Sana** zamindar!' cried Chakori when she recognized his face and ran away crying in shame.

'You too are here? She's a lowly dasi; they're messed-up harlots. I came here for her trial. You needn't worry about her. I've fixed your marriage. Never step into this place. Get out of here,' he said hurriedly but slowed down and repeated, bewildered. 'How long have you been standing here?'

Diganta Keshari couldn't blink in his dismay. His gaze remained fixed on the zamindar's face. Truth, and nothing but the truth, mirrored in the zamindar's eyes. The fire emitting from his gaze was complex; lie, hatred, violence, bigotry and vengeance flared from that inferno. An apparent calm exterior failed to cover up the sinful thoughts of lust, anger, revenge, fear and doubt smouldering beneath that look. He leaned forward and whispered to his son, 'I'll fix this bitch.'

---

*young

Both the shadowy figures moved in tandem, and then separated into the darkness. Inside, Chakori cried in shame and self-hatred, 'My lord, little master! Sana zamindar!'

The zamindar's palanquin rose from the shadows of the garden and merged into the dark road going towards the palace. The progeny didn't follow and implored, 'What's the right path?' The dilemma roiled his mind.

'Rise from the darkness! Awake and lead through light and attain the bliss of nirvana,' urged a powerful voice inside him.

The resounding cry 'Revolt! Revolt!' filled the air. The powerful collective voice of the disenfranchised asked him to rise against the status quo and dismantle the corrupt behemoth. The roar merged with the motherland's call asking him to wake up from the stupor and join the movement to liberate her.

The epiphanic moment entreated Diganta Keshari to galvanize and awaken people for the uprising. Without awakening, liberation was wishful thinking. The journey through awakening leads man to meet Brahman—the absolute reality. The Upanishad called that sanctified path *Uttaramarga*, where the soul is no longer chained to the miseries it had seen in the world. The path before it is lighted; it has no confusion or deterrence with regard to finding the place 'where freedom reigns' eternally.

The choice emerged incisively clear before Diganta Keshari's eyes. The rumbling terror and aching regrets of the past moments were gone. He wanted to lead posterity through that path of enlightened awareness that would never lead them back to slavery, despotism and oppression. Chakori's cries echoed from every direction like countless human beings asking for liberation. In that most definitive moment, Diganta Keshari stepped forward, leaving zamindar Graharaj's palace behind.

The sky in the east was red like blood. In the glowing brightness of the dawn, the exalted path of awareness emerged clear before his eyes.

Chapter V

Diganta Keshari drifted beyond the familiar topography and stood quietly on the sands of the dead river Vasanta Patali like the *Saptarishi* constellation, etched as a question mark in the night sky. Countless thoughts bellowed in his mind like the tiny particles of sand swept by the wind. He didn't want to submit to the idea that questions that haven't been raised should remain unuttered. He was ready to move forward and embrace the unknown. Standing on the sands of the Vasanta Patali, a branch of the mighty Devi River, he revisited the numerous bits that had gone into creating his past—his heritage, recent and remote. He was close to Kosida, his maternal village, some eight miles away from the historic Harishpur Fort which welcomed the first British agent and his group of eight merchants who came with a cache of splendid presents to the friendly state of Odisha in 1633. *Boita kulia muhana*—the harbour suitable for anchorage—was the name of the point where the river entered the sea. The wanderer chose the place as the point of his rebeginning on the exalted path of freedom.

The river had washed away countless footprints, but the numerous interesting stories he heard about the river's past from his maternal grandfather were still alive in his memory. His stepmothers didn't let him visit his grandfather often, but their cruel restrictive hands couldn't stop him from remembering the tales of the kings, ports and merchants that he heard from him. The warrior king Muhana Kimbhira Madhi Mangaraj* was the ruler of two forts—Harishpur and Mirichipur. Harishpur in Balikuda and Mirichipur in Kakatapur were prosperous ports of their times. Portuguese ships anchored there regularly and traded happily with Odisha. Initially, independent rulers controlled the forts, but when one of the rulers died, having no successor, Mangaraj took charge of both places. There were eight Odia feudal states, namely Olara, Mirichipur, Harishpur, Visunapur, Kujanga, Paradeipur, Ali and Kanika, on the eastern coast. These eight states on the river strongly resisted the invasion by external forces coming from the sea. The king of Kalinga had bestowed powerful titles upon them like Muhana Kimbhira (the crocodile at the confluence) and Muhana Chouka (the guard at the confluence).

The walls of Sunagarh, the capital of Harishpur, were covered with gold, and dazzled in the morning sun like a fort on fire. People were sufficiently warned not to stare at the radiance of their capital for long. The king had decreed that if anyone looked at the splendid fort for long, the pupil of their eyes would be poked with burning iron nails. The fear of losing their eyesight made the subjects of the twin states—Harishpur and Mirichipur—always look to the ground.

Nobody could say exactly how big the Ranigarhia pond in Sunagarh was. But surely it was built after the demolition of countless pieces of farmland, homes, gardens, orchards, temples and inns belonging to commoners, using free labour. The water in the pond was pink like the lotus; it tasted slightly saline as the

---

*Mangaraj is a common title used to refer to the kings in the coastal area.

water of the salty Luna River seeped into the soil and entered the reservoir. But some said that the blood of the countless people who died while digging the pond gave the water its pink hue; their tears, sweat and blood made the water salty. Queens used to take bath in that pond; the king demolished the nearby homes to ensure the privacy of the queen who frolicked in the water. Even a cuckoo wasn't permitted to build its nest on trees, to keep the bathing of the queens and princesses undisturbed. The beautiful princess exclusively used the west side of the pond with silver steps. Even the rising sun was scared to rush; it hid its rays from touching the princess as she got down the silver steps of the palace and gently entered the pearl steps of the pond to take a bath. The water of the pond, tainted with people's tear, sweat and blood, was murky. None of the subjects ever saw the princess. Some say that the spirits might have seen her.

There was no trace of Sunagarh; it sunk in the rising tides of the Luna River. But the lores of villages like Suliapada and Narahana are still alive in the popular imagination. Years ago, two brothers from a noble family in Talcher escaped their cruel ruler, reached Harishpur and Mirichipur, and took control of the two ports. They used Suliapada, the ground for gallows, to kill scores of innocent subjects. Per lore, Narahana, the site for human sacrifice, was a huge open amphitheatre; it hosted ghastly executions on special days of the year and decapitated those subjects who dared to oppose their ruler. Royals and commoners joined the event. People claim that the cries of those killed rumble through the air in the dead of night in both places, even today.

Zamindar Graharaj Chaudhury, impressed with their glorious legacy, chose a bride—his first wife and Diganta Keshari's mother—from the brave Mangaraj clan. Odisha in those days was the centre of trade and commerce. Boitakulia and Devidana were two famous ports at the confluence of Devi River, and Harishpur and Mirichipur were prosperous in river Basanta Patali. Odias traded with the outside world; and its rulers, who dealt with the Portuguese traders, were courteous and knew how the world worked.

Activities on the coastline began to change with time. Traders from other foreign countries sniffed Odisha's money and showed up. The English stationed in the Coromandel coastline sent a delegation with eight representatives led by William Bruton and Ralph Cartwright, to Odisha. They anchored at the Boitakulia port in Harishpur on 21 April 1633. The British understood that entry to Harishpur would be easy, and that it would be even easier to obtain a trade permit from the Nawab stationed in Barabati Fort, Cuttack, with the help of local leaders.

The English planned to greet the king of Harishpur with impressive presents as a gesture of goodwill and self-introduction. However, they faced stiff resistance from the Portuguese traders who were firmly rooted in that area. The fight between the Portuguese and the shrewd, aggressive English in the sea was tough. King Madhab Mangaraj—the crocodile at the mouth—didn't like hostility between the European rivals in his waters. He was overtly friendly towards the foreigners, intervened in the battle between the two trade rivals, rescued the English merchants, and helped the wounded recover in his guesthouse. On their part, the English merchants didn't forget to please him with valuable gifts. Mangaraj mediated for the English to meet Nawab Agha Mahammad Zaman Tirani at Barabati Fort and obtain the trade permit. Four of the eight

English traders stayed in Pataligarh. Bruton, Cartwright and two others headed for Cuttack. On the morning of 26 April, they packed valuables like gold, silver, clothes and spices from their ship as gifts for the Nawab, and set out for Balikuda in a boat. The ruler of Balikuda welcomed them with traditional pomp and grandeur, accompanied by music and singing. He supplied coolies to carry their goods, and horses for the Englishmen to reach Cuttack. He walked some half a mile to see them off. The scorching April heat was unbearable for the English; they stopped next at Hariharpur. In those days, Hariharpur was famous for cotton clothes and silkwear. Impressed with the prosperity and development of the place, Bruton and Cartwright thought of establishing their main trade office there, if granted permission from the Nawab to trade.

The English delegates got permission to meet Nawab Tirani in the Barabati Fort on 1 May, and they waited with other visitors for the meeting. Cartwright was not just impressed with the wealth and grandeur of the fort; he was swept off his feet with greed to possess whatever he surveyed. When the Nawab entered the hall, followed by the courtiers, the audience stood and lowered their heads in deference. Cartwright and his team stood up and did the same.

Everybody sat down after the Nawab took his seat. As the leader of the delegate, Cartwright got the first opportunity to submit his application. The Nawab smiled briefly. The Englishman extended his arm to shake his hand but was confused when the Nawab removed his left foot from his shoe and extended it towards him. Cartwright was dismayed; a servant bent down and held the Nawab's foot. Some officials made Cartwright understand that he should kiss the Nawab's foot. He was in a fix. He wasn't ready to kiss; he gestured his unwillingness twice. The Nawab was haughtier; he refused to look at Cartwright's application. It's not certain if the Englishman knew anything about the culture of India, but he was smart enough to remember the episode where Lord Krishna didn't hesitate to kiss the foot of an ass in the time of dire need. Suddenly, he bent down and kissed the Nawab's foot vigorously. The audience hailed his gesture, and the chamber resonated with laughter, cheer, clapping and loud greetings. He obtained the trade permit instantly and forgot the shame of kissing someone's foot.

After signing the trade agreement, the four English traders returned to Hariharpur and started building the factory, a warehouse for trade purposes. Cartwright had examined the cotton and silk products of the area and guessed that Hariharpur was already developed, and they need not work hard to change it to a modern city. Calcutta had not emerged in the picture yet. The Englishmen started the work; the width of the foundation of the proposed factory was eight feet. He had dreamed of erecting a multi-storied building over there. In the Bengal-Odisha division, Hariharpur was the first factory. Ships sailed smoothly through Boitakulia and Devi ports over Alka River to Hariharpur. Trade flourished. Hariharpur and Balipada were on the verge of becoming great cities, and in all probability, Calcutta would've been remembered differently in modern Indian history. But God willed otherwise.

Large-scale sand deposition filled the Alka River in a few years and severely limited its depth. Large ships couldn't manoeuvre in the shallow water. By the year 1641, the factory was almost defunct. Cartwright widened his search for a suitable river port. He treasured the hospitality, love, affection and respect of the king and the people of Hariharpur, Balikuda, Harishpur and Mirichipur in his heart. He moved the factory to Calcutta on the mouth of Hugli River. Soon, Calcutta emerged as a prosperous city. Hariharpur and Balikuda got stuck in time as two mofussil towns of Cuttack in Odisha.

Those descendants of Muhana Kimbhira Madhab Mangaraj who took pride as the pioneers in welcoming the English to Odisha, were finally duped of the treasured gold plates that covered the interior of their palace, by the same English. Cartwright always remembered that the Portuguese and local goons attacked and harassed him in Harishpur, so he called it Harasspur. He learned of the merciless abuse of the rulers of the people in Mirichipur and twisted the name to Mercipore. After Madhab Mangaraj's death, his two sons, Narasingh Mangaraj and Padmanabh Mangaraj, became the rulers of Harishpur and Mirichipur. They surpassed the father in their oppression of the subjects. By the nineteenth century, except for the memories of the harrowing tales of bloody repression and suffering, there was no sign of the glory and opulence the two places enjoyed at the beginning of the seventeenth century. Per 'sunset law', a major chunk of the Harishpur zamindari was acquired by some Zamindar Laha from Calcutta. Mirichipur zamindari was split into fifty small chunks that tiny officials like the Mamalatkar, Makadam and Gumasta bought as zamindari. Diganta Keshari's uncle was in charge of a tiny area of Harishpur.

People in that area still believed that the oppressive Mangaraj rulers reincarnated as crocodiles and attacked the unsuspecting people ferrying across the Devi River. People's unquestioning surrender to such beliefs vexed Diganta Keshari. He doubted if their minds, sealed by the darkness of ignorance, could ever see the flimsy base of those beliefs. He also thought of the English who came to the shores of his land for trade but occupied it. No one in their wildest of imaginations ever thought that the 218 traders who came for trade with India under a one-sided decree from Queen Elizabeth of England would instead rule over India for two hundred years. Those traders who asked for permits from native kings to build trade houses in different parts of the country were greeted warmly as guests from outside. He wondered if extending a warm welcome to strangers was a crime. The foreigners looked at the warmth as India's weakness. The English, who coveted the wealth of others, grabbed power and ruled for years.

After the death of Aurangzeb, the heirs to his crumbling empire were mired in a decadent life of laziness and over-indulgence, and the English entered the scene to take control. In 1775, an inefficient monarch Shah Alam II sold the Diwani—the ownership over the revenue of Bengal, Bihar and Odisha—to the East India Company. Lord Clive, the British general, bought that permission from the emperor of Delhi for twenty-six lakh rupees. In 1803, the British took over the administration of Odisha. Puri, Balasore, Cuttack, Kujanga, Kanika and Harishpur came under their direct control. Their doctrine of lapse, virtually an annexation policy, aimed to end the ownership right of Indian rulers over land and revenue. The collector's office and the zamindari system systematized revenue collection from the land that people owned.

The proof of indemnity or the decree of no tax, issued by earlier kings, saved some from giving taxes to the British; those who couldn't produce the proof gave taxes on their income from the land. The infamous sunset law doomed the fate of many. If the taxpayer couldn't pay the taxes at the Calcutta office before the sunset of the given date, their land automatically got transferred to the East India Company. The law disenfranchised scores from the ownership of their land. Shrewd Bengalis in Calcutta purchased the auctioned zamindari from the company and overnight became owners of huge chunks of land in Odisha. The Laha family of Calcutta thus purchased a large chunk of the zamindari of Harishpur. Dolamani Srichandan Mahapatra, the petty revenue official, was instrumental in implementing the sunset law in the area. He was one of the few who understood government laws in those days. Those who went to him for help, he misinterpreted the laws and by-laws, and bought the revenue rights over the lands of many gullible victims. The sunset law proved lucky for him. A huge portrait of the setting sun adored his drawing room in a symbolic salutation to the law that made him a zamindar.

Dolamani came from a poor sharecropper family. He left home for Calcutta in search of livelihood. Calcutta made him wise. During his stay there, he came in contact with some Company peons and could carve a future by bribing one. The English sought low-level native employees to run daily office errands in rural areas. Dolamani got the information and returned to his village. Some say that rays of strong optimism made one of his eyes permanently crooked.

A sahib from Calcutta camped in Harishpur to recruit some locals. On his horse, he rode by Dolamani's village; two donkeys loaded with turbans followed him. Curious villagers of Balikuda were out as spectators. Dolamani having the recruitment information beforehand, sat silently on his veranda, posing as one able to read and write with his stack of palm-leaf texts and scribbler. He didn't know how to write even his name. The peon friend from his Calcutta days whispered to the sahib to hire Dolamani; the sahib got off his horse, grabbed a turban from the donkey's back, and anointed Dolamani as *muktar*, a petty official in the revenue department. Dolamani drew a sickle and tiller symbolizing farming—his occupation—for his signature, and someone signed below to validate. He rose from the ranks and became the zamindar of Balikuda; his last name changed from Swain to Srichandan Mahapatra.

People of that rural area knew each other. Dolamani was a distant relative of Diganta Keshari from his mother's side. The nowhere wanderer decided to stop at his place in Balikuda that night and seek his recommendation to join as a teacher in Alakasharma, an ideal residential school in Jagatsinghpur. The young freedom fighters, who dropped out of college, taught some 120 students there. The school sat inside a dense mango orchard flanked by the Alka River on one side and a huge canal on the other. Diganta Keshari planned to join there and work with leaders like Gopabandhu Chaudhury and Ramadevi.

Dolamani supported the British blindly for retaining his zamindari, but didn't oppose the nationalist leaders either. He feared that if the nationalists won the freedom struggle and the British left, he would need the support of the nationalists to thrive. Dolamani listened and understood the young man's intention of coming to him. He feared that Diganta Keshari's stay with him might bring him under the radar of the British and said, 'Listen, my son! Give up these mad ideas. Don't be swept by the euphoria! You've everything. Don't stand against the British. Those who have time, let them. Enjoy the gifts of zamindari. Live your life. Don't worry over the fate of the generations coming after you.'

Diganta Keshari didn't argue and left with a genial smile towards the Balikuda bazaar. The marketplace was small. His aimless moves on the patchy, muddy rut caught the attention of Parshuram, the headmaster of the local high school. At the end of the strip of shops and beyond the Machhagaon Canal, ran a narrow road through the vast stretch of paddy fields to the high school. Parshuram Das, a brilliant science graduate, refused to join a well-paying corporate job with Tata Iron and Steel Company, and joined the school as the headmaster with a meagre salary of thirty rupees a month.

Parshuram was from the village Alabola, one and a half mile north of Balikuda. The son of Balakrishna Das, a renowned Sanskrit pandit and Ayurvedic practitioner, his home was known as the Adhikari's place. Balakrishna, the Vaishnava, used to christen brides, grooms and boys, and whisper their names to their ears in marriages and thread ceremonies. People lovingly called him the whispering Vaishnava. He had a huge temple for Lord Krishna in his home, and he observed every ritual associated with worshipping Jagannath, Balabhadra and Subhadra.

Balakrishna spent his whole day in that puja room; he had two simple meals daily and spent his time reading Sanskrit scriptures. He treated people for free with his potions; the patients brought him some humble gifts like a few drumsticks, brinjals and plantains, or a tiny bottle of homemade ghee. He headed a noble, scholarly joint family and owned a few acres of good land to run his household. But he didn't care much for worldly belongings and was detached from mundane worries. His wife died years ago when Parshuram was twelve. After her death, he kept himself busy with puja, chanting, reading scriptures and studying medicinal plants. He didn't care much for his land or children—Parshuram, Batakrishna and Ahalya. Uncles and aunties in the joint family looked after the children. He loved music, and when the world was too much for him, he retreated to the small house away from his joint family. He stayed alone and cooked while singing in devotion to Sri Krishna. Once, he stirred hard and busted the earthen pot with dal over the stovetop. His love for a one-and-a-half-foot-long blue tin box with a big pink rose was another funny story about Balakrishna Das. The box, a gift from the husband of a woman he cured, was the most valuable gift he ever received. For him, nothing mattered except music and love for man.

'Love for man', the message of the tiny blue box, guided the rhyme of teacher Parshuram's life. The strings of love for his people thrummed hard in his heart. He, therefore, refused the high-paying job with Tata and vowed to educate the people of his area. He founded the middle school, wrote songs, dramas and musicals, and acted and staged them to raise funds for the high school. He took a nominal salary and laid the foundation of Balikuda High School.

Parshuram was a brilliant student. He finished middle school with a merit scholarship, but no one took care to send him to high school. He spent time acting and staging folk musicals and dance dramas in the village. His teacher persuaded Parshuram's uncle Dinabandhu to take the bright boy to Bhadrakh, and put him in high school. Bhadrakh brought a turning point in his life. He stood first in the district in the final high school exam, joined Ravenshaw College in Cuttack as a science student, and passed out from Patna University. Dinabandhu, a top police officer, wanted his nephew to join the police service. But Parshuram declined politely, saying that he wanted to join the freedom movement with his friend Govinda Das. The dedicated police officer made young Parshuram understand that, like any other sensible Indian, he didn't want the British to occupy India. Still, the job was valuable to him in raising his children. Parshuram assured him that he wouldn't directly participate in the freedom movement and jeopardize his position. He decided to teach, educate, make people aware, and indirectly contribute to the freedom struggle. He returned to his village. Besides uncle Dinabandhu, his beloved guru, Professor P.K. Parija, wrote a letter asking him to start a high school in Balikuda:

Dear Parshuram,

Balikuda needs your attention urgently. We can start a high school in the village with your sincere effort and dedication. I still remember your memorable line from college days; you said that keeping in mind the current situation of our country, it's more useful if we can enable the masses to hold pens rather than asking them to hold guns in their hands. I'm simply reminding you of your own words.

Lovingly,
P.K. Parija

That letter was an order from his guru. Parshuram never dishonoured the wishes of his revered guru and started the Balikuda High School. Parshuram's marriage to Manorama, the only daughter of Zamindar Dhaneswar Mahapatra of Pariya Patapur of Puri, was also a strange coincidence. Manorama lost her father in her childhood and grew up at her maternal uncle Rajkishore Mahapatra's home. Rajkishore was a police official and a good friend and neighbour of Dinabandhu in the police colony. Dinabandhu's wife met Manorama at Rajkishore's house. Impressed with her beauty and finesse, she solemnized the marriage of nephew Parshuram with her. It was a union of two wonderful people. Parshuram never eyed the property Manorama was to inherit as the lone survivor, and she followed her husband dedicatedly. Parshuram's nationalist ideology never came between his cordial relationship with his uncle Dinabandhu and Manorama's uncle Rajkishore, who held sensitive positions in the British police service. He silently kept alive the momentum, secretly collected funds to support the freedom struggle, and sent that money to Cuttack office biweekly.

Parshuram created the spirit of nationalism in the young students. The village folks sought his guidance in day-to-day matters and asked him to mediate disputes over properties, especially land. Two other friends, Govinda Das and Harekrishna Bishwal, often joined him in resolving familial conflicts, and helped people of the surrounding villages live in peace and harmony. The three friends shared a very strong bond, and when they moved together, people compared them to the trinity—Brahma, Vishnu and Maheswara. Their motto was to see the end of the repressive regime of the kings and zamindars, the independence of the country, and a just society where everyone lived peacefully.

The zamindar and his middlemen in Balikuda didn't like Parshuram. They knew he was a threat to their monopoly over the matters of the area. They feared that the students who passed from his school were conscious of their rights and might revolt against the rules the zamindari system imposed on them. Even Dolamani, who overtly maintained a friendly relationship with

Parshuram, wasn't happy inside. But the popularity of the new teacher in that area prevented him from opposing Parshuram.

The journey of a small river that aims to join the ocean is never smooth, but it never forgets its mission when stuck halfway; it helps trees and grassy lands thrive. Parshuram was aware of the challenges to his goal to educate and inspire the masses towards self-awareness. Music and love for humanity were gifts he inherited from his father, and he often used them to educate his pupils. The first question he asked someone joining his school was if they knew how to sing. He believed that singing was a gift that could make anyone learn faster. The learning in his school started with the basics of music, and then moved to subjects like mathematics, science, Sanskrit, English, literature and geography. Though a science graduate, he could impart lessons in other subjects and routinely hosted musical gatherings in his home in the evenings. Music and love flowed together. The personality of twenty-eight-year-old Parshuram could be summed up as someone always cheerful, one who made the people around him cheerful too.

Diganta Keshari had heard much about the great teacher but hadn't met him in person. During the few days he stayed at Dolamani's place, he heard nothing but serious allegations against the headmaster. God's will made him wander into the Balikuda bazaar as a stranger that day and meet Parshuram.

'I'm Parshuram. I think I saw you sitting at Dolamani's porch some days back,' he said as an introduction.

Diganta Keshari greeted back politely. As they talked, he found the link between Diganta Keshari's family and that of his wife, Manorama. He invited the young man to his home. Anyone who had been to his place even once became a part of his family. Manorama was very hospitable too. While he playfully teased his wife for her zamindari hauteur, she proved him wrong with her warmth and politeness. She made a few extra dishes for the visitors and served it alongside rice, dal and vegetable curries. On average, they had two or three guests in their home daily. They were generous hosts.

After making the guest comfortable in his home, Parshuram wanted to know the purpose of Diganta Keshari's visit to Balikuda. The young man said he ran away from home and didn't want to return to his father, Zamindar Graharaj Chaudhury. The couple assured him of safety in their home and promised never to disclose his whereabouts to his father or his identity to anyone. As per the plan, Diganta Keshari stayed in their home as a follower of Hari Bishwal, an erstwhile revenue official, a follower of Gandhi, and a well-known freedom fighter in the Balikuda area. From that moment, he was renamed Digdarshi, and was assigned to guide the young men and galvanize them to fight for the country's freedom.

※

When Digdarshi wandered on the sands of Basanta Patali in long soul-searching deliberations on his immediate life goals, the freedom struggle was in a critical stage. At the Lahore session, the National Congress decided to violate the salt law as the first step of the civil disobedience movement. Gandhi started the Dandi March to defy the salt law. In Cuttack, Gopabandhu Chaudhury, Acharya Harihar and many other nationalist leaders gathered for the Salt March to Inchudi and enlisted as volunteers. Gopabandhu Chaudhury's wife Ramadevi came to Balikuda to gather volunteers. Four young men, Govinda Das, Hari Bishwal,

Kshetramohan Kanungo and Narayan Prasad Das, joined the move. Birakishore Das, a well-known name from Balikuda, also played a lead role in the non-violent movement.

Satyagraha, a non-violent movement, swept the nation like a powerful current. The call didn't just inspire men; it also brought out women held behind the four walls of homes in droves. Ramadevi reached Balikuda to host a public meeting. She started her journey from Govinda Das's house in Alabola. Before her arrival, people were aware that Ramadevi, the daughter of Gopal Ballhab Das and wife of Gopabandhu Choudhury, was going to address the people in the *Melan Padia*, the ground where the annual retreat of the gods from local temples took place in spring. People who had so far not seen a woman address people in public were extremely curious to see her speak. The deprecating question in their eyes was, 'What kind of a meeting will a woman have?'

On top of that, they wanted to see someone—the daughter and daughter-in-law of zamindars—out without covering her head and talking to people in the open.

Pranakrishna Das's wife Nishamani, known as Nishapa, led the trail of women who came out to join Ramadevi's march. Women were encouraged by her example, and they joined one by one. The ceaseless flow of humanity seemed like a mighty river running fast to join the ocean. They sang patriotic songs written by poets like Birakishore Das and others:

> Rise, oh freedom fighters!
> Rise, the brave minds!
> We'll throw the English out
> Let's remember our heroism.

Momentum picked up among the masses. They didn't care for the scorching sun overhead and walked miles to attend Ramadevi's Salt March. Travellers forgot their destination, buyers forgot to buy their goods, and students forgot their studies. Everyone marched towards the ground to hear her in Balikuda, as if under a spell. A twenty-five-year-old young man Sama Puhana, who was plowing in the field, watched the unusual sight with awe. He had never seen something so interesting happening in his village. He couldn't simply make out the fervent march of those people queued behind a pretty woman whose face dazzled in the bright sun. He heard them sing:

> Let's march to make salt!
> Obey the Mahatma's call, dear brothers!
> The sea surrounds our village, it's ours.
> They say we can't take a handful of salt!
> That's so unfair!

The crowd chanted in a chorus between each line, 'Long live Mother India!' The force of that unified voice frightened the bullocks that dragged Sama's plow. Sama, on his part, forgot his job at hand, forgot the animals, and ran to join the people chanting 'Long live Mother India'. His torso remained bare; he was hungry, and a simple turban covered his head. The illiterate rustic instinctively knew that the British occupation of his beautiful motherland was wrong. Ramadevi conjured up the image of Mother India for him.

'Mother India! Where is your golden crown? Did that English snatch that off your head? I promise I will work hard and bring it back to you, or else I'll never marry,' declared Sama Puhana falling at Ramadevi's feet.

Sama's action shocked people. They thought he was mad. Govinda Das came forward and urged him not to hurry for the freedom struggle or vow to remain single until the British left. Govinda Das knew Sama, the illiterate simpleton from his village, well. He was brave and free-spirited, and despite being poor, he didn't care for the king or the zamindar. Sometimes, a strange idea overtook his mind, and he set free his livestock. Claiming that the animals shouldn't be chained, he used to let them roam free. He was tall and strongly built. With an even bigger heart and an open mind, he had come forward to marry Sebati, the frail petite seventeen-year-old who was abused by her stepmother. Since her mother went mad and died, no family was willing to take Sebati as a bride for their son. That day, when he promised to bring back the crown that the British had taken away, his eyes met Sebati's eyes. She stood in the crowd with tearful eyes, and silly Sama was convinced that there shouldn't be any special hurry to marry her; that girl would wait for him.

As Ramadevi and Annapurna Maharana reached the Balikuda ground via Nagpur village, seven thousand people had sprung to the ground leaving behind whatever they were doing to listen to her. Hand-woven khadi, popularized by Gandhi as a symbol of self-reliance, was sold to people there. The people were frenzied with enthusiasm.

The government had taken tacit measures to disrupt the meeting and misdirect people's attention. Sadhabananda Mishra, the deputy magistrate from the British government, stayed at the inspection bungalow to see that the crowd was taken away from Ramadevi's meeting. He had arranged the Gotipua dance, a popular folk performance, to distract the rustic audience from attending the meeting. But the unified voice from the meeting resounded like a chorus. 'Let's go to make salt' and 'Friends, follow the Mahatma's call' boomed in the air. The people didn't fear brutal flogging and stayed in the meeting. The deputy magistrate was the sole audience of the folk singers' parody of the Salt March. The seven-thousand-strong crowd listened to Ramadevi's inspirational speech for two hours. She urged for donations to fund the national movement. Women voluntarily gave away their gold and other valuable jewellery, and she stood before the crowd holding the things on the end of her sari.

After the meeting, Ramadevi stayed with Raghabanada Das's family. Birakishore's mother was in charge of the kitchen; she was proud that her son had joined the freedom movement. She cooked and fed the freedom fighters happily. Ramadevi sat on their elevated porch and talked to allies like Hari Bishwal, Kshetramohan Kanungo and Govinda Das. Sama Puhana showed up, challenging the British to return Mother India's crown. He sang, 'Long live Mother India! Long live Mahatma Gandhi! Long live Ramadevi!'

Ramadevi saw a young boy sitting in a corner and watching the activities. Bony and shining like a straight golden stick, he had large, glistening bright eyes and a sharp nose. His face was soft like a fresh flower. A school bag hung from his shoulder. He had been staring at Ramadevi with admiration, and without blinking his eyes. She called the boy and patted him gently on his back, and said, 'I've marked you sitting in the front row of the meeting today. It's already getting dark. Why didn't you go home? You are from which village? What's your father's name?'

'The name of my village is Kania, and my father's name is Purushottam Mohanty.'

'Which class are you in?'

'I finished seventh and am going to eighth this year.'
'You may go home now. Aren't you hungry?'
'No. Bira babu's ma fed me well. I'm full.'

The boy opened up after the conversation and expressed his desire to join the freedom movement. Ramadevi said that he could join the Banar Sena, the group for the children. She warned that the volunteers might be beaten hard; Deputy Magistrate Zahid Sahib lashed twenty-five blows to the young fighters and often got their palms bloodied. She thought that, frightened, the boy would go home. But he rose from his seat passionately, spread out his hands towards her, and began singing loudly,

> Hit me as many times as you want
> We're here to die for our motherland
> Can you scuff such a tough band?

She folded the boy in her arms and kissed his cheek tenderly. It convinced her that the future of the freedom movement was secure in the hands of brave warriors like the little boy. She asked him to go home and ask his parents if he could come to the Alakashrama and join the Banar Sena. The boy touched her feet and was ready to leave. She called him from behind and asked, 'I didn't ask your name, dear boy. What's your name?'

'Baikunthanath Mohanty, people call me Bai,' he said.

The boy moved ahead in the darkness—not towards his village but towards Jagatsingpur. His shoulder was burdened with the load of the school bag, but a mightier responsibility awaited him. He threw the bag with all humility to the waters of the Machhagaon Canal, and became free. Gopabandhu Chaudhury, who had resigned from his position as a deputy magistrate, was waiting desperately to bring together the Banar Sena in

Alakashrama; he needed the support of the young freedom fighters in his mission to remove the Ravana-like oppressive British rule. Baikuntha was the humble squirrel that carried little sand for building the Setubandha over the sea in the Ramayana. He, too, should do his bit in making the bridge to free the motherland.

Chapter VI

A single watershed moment defines the goal people want to pursue in life. Digdarshi's vow to fight against the painful shame of being an outcast in his motherland came at a rarified moment when he found the analogy of India's suffering under British occupation in Chakori's plight as a dasi. He saw that the young dasi, forced to live beneath her father's roof as an illegitimate child and a voiceless slave, wasn't different from the cries of an entire nation caught by the powerful tentacles of colonial British rule. Digdarshi's voice of resistance became powerful and transformed into an insuperable wave of protest against imperialism. His awkward adolescent dream to set free the daughter of a dasi led to a fiercely determined goal to fight for the nation's freedom.

He couldn't reconcile that the British, a foreign power, denied people the right to oppose its repressive rule. The desire to challenge the Raj overpowered him. He united scores of young men to fight for freedom. Like the powerful pull of the full moon stirring the heart of the ocean, calls from Ramadevi and Saraladevi, too, added to the surge of patriotism in the people of Balikuda, Jagatsinghpur and Erasama. The freedom fighters sought volunteers to work in remote villages, stimulate the masses, and make them aware of their right to oppose peacefully. The momentum was flagging at times and wasn't effective in arousing the villagers from the deep slumber of ignorance and inertia.

'Music would be a magical medium to stir the dormant minds of the masses,' said teacher Parshuram. He quickly composed and recited two rhyming lines in his beautiful voice, *'Ama ghara chabi ame karu dabi* (we ask you for nothing but the key to our house).' The young volunteers followed. He composed a few nationalistic verses overnight and set the tune. Digdarshi, Kori, Madan, Baikuntha, Hari and Govinda didn't sleep the whole night, and learned to sing. Manorama stayed awake and provided tea and snacks for them all. By daybreak, all those amateurs became expert singers.

'It's dedication. One can achieve the impossible with sheer dedication,' said Parshuram.

'Yes, dedication—not just for music, it should be for the country and the nation,' replied Digdarshi.

The team held meetings accompanied by music and singing in every village, and played *nagara* for every announcement. As the nagara players were afraid of the police, Digdarshi took the instrument in his hands and began playing like a professional. Dolamani watched the scene on the village road and mocked the move as the misfortune of a rich zamindar's son, hanging the nagara made from dirty animal skin on his neck and playing like a poor piper to make a living.

Law-and-order officials followed Digdarshi's team wherever they went to spread the message of the non-violent movement, and urged people to deny them food or shelter. The volunteers had to go without food for some days. They rested under the trees but didn't beg for food or drink from the people.

One night during the journey, the volunteers heard about free food for the poor offered by a Brahmin, Udayanath, after his father's death in Chandrakhati village. Digdarshi and three others—Hari, Madan and Govinda—who had been hiding from the police and were without food for more than a day, rushed there uninvited. They made plates for themselves from the leaves of the roadside *baigaba* tree, and managed to eat. Until then, Digdarshi didn't know the plucking pains of hunger or the greedy gulps taken by the hungry. That day he experienced the hungry man's disregard for status, wealth, caste or class. After eating, the friends spread hay and slept peacefully in a nearby barn.

Darkness engulfed the whole place. He lay on the bed of hay and stared at the vast and clear April night sky that seemed to take pity on the zamindar's son and cover him gently. Chakori and his dream to see her free, flashed before his eyes. He thought of the boundless sky moving free and the moon watching the *chakori*—the bird believed to be crying for her missing mate at night.

Digdarshi heard someone wailing and determined that it came from Udayanath's backyard. He rose and began to walk in that direction. A middle-aged woman wailed in the shed. None of the family was around her. Seeing the stranger in the middle of the night, she became silent and thought that he might be there for the free food. Digdarshi introduced himself as a wandering priest, performing havan and puja; the name of his ashram was Sarvadharma Ashram and his guru was Parshuram. She believed whatever he said and urged him to save her daughter's life, who remained unresponsive. The Brahmin's wife claimed that her daughter was dying from hunger since the father, Udayanath, didn't allow the girl, Maiya, to eat anything that day. She asked him to recite the *Sanjivani* mantra that might restore life to her.

She further clarified that Maiya was a child widow who, in the holy month of Kartik, was expected to eat one meal in the evening and bathe before sunrise. She was supposed to fast that day if anything went wrong while making the meal. The rigor of the practice took a toll on her health, and she became sick. It was Ekadashi that day, and she was supposed to fast without swallowing a drop of water.

'Her eyes don't move. She will die any moment. Death may save her from this dungeon forever,' the mother cried.

She was pale with fear for her daughter's life. Digdarshi further learned from her that Maiya was given in marriage as a child. The groom had tuberculosis and died days after the marriage; she had never been a bride. She was seventeen and had been observing twenty-four Ekadashi in a year without drinking water for the last eight years. While the father fed the poorest of the poor in the free community feasts as a mark of remembrance for his father, the daughter almost died from starvation. Digdarshi pacified her and wanted to check her pulse. The mother prohibited him, saying that the orthodox father thought that if any man from outside ever touched her, his five generations would rot in hell. He asked the mother to get permission from Udayanath, so that he could treat the girl. When he finally entered the house, he saw the father pouring drops of water into the girl's ear.

'Why do you pour water through her ear? She's almost dead! I'm a yogi and have saved many lives. I know quite a bit of medication,' Digdarshi said.

'If you're a yogi, you should've known that a child widow from a Brahmin family isn't supposed to have even a drop of water on Ekadashi. If she's dying, the holy water for salvation should be swallowed via the ear. What kind of an enlightened person are you?' replied Udayanath, irritated.

Digdarshi was in disbelief. Udayanath's behaviour stunned him. But he continued his plea calmly, 'How do you predict that her death is imminent? I can see that she has a long life. Give me a chance. I'll try to save her.'

The father allowed him inside. Digdarshi asked everybody except the mother to leave the room. He asked her to bring some milk and said that he would bathe the milk with a mantra and then offer that to the earth so that the girl would rise. He agreed with the father not to give food, milk or medicine to Maiya. The mother locked the door from inside. Digdarshi saw that the girl was conscious but was extremely weak from not having food for a long time. He sought the mother's permission to add some sweet potions to the milk and let the girl drink. She didn't object. Digdarshi added some glucose to fortify the milk and offered her. The freedom fighters often carried glucose packets to stave off hunger when they didn't have food for days. They also saved some emergency drugs for cold, fever and diarrhoea, in their bags. He gave a tablet to reduce her fever. He poured some water on the ground to give the impression that the milk was being offered to the earth. In minutes, the girl opened her eyes and called for her mother faintly.

'How do you feel, my girl? Do you feel a little better, my dear Maithili?' asked the mother.

Digdarshi understood that the girl was Maithili—another name for Sita—the goddess who married Rama and endured every injustice heaped upon her as calmly as the eternally forbearing earth. Like her namesake, the girl didn't know how to complain and stand up for herself. He quietly felt the irony in her name. Maithili opened her eyes, extremely surprised to see the stranger standing there.

'I'm Digdarshi from the ashram nearby. If you want, you can join the ashram. Many girls like you, who aren't treated well by society and want to escape the system, have joined the ashram; they work for the country's independence. Bye for now! I've got to go—I must embark on my journey before daybreak,' he introduced himself and his mission, and left.

Digdarshi had a final, gentle look at that pale, sick, innocent face. Maithili raised her trembling, frail hands, and folded them in gratitude for the man who gave back her life. It was dawn, and to Digdarshi's eyes, the pole star looked like a resplendent drop of tear on the rosy cheek of the sky.

∞

Maithili had cried hard the day jewellery pieces were removed from her body. Someone wiped off the red dot from her forehead, chopped her long hair, took away her colourful sari, and wrapped a white one over her. She cried for her cherished bangles, bracelets, earrings and anklets. She cried for her silk sari with colourful domes on the border. She cried for her kohl, vermillion and long hair. The nine-year-old never understood why her parents, aunts, uncles and other relatives were crying after they took away all her favourite stuff. It wasn't the age for her to understand the things happening to her.

'My darling, you're no longer going to eat fish or wear bangles,' said her mother sobbing.

Little Maithili thought her father had become so poor overnight that he couldn't buy bangles or fish for her.

'If all of you can have these adornments like vermilion, jewellery and bangle, why not me? Why can't I eat fish if the rest of the women can?' she later asked her mother and the women in her family.

The mother had no answer except her tears. Finally, it was her uncle who came forward with an answer, 'The man you married is dead. You're a widow now, and a widow can't have all these things. Control your mind, dear child! There're many women in our village who have got a similar fate.'

Maithili didn't give in easily. She thumped her foot on the ground and cried, 'I don't know him at all, never even met him. Why am I not supposed to eat fish and wear jewellery if he dies? Did he or his father feed me?'

The protest didn't go well with her father. He silenced her with a thunderous howl, 'Be silent! Ill-fated female! Don't cross your limits by asking too many questions. Remember! You're fated to be a widow and must bear with the misfortune. Nobody here widowed you!'

He screamed while wiping out his tears. The nine-year-old was stunned to hear the word 'widow' from her father. It was revolting for her to imagine herself as one of those pale women draped in a coarse white sari without any makeup or zest, for the rest of her life. She knew those women weren't allowed to attend celebrations like marriage or thread ceremony. The girl rolled on the ground, questioning if her mother, aunt or any other woman in her family wasn't a widow, why should she be?

The crazy behaviour of the girl upset everyone. Her grandmother warned that those questions were a bad omen for the rest of the womenfolk in the family. The old woman slapped hard on Maithili's tear-soaked face and calmed her down. 'Ill-fated witch! Your bad karma killed your husband. Your fate is sealed. Don't curse your mother and aunts.'

Initially, Maithili looked for her bangles; she didn't like her bare wrists, but slowly, she got used to that rule. Some fourteen or fifteen widows in her village lived without wearing bangles; no hint of colour appeared on the white sari they donned. She forsook the bangles and colourful saris, but still craved fish. Nobody in her home dared to offer her fish. It violated the pious life that a widow was mandated to follow. It was a sin to feed fish to her. Maithili's father, Udayanath Panda, who taught in the Sanskrit school, mandated her to follow every practice that a Hindu widow was supposed to follow; his daughter was no exception.

Maithili had no bed; she slept on the bare floor and her hair was regularly chopped. She was barred from attending celebrations and enjoying songs, dance, music or theatre. Restricted from eating moringa leaves, onion, garlic, gourd, cabbage, cauliflower and other vegetables, she survived on bare vegetarian food. She ate a single meal in the months of Baisakh, Kartika and Magha. She had the limited choice of eating whole mung bean boiled with taro, *agasti* spinach, plantain, and a little ghee with rice. Yogurt and salt were additional. The father used to supervise if she followed every practice.

The father hit Maithili hard if she wished to eat fish with her cousins. Hurt and humiliated, she refused to eat some days and went to bed hungry. The house witnessed a lot of tension surrounding the poor girl. Initially, she was a very picky eater, but things changed drastically. The mother was traumatized to see Maithili constantly craving food. The miserable life of the daughter made her very sad. She, too, didn't care for her looks. She stopped wearing bright saris or putting vermilion on her forehead. She was extremely awkward about wearing jewellery as Maithili went around without embellishment. She managed clothing and other external things, but the food aspect of it was different. Being a married woman, she couldn't fast on Ekadashi or shun eating fish, for those were believed to be practices of a wife to assuage huddles to her husband's long life and wellbeing.

Udayanath, the hardliner, warned his wife to watch over Maithili. The mother often thought that it would be better if they stopped bringing fish home, but Udayanath couldn't manage to eat without fish. The least he needed on his plate was a little bit of fish curry on the side. When the smell of fried fish wafted in the air, Maithili would rush to her mother and beg for a piece passed on to her secretly; otherwise, she would threaten to go without food. But her mother didn't dare to defy the rules for her naive daughter. When Udayanath and his younger brother Balunkeswar sat on the floor and relished the lush gravy of the fish curry elaborately served to them, poor Maithili stood at the threshold and watched their feast without flapping her eyes. Often, the mother stopped serving food to the brothers in between, and asked the girl to go outside and play. The mother would touch a bit of the fish curry to her tongue, and join her daughter for a bland dinner. Tears from the quirky girl's eyes and the tears of a mother who couldn't violate the dictums for a widow, mingled with the food on their plates. The girl cried non-stop for fish and often choked, while the morsel of rice went cold in the mother's palm; they were half-starved and got weaker gradually.

During the sacred months of austerity and fasting on Ekadashi, the mother hardly ate while the girl sat in a dark room without water. Udayanath had once hunkered down and slapped hard on Maithili's tender cheeks for picking a few morsels of puffed rice from the floor and eating on a day of fasting. He never tolerated violation of rites related to faith. He feared more for the sin of deviation that might push his forefathers to rot in hell. After that incident, Udayanath started locking her up in his bedroom. The girl cried non-stop inside; she begged for food and water. The smell of tempering on curries made her crave food; she begged for a few drops of water to quell her thirst in the terrible heat of April. The Brahmin, who gobbled a huge bowl of rice seasoned with yogurt, burped happily. If he heard his daughter asking for food and water, he said with concern that Maithili had to bear the misfortune of a widow because of the sins she committed in her previous birth. He warned the poor girl that if she didn't follow the practices meant for a widow in this life, the misfortune would follow her in the next birth too.

The mother didn't care for the punishment in the next birth or the sins committed against previous generations. She was convinced that she didn't give birth to a daughter to see her go through the misery in her present life. She hid water in a pitcher, and snacks and bananas under the bed. Maithili didn't cry for food after that. But neither the girl nor the mother were careful enough to throw away the banana peels tossed under the bed. The father caught their crime, hit his wife cruelly, and checked the room thoroughly before locking up Maithili. Once more, the mother looked for an opportunity to feed her hungry daughter; and since no transaction, good or bad, could be a secret forever, she was caught by her mother-in-law while stealthily delivering some food in a pouch through the window. The old woman was horrified by the lack of piety in their conduct. She screamed that if she, a seventy-year-old senile, could withstand hunger, then why not young Maithili? She declared that the co-conspirators were bent upon sending the ancestors to hell.

The old woman's two sons rushed to check. The mother stood hunched like a culprit awaiting the verdict. Distraught Udayanath atoned for the sin by offering water to pacify the souls of his ancestors. He vowed to send Maithili back to her in-laws' place, where she would toil like a slave. The mother fell at his feet and urged him not to push the widow to that place of unspeakable suffering.

The mother and daughter were locked in two separate rooms on every Ekadashi. The father told Maithili the story of a sati in his clan who, years and years ago, ended her life after the death of her husband. According to him, every Brahmin girl needed to know the glorious practice of sati. He criticized the British for abolishing some sacred Hindu traditions like sati and child marriage. He believed that their stringent law prevented countless women from reaching heaven, and was upset with natives like Raja Ram Mohan Roy for joining hands with the foreigners to end sati. He scolded Gandhi, who came from Africa and fought relentlessly against child marriage and encouraged widow remarriage. He looked deep into Maithili's curious eyes and pointed at the sati ground in his backyard and the *sahada* tree, beneath which his father's auntie attained sati at age eight. The pandit was proud that someone from his ancestry did such a pious deed and rose to that exalted status.

While fantasizing about heaven, Maithili felt terror listening to the details of the sati's ascent to that dreamland. Udayanath asked her to sit close to him and listen to the story. The pandit elaborated that the legendary auntie was married at seven to a man as his fifth wife. Before the union was even solemnized, the old man breathed his last. He was from the neighbouring village, and when his pyre was readied, the girl was decorated as a bride. Excited, she wanted to know the purpose of the arrangement.

'You're going to heaven. God has already opened the door for you!' said a relative. The girl was excited to go to heaven and meet the gods and goddesses. But she couldn't make out when the people said that someone who had joined her for eternity—for uncountable births and rebirths—would be waiting there for her. She began to recall the person close to her; none of her parents, uncles, aunts or siblings had been to heaven. She was curious about the person who waited for her in heaven.

'Am I going alone?' she asked.

'Yes, darling, going to heaven is a lonely journey,' said someone.

'Not even my parents?'

'No! Your parents aren't that blessed.'

Petrified, the girl clung hard to her mother. She panicked and cried miserably, 'No, Ma, no! I won't go to heaven. I'll be too scared among strangers. I'm scared of the darkness and can't sleep alone. How can you send me there all alone?'

The mother sobbed and choked miserably; they held each other tight. Someone pacified her from behind. 'Why're you so scared? Your husband is in heaven. You're married to him. He died yesterday and has already reached there. He has been waiting for you there. Your real life will begin there. No need to suffer in this sinful world. It's all God's grace,' explained someone.

'Ghost! Ghost! That man became a ghost after death. Why should I go to that stranger? I can't recognize him. Ma! I'm so scared of ghosts. I might die, but I won't go to heaven. I'll be with you…,' screamed the girl.

Before leading the eight-year-old to the pyre, the priest at the cremation ground made her drink a bowl of a concoction made from a mix of poisonous *dudura* seeds and bhang. Most satis were forced to drink that concoction. How can the journey to heaven be enjoyable without being intoxicated? While she was taken to the cremation ground, the girl was delirious. Under the influence of the drink, she giggled uncontrollably in euphoria one moment, then fell on the ground and cried hard, refusing to go to heaven the next. The uproar from the combined mix of drum beats, conch blows, ululation, cheers and singing the praise of God, drowned the shrill cries of the girl.

As soon as she saw the leaping flames of fire, she became aware of their intent. She held on to her uncle—who was leading the procession—tight, hid her face in his chest, cried hard, and howled, 'I don't want to go to heaven. Don't burn me for that dead man. I'm so scared! Please let me go! I'm begging for my life!'

The girl, who clung tight to her uncle's chest in fear for her life, was forcefully taken to the pyre. Four men flung her to the flames and pressed her body hard with bamboo poles against the rising fire. The spectators were desensitized to the roiling sight of a sati burnt before their eyes. The barbarism was sealed from them by pouring enough ghee and incense into the flame that covered the place in smoke and smog. The roar of drums and bells, and cries of prayer, drowned the painful wails of the girl being burnt alive. The spectators glorified her attainment of sati with cries of praise for her. It was hard to determine if the tears in their eyes were tears of joy for her attainment of satihood and ascending heaven, or of their unspeakable guilt.

From that day, the area was known as the sati ground, and it became a place of pilgrimage for the scores of villages surrounding it. The memorial that glorified Udayanath's clan became the site of an annual festival; actors dramatized the event to drive home the concept of sati to young girls. Tender Maithili cringed in pain and guilt while she heard the horrible atrocities inflicted on her great grandfather's sister to make her a sati. She seethed in anger against the inhuman practice, and her tender rebellious heart crumbled into innumerable tiny pieces in disapproval of the barbaric custom. It wasn't an isolated incident related to her family; sati was a practice very much alive in other parts of the country. Many innocent souls were, thus, purged in plain sight with no qualms because people refused to give up their heinous prejudice against a woman when she became a widow.

Goddess Sita, in the Ramayana, was asked to prove her purity before Rama, and had to enter the fire several times. Draupadi, in the Mahabharata, had to cleanse herself in fire every day before she entered the chambers of any of her five husbands. Fire is elemental for a woman to prove her chastity and faithfulness to the man she is given out to in marriage. These reflections crushed young Maithili's rebellious mind. She was a hapless, young ignorant widow, absolutely powerless. The revolt, however, agitated her heart unabated.

Chapter VII

Twelve years later...

In the ceaseless flow of mighty time, twelve years fizzle out like tiny, insignificant bubbles. Twelve years in the life of a nation disappear in the blink of an eye, but twelve years for a person waiting for the return of a dear one slowly reduce to a lingering, painful sigh. Each moment is a fraught pause, an aimless wandering in the corridor of darkness, completely disregarding the hope of the return of the beloved person. Zamindar Graharaj Chaudhury waited twelve years for the return of his missing eldest son. Years passed, and the curtains slowly began to draw over the haunted nightmare. Nobody knew if Diganta Keshari was dead or alive. It was customary for the father to bring closure to the case by following the rituals observed for the dead. The zamindar performed the last rites and reluctantly accepted that the young man was no more alive.

The other person caught in the tense drama surrounding Diganta Keshari's missing was Devaki, the stepmother. She prayed earnestly that he shouldn't ever return. It was hard to read the zamindar's mind. While the officials investigated Diganta Keshari's role in many anti-government activities and searched for him, Graharaj informed them that his son had dropped out of college, joined the non-cooperation movement, and had been missing for a long time. He testified that a rebel had no place in the palace of a British loyalist. He declared that he banished his son and wouldn't allow him to enter his territory if he didn't stop opposing the Raj.

But whether the zamindar had legally dismissed Diganta Keshari as his heir remained a mystery. He talked vaguely to the authorities, 'Almost decided. If he doesn't mend his conduct…'

He was decorated with the title 'Rai Sahib' for his loyalty to the British. The honour brought some reprieve, but the emptiness in his heart was unbearable. He often checked Diganta Keshari's room and asked the servants to clean the furniture and change the bed sheets. They arranged fresh flowers in the vase, scented the room with rose and sandalwood water, cleaned and stacked his dresses in the almirah with camphor, and kept his books and other things in order. Suddenly, he seemed very sentimental, and assigned the daily maintenance job of the room to Chakori.

Chakori lived in the outhouse only for four months. Practically, Devaki couldn't run the household without her. Also, she couldn't tolerate the dasi enjoying a good life, and wanted her to return to the palace and slave around following her orders. The saying goes, if you want revenge, keep your enemy alive. Per her order, Chakori would arrive at daybreak, get off the palanquin, and leave the palace at midnight every day. When sick, she would sit back and nap on the veranda, but was often summoned back to work in minutes. She was Devaki's prey.

Chakori counted each passing day. She kept alive the hope that Diganta Keshari would return and the day of freedom would dawn, but she didn't know when. She was sure he would never excuse her for the illicit relationship with his father, and her resulting pregnancy. She suffered unspeakable guilt for the young man going missing. But she had no answers for his stealthy appearance at the outhouse that night. In this never-ending conflict in her mind, she heard him scream, 'What did you do, Chakori? Is this the freedom I've been looking for you?'

'Master, I didn't have any choice. A dasi is always the easiest prey. Chop my head for the unforgivable sin and set this dasi free,' she said to herself.

Chakori told Devaki with much hesitation about her strong feeling that Diganta Keshari was alive and the family should wait a few more years before declaring him dead; also, people shouldn't blame her, the stepmother, for hastening the process. Devaki never wanted Chakori to meddle in family matters. She feared that Chakori performed black magic to control the senile zamindar. She was relieved that the disappearance had cleared the path for her four sons to inherit the zamindar's wealth. Dakhinray, the father, constantly reminded her to use the missing stepson in their best interest. It was futile waiting for the missing son. He insisted that even the socially mandated practice of twelve-year wait period let a wife voluntarily take off her bangles and vermilion to become a widow.

Dakhinray's rise from rags to riches had an interesting backstory. The journey of a humble peasant to the rank of a zamindar had a checkered path. His grandfather, Balamukunda Jena, was a lay farmer with very good looks; his elder brother was the zamindar's bookkeeper. Handsomeness and the elder brother's stature helped his marriage into a rich family. His wife was gifted eight acres of land for her expenses for cosmetics, known as outlays for turmeric in those days, which became the 'seed' of Jena's wealth. His son, Parikshita Jena, became a sub-deputy under the British; the villagers called him Raja Sarkar. Later, as an assistant settlement officer, he collected excess paddy from the farmers and loaded his granary that became the second layer of his wealth. During his stay in Banki, he obtained boulders and wood illegally to build a concrete home in his village. When he joined as the manager of Puri Jagannath Temple, he defrauded and took away a huge cache of gold to enrich himself. To make a long story short, when he served in Chamaparan, he propitiated British officials well and got the title of zamindar. He bought the zamindari from Mahikanta Bishwal with the wealth he amassed. Devaki's father was one of his inheritors.

Devaki and Dakhinray successfully persuaded Zamindar Graharaj Chaudhury to remove Diganta Keshari's name as the legal heir of his estate. He was officially declared dead. Graharaj spoke publicly that his eldest son was the black sheep of his family and therefore he decided to disqualify him from ownership of the zamindari. But deep inside, a faint voice often reminded him that nothing other than his debauchery had traumatized the son so deeply that he left home in rejection of everything that the father stood for. That night, when he came face to face with the fallen human masked behind his ideal persona at the steps of the outhouse, it gave him a shattering jolt. Diganta Keshari's imagined hateful thoughts echoed in Graharaj's ears like prophecies echoing in the air. At times he felt it was better that his son went missing. Facing the son who carried a sullied image of the father would've wounded his pride in fatherhood and masculinity. It wasn't unusual for a zamindar to have mistresses. Had he been open from the beginning about his relationship with the dasis, mistresses, prostitutes or court-dancers, the impact wouldn't have been so devastating upon either of them. He had the painful realization that the self, cloaked in a false garb, might come off someday and ruin a man's self-image mercilessly.

When Diganta Keshari was gone, the zamindar made his relationship with Chakori public. He didn't wear the mask of piety. He visited whores like Narmada and Sunila, and didn't hide the names of the corners he visited to seek pleasure. Initially, there was a tiny flicker of hope in him that Diganta Keshari—the sensitive young man—would get over that phase of disorientation over his inappropriate conduct, and return home.

In the meantime, rumours were rife about Diganta Keshari's subversive activities in the area. Dakhinray had a police informer who spied on Diganta Keshari and churned out those stories. Devaki knew from her father that Diganta Keshari mobilized farmers and labourers against the zamindar, spread the message of the non-cooperation movement, enlisted volunteers, and galvanized the youth against the British. She informed everything to her husband, including his arrest and torture in the lockup. It wasn't a secret that Diganta Keshari was instrumental in spreading Gandhi's teachings in remote corners of the state; he worked alongside terrorists who incited violence, and read out passages from books confiscated by the government.

Graharaj knew that his son trained under Gopabandhu Chaudhury and Ramadevi, and spearheaded the non-cooperation movement in Balikuda, Erasama and Jagatsinghpur; he also visited Bari, Balasore, Koraput, Ali and Sonpur. The police arrested Diganta Keshari when all the top leaders of the freedom movement in Odisha were kept behind bars, and angry students of Ravenshaw College burnt down the college office in protest against the police. The rage leaped beyond the campus and engulfed other towns and villages in the state.

During that period, the number of police shootings in parts of Odisha surpassed the record from other areas of the country. Twenty-five protesters were killed in Eram, and people began saying that the police killing on the bank of the Turee River in Koraput was no less harrowing than the Jallianwala Bagh massacre. Nineteen people were killed in police firing. Of the hundred and forty freedom fighters arrested, ninety-two were ordered to be hanged. Graharaj learned that Diganta Keshari was very much involved in the arson at Ravenshaw College. But he smartly escaped the watchful eyes of the police and reached Koraput. He galvanized the tribal people. Graharaj got confusing news that either his son was killed by the police or would be hanged on charges of treason.

Graharaj knew that Diganta Keshari was a lion's cub in a fox's dale and hated the British rule. He knew it was hard to contain the fire of patriotism in his son's heart. He recalled one episode from the boy's childhood. Sometime during the 1920s, police superintendent Smith was on a visit to verify the impact of an anti-establishment speech on the rural folks, and stayed in Graharaj's guest house. British officials visited on horseback, but Smith sahib was an exception; he came on a bicycle. Most of the villagers hadn't seen a bike till that day. They called it *sungadi*, the zero cart; possibly the analogy was for the big wheels. They were familiar with bullock carts with two wheels side by side, but they hadn't seen a cart with two wheels moving fast against each other without crashing. People thronged the road from the previous day to glimpse the magic vehicle.

Diganta Keshari studied at Cuttack Collegiate School then, and was on vacation in the village. He stood on the rooftop terrace and was hurt to watch the rousing reception that the naive folks gave to Smith. He felt that people should have a sense of dignity. Smith sahib ambled out on his bike in his khaki shorts and a fedora hat. People cheered him with excitement. Smith sahib might have been making fun of the poor Odia simpletons, 'Fools, haven't you seen a bicycle yet?'

He rode leisurely to help the people have a closer look. Bodyguards ran by his side. He seemed to think that without the British colonizing several countries, perhaps many parts of the world would be in darkness and remain backward. While he was extolling in his mind the contribution of his race in civilizing the world, a stone came with the shower of flowers and hit the left side of his forehead. He screamed hard from the injury and lost the grip on the handles, and fell off the bicycle. The zamindar's people came and took him inside the palace. All the innocent schoolchildren were questioned and beaten hard to find the culprit. Strangely, none of the devils came forward with a confession.

Zamindar Graharaj Chaudhury apologized that some low-caste urchin might have done the mischief. Diganta Keshari pushed through the crowd and admitted that he threw the stone, and that no innocent child should be punished. Graharaj was humiliated and lost his temper; he might've killed his son right there. Prapancha Mohanty came to the immediate rescue of the boy with his quick wit, calling the zamindar's son a kind soul who could not stand the whipping of the innocent kids and took the blame upon himself. Before Diganta Keshari explained further, the zamindar looked sternly at Prapancha Mohanty, who took the boy inside.

'I'm sorry for the mistake. The stone missed the target and hit his forehead. I wished it hit below his ear and the peppy trader in the bicycle died right there!' he told his father.

That day, Graharaj counselled his son patiently. Later in life, Diganta Keshari grew to be a very calm, gentle and obedient young man. But his hatred for the English was never gone from his heart. Episodes from the past thus swam in his mind when he was in a pensive mood.

⚭

The sun rose. Darkness ebbed at daybreak and life seemed new. But for Chakori, there was no daybreak; the darkness never receded, and there was no end to her misery. The unbearable burden crumbled her every day, but she never let dejection overtake her grit. A strange desire propelled her to push ahead and keep rolling. She reflected if Diganta Keshari ever returned to the palace, would that change her fate? She never thought of it in terms of gain or loss and prayed silently for him to return. Midnight was the usual time for her to return to her shack. She dragged her tired body and the broken heart inside mechanically.

Graharaj would often reach there earlier, spend the night with her, and leave in his palanquin before daybreak. Ranidhai, the midwife, sometimes came at night to check on her and cleanse her unwanted pregnancies as ordered by Graharaj. Her shrill, painful cries burdened the darkness of the night with a sombre note. She would get up in the morning, return to the palace, and look after Devaki and her children. She often fell at Ranidhai's feet and urged her to spare the unborn in her womb. She wanted to be a mother and hold a living, breathing bundle of flesh and blood in her arms and didn't care if it was a boy or a girl.

Grinning in her familiar manner, Ranidhai made her understand that if she gave birth to a girl, she would be a dasi like her, and a son would be a golam, who would always be shamed for his dubious origin. She warned that Graharaj would never give the rights of an offspring to someone born to a dasi. Her cries for motherhood didn't move Ranidhai's cold heart, nor did her tears dig a line on her parched mind toughened over the years; she mechanically removed the foetus like a fruit or flower plucked from a tree.

Chakori was continuously sick for a while; she could no longer rise and go to the palace for work. Graharaj visited her less. He was interested in the young dasi because his wife had lost her charm due to repeated childbirths. With frequent abortions, Chakori became sick and looked less attractive. The zamindar's palanquin then stopped regularly at the doors of young whores like Narmada and Adara.

The dream of becoming a mother didn't leave Chakori's mind. One night, she went to Ranidhai, kept some small gold and silver jewellery at her feet that the zamindar, his wife and her mother Sahabi had given her over the years, and prayed for help. Ranidhai heard her patiently and tied those pieces on the end of her sari, saying, 'Here's the deal! For nine months, you'll pretend to be a patient of ascites and say that the swelling is due to the abnormal fluid buildup in the abdomen. But when you give birth, it won't be a secret. What action the zamindar would take against you, I don't know. But he might chop my head for enabling the whole thing.'

Chakori held on to the midwife's feet and begged that she didn't care for her life. She pleaded with Ranidhai to plan something to avoid the wrath of the zamindar. The midwife decided to leave the village for six months and return once the baby was born. For the rest of the world, Chakori had ascites and gained weight; her hands and feet swelled, giving the impression that she was battling death. Graharaj stopped visiting her and instructed his servants to cremate her if she died. Devaki worried that her children would miss her care if she died. She didn't care to visit her but never wished her dead. Chakori was the only person grateful to God for helping her in the mission.

Death, however, wasn't in the offing. Life bloomed in the darkness in the farmhouse. Dina Rout's wife took care of Chakori for finding the connection. The cries of an angel overpowered Chakori's agony, and the news of the birth reached every corner of the area. It was a terrible blow to arrogant Graharaj. A dasi could be his mistress and warm his bed, but she couldn't be the mother of a child with his name. Devaki, too, seethed in anger. Graharaj coldly explained that Chakori was immoral like her mother Sadhabi, and wasn't happy with him. She had affairs with scores of employees, servants and caretakers, whoever visited her. Her baby was a bastard. He convinced Devaki that if the country became free following the freedom movement, zamindar families mightn't find people to work for them, but Chakori's son would be a good house attendant to work for them for free.

Dina Rout's wife, who was attending the labour, took the newborn still wrapped in its umbilical cord. She asked Chakori to give the baby away to her sister—who didn't have a baby—for adoption. The mother's weary hands pulled the baby away from the woman.

'I won't give my son even if someone kills me. 'I'll leave the zamindar's area and may even start begging on the streets to raise him,' she vowed.

She pressed the baby to her heart. Tears rolled down her

cheeks. She had never asked anything from God, but that day, she prayed to him to save her son and let him thrive in the world. He could be a golam or a beggar, and she didn't care; she wanted him to live. She named him Arkhitia.

Chakori didn't hesitate to come and resume work in the palace. Gradually, she was comfortable bringing her boy to work. She laid him on a rag in the corner, worked in the palace, and held him if he cried in hunger. Motherhood kindled a tenderness that made her forget every hardship. She imagined Diganta Keshari's reaction if he came and found her with a baby. He looked exactly like Graharaj but resembled Diganta Keshari quite a bit. She wondered if the supposedly dead younger zamindar was born as her son. She was proud to imagine carrying him in her womb. She looked into her son's powerful eyes in admiration, and heard the young zamindar's voice in his cries, promising her, 'I'll set you free. Days of freedom are very close. The sun comes out only when the sky blushes with redness. I'll bleed and herald the sunrise.'

In the darkness of the night, she pressed her son to her heart and declared that she didn't want to be free, and didn't wish to see the young zamindar bleed to bring freedom. She prayed for him to be safe and was ready to hold him like her son on her lap, if he was dead. The sun never cared for her prayers and rose resplendent with bright saffron rays splashing across the eastern sky; the air resonated with cries of 'Long live India' and 'Long live Mahatma Gandhi'.

∽

Arkhitia started to speak a few words and ran all over the palace with small, unsteady steps. Graharaj, at times, watched him carefully, and felt the shadow of his missing son in the boy. After Diganta Keshari went missing, he feared that the illegitimate Arkhitia was the proof of his and Chakori's union in the farmhouse. The zamindar looked unforgiving. Chakori looked into his stern eyes and said, 'Master! My son and young zamindar carry the same blood in their veins. The resemblance between the two is obvious.'

Tears rolling down, her chest could not unburden the pain sealed deep within. The zamindar knew she told the truth; he knew of the truth from the beginning. But he didn't like the dasi telling him on his face that he had fathered her son. It was an affront to his authority, pride and machismo. He couldn't stand her claiming that her son carried the zamindar's blood and potentially claiming a share of his property later. He warned her to keep the paternity a secret and ended the conversation with a cryptic note of the ominous. Chakori could construe the threat. She fell at his feet, saying, 'I ask for no favour. Don't harm him! Let him live! He'll serve you, your sons and their sons as a golam. I beg this much from you, master.' She hummed, 'I'm a fallen woman, and my son's a bastard, an illegitimate golam.'

Graharaj sat at an elaborate lunch spread on the floor, and Chakori sat beside him with a fan in her hand. Arkhitia looked at his food greedily without a beat of his eyes. Chakori stopped him from reaching out to the plate with her stern peeks. The kid's eyes rhythmically followed the zamindar's hand moving from the plate to his mouth and back again. Graharaj threw a little food at Arkhitia carelessly as one would throw at a pet. Chakori humbly took the food and fed it to her son, as if it was an offering from God, and asked the little one to leave the dining area. He gulped the bite hurriedly and showed up at the threshold in no time. Devaki asked her to serve him on a separate plate away from the zamindar and let the master eat his meal peacefully.

Arkhitia sat at a distance with his small plate and happily ate the zamindar's leftovers. Devaki, too, piled pieces of sweets and cake not eaten by her children on his plate. When Chakori worried that those things might upset the poor kid's stomach, Devaki grinned, saying, 'Nothing happens to the least important lives. Look how chubby your son is, and how skinny are mine despite all my care and attention!'

Chakori hoped that no evil eyes should ever harm her son. Arkhitia was very playful. He called Devaki 'Ma' following Devaki's children. The zamindar's wife was Devaki, or Ma Devi Lakshmi—the generous goddess of wealth who folds every poor and helpless in her arms. The boy grew as fast as an unwanted shrub that no one wanted. Chakori wished that they would be able to move to a different place when her son became a young man. He would work, make some money, build a home, and she would spend the rest of her life with his children and grandchildren.

But the day the boy grabbed the end of Graharaj's dress and called him 'Bapa', gently snuggling his face against him— everything changed. The servants were awkward. Graharaj slapped the boy hard, pushed him away, and disengaged himself; the boy cried non-stop. Devaki's wide eyes were clouded with distrust. The palace people feared a face-off between the couple. Graharaj appeared at Chakori's place at night and asked her to teach her son not to call him Bapa. She tried to convince him that calling the provider and the saviour of all in the palace Bapa was not bad behaviour. The zamindar didn't get carried away by her compliments. He claimed that Devaki might be the mother of the poor, but he was Graharaj or Vishnu—the lord of the universe. The boy must behave, or the consequence of his mischief would be dire. Chakori was worried after the warning and tried hard to teach Arkhitia to call the zamindar 'Hajur', but the boy didn't care to learn to call the zamindar Hajur and kept calling him Bapa.

Devaki's father, Dakhinray, was embarrassed to see Zamindar Graharaj's filthy secrets with the dasis coming out in the open. Chakori tried to ease the tension, saying that once the innocent boy grew up, he would call the zamindar 'Santa', otherwise she would chop his tongue. Dakhinray hated Chakori, and her young son Arkhitia a thousand times more. He dreaded the boy hanging around her daughter's neck like a dark snake, and feared that with the freedom movement banging at the door, he might demand a share of the wealth that should've rightfully belonged to her grandchildren.

∞

Alaka, meaning lightning, is a thin, sparkling branch of the Devi River that rushes past Balikuda. There was a huge, ancient banyan tree on the river bank called *handidia baragacha*. Under the shed of that banyan tree, people offered food to the dead in earthen pots during the rites for the dead, hence the moniker. Beyond the wide canopy of the tree's shadow was the area where the cowherds tended their cattle. They said that foxes howled after sunset in that dreaded prohibited area, witches alighted and put out light intermittently at night, and spirits kept their babies warm in that fire. Near that godforsaken place, the Utkal Pradesh Congress Committee bought a fifty-two-decimal-long land in Gopabandhu Chaudhury's name, and volunteers from the party built a rudimentary office. It had seven rooms; some were used for training the volunteers and some for spinning cotton in the *charkha*. Govinda Das of Alabola and Harekrishna of Nagpur were supervising the training. When those two were unavailable, Digdarshi remained in charge of the training camp; the unseen protective hands of guru Parshuram hovered over his head constantly.

Digdarshi lived in that camp with a few young volunteers of the non-cooperation movement. Baikuntha Mohanty led the Banar Sena, the team of young party workers who, like the humble squirrel in the Ramayana carrying sand in his fur to help build the Setubandha over the sea, did their bit for the freedom movement. Mohanty loved to spend some time with Digdarshi in the Alaka camp. In the silence of the night, villagers claimed they could here the rustling footsteps of ghosts and spirits coming from the direction of the tree. But the two friends had no such eerie experience. Baikuntha was artistic; the young man loved music, dance and theatre. The two spent the whole night dreaming about freedom, self-rule and the end of British colonialism.

Gopabandhu Chaudhury, the leader of the Congress Party, opened the Swaraj Ashram in his Bakhrabad house in Cuttack. Workers arrived there in droves. Sama Puhana, too, reached there with Baikuntha Mohanty. He fell at Ramadevi's feet with devotion, and declared that he had left home and didn't plan to marry till Mother India was free from the British. She remembered Sama from when she led the procession from Alabola village to Balikuda. She knew that his soul was filled with love for Mother India and he cried to see the country free. Jagiri Swain, another youth from Dhumata, was obsessed with India's freedom. He left his village, home, wife, family—everything, and spread Gandhi's message like someone possessed. Many people in his village, too, thought of Sama to be a little crazy. Ramadevi's husband Gopabandhu Chaudhury, a deputy magistrate, resigned and joined the freedom movement; people thought he was crazy too. Every day, people who were passionate about the freedom struggle reached the ashram.

Ramadevi didn't want to drive away Sama. She patted his back and asked him to go and help the people in the villages understand the non-cooperation movement. Govinda Das placed a Gandhi cap over Sama's head and pushed a tricolour in his hand. The messenger of freedom walked proudly, chanting, 'Long live Mahatma Gandhi, long live Mother India, and long live Ramadevi.' He was not the Sama from the nondescript village of Alabola anymore, but was one among the millions of Indians crying for freedom. The great patriot marched ahead, loaded with confidence. In contrast, there was Naba Das, who became a gatekeeper of the Empire and arrested countless freedom fighters who violated the government order and participated in the Salt March. Earlier, Naba watched cattle, but of late, his job had been to watch human beings. Infamously, the man arrested and sent to jail Upendra Mahapatra and Jayaram Mahapatra, who had shown the process of salt making to a group of unsuspecting villagers. The arrest created tension in front of the Bhagavati Temple in Parahata village.

During the hullabaloo near the Bhagavati Temple, Udayanath Panda and his family were inside the temple. Panda was enjoying a drink laced with bhang before having a sumptuous feast of meat and other delicacies. His daughter, Maithili, sat with her stepmother and aunt and listened to the noise outside. It was Ekadashi, a day of fasting without water; she wasn't supposed to touch even the *prasad* from the Devi. Maithili looked at the vast open sky and thought that there was no meaning in a life of ceaseless suffering; she couldn't eat, wear, adorn, marry or live a normal life. In another bullock cart in the shed of a tree sat Sebati, the young woman once betrothed to Sama. Her stepmother had gone to the temple with her son and daughter to seek blessings for them. Sebati sat there looking after their belongings. Since her marriage couldn't be solemnized with Sama Puhana, she was known as the 'ill-fated bride'. The name-calling and mockery of her neighbours made her life miserable. She wanted to run away but didn't know where to turn. She was ready to go to Sama's parents and serve them all her life. But since he vanished a day before the marriage, the parents thought that something inauspicious in her fate had removed their son from their lives. Sebati was so hated that she feared the villagers might not give her a proper cremation if she died; life and death seemed the same for her. Sama, the groom, in her reveries, walked on the floating clouds. She admired his wide masculine chest, strong, shapely arms, nose and eyes. Her mind created such fleeting illusions that there was hardly any line separating reality and imagination.

While Sebati struggled to comprehend her fate, Maithili, nearby, was slowly dying in the dry, hot afternoon sun. She didn't sip water the entire time and couldn't open her eyes. Her aunt, who tried to wake her up, was upset with the father for dragging the girl on that trip to the temple on the day of Ekadashi. She feared that Udayanath probably waited for his daughter to die. Sebati heard the commotion beside her and rushed to save the girl's life. She didn't wait for anyone to explain that she was a child widow and the fasting took a toll on her life. She could guess it from her plain looks, especially her hands and feet without adornment, and the white sari she wore.

Maithili's mother was dead by this time. She couldn't stand the misery of her young daughter as a widow. After his wife's death, Udayanath, the Sanskrit pandit, was caught in a huge dilemma. He stayed away from home and spent his time discussing scriptures outside. In a year, the widower felt that he needed someone at home to look after Maithili. He found a bride who was one year older than his daughter, and brought her home. Ironically, he asked the daughter to take care of the bride. He ensured that the bride, who was thin and rickety, and her knees bumped against each other when she walked, was fed well. She quickly became strong and rounded to take care of the household. Maithili was kind and rather pitied the poor girl who married her old father, thinking she might become a miserable widow like her. If his wife was late for eating, or her hair wasn't combed, or if she lifted a pitcher of water or served him food, he shouted at Maithili. The new-Ma did no household chores; Maithili cooked even while she fasted and served meals to the family. The father bought saris, jewellery and vermilion from the bazaar and asked his daughter to encourage his wife to dress well and walk around cheerfully, like a bride. He reminded her that the new-Ma was not a 'poor unlucky widow'. The phrase sent a chill down poor Maithili's spine and brought tears to her eyes. One day, as she picked up the new sari and adornments from his hands, the tiny urn of vermilion fell off her hand and spilled on the ground. The Brahmin got very upset and accused her of being jealous of the new-Ma. He raised his hands to slap her. Maithili didn't want to remember the painful episode but couldn't stop the events from recurring in her mind.

When the eyes of Maithili and Sebati met, both girls knew that their situations were desperate. They instinctively knew how dire their situations were. They were strangers, but could fathom the pain, misery and loneliness surrounding their lives. People say the sea doesn't overflow when rain water pours in. Likewise, the misery of one didn't overwhelm the other. Their ocean of suffering was full. Instead, the magic of love touched their two hearts. The common questions in their eyes were, 'How long will our lives be hung like this? What is the goal of our lives? Do we deserve this? Where should we escape when there's nothing but darkness ahead?'

Strangely, they found a luminous ray that brightened their possible path of escape through the all-pervasive darkness. Udayanath's young wife had gone to share the prasad offered to the goddess. Left to themselves, Maithili and Sebati began to run instinctively. They joined the throng of female workers of the freedom movement who had gathered to protest the arrest of their leaders, Upendra and Jayaram Mahapatra.

'Where're they going?' Maithili asked Sebati.

'Balikuda,' she replied.

'Why?'

'They'll first reach Sarvadharma Ashram. They'll be counselled there and then dispersed to work for the freedom movement,' replied Sebati.

She was more informed and aware about the current events. After Sama followed the movement and left the village, Sebati was aware of the things happening in the country. Maithili listened to her carefully and asked, 'Shall we go with them?'

'Where?' asked Sebati.

'For working with the Congress Party and the freedom movement,' replied Maithili.

Those two pairs of feet stepped up and, like pouring rain dissolving into a pond or a river, seamlessly merged with the march. They left behind their pain, misery, and the untold story of the senseless burden of tradition imposed on them. Pages of a new history slowly opened before their eyes. They felt that life had immense potential. Traumatized in the battle of life, the pair suddenly realized that there was a higher purpose behind their ridiculous suffering, and that they were poised to be rewarded handsomely for all they had gone through. Once they reached the Balikuda marketplace, they looked at each other and asked, 'Where should we go now?'

Someone from the crowd pointed towards the official residence of high school headmaster Parshuram Das, and said, 'Go there, you'll find the right direction from that place.'

Once the two friends reached Parshuram's Sarvadharma Ashram, they were closer to their goal. Sebati, who had been looking for Sama desperately, couldn't trace him. Parshuram didn't know about Sama's whereabouts. Sama went to Cuttack as a volunteer, and was arrested and jailed by the police. Hundreds were arrested every day. How could anyone keep a track of them? Sebati no longer looked out for Sama but searched for her life's meaning. Maithili's perspective on life changed too.

Chapter VIII

Like the moon uncle and tiger uncle in folk tales, Jayaram Mahapatra was lovingly called Tungamamu. He gave up his job as a guard at an irrigation project, and joined the freedom movement. During the Salt March, he and his friend Upendra Mahapatra were arrested from Parahata village and sent to Patna Camp jail. Tungamamu recorded with the police that he was an I.C.S. officer, one of the highest-ranking bureaucrats in the administration. He had bluffed to scare the police and get out to work for the freedom movement. The arrest of a top official created a furor, and an immediate investigation followed. Poor uncle didn't foresee the consequence of his prank.

The Patna jail was a threadbare encampment with a low tin roof and a regular fence like a cowshed; horsemen guarded the place. It was very cold inside, and food, blankets, and other essential items for the inmates were in short supply. Tungamamu and many others who were arrested got sick from typhoid. The inquiry didn't stop, however. The police came inside and repeatedly asked him if he was an I.C.S. officer, holding the entire list of civil servants in his hand. Sick Tungamamu threw his usual tantrum and replied, 'Bloody fool, I worked in Indian Cooking Service. Give me mutton and masala, and you'll see how great a cook I am. All will eat and testify what the I.C.S. officer can cook,' he mocked while the bystanders laughed.

He didn't like the shoddy food served to prisoners. He was a great cook and loved good food. The jailor asked him to make mutton curry. While cooking, Tungamamu ate away half of it. The jail officials punished him for his misconduct, and asked him to do some of the toughest jobs. His condition deteriorated, and he was released on account of his failing health. He carried Nabakrishna Chaudhury's message to his wife, Malatidevi, asking her to keep up the civil disobedience movement and continue salt-making at Kujanga. Sama Puhana was also released from jail. He took great care of Tungamamu in Cuttack Swaraj Ashram, and carried him on his shoulder to his home in Balikuda. On their way, they stopped for one night at Alakashram.

The inmates of Alakashram had retired to their rooms after spinning cotton till late that night. Seba's soft hands touched Ramadevi's feet for a massage; she wasn't well. She withdrew her feet, telling her that the girls who had been tirelessly cooking, cleaning and serving food on top of spinning cotton, needed care and rest. She asked Seba to take care of her friend Maithili who worked sincerely even on days when she had her fasts and prayers meant for a widow. Malatidevi, the loving, caring leader, was Ma to everyone around her. She had changed Sebati's name to Seba because of the girl's readiness to serve others. She graciously asked her to make some barley for the ailing Tungamamu in the morning before he left for his village. She praised her, saying that service to humanity was the motto of the people from Seba's village, Alabola, and mentioned that Sama from that village carried Tungamamu on his shoulder from Cuttack, and would take him back to his home the same way in the morning. Sebati was proud to hear Sama's tales of generosity and heroism. Once betrothed to her, Sama postponed his marriage and left his parents behind when the freedom movement possessed his mind. Old memories flashed before her eyes, and her heart thumped hard. Tears welled in her eyes; she wasn't sure if it was from joy or sadness.

A deep sigh shook her heart; she didn't know how long she sat motionless at Malatidevi's feet. She rose and moved towards her room to sleep, but stopped momentarily near the guest room. It was dark, but a dream alighted the path towards a new possibility that night. She thought of making some noise to draw Sama's attention, who slept inside, and let him know that even though she couldn't be his wife, she had followed his footsteps, left home for the country, and joined the freedom movement. Betrothed to Sama, motherless Sebati wasn't a lifeless toy but a young woman of flesh and blood with feelings and sentiments usual for her impressionable age.

She heard someone turning on the bed inside and rushed to her room quickly. She feared that Sama mightn't appreciate her standing outside in the darkness. He might wake everyone and say that the girls in the ashram were cheap; they left home on the pretext of working for the country but were shameless sluts. She returned to her room, and decided to bring barley for the sick guest, and meet Sama gracefully in the morning. Maithili wasn't asleep, but Sebati wasn't ready to talk to her friend. She turned to the bed, saying, 'Wake me up early in the morning. I've to make some barley for the guest. I don't want to be late.'

'No worries if you're late, I can make barley. No worries. You aren't supposed to do everything by yourself, my friend!' said Maithili.

'Let me do it tomorrow for my good old friend.'

'What's so special?'

'He's my…' Sebati stopped halfway.

'What's he to you? Who're you talking about?' implored Maithili.

'Jayaram Mahapatra is related to me—he's Tungamamu; he's very sick. So I want to make barley for him,' Sebati said in a muffled tone in the darkness.

'All right, I'll call you,' said Maithili and turned to sleep.

Sebati looked through the darkness and saw so much! Who says darkness is opaque? She couldn't sleep the whole night. She rose early on her own and made barley. She covered her head and carried the bowl to the guest room. The place looked bright in the morning light. Tungamamu sat alone cross-legged in his bed. He appreciated her for bringing barley for him.

Sebati's eyes searched for Sama everywhere. Tungamamu said that he felt better and was ready to go to his village alone; he had sent Sama back to the Congress Party's Cuttack office early in the morning. He called Sama a very emotional young man but the most honest and dedicated worker, rare to find among the youth of his age. Sebati's wide-open eyes were vacant; she stared at the road that led to Cuttack. Nothing stood still. The world before her was caught in an unending flux. The wise have said aptly, *sansarati iti samsara*, or something that's constantly in flux, is called the world.

When Sama left the village, and Sebati's marriage with him didn't materialize, people said that her life was over and the world had ceased to move for her. But the day she left everything behind and ran away with Maithili from Parahata and reached the Alakashram, she realized that life moved unrelentingly, and that no one's world ever stopped spinning. As long as she breathed, the world around her was alive. She felt that a woman's world wasn't simply limited to her husband or children. Everything in her proximity—birds, animals, trees, creepers, hills, rivers, the known, unknown, friends, foes, air and water—become inalienable from her existence.

For Maithili, too, Alakashram became the world, and the meaning of life changed. She was meticulous, and Ramadevi had assigned her many responsibilities in the ashram. The strings of love bound her to the place; she worked hard from daybreak till midnight and had no time to pay attention to her looks or clothes. There was magic in Maithili's personality; she could easily persuade others to accept her views. Ramadevi often entrusted her with the responsibility of resolving conflicts between people. From her childhood, she had questioned the irrational postulations of her father. While she had lacked the courage to raise her voice against an authority figure back then, the freedom she enjoyed in the ashram gave her the courage to resist injustices and wrongdoings. Alakashram offered shelter and trained many children and young widows deserted by their husbands and families. Initially, Maithili thought of remarriage to avenge the discrimination she faced from her father. But once she came across hundreds of women caught in the same predicament, she felt that a lone widow marriage wasn't enough to open the eyes of a society that perpetrated such shameful injustices against young women. She knew that the number of widows below the age of fifteen was some 300,000. She secretly vowed to see some perceptible changes in the status quo.

Meeting Digdarshi, the young man who had saved her life as an angel a few years back, again in Alakashram, amazed

Maithili. She was no longer a child but a sensible, mature woman, who understood and appreciated his inspiring words and advice. Digdarshi expounded that women's liberation was the main goal that forced him to leave home. But working in rural areas for the freedom struggle made it clear to him that women's liberation was impossible without removing illiteracy and deep-rooted biases. Political freedom didn't hold any meaning if humanity didn't eliminate superstitions and biases. She had a strong premonition that Digdarshi would one day give direction to the masses mired in superstition and stale practices. She believed that Mohandas Karamchand Gandhi or Subhas Bose alone could not single-handedly change the fate of a nation. Gandhi, Nehru and Bose needed countless dedicated people like Parshuram, Hari Bishwal, Govinda Das, Digdarshi and Ramadevi to realize the country's dream of freedom.

Maithili also met Digdarshi's two other friends—Madan Jena and Sama Puhana—in Alakasharm. The trio moved together. Madan and Sama were at his beck and call and acted as his right and left hands. Their stay in Parshuram's house, Sarvadharma Samannoya Ashram, had transformed them completely. In that secular sanctuary, they learned to abandon many of their reservations on caste, class and religion. Madan, especially, adopted his guru's humanism wholeheartedly and became saintly. Digdarshi often wondered that if there were more people like Parshuram, Gandhi's teachings could be popularized in the villages easily. The friends often recalled an unforgettable episode during the Salt March days when Madan Jena led the protesters at Orando Chatura Mundai. Excise inspector Sadhucharan Mohanty was in charge of restraining the protesters. He beat Madan very hard until he became unconscious. Digdarshi was swiftly pushed aside before he could do anything to rescue his friend, but he still pleaded with the villagers to get some water to wake Madan up. No water was allowed inside, and instead, Sadhucharan asked Sehmat Mia, the peon in his office, to pee in Madan's mouth in public. Everyone watched the dastardly act in utter dismay. Madan rose; he didn't vomit in revulsion and thanked Sehmat Mia for his promptness in saving his life, saying, 'Brother, I can't forget your generosity. While no one in the village offered me even a few drops of water, I'll remember you forever for this great act of kindness.'

Maithili was one of the female volunteers in a group under Digdarshi's supervision that marched to Kujanga to demand the right to make salt. She remembered that passionate adventure with high drama and hilariously comic events. She couldn't forget the blunt and foul-mouthed deputy magistrate Madhab Panda, who was in charge of peace and order during the march. Panda used offensive words like *sala* indiscriminately. Sala was the prefix and suffix to his name: sala Madhab Panda sala. The horse he rode acted irate and seemed wilder than his master. One day, Panda rode his horse to supervise the marchers rushing to Kujanga and lashed the animal repeatedly to move faster. Some eight to ten gasping barefoot bodyguards ran alongside, carrying their guns on their shoulders. As the horse galloped with Panda on its back, the scene resembled a race between men and the beast. Panda lashed the bodyguards mercilessly if they failed to keep pace with the horse.

Digdarshi took photographs of the march with his camera. As they reached to cross a rising river, he saw the horse refusing to enter the waters and knelt on the sand so hard that Panda was taken off its back. Guards and peons rushed, lifted Panda on their backs and took him to the other side of the river. He was angry that Digdarshi took photos of those embarrassing moments and ordered the attendants to snatch the camera from his hands. Madan rushed, grabbed the camera from Digdarshi, and took to the *kaccha* road beyond the paddy fields. When the chasers tackled Madan, he held the camera over his head and warned, 'I have a gun, a three-barrel shooter! Be aware! Don't come to me. I'll shoot.'

He unlocked the folding camera box that opened with a scratching mechanical noise. The guards feared for their lives and laid down in total surrender keeping their turbans on the ground. Madan escaped to the nearby woods. Panda knew that his men were fooled; furious, he whipped them hard. Maithili pitied those poor guards and screamed at Panda not to hit the innocent men. Her slim, fair body turned red like copper in anger, and her large eyes opened wide like Goddess Durga's. Astounded, Panda didn't like being chastised by a woman. He lost his sense of propriety and spewed obscenity at her in rage, 'How dare you whore talk to me? Destitute and widows like you left home and gathered at Alakashram to engage in illicit love affairs...'

The word 'widow' was so derogatory a term to Maithili's ears that it always made her numb, and that day, it put out the rising fire in her momentarily. Before Digdarshi could react to the situation, Malatidevi, who was behind him, came to the fore. She stood in front of Panda and grabbed the whiplash from his hand. Panda got off the mount in a hurry.

'Don't you have your daughters and sisters? These women are like your daughters. I'll ask this girl to slash your tongue and see that you no longer use such foul language for women,' warned Malatidevi.

Other marchers surrounded Panda. He shook in fear for his life; his guards were too petrified to use their guns. Malatidevi asked him to fall at Maithili's feet and beg her forgiveness. Maithili moved away. Madan reappeared and handed the camera to Digdarshi to take a photo of the magistrate stooping on the ground. The drama didn't end there. As he started on his horse towards Kujanga, followed by his attendants rushing to check the safety of the dilapidated log bridge, the young freedom fighters of the Banar Sena, hiding beneath the overpass, rose with tricolours in their hands and shouted, 'Long live Mother India'. Panicked by the commotion, the horse ran away, crashing Panda to the ground. A young marcher teased him, saying, 'Brother Madhab, you're late! People're making salt in your absence.' Wounded and bloodied, he couldn't rise from the ground. Again, the kind-hearted Maithili rushed to him and wiped the blood off his nose and mouth, but he removed Maithili's concerned hand in denial.

∞

During that time, Digdarshi was underground for a while but was soon arrested. Later, following the agreement between Gandhi and Irwin, he was released along with the rest of the political prisoners. The government subsequently lifted the ban on salt-making by the common man. The freedom struggle was politically eventful, but it became memorable to many for some fine instances of friendship and loyalty. Time flowed, never making people's joy in small things irrelevant. Parshuram's friendship, for example, with his Muslim friend Aziz Khan from his school days in Bhadrakh, remained his most cherished relationship; he didn't care for the remarks of the Hindu friends opposed to it. Aziz was a regular in his Sarvadharma Ashram.

They loved to revisit a funny incident following Parshuram's marriage to Manorama, the most beautiful bride in Alabola village. People talked more about her beauty than the dowry she brought with her. But since they were from a conservative Vaishnav Karan family, an outsider like Aziz wasn't supposed to see her. Parshuram was a little proud of his pretty wife and wanted Aziz to have a glimpse of her. So he asked Aziz to stand quietly, a little away from the back window of his bedroom at night. Parshuram entered the room and closed the door from inside, keeping the lantern on the window sill. He gently pulled the veil over Manorama's face so that Aziz could see her in the lantern light. But the shy bride didn't let him remove the veil. The couple went back and forth in the veil-drawing act. Aziz, who stood outside and watched, couldn't resist but laugh. Fortuitously, Manorama found Aziz standing outside and screamed, 'Ghost! Ghost!' She fainted in fear. Parshuram tried to revive her. Her cries alerted the servants of the house, who chased and grabbed Aziz, who was running for his life; they thrashed him brutally. When Parshuram reached there to save his friend, Aziz was hit on his head and was bleeding. The scar from the wound remained on his forehead as a lasting memory of that episode.

Aziz, like a comet, regularly surfaced in Parshuram's house from nowhere, and the two friends discussed for hours behind closed doors. They ate from a single plate. Manorama was initially reluctant to clean the plate after they finished eating. A Hindu upper-caste woman wasn't allowed to touch the plate of a Muslim. Her liberal husband asked Manorama not to go by religious biases. She accepted his views but didn't like the long lectures he gave on religion and caste, which Aziz might overhear.

The bond between Parshuram and Aziz Khan was instrumental in furthering the freedom movement in areas near Balikuda. Parshuram popularized the message of freedom through education; Aziz travelled the nooks and crannies and collected information as a secret agent. Aziz once informed that the police had seized the Cuttack Swaraj Ashram, and the building needed to be reclaimed by the freedom fighters, who must hoist the Indian national flag over it. Baikuntha, Jayaram, Digdarshi and Shankar Das from Balikuda immediately set out on the mission. These volunteers in Cuttack aimed to implement total prohibition in a peaceful way. They wore red shirts and white Gandhi caps. While some lay on the ground, the rest picketed, urging the owners to shut down the liquor stores. But the angry supporters of liquor consumption walked over those peaceful protesters on the ground, which led to a confrontation between the two groups. The police reached the site, arrested the volunteers, and put them behind bars in dirty, mosquito- and bed-bug-infested rooms. Zahid sahib, the jailor, flogged them with twenty-five strokes on their palms and asked his peon to flog with another twenty-five. Their hands cracked and bled, but tears didn't roll down their cheeks; a strange power inspired them to remain calm and bear the torture stoically. They were ready to sacrifice their lives for the motherland. An Irish jailor was a little lenient; he slapped ten lashes. When the volunteers were released, the crowd waiting outside greeted them with great love and took them back to the ashram in a procession. Ramadevi hugged them there like a mother and fed them well. She told stories of brave heroes to keep their morale high.

The Banar Sena was determined to plant the national flag on Swaraj Ashram. Digdarshi, Madan and Baikuntha led the mission by holding the tricolour. Madan was beaten severely by the police and he fainted from the brutal lashing. Sama snatched the lathi from the police and beat several police officials who tried to prevent them. Lane saheb took the gun from the police and pointed it at Sama; he raised his hands and surrendered. The police pushed him to the van and took him away. Digdarshi and Baikuntha ignored the police and hoisted the flag over Swaraj Ashram. Lane saheb pushed his gun into Baikuntha's shoulder pit, and the bayonet pierced through the shoulder across his back, causing a deep wound; he fell while still holding the national flag. While in the hospital, leaders of the Congress Party told Baikuntha that Madan and Sama were caught by the police and thrown into the tiger-infested dense forest of Chandaka, and that Digdarshi was captured and put in the Patna jail for a year.

∞

On the sixth of May 1934, Gandhi came to Odisha and marched into the slums where the untouchables lived. Women from rich conservative Hindu homes joined Gandhi; Ramadevi was the most notable person in that mission. These women took up sanitation jobs which the lower-caste untouchables did. They cleaned latrines, open drains and garbage bins alongside the male volunteers. This drive for assimilation in a highly segregated society made people feel that there would be no difference between the rich and poor or upper- and lower-caste people.

The assimilation initiatives, however, bothered Zamindar Dakhinray a lot. He feared that the move to remove the lines between the high and low castes would have a different ramification in daughter Devaki's life. He worried that dasi Chakori's illegitimate son Arkhitia, fathered by his son-in-law Graharaj, might cite some inheritance law and demand his right over the zamindar's property. He felt that none but Devaki's sons were the exclusive inheritors of the estate. He stayed for a few days at Graharaj's, assessed the situation carefully, and had a secret meeting with his daughter.

Chakori's son Arkhitia didn't wake up one morning; he didn't run around playfully or call the zamindar Bapa. He had eaten a lot of sweets the previous night at the feast to mark the zamindar's youngest son's birthday. Everybody enjoyed the feast, but something went wrong with the little one. He couldn't rise from the rags. Chakori found two streaks of poison from his nose on the bed; his body was blue and lifeless.

Nobody knew how long a shattered Chakori took to gather herself and rise after her son's death. She wailed 'Arkhitia' repeatedly for days, banged her head against the wall, and injured her forehead; her eyes dried. Devaki didn't summon her to work. Graharaj's palanquin didn't stop at her door. Devaki reportedly told everyone to let her cry and grieve as long as she wanted, and that she shouldn't be forced to come to the palace to do the chores. The unusual generosity hardly made any sense to Chakori. She remembered the countless instances where she was dragged to work in the palace even in extreme sickness, when she had no power to carry herself. She recalled the beastly advances of the merciless zamindar who stirred her sick body for pleasure. She sincerely doubted if a sense of guilt ever overtook those ruthless people and pushed them to reconsider the barbaric practices in their palace. She searched every nook and cranny for answers. She remembered Digdarshi desperately, and thought her son's life might've been saved if the young zamindar was in the palace. The grief of losing her son joined the pain of not having the young zamindar in the palace; the two streaks of grief became inseparable in her mourning. The death of Arkhitia was the death of hope.

'Who'll set me free? Who'll I look up to and how will I dream of my release from the enslaved life of a dasi?' she wondered.

Chakori sat alone and grieved. On one particular day of mourning, she was surprised to hear a soft tap on her door in the darkness. She made out that it wasn't Zamindar Graharaj's typical knock. Also, she wasn't sure about the stranger who whispered her name. She rose and opened the door cautiously. A shadowy figure hastened inside and closed the door hurriedly. Before she could scream, he put his hand over her mouth and asked her not to scream.

'The police are after me. If I hide here, they won't find me. I'm Dukhabandhu! Your brother Dukhia. I've joined the freedom fighters.'

Chakori stood in shock and disbelief, seeing her half-brother after so many years. She couldn't believe her eyes. She leaned against his shoulder and cried, 'Arkhitia…Arkhitia…Arkhitia'.

Dukhabandhu listened to the account of innocent Arkhitia's death, enfolded in Chakori's tears and sighs. He comforted his grieving sister, saying that God was very kind to have saved her son from the pain of living his entire life in guilt, inferiority complex and pain, with the seal of a golam over his head, and the knowledge of being a bastard born to a dasi hounding him eternally. He urged his sister to forget her sorrows and join the struggle to liberate the country from the British. He said that as long as the country was in bondage, their freedom was not possible. She couldn't understand everything her brother said. She knew she had no road to escape from the hell that was the palace. Chakori asked if it was true that all would be free when the country became free, and if she would be released from the clutches of the zamindar after freedom. Dukhabandhu believed in the ideals of Subhas Bose, not Mahatma Gandhi. He was hiding in the forest for twelve years. He looked for answers to her questions in a pensive mood. He assured her, saying, 'Let's first strike at the root; once the stubborn core is uprooted, the branches and stems will die down automatically. There won't be any rulers and the ruled. Have faith…'

He said that Diganta Keshari was alive and very active in the freedom struggle. He followed Gandhi, worked in the Balikuda, Erasama and Jagatsinghpur areas, and popularized the khadi movement in villages. Pointing at the rail track behind the outhouse, he said the angry government had arrested hundreds of freedom fighters and sent them to the Patna jail. Digdarshi might have also been moved with those people. Hearing that the young zamindar was alive, her hands rose in gratitude towards God. She sobbed uncontrollably, saying, 'I, too, believe he is alive and will return someday and remove the pain of the poor. People in this area have been waiting for him desperately.'

Chakori's large eyes were fixed on Dukhabandhu. The pupil of her eyes glistened in unwavering determination, like bright stars in the darkness. She wasn't sure if she, a poor dasi, could do anything for the country's freedom. Dukhabandhu held her hands softly, asking for a favour. He asked her to let him and some of his revolutionary friends hide in her home once in a while and never give away the information to the police, even if they threatened to chop her head. The garden and the outhouse belonged to Zamindar Graharaj, a supporter of the British; there was no fear of a raid of that place. If she agreed to provide that help, that would be the greatest service to the motherland. Chakori was scared. Nobody dared to enter the outhouse except Zamindar Graharaj. If the information reached him, he wouldn't hesitate to chop her head and the heads of those hiding there. Dukhabandhu could make out the thoughts bothering his sister. He said that even Diganta Keshari might come to seek shelter there. The police were running after him.

'I vow three times in the name of truth that I won't open my mouth even if someone threatens to behead me. If so many people are ready to sacrifice their lives for the country's freedom, why should I fear for my useless life? I'll be saved if my head is chopped…' Chakori declared spontaneously.

Chapter IX

Darkness never washed away completely from Chakori's firmament of hope, nor did it let the sunrise arrive in absolute glory. Confoundingly, the morning star kept on looming bright, beckoning imminent daybreak. Life is fleeting; it burns out slowly. After meeting Dukhia, Chakori clung to the faint hope that Diganta Keshari was alive and would appear someday at her doorstep. She dreamed of washing his feet and inviting him inside. Caught between hope and despair, faith and doubt, she kept alive her tenacity and debated whether her son Arkhitia's life would've been saved if the young zamindar was around. She thought she would be free only when the soul left her mortal body. She wished to meet him at least once before death, grab his feet without fear and shame, and declare that she wouldn't accept freedom even if set free; she owed her life to the senior zamindar and would serve him till death. She wailed alone in that dark room and repeatedly called out Arkhitia's name.

Zamindar Graharaj's five sons were grown and resourceful, and the father had no control over them. Devaki, the proud mother of sons, was disposed to a life of idle luxury. She stood with them if the zamindar complained about their indulgence in debauchery and wished to control the money they wasted over Narmada, Sulochana and Urmila—the so-called women of ill-repute.

'Lechery is no sin. It can't be separated from the zamindars—it's a sign of their legacy and masculinity,' she said, defending her unruly sons. She favoured the intrepid zamindars who openly enjoyed visiting brothels and had concubines and dasis as sex slaves in their palaces; she knew such men in her paternal home. Instead, she hated the hypocrites who secretly harboured whores and mistresses and stealthily visited those places. Thus she vented her long-held hatred for her husband, Graharaj, for his double life behind the mask of a strict zamindar and an upright person.

The old zamindar was isolated in the palace. Devaki defended the permissive conduct of her sons, and their disagreement with the father slowly appeared as bitter hostility between them. Their three sons lived outside for their studies and spent five times more than they were supposed to. Every month, the zamindar verified the expenses with the accountant and blamed Devaki for making them lax and irresponsible. He often compared them with Diganta Keshari, his missing ideal son. Devaki could handle any insult except the comparison of her children with her stepson. Small squabbles between the old couple often flared up into lingering disagreements.

Prapancha Mohanty, the estate accountant, often aggravated the situation. He changed sides according to convenience and stoked the fire. At least two sons took Devaki's side if she fought with the zamindar; Graharaj kept quiet like a wounded lion and seethed in anger. Poor Chakori witnessed the vulnerability of the zamindar, who, years back, used to be extremely aggressive and arrogant. She remembered a timid Devaki pushing her as the shield when he was angry. But the tables had turned against the strong man; the macho man cowered before his wife. Chakori took pity on him and forgot his earlier abuses. After all, he was the only man in her life and the father of her son Arkhitia. Being a dasi, she couldn't come to the zamindar's defence. The zamindar's sons called her *dhaima* (nanny)—the caregiver; she had raised them and borne all their tantrums and mischiefs. She looked after them and cared for their health and wellness. She knew the food each one liked to eat and the dress each loved to wear. She dealt with them according to their moods and needs. She remembered the birthmarks, bruises and moles in their bodies better than Devaki. Devaki gave birth, but like Yashoda, Chakori raised them. But she didn't dare to look at them straight in the eye once they grew up. Once they knew that she was their father's mistress, they didn't call her dhaima, and, like their mother, they too addressed her disdainfully by her name, Chakori.

The zamindar couldn't handle the pity he saw in the dasi's eyes; he wasn't a bruised kid needing her sympathy. He screamed like a wounded tiger and asked the wretched dasi to leave the palace. He threw at her whatever he could lay his hands on. Following Graharaj, Devaki and her sons shouted together to take her down and save the so-called family reputation. Chakori was used to such abuses. Someone who didn't carry her father's name and lived as a mere mistress perhaps couldn't have a sense of self. Shame had no meaning for someone without a sense of self.

Sometimes Chakori felt tempted to disclose to Zamindar Graharaj that Diganta Keshari was not dead as presumed. She wanted to confide that he might return any day and show up at the outhouse for refuge. She thought that the information might lessen the worries of the zamindar. Her spirit then cringed, thinking that Dukhabandhu hadn't even seen Diganta Keshari with his own eyes; no one could determine if the rumour was true. If the matter ended with the police, they would look for Dukhabandhu and put him behind bars. She kept the thought to herself.

She remembered Dukhabandhu's words that Diganta Keshari and other freedom fighters might pass her area by train on their way to Patna jail. So she went out and stood near the rail line running across the river beside the outhouse. The gigantic locomotive hurried past her, puffing gusts of steam into the air. The passengers gazed out from inside, surveying the passing panorama of villages, mountains, hills and rivers. The tender rays of the early morning sun shone on their faces like the colour of Holi. She often stood there, hoping to catch a glimpse of him, and waited till her eyes could no longer see the train's last car. Some days, the train was late, and Chakori would be delayed for work in the palace. She'd be scolded harshly, but she gave no explanations.

∽

The police razed the Handipakabara Ashram in Balikuda to the ground. Parshuram assured the workers that there was no reason to worry and asked them to continue the meetings of the Congress Party in the Sarvadharma Ashram. He was friends with the rich, the poor and the powerful, like the police. The police were aware of the presence of the freedom fighters in his ashram but did not arrest them. Distinguished leaders like Acharya Harihar, Gopabandhu Chaudhury, Harekrishna Mahatab, Nabakrishna Chaudhury, Surendranath Dwivedi, Nityanand Kanungo, Bhagirathi Mahapatra, Sarala Devi, Ramadevi, Hari Bishwal and Govinda Chandra Das came and attended meetings in his place. They discussed the Gita, Aziz

Khan recited the Quran, and someone else used to read the Bible. Wandering mendicant Brahmachari Nabanana used to discuss the Ramayana and the Mahabharata. The police knew everything but couldn't prevent it because it was a friendly gathering devoted to discussing religious scriptures.

In such meetings, the team determined the course of action for members like Sebati, Maithili and Digdarshi. Along with Govinda Chandra Das, Harekrishna Bishwal and Birabara Das of Balikuda, workers like Digdarshi, Sebati and Maithili went out to popularize the message of freedom. The police followed and asked the villagers to deny the freedom fighters food, water and shelter; they warned people of severe punishment if they defied the order. Madan Jena, Digdarshi, Sebati and Maithili were in one group and they worked tirelessly to reach out to people. One time, they stopped at a school in Erasama to rest for the night. One of the teachers, a sympathizer of the freedom movement, went to the school's president to get permission to accommodate the group. The president called the freedom movement a farce of the scoundrels, notorious for letting widows and women deserted by their husbands join the call. He ordered them to be ousted from the campus immediately. The group left the school silently, headed to the village cremation ground and sat under the banyan tree. The night was clear and bright.

A soft breeze brushed against them. Fire still smouldered in a nearby pyre where someone was cremated earlier that day. The funky smell of cremation hung in the air. They were all exhausted. Digdarshi was worried that Sebati and Maithili could be very hungry. Maithili said that she was used to fasting without water during Ekadashi, since the age of nine. So she didn't care for food. With a sigh, Sebati said that growing up in a poor household with a stepmother, every day was an Ekadashi for her, and it was not unusual for her to spend a day without food. Maithili said that fasting must be challenging for a zamindar's son who was used to comfort and care. Digdarshi replied that he had forgotten his home, village and even his father's name. He understood that India was his motherland and his religion was to fight for her freedom. He also asked the two women to remember that they were the ashram inmates, working for a bigger cause, and personal matters shouldn't be a part of their discussion.

Madan Jena was hungry and asked if they should arrange for something to eat, or talk to the villagers for food. During their discussion, the school teacher showed up with some fine, fragrant Balami rice and vegetables. Madan grabbed one earthen pot that people had discarded after performing the last rites. He brought logs from the pyre that was still alight and arranged stones for a working stove. He laid the rice and vegetables together to cook. The aroma of Balami rice wafted in the air, making them even hungrier. When things started looking up, Nawab Das, the guard, rushed there and smashed the pot, and the dinner in the making fell on the fire. The group spent the entire night starving, sitting beneath that banyan tree in the cremation ground.

Sebati didn't understand splendid concepts like freedom, country or nation. She understood that whatever path Sama Puhana chose was right, and that she must follow in his footsteps and remain on that path. She believed that if she stayed resolute in her mission, their paths would converge at some point and bring her face to face with Sama someday.

Zamindar Graharaj Chaudhury's outhouse, the ultimate symbol of sin and debauchery, gradually emerged as a shrine of refuge during the freedom struggle. Some shadowy figures emerged from that place and fizzled out in the darkness, and they re-entered in the dawn without a stir. Graharaj's palanquin never stopped there during the daytime. So, it was safer for the rebels to avoid the watchful eyes of the police during the day and hide there; they used to decide their course of action sitting inside. Chakori stole rice and provisions from the zamindar's pantry and made some simple food for them.

It was by chance that Devaki caught her stealing. She was puzzled as to why someone who spent her time in the palace from daybreak till night and went out after having dinner needed to steal from the palace. The suspicious zamindar's wife thought of countless probabilities. She feared that Chakori might be part of a conspiracy and had joined a group of rebels against the zamindar. She entertained some secret lover other than the zamindar, or she was busy making money by selling the stolen produce outside. Chakori didn't answer when questioned. They scolded, kicked, stripped and searched her.

Zamindar Graharaj's doubts had a different shade. He was reminded of the adultery of Chakori's mother, who, despite having a comfortable life in Dakhinray's palace, went out at night and cheated on him. He felt she might've opened the door to find new paramours. He looked for a confession and went on whipping her hard. Chakori cried in pain, saying that she stole the rice and dal to feed the poor and do some good karma. He made fun of her supposedly righteous conduct by stealing from others for charity, and asked Prapancha Mohanty to keep the outhouse under strict surveillance.

The physical abuse didn't seem to bother Chakori. She was more worried about the strict watch the master had ordered over her place. She thought it would be a disaster if the freedom fighters were caught at the outhouse, and the dream of having Diganta Keshari as a visitor would never be a reality. She warned the freedom fighters to be watchful for a few days.

Dukhabandhu didn't come for quite some time; the other members also didn't appear. Chakori had bought a charkha sometime back and learned to spin and make threads from cotton. She, too, planted some cotton in her backyard. Dukhabandhu had said that Diganta Keshari had become a disciple of Gandhi. He made the thread in a charkha and wore homespun khadi to spread the message of khadi in the villages. Hearing about the mission of the young zamindar, Chakori lovingly adopted the practices. She returned from the palace late at night and sat down to work with her charkha. Dukhabandhu taught her the art of making thread with the charkha. He later gave up the path of non-violent resistance and trained with the extremists who thought of armed resistance as the alternative path to freedom from foreign rule. He vowed to kill all the Englishmen and smear his forehead with the blood of the native kings and zamindars.

Chakori didn't understand which of the two was the correct path. She knew that Diganta Keshari never rushed to a conclusion and deliberated calmly over matters before making any decision. She believed that his adherence to the non-violent path was right and silently followed him. The days Graharaj didn't come to her place, she spent the whole night spinning cotton and making threads. She saved the rolls carefully in a box and wanted to gift those to the young zamindar, who she heard made khadi out of them. She wanted to wrap a khadi sari herself, but it wasn't allowed in the palace. Her devotion to the elusive Diganta Keshari was unwavering. She was like Ekalavya in the Mahabharata, who never met his guru Drona but perfected his archery skills by looking at his image. She didn't meet Diganta Keshari all these years but followed his teachings faithfully.

Chakori rushed to her backyard in the morning and waited for the train to cross her area. She wasn't sure if she saw him that day. For a moment, her eyes chanced upon meeting a face obscured beneath the cover of his beard, leaping out of the compartment; his pair of eyes roved beyond the river, forest and green fields and rested briefly over the zamindar's palace. His look was dispassionate but deep, and stopped momentarily like a calm, compassionate but resolute vow over her tiny outhouse.

Chakori stood there like a shadowy figure with a pall over her head. The train moved fast as she stirred and struggled to look carefully into his eyes and be sure that it was the man she had been waiting to see all these years. It was a familiar face. She began chasing the moving train like a woman possessed and screamed out hysterically, 'Little Master!' She stood there for quite some time, tired and puzzled. Everything looked hazy to her eyes moist with tears.

∽

In January 1931, Lord Erwin withdrew the infamous proclamation that declared the National Congress Party illegal. The ruling enabled the British government to arrest all party members as political prisoners and keep them behind bars. Soon, Gandhi met Lord Erwin in New Delhi, and the duo signed the Gandhi–

Irwin pact on 5 March 1931. All political prisoners except Bhagat Singh, Sukhdev and Rajguru were freed on 23 March. The government didn't lift the death sentence imposed on the three and acted in unusual haste to hang them. Digdarshi came out with scores of other freedom fighters held up in prison, but the time he spent inside the jail deeply wounded his spirit. He tried to talk to Dukhabandhu, who was kept in a high-security cell, while walking through the corridor.

As a political prisoner, Digdarshi enjoyed certain freedoms denied to other hardened criminals. He was allowed to borrow books from the prison library and read. He could write one or two letters to his family in a week. But he didn't have a family per se; the few letters he wrote were addressed to Parshuram. Brief but symbolic, the meaning of those letters was understood by the receiver alone. He didn't care much for the food in the jail, nor did he hesitate to use the single iron bowl for eating and in the washroom. Inside the cell, a raised bed of five feet by two and a rugged blanket were left for the inmate's use. He had the choice to use his bedding, but Digdarshi didn't want to use anything special. He felt choked inside the narrow confines of the cell and longed to get out in the open. He used to get information about the outside world from Parshuram's friend Vibhuti, the assistant jailor of Cuttack.

He was surprised to hear from the jail warden about a relative waiting to see him. He went out and saw Maithili in the visitors' room. He wasn't excited but rather puzzled, and accused her of using the fake identity of a relative to meet him. He was not prepared to hear Maithili explaining in a roundabout way that she was there to meet him as someone close to her soul, or that he was the guru who gave her a rebirth and remained the greatest inspiration of her life. He reminded her of the life of detachment the ashram inmates needed to aspire to. Her face turned red in anger and shame.

'My best wishes aren't cloaked in any vested interest. The needs of a physical body do not limit Maithili. She's a free soul beyond the body…,' she declared calmly; her eyes dazzled brightly like the morning sun.

She was there to tell him about the first widow remarriage of Rupendra from Parahata village, who met his wife—also a freedom fighter—in jail. But the marriage was not accepted, and the couple was barred from entering his home. They were asked to go from door to door seeking forgiveness. Parshuram took them to Sarvadharma Ashram, and he, too, was shunned from sharing water and fire in the community. Digdarshi was unhappy to hear the commotion over widow remarriage and expressed that the freedom they fought hard for might not last long if people did not change their mindset. He said that scriptures like Parasara Samhita, Narada Samhita, Atharva Veda, and Rig Veda, and sages like Jaabaali, Agastya and Vaishampayana favoured widow remarriage.

'As long as the rules are different for men and women in our society, freedom isn't what we should look for. Gandhi has also raised his voice about this matter,' said Digdarshi and stopped.

The call to join the freedom struggle was a rage—inviting and irresistible. However, the freedom fighters who left everything behind on a whim and didn't care to look back weren't spared the demands of the real world. While in jail, Govinda Das learned of his father's death, the auction of his home, and his inability to save it. Madan Jena lost his wife. None of them got parole to join their families for the last rites or the funeral.

Sad and numb, they mourned privately, powerless to talk to the jail authorities.

The cries of inmates tortured in the prison never left Digdarshi's mind. He couldn't forget the scene of Dukhabandhu being brutally smothered under a blanket. The punishment was called 'blanket wrapping'. Digdarshi joined the queue of inmates who held their plates and waited to receive their breakfast. Standing in the queue, he heard the buzz that Dukhabandhu was caught while trying to jump over the prison wall and escape. Some four or five sturdy jail wards wrapped him in a blanket and pounded him hard as if they were removing paddy from the stacks. Digdarshi couldn't stand the cruel sight and walked away without getting his breakfast that morning. He learned from a fellow inmate that Dukhabandhu was identified as a dreaded terrorist. Police charged him with arson and murder, and kept him in a small cell in solitary confinement. He was often force-fed a porridge with equal portion rice and salt. In other instances, he was thrashed mercilessly on his butt till it spilled blood. His arrest was political; he rebelled against the British but was treated like a dreaded criminal inside the prison.

After 'blanket wrapping', Dukhabandhu was pushed to a dingy, tiny cell without a window; the surveillance over him became more severe. A small hole in the door carried little air inside for breathing. The inmates saw just his bright fiery eyes as they walked past the cell. He urged Digdarshi while he crossed the cell to inform his sister Chakori that her brother had been freed from every kind of slavery. He urged the young zamindar that if he understood the miseries of slavery, he should fight against the system till he breathed his last. Dukhabandhu's eyes, he felt, were bright with the vision of an idyllic land where man was free from every fetter that chained him to the miseries in the world. He could not see his face, just a pair of bright eyes through the hole that congealed into two balls of fire in readiness to guide him through the darkness towards a lighted path.

⁂

Parshuram's house, aptly named Sarvadharma Ashram, sat in the heart of the Muslim neighbourhood in Balikuda. For the school to be built there, some Muslim families had to give up their ancestral homes and re-root themselves in the low-lying areas of the Machhagaon Canal. They even dug out some of their near and dear ones from the graves and buried them elsewhere. So, Parshuram often felt that the sacrifice of the Muslim community was greater than his own towards building the school in Balikuda. The school's boundary touched the lanes of the untouchables in every direction; the Bauri people lived close to the west side; the Mehentaras lived in the east; and the Chamaras and Rajaks lived in the north. So, Parshuram's closest neighbours were Muslims and other communities in the lowest rung of the caste ladder. He was the first person to invite them to the various celebrations in the school and offered them seats in the front row with other invitees. Their presence justified the name Sarvadharma Ashram, meaning the abode of people of every religion. Manorama's loving nature helped her to forge a deeper bond with those people, and she invited them as friends during family events. This liberal conduct of the family wasn't, however, appreciated by upper-caste people in the village—especially Dolamani Srichandan, who was proud of his high caste in the hierarchy. He clearly disapproved of

Parshuram's blending with the lower-caste people; but he wasn't vocal in his resentment, he feared backlashes since the headmaster was very popular.

In the year 1931, the British government planned to have separate constituencies for the lower-caste people to widen the rift between the upper-caste Hindus and the untouchables. The news pained many people in the country, and Gandhi immediately started fasting to death inside the jail to protest against the divisive policy.

When caste-based tension was rife, Rajan Behera, a cobbler's son from Balikuda Chamara lane, returned from England after completing his education successfully. Dolamani had earlier opposed lower-caste Rajan's admission to the middle school where his children read. He further argued that since the school was built on land donated by an upper-caste zamindar, an untouchable wasn't allowed to go there. Parshuram was willing to admit the boy, but the father feared for his son's life and removed him from school voluntarily. The removal deeply hurt Rajan, and he left home in anger, shame and disgust. But in a dramatic turn of events, he jumped into a ship heading to England. He worked as a sweeper on the ship and reached England by dint of his extraordinary courage, intelligence and ambition. He stayed there for five or six years, did his studies, and finally, one day, appeared in the Balikuda market fully dressed like an Englishman. Rajan looked completely different. He had a lighter skin already, and his stay in England had brought the mark of a sahib in his personality. He had become tall, robust and handsome in those few years. In suit, pants and tie, he looked almost like an Englishman. He spoke very good English.

Parshuram wanted to felicitate Rajan for his successful sojourn in England. Some objected that since the country was fighting hard to remove the colonizer from Indian soil, honouring him would display the native's subservient attitude. Parshuram explained that the felicitation wasn't for his journey to England but for his decision to return to the country. The headmaster felt that Rajan's patriotism was exemplary. He arranged a meeting in the school playground. Zamindar Dolamani and a few others opposed the event. He ordered that no student should come to the school that day. The parents of the students were Dolamani's subjects; they didn't violate the order and locked the kids inside their homes. Most kids defied their parents, somehow sneaked out, and reached the school by noon. Aziz Khan presided over the meeting. Rajan Behera sat on the podium. But none of the pupils came forward to garland him. They were there to listen to him and the stories of his experience in the country of the sahibs, but were scared that if they put the garland on the untouchable cobbler's neck, they would lose their caste. Parshuram decided to put the garland himself and start the meeting.

Something unprecedented happened momentarily. Sushila, a nineteen-year-old petite inmate, new to Parshuram's ashram, rose with a garland of regular white flowers and hung it around Rajan's neck. She was a Brahmin child widow from a nearby village who had fled her home a few days back, joined the Congress Party and sought refuge at Parshuram's place. Her action stunned the audience. For the elders in the audience, the move was a sacrilege; they closed their eyes in disgust and chanted the name of Lord Rama. Youngsters giggled and clapped. The general assumption was that her garlanding not just violated the caste order but also validated her voluntary acceptance of an untouchable as husband.

Sushila's story was layered. She ran away from home and was determined not to give out the names of his parents or of her village. Instead, she gave a long statement that summarily said that Ramadevi and Sarala Devi held meetings in her village and talked about Gandhi and the ideology of the Congress Party. The duo explained the great man's views on the caste system, untouchability and widow remarriage. They asked women to come forward and work alongside men in the freedom movement. Their words inspired her deeply, but she was extremely upset when her father and brothers—her family's male members—scolded Ramadevi and Sarala Devi in foul language. When she objected, they beat her mercilessly. She got a fever that night, and while she was delirious, she met Gandhi in her dream. She had never met Gandhi in her life, but strangely, whatever description of Gandhi she had heard, matched the man she met in her dream.

In her dream, that person from heaven gently touched her warm forehead and uttered, 'Sushila, be awake! In one of my addresses to the students in Madras, I spoke about widow remarriage! That doesn't mean that all widows are bound to remarry. I meant to say that God has created both men and women; therefore, both should be respected and be able to enjoy equal societal rights. Wherever the scriptures or the sages have berated women and advocated her subjugation and shaming, I've opposed them. If a man isn't denied the right to marry after his wife's death, why weren't the men who made the rules ashamed to stop a widow from remarrying? The horrendous beating you got from your father and brother isn't an isolated case; it's symbolic of man's abuse of women for ages. You've every right to protest this wrongdoing. I've seen the miserable lives of the child widows, and the best choice will be to never regard those girls as widows. A woman is an equal partner to a man; she's gifted with intellectual abilities similar to a man; she's unique, having her independent identity. The hackneyed practices of society give enough power to even the weakest and the most ignorant man. Emboldened by tradition, men subjugate and control the most powerful women and enjoy a status of superiority. Most of the movements of our country couldn't be sustained because of the precarious position of women in the scheme of things. Now, at this critical stage of the freedom movement, we may not be successful if women don't participate wholeheartedly. Millions of illiterate women, who can't read, write or do sums, can contribute a lot to the great cause through the power of their inherent goodness...'

Sushila woke up overpowered by emotion and excitement from her encounter with Gandhi. She sweated profusely. Whatever she had heard the previous day in Ramadevi's address revisited her in the dream as words from Mahatma Gandhi. A strange power transformed the timid, frail young girl into a fearless, strong woman. She opened her mother's jewellery box, separated her gold ornaments, held them in a pouch and began running away from her home at a fast pace. She wasn't scared of ghosts, spirits, witches, thieves or criminals.

It was almost daybreak; she heard some footsteps rushing nearer. She quickly sat down behind a *kewda* bush and remained hiding there all day. Around midnight, under the cover of darkness, she walked to the home of a Congress Party worker and begged him to help her reach Ramadevi's Alakashram. The thorny edges of the kewda leaves had bruised her all over, and she was covered with blood. The Congress worker brought Sushila to Parshuram and left her in his care. Manorama remained in charge till Ramadevi was released from Hajaribagh jail in two weeks. Parshuram decided that if her family didn't look for her in the interim period, he would send her to Alakashram. On her part, Sushila was determined not to go back to her paternal home; she had decided to fulfil the mission of Gandhi as she heard in her dream. The child widow was frail from lack of proper nourishment and the rigorous fasting rituals during Ekadashi, but still, she had retained a tender, fragile grace, and her looks emitted a certain mystical aura. Parshuram could feel the hidden sparks of fire beneath her calm exterior. It wasn't surprising that the young woman who took that spontaneous step to garland Rajan Behera and stunned the audience was none other than Sushila. She didn't think that her action was a violation of some sacrosanct norm.

History and the lives of people were yoked together in subtle ways. Changes that the Empire thought might strengthen its position, created ripples in the people's lives, and they became aware of the things at stake. For example, when Ramsay MacDonald, steadfast in his goal to divide the country along caste and communal lines, redrew just two separate seats for the untouchables and Muslims in state assemblies, Gandhi felt that the law undermined the interest of the untouchables. He sat on a fast-unto-death protest against the law in Yerwada jail near Poona, forcing the government to agree to carve out more constituencies for the untouchables within Hindu constituencies. It empowered the Dalits and led to the formation of the All India Organization to Remove Untouchability and Seba Samaj for Untouchables. The Congress Party gained greater sway over the British government and the people's minds. Leaders in Cuttack formed a committee to abolish untouchability. The women party workers who returned from jail joined a cleaning drive in the slums of the lower-caste people—a novel initiative that inspired similar action in Balikuda. Hari Bishwal, Parshuram, Govinda Das and others founded the Sarvasamya Committee and led the initiative to clean areas where untouchables and Muslims lived predominantly.

Sushila loved these progressive initiatives around her. She had no regard for untouchability as she came forward to garland Rajan that day. Parshuram understood that it wasn't romantic love—the stereotypical inkling of attraction between a young woman and a young man. But unfortunately, for the people gathered there, the act was bold and offensive; they questioned Sushila's motive and morality. Parshuram was calm; he thought that if Sushila and Rajan decided to marry, the union would take care of two very dogged issues—namely, widow remarriage and marriage between high- and low-caste young men and women. But he wasn't sure if Sushila would marry an untouchable or Rajan a child widow.

Sushila stood silently before Rajan. He looked quite self-conscious with the garland still hanging over his neck. While the laughter and the claps died down, Rajan said 'thank you' in a soft tone. Sushila raised her head and their eyes met, and that rare moment chiselled an unshakable bond between the two. But, before she could leave the stage, the mob began pelting stones. Rajan rushed forward to protect her; the mob was violent. Hari Bishwal, Aziz and Parshuram came forward to pacify them; they, too, were wounded from the pelting. Police reached the site and arrested Rajan and Sushila. They were detained at the police station for inciting violence. But ironically, the chains that handcuffed them inspired them to accept the chains of marriage that day. After they were freed from jail, Rajan and Sushila came wearing hand-spun khadi to Parshuram's ashram to convey their love and gratitude to him and inform him of their decision to marry. Tears of joy came to Parshuram's eyes; he wanted the marriage to happen fast. But the couple declared their intent to remain single till the country got her freedom; if freedom didn't come, they would not marry and wait for another birth.

※

Non-violent resistance was on hold during the the year 1933. The sudden plunge in the momentum gave Digdarshi ample time to think over truth and reality. A detached karma yogi, he didn't look for the fruits of his action but never devalued the need for action. Since non-violent resistance was suspended temporarily, Gandhi urged the freedom fighters to keep up creative and constructive work throughout the country. The field was vast and open; therefore, Digdarshi couldn't sit idle. Initially, he was interested in joining his friend Baikuntha on a tour of India by foot for five long years. The Party had entrusted him with the responsibility to supervise the services initiated for the untouchables in the area. The khadi movement was also not supposed to lose momentum in the villages. On top of that, the atrocities of the zamindars in Harishpur and Mirichipur over the peasants rose daily; Dolamani's misdeeds were insufferable. There was no respite for Digdarshi, but his mind never lost its focus on the higher goal that inspired him to leave home and face the challenges of the outside world tangled in many issues.

The tragic death of Kulachandra Das in the meantime shocked him to the core. The son of a dasi for a small zamindar near Harishpur, Kulachandra was very intelligent. Some generous people helped him complete his study of law in Calcutta and become a lawyer. The zamindar, old and ailing, was very fond of him, but the bond between the two didn't go well with his spoilt, good-for-nothing sons. Alcoholic and lewd, they didn't mind influencing the zamindar to raise taxes on the subjects if they needed more money. Those haughty young men were extremely jealous of Kulachandra; they feared that, being a lawyer, he might invoke the law and take away the ownership of the estate. But Kulachandra was a man of integrity; he was very kind and caring towards the ailing zamindar on his deathbed.

The zamindar's sons, his legal heirs, planned an open showdown with Kulachandra, and invited family, friends and guests, including police officials, to the palace. Kulachandra was a patriot and appeared in traditional khadi at the gathering. The zamindar's sons knew of the British aversion to Indian attire and assumed that he wore khadi to embarrass the zamindar's family.

The zamindar's eldest son asked for Kulachandra to join the guests, but as he proceeded to take his seat, the son said, 'Hey! I didn't invite you to sit with the esteemed guests. Being the son of a dasi, and a bastard, you must know where you stand. Clean off the dust on my shoes,' he ordered like a master.

Kulachandra wasn't provoked. He replied calmly, 'Those present here are all slaves, and you're the biggest bootlicker of the Englishmen amongst all!'

The zamindar's son, on the offensive, was furious; he pounced upon Kulachandra like a hungry tiger. The audacity of a dasi's son who talked so disrespectfully of the British officials and of him in a special gathering enraged him. He screamed, 'If I'm a slave, you're the slave of a slave. Don't forget that you polished our shoes in your childhood and ate the leftovers from our plates. How soon have you forgotten your past! Sit down now, polish my shoes or else be ready to go to the torture chamber for a treat.'

Two henchmen quickly pushed Kulachandra from the back to sit on the floor and ordered him to start working with the shoes. They warned of dire consequences if he didn't carry out the order. One of the guards held a spear-like sharp weapon pressed against his back. If he defied their order, he might be killed before everyone and his death would be made to look like a natural death. Kulachandra had no choice but to lower his head and polish the shoes amidst the ring of laughter from the guests.

The next day, Kulachandra's dead body was found hanging from the branch of a *bakula* tree. A letter he wrote and addressed to Parshuram was found near him:

> No one should think mistakenly that I couldn't handle the shame inflicted upon me, and ended my life. My death should be a wake-up call to every countryman. I know my name won't be on the glorious list of martyrs. The goal of my death is self-rule—freedom. As long as this country isn't free, its rule by the privileged feudality isn't going to end. As long as society is stratified in the layers of kings, zamindars, subjects and slaves, humanity will be mired in the sufferings of hell. Thousands of enslaved people like me get killed or kill themselves in misery, pain or shame. I'm just an example. My soul will be at peace if my death is understood as a challenge at a time when the enthusiasm for the freedom movement is at its lowest point. I'm dedicating my life to the liberation of humanity as I end my life and embark on the path of the final journey.

Kulachandra once was a very dear student of Parshuram. He was Digdarshi's friend from college. Parshuram passed the letter to Digdarshi and said that in spirit it was meant for him. Kulachandra, the symbol of protest, urged his friends to dispel the ignorance festering people's spirits.

Digdarshi was deeply moved by his friend's suicide and understood that man is the cruelest and the most violent creature. He's thrilled to attack another even when he's not hungry, or there's no threat to his survival. He sits on his heap of wealth and seemingly enjoys the cries of the poor! Buried in stinking riches, he feels powerful like God, and thinks of himself as someone above death. The zamindar's son was eyewitness to many such harrowing cruelties. He remembered with penitence the cries from the torture chamber, *mridanga ghara*, and the pillar of punishment, *majhi khunta*.

People relate countless tales of torture in the mridanga ghara and majhi khunta. The maids and slaves condemned to punishment at majhi khunta were tied to the pole in the middle of an open yard and beaten mercilessly. If the violation was stark, they got the severest punishment in the mridanga ghara. The rebellious and the arrogant met with the severest forms of corporal punishment. The painful cries of the victim weren't supposed to be heard by the outsiders; the perpetrators smothered those painful wailings with the incessant beating of drums or the mridanga. It was a blessing if someone died; he was released permanently from torture, and his soul moved beyond pain and suffering.

Chapter X

The situation following Kulachandra's suicide was stifling. The uneasy calmness was like the stillness before a storm. Rain was imminent; the loaded droplets in the mist hung in the air, waiting for a powerful push from a mass of monsoon clouds for a mighty collision against the mountain, obstructing its move.

The mountain stood there from time immemorial; it's the insuperable mountain of pain, suffering and misery, and the freedom movement—the monsoon wind—slowly moved towards it. Its touch gradually awakened the masses and readied them to merge with the larger national movement.

Sitting in a separate room in the Sarvadharma Ashram, Hari Bishwal, Govinda Das, Parshuram and Digdarshi tried to determine the common goals to galvanize the freedom movement at the grassroots. They focused on challenging the nagging issues of caste system, untouchability, repression and abuse of women, and determining ways to remove these deeply embedded practices. Service to the Harijans, freedom for women, and the spread of mass awareness became their primary goals.

Kulachandra's death had infuriated the people, and when the zamindar of Harishpur raised the taxes, the burden on the aggrieved was like adding ghee to the fire. Harishpur zamindari came under the pakki mahal taxation, and it was illegal for him to impose random additional taxes. Digdarshi urged the subjects to protest. Reading Maxim Gorky's *Mother* and Lala Lajpat Rai's *Young India*—which he got from guru Parshuram—gave him a clear understanding of revolution and patriotism. *Mother* showed him the courage of the common man against the oppressive rule of the Tsars and his role in making the Russian Revolution a reality. *Young India* filled his heart with a deeper sense of patriotism. He felt that the suffering of people in the Gadajat, Zamindari and Mugalbanai areas was no less harrowing than the hardship of the Russian people. He revisited the history of the peasant revolt in Kanika, and the role of the young leader Harekrishna Mahatab in that movement. The king of Kanika copied the lavish lifestyle of the English, and when his expenses went out of control, he imposed newer taxes on the subjects resulting in sixty-four types of taxes at one point in time. A loyalist of the Raj, the British decorated him with titles like 'Sir', 'Rajabahadur', 'Knight' and 'Order of British India'. The peasants rose against the exploitation by their ruler, but the king misinformed the British that the popular revolt was against the Raj. The attack on the rebels that followed was two-pronged, and the brutalities of the British surpassed the repression of the Kanika ruler. Several people lost their lives; women were molested and homes were looted; many ended up as paupers on the streets. Digdarshi, then a student leader from Ravenshaw College, was actively involved with the Kanika peasant revolt. That experience gave him a lot of courage to lead the revolt against the Harishpur zamindar.

At that time, Gandhi had kept the non-cooperation movement at the national level on hold, and asked his followers to invest their energy in rebuilding the institutions at the grassroots. Digdarshi taught the people of Harishpur and Mirichipur to oppose injustice; he found them meek and servile. The zamindar smelt the discontent and rushed to curb the uprising pre-emptively. The clampdown was horrible, but leaders like Bhuja Malika, Narana Jena and Suryananda Swain did a great job. Peasants in Dhenkanal, too, revolted against their ruler. Other zamindars united against the momentum and reproached the Congress Party leaders for inciting the commotion. They exaggerated the protest as treason, and tried to get every possible help from the British to put down the revolt. Topsil sahib, the commissioner of Odisha, didn't get a correct picture of the peasant movement from his subordinates. The corrupt officials below the hierarchy were close to the zamindars and presented the popular revolt as a new type of protest imagined by the Congress Party.

Listening to Jayaprakash Narayan's talks during his prison time in Nasik Central Jail on raising mass consciousness against the British, planted the seeds of socialism in Digdarshi's mind. From a young age, he thought of organizing the exploited masses against the exploiters. It was his opportune moment to talk to people about a classless, egalitarian society. Meanwhile, prominent leader Nabakrushna Chaudhury convened a secret meeting for deliberation over social equality; at the end, the participants announced the creation of the Utkal Congress Samajvadi Sangathan. It became the foundation of a socialist organization in Odisha. Surendranath Dwivedy declared himself a socialist there, and removed his sacred thread—the symbol of a Brahmin. Malati Choudhury sold her jewellery and donated six thousand rupees to the organization. They published *Sarathi*, the first magazine dedicated to the workers, on 1 May 1933.

Dwivedy regularly came to Balikuda and held discussions with his friend Parshuram. Digdarshi was inspired by the socialist ideology and published *Dalitara Dabi,* a handwritten journal edited by Parshuram. He ensured that the journal was distributed in Harishpur and nearby areas. All the contributors used pseudonyms, and those who copied the writings into the journal were from other villages. They worked secretly and vanished under the cover of the night. The journal created a lot of confidence in the people, but Zamindar Dolamani wasn't happy. Socialism didn't deviate from the Gandhian ideals of passive resistance and universal love. Still, a handful of unscrupulous Congress Party workers like Dolamani found it the best thing to create a rift in the Congress Party.

Dolamani was good at distorting facts and engendering doubt through propaganda. He called a meeting of the village people, and explained that socialism was the enemy of the poor and would do no harm to the rich and the privileged. He implanted the fear that the socialists would take away the land and home of the poor, provide a communal kitchen, and ask all to sit together and eat; there would be no line separating people based on caste, creed, sex or social status. He warned that all wealth would become communal, and no one could claim a personal home, wealth, wife or children. Dolamani got some astounding results. Upper-caste people believed that God ordained untouchability and, therefore, saw it as inviolable. They couldn't think of abandoning their caste, and their wives as communal property, or having bastards as their offspring. They found the ideology a dangerous agenda. The average villager looked at Digdarshi, Govinda Das, Parshuram and Hari Bishwal with suspicion.

The primary aim of the Socialist Congress Party in Odisha was the abolition of the zamindari system. Krushak Sangha, the association of peasants, held its first meeting in Cuttack Town Hall. They wanted a peasants' association in every village that worked closely with them and the peasants. Harekrishna Bishwal started the first peasants' association in his village, Nagpur, and included many young men in the group. Those young men urged the peasants to sign a memorandum appealing to the government to reduce taxes.

Gandhi, who, for many, was an avatar of God, came to Cuttack with a mission to remove untouchability. He vowed in the name of Jagannath and marched to the slums of Harijans, accompanied by leaders like Ramadevi. Gandhi had a strategy. He didn't want everyone to join the front line of the non-cooperation movement, defy the law, and get arrested. He wanted some workers to stay back and keep up the momentum. Some volunteers were conspicuous in their leadership positions in the protest marches and went to jail. At the same time, some stayed back and took care of the organizational activities, supervised reformative initiatives, and worked closely with the masses. He urged young men and women to leave the cities and go to the villages. Gopabandhu Chaudhury and Ramadevi built their ashram in Baree; they named the place Sebaghara. Hari Bishwal, Govinda Das and Keshtramohan Kanungo found a permanent office for the Congress Party to serve the people. It sat between the Muslim and the Harijan neighbourhoods, and those people came forward to help build the place. It was named Gandhi Sebasangh. People also joined hands to build the Gandhi ashram in Ganeswarpur. Every village was eager to join the movement; enthusiasm returned to the masses.

The reformists made the simple village folks understand that ignoring Gandhi's advice was akin to ignoring God's words, which would bring greater misery upon them. It worked well. Maithili, Sebati and others walked to nearby villages and talked to people about initiatives like khadi, service to Harijans, women empowerment, basic education, prohibition and adult literacy. During their visits, many women were inspired to join the cause. They formed smaller groups with men and reached out to people to bring change in the villages. The move certainly stirred sleepy villagers but didn't impress the zamindars. The volunteers worked sincerely for village rebuilding and stayed away from violence. The zamindars didn't welcome the activities and summoned many of their subjects, punishing them on unfounded charges to discourage people's participation.

Zamindar Dolamani's sharecropper Sunamani was thus beaten so hard that he fainted that day. The two musclemen choked his mouth with a bundle of rags and continued flogging him non-stop. Suna's crime was joining the peasants' union and coming out in the open against the new taxation in Harishpur. He was framed for the serious offence of stealing valuable gold jewellery belonging to Dolamani. Suna had been to the zamindar's place in the morning while barber Jagu Barik was giving an oil massage to the master. The zamindar had removed all jewellery off his body; he didn't want them to get greasy or come in the way of the barber's hands reaching every nook and cranny of his body. The charges stated that Suna sat at the zamindar's feet, talked to him, and took away the valuables while leaving. Four guards from the palace followed and arrested Suna for stealing, even though he claimed his innocence and clearly stated that he had not seen any gold jewellery in the palace. Dolamani claimed that Suna sold the gold chain and ring, and donated the money towards his membership in the peasants' association. Suna saw the chain hanging on his neck. He said, 'Master, the gold chain is on your neck! You were busy listening to people. So you might have forgotten about it.'

Dolamani crackled, and the men around him burst into laughter. One of his *chamcha*s said, 'Do you think the lord has just one gold chain like some wretched of the earth, as you or me? His neck won't be bare if a single one is missing. If you start counting his pool of necklaces, perhaps your entire life won't be sufficient... Do you understand?'

Nobody paid any heed to what Suna spoke in his defence. He was dragged to the punishment chamber, beaten hard, and left on the floor unconscious. In the morning, the zamindar ordered his people to brush Suna's teeth. It was code language; he ordered that Suna's mouth be filled with faeces. The pattern wasn't something unusual. If it was ordered to shower someone, they were doused with pee and poop. If someone screamed in pain, they were ordered to have sorbet, meaning someone would pee directly into the victim's mouth. During those operations, the violent screams and mad sadistic howling of the zamindar, like that of wild tigers and lions, sent shock waves through the hearts of the executors; they trembled in fear that the same might be their fate any day.

Suna's punishment didn't end there. The zamindar decided to hand him over to the police. Everybody understood what might happen to someone who dared to steal the zamindar's valuables. The police were the zamindar's fawning yes-men. In the presence of all, the zamindar removed the ornaments from his body and asked someone to knot those to one end of Suna's rag. His hands were tied behind him, and he was walked to the police station in public view. The police who retrieved the so-called stolen jewellery were rewarded publicly for their prompt action. Nothing was a secret. The practice aimed to terrorize the peasants and demonstrate the power of the zamindar. The master was omnipotent, he could easily make a sadhu look like a looter, and no one could challenge him.

The zamindar appeared on the scene a little later. He was ready to bail out Suna and declared that he was also ready to pardon his crime. That night, Dolamani entertained the police in his Rangabhavan.

∽

Digdarshi planned a *havan,* the ritual to ward off evil. A religious event, he knew, was the easiest means to attract the naive village folks in droves. And it was better if, in the gathering, a sadhu could inspire courage in them by citing examples from the scriptures. He vanished from the scene, and the friends spread the news that he had left the ashram to take charge of activities at another site. He wasn't a very familiar face in the new site.

In two months, from nowhere a mendicant appeared and arranged a havan on the dead riverbed of Patali. The people nearby came to know that some Digbaba from the Himalayas had come and planned for a havan on the sands of the river. They reached the site slowly, and began to join the baba with love and dedication. The baba's face was covered with a thick beard, and his two powerful eyes glowed bright, adding grace to his beautiful face. He lived in the Shiva Temple on the riverbank, but sometimes walked leisurely towards the peasants' association office and discussed religion with the workers there.

The havan began; the baba read out lines from the Gita and

explained the meaning to the crowd. People from everywhere joined the eight-day-long event. After the completion of the havan, the baba vanished mysteriously; but he didn't forget to explain the real meaning of the havan before he left. A few days after the baba's disappearance, Digdarshi, the Congress Party worker, appeared in the scene, and explained the baba's teachings to the people in simple terms that touched their hearts. The message united them, and finally, they decided to revolt against the injustices they had endured all their lives.

∽

In villages, the rich upper-caste people guarded their cultural mores zealously. They didn't like it if others tried to appropriate their exclusive manners of clothing, talking and cooking. They made it a point that during festivals others shouldn't decorate homes and yards with the type of rangoli they drew, or prepare sweets and cakes typically made in their homes. The zamindars had made it a punishable offence if people below the feudal gentry aped those upper-class practices. Zamindar Dashanana Mahapatra's bookkeeper, Srikhandi Mahapatra, saw a gorgeous drawing on peasant Bhuja Rout's verandah in Harishpur. It was anathema and a violation that made him mad. Srikhandi was a devious sycophant. He swindled a lot from the revenue he collected for the zamindar and made his wealth. He was ready to blow the matter out of proportion and please the master at the expense of the ignoble victim. He convened a gathering where sumptuous food and drink were to accompany the swirls of the dancing girls. On top of that, the crude sardonic mockery of the scapegoat Bhuja was to be the extra kick. He also planned to get dancers from Calcutta to the party.

The zamindar's guards arrested Bhuja Rout. He had been under watch for his role in the peasant movement. They were ready to frame him for his disrespectful conduct towards the zamindar. Bhuja Rout pleaded, 'Master! We're poor peasants. We don't know how to draw such elegant rangoli. Sister Maithili drew this in my front yard. She goes from village to village and teaches skills like drawing rangoli, making sweets, farming bees and caring for cows.'

Zamindar Dashanana didn't listen, and said that the blame would go to him as he was the house owner. He called him the mastermind who knowingly violated the rule and loved to pose as a leader working for the Congress Party.

Immediately, the guards began throwing green coconuts at the poor victim. He gasped in pain from the incessant beating and couldn't move. He was dragged and thrown unconscious in front of his home. The peasants were scared to oppose. Severely battered, Bhuja Rout took a while to recover but couldn't walk afterwards.

The reformists, in the meantime, had built a temporary shed on the bank of the dead river Patali, popularly known as Patua, a tributary of Devi River. There were two rooms in the shed. They used to run the office of the peasants' association from one, and Digdarshi and Madan Jena also lived there; Maithili, Sebati and Sushila occupied the other room. The peasants of Harishpur were a little sceptical of the effectiveness of their revolt against the zamindar. After Kulachandra's tragic death, the reformists selected the area for their activities, and settled there.

The deadly punishment for Bhuja Rout—stoning green coconut at the poor man—made Maithili very sad. She didn't know that a mere rangoli she drew in his yard would result in such severe punishment. She couldn't stop crying once she came to know of the aftermath. She understood that as long as fear and ignorance clung to the minds of the poor peasants, nothing could be done; not even the British political agent could do anything for them.

※

Bhuja Rout's suffering overwhelmed his fifteen-year-old daughter Kanak. She couldn't stand the pain of her father, who remained paralyzed in bed. Digdarshi and Maithili stood by Kanak and counselled her to tell the political agent everything if asked to testify.

'We're with you. Nobody can harm you. If you can tell without fear whatever you've seen and experienced so far, then only justice will be done in your father's case,' advised Digdarshi.

Kanak was impressed with the work of the reformists of the Congress Party. With encouragement from Digdarshi and others, she found the courage to raise her voice against the injustice done to her father.

※

Time was very critical. Sarangadhar Das reached Parshuram's home during one such day. The peasant movement had gained momentum in Dhenkanal and other Gadajats of India. The All India Gadajat Praja Sammilani was instituted under Pandit Nehru and Pattabhi Sitaramayya. Sarangadhar Das was elected as a member of that organization from Odisha. A native of Dhenkanal, he went to the US to complete his education as an agriculture specialist and returned home to work to improve the farming sector. He was often put into trouble by the local king but had vowed to serve the poor peasants. He assumed the pseudonym Landa Dehuri and wrote about the atrocities perpetrated by the rulers in the Gadajat areas. Once he learned about the brutalities against the peasants in Harishpur and Balikuda, he rushed to take stock of the situation. He presided over the meeting held on the sands of the Patali River. It was decided unanimously not to withdraw the peasant movement. The meeting and Sarangadhar's walk through the villages inspired confidence in the people.

∞

Late that night, Digdarshi sat on the floor in the dimly lit room with his knees folded, and spun thread in the charkha calmly. He was so engrossed in his work that he didn't feel the presence of the woman who entered the room like a shadow, and sat beside him. A soft sigh escaped her heart and stirred the lone lamp inside the room. He got distracted, and quickly raised his head and asked, 'Who're you here at this late hour of the night?'

'I'm Kanak,' she said.

'What's the matter? Is everything okay?' he asked anxiously.

'My father passed away,' she said, falling to his feet and crying inconsolably.

Digdarshi stood in shock for a while; he understood her agony and let her cry. Moments passed. He urged her in a calm but firm voice to overcome grief and be resolute, saying that her father's death was an irreparable loss, and she should consider it as a release from extreme suffering for the incapacitated man.

Kanak was desperate. She was there to tell that the zamindar had ostracized her family and had ordered that nobody in the village should help her remove the dead body or join the cremation. Her brother, afraid of the zamindar, wasn't able to take any decision. She wanted the body to be cremated with dignity. Digdarshi needed no further explanation to understand that she was there to beg for help for the last rites. He rose, saying, 'Let's go to your place.'

He informed Maithili and Sebati, and asked them to send Aziz Khan and Madan Jena to Bhuja Rout's home upon their return to the ashram. Kanak followed him; her slithering sighs bounced against his heart. 'We have to get over this darkness patiently,' he said.

As they walked through the village road, Srikhandi Mahapatra came across them. He turned up the faint light of the lamp in his hand and saw Kanak and Digdarshi walking side by side.

'Oho, Kanak? Hi, hi,' he said.

He gave an obscene shriek, saying that kings went out in the dark in the old days, but it was strange that a peasant's daughter roamed at night with a Congress Party worker. The patronizing old man advised her to rush home and make arrangements to send her father's soul to heaven.

Bhuja Rout's body was cremated at dawn on the sands of the river, not in the village burial ground, because the zamindar prohibited the dead body, touched by Aziz Khan, a Muslim, from being taken there. Digdarshi, Madan and Aziz did the cremation, bathed in the river, and ate some puffed rice with jaggery, following the Hindu tradition. Kanak was grateful to them for bidding an honourable farewell to her father like a son. Aziz assured her that they would always be with her. That moment forged a great bond. Digdarshi asked her to join the Congress Party and work as a volunteer to help fulfil Gandhi's dream of a free country without bias against women, lower castes and the poor. She was supposed to come to the ashram after the twelve days of mourning.

Standing on the ashram verandah, Maithili could see the fire slowly fading at Bhuja Rout's pyre on the river bank; her heart sighed in remorse. She was guilty that the rangoli she drew caused the conflict, and the poor man succumbed to the blunt trauma he got from the green coconuts thrown at him. She felt responsible for his unwarranted death. She was disturbed that none in the village who witnessed the entire sordid drama came forward to testify that it was a brutal killing by the zamindar's people. The guarded silence of the public, she felt, made Bhuja Rout's murder pass as a natural death.

Digdarshi was deeply moved after conducting Bhuja Rout's last rites and returned with a heavy heart. He tried to rein in his restless mind and sat down on the verandah with his charkha to spin some thread for a khadi sari he planned to weave for Kanak. The day he carried Bhuja Rout in his arms to the pyre, he felt the subtle bond of a brother with the poor girl, and he vowed to honour that responsibility. Maithili sat across him, busy turning her charkha. She appeared like a heap of grief; her look was quite humbling. He was lost in his thoughts while working at the charkha. Her eyes silently scanned the Patali River that ran by the ashram; her mind, too, was distracted by nagging thoughts. The curl of smoke from Bhuja Rout's pyre no more rose through the sky.

The mind is a strange place. Thoughts relentlessly ebb and flow there, but some nagging ones flash regularly in the stream of consciousness. Digdarshi wanted to talk to Maithili, who was lost in her contemplation of their social reform agenda, like service to Harijans, unification of peasants, and reform in old practices. Nothing seemed well-coordinated. Maithili defended their progress in sanitation in slums, the making of khadi, women empowerment, and basic education. But she wanted the reformists to lead by example. 'Some of us from the reformists—the advocates of change—should marry from the untouchable community, marry someone outside our religion to promote religious tolerance, and marry widows to remove the stigma of widow marriage.'

He confided in her that Aziz was in love with a Hindu girl and had decided to marry her. Leaders like Ramadevi, Parshuram, Haribhai and Govindabhai wished that more and more of the young volunteers would set the precedence for widow remarriage. He was pleased to share that many cultured young men, inspired by Gandhi's essays in *Young India* and *Harijan*, had vowed to marry child widows. People's attitude toward untouchability was changing too. Maithili knew that Gandhi believed that *swaraj* or freedom was the birthright of every nation, and he emphasized that women should be free from social inequality, prejudice and stigma before achieving that goal. Gandhi said that if half of a country's population consisted of women, and if they were variously repressed and neglected, freedom for that country made no sense. Similarly, without granting equal rights and privileges to Harijans or the untouchables, the country couldn't be free in the real sense of the term. She agreed that the pathetic instances of five-year-old widows who are fasting without water on Ekadashi should stop. She wanted to take the lead in fighting these age-old evil practices and root them out.

Digdarshi had a different vision. He wanted Maithili to marry and set the example that a child widow could marry and begin her life anew. Maithili worried that if she married, her father might think of her as an impostor who left home to marry someone of her choice, rather than follow the path shown by Mahatma Gandhi.

Digdarshi disagreed and said that if she feared her father, she couldn't bring confidence in other widows to remarry. He asked her not to fear the so-called stakeholders of society and succumb to their wishes. Maithili looked straight into his eyes and declared that if she were going to be an inspirational example, she would be a friend to her supposed partner and marry him after the country became free. Digdarshi declared that every Congress Party worker wanted to marry her, and her brown cheeks went rosy as she blushed. He sought her consent to discuss the marriage with his guru Parshuram's wife, Manorama. Maithili wanted to know who the groom was. He guaranteed that she wouldn't be disappointed with the suitable man he had in his mind. The two sat down with their charkhas; four hands moved simultaneously, and the fine threads of their thoughts began winding separately.

Where life failed to extol someone, death heralded glory for him. Bhuja Rout lost the battle with life, but death made him a potent symbol that rekindled the dying flames of the freedom movement. Govinda Das and Hari Bishwal ensured that the political agent should hear from the peasants and the zamindar in deciding the fate of the peasants' protest. Both sides readied witnesses and proofs, and the general perception was that the judgement would be impartial.

In the meantime, within a week of Bhuja's death, Kanak was rumoured to be missing from the village. People stated that she was taken to the zamindar's palace. As planned during her father's last rites, she was supposed to join Digdarshi's ashram as a Congress Party worker. Kanak's abduction seemed uncalled for. Digdarshi, Madan Jena and Aziz Khan rushed to the village, and Maithili and Sebati went to her home to verify.

From their discussion with the family, Maithili's group determined that Kanak seemed to have lost her mind after a sickness. She wanted to overcome the nightmare leading to her father's death and was determined to join the Congress Party. She wanted to wear khadi and live in Ramadevi's ashram because she feared it would be hard for her to continue as a freedom fighter in the village. In the meantime, interrupting her imminent move, came the summons from the zamindar's palace asking her to go there and receive money for her father's last rites. Her family said that she went and never returned from the palace. Maithili and Sebati also verified with the villagers, who told a different story. They informed that Kanak was summoned to the palace, and upon reaching there, the guards and attendants gang-raped her. She was ruthlessly beaten in the torture chamber and went missing from the village after that. Kanak's brother wasn't bold enough to oppose and find out his sister's fate. The villagers were aware of the sinister abuse of the poor young woman but were afraid of the zamindar and the police, and didn't dare to come forward to tell the truth.

Digdarshi was deeply hurt. He could make out that Kanak was punished badly for her desire to join the Congress Party. Congress workers took the matter seriously and felt that the zamindar's high-handedness had crossed the limits. They mulled over the idea of storming the palace. At this juncture, the palace notified him that the zamindar had convened a hearing on Kanak's case in the presence of the police and the magistrate.

Upon arrival, Digdarshi could sense that the zamindar had planned to erode public confidence in Digdarshi's integrity, remove the Congress Party workers from his jurisdiction, and retain his absolute authority over the subjects. In the alleged chargesheet, Digdarshi was Kanak's molester, and she was supposed to identify him as the criminal who violated her. The victim was warned of severe consequences if she spoke otherwise. Death threats for her and her brother's family had forced her to succumb to the pressure tactic. Rumour was that the zamindar promised her enough cash and a job in lieu of her testimony. Digdarshi wasn't afraid of the investigation but was worried about Kanak's fate. Her vulnerability pained him; he was deeply sorry for the prey being pushed into the trap. Kanak—the other name for gold, he believed, molten in fire, would shape into beautiful jewellery. Like gold, she would singe in the fire of shame, tolerate all the harsh poundings and abuses, and dazzle at the end. He appeared for the trial. Zamindars from nearby areas, including Dolamani, were present in the audience.

'Oh! I didn't know you're tangled in such acts!' Dolamani said with a huge pinch of sarcasm.

Kanak was dragged to the hall. He couldn't look into her eyes. She wasn't the woman he knew; she seemed like a ghost of her former self. Her body was pale like the dying moon, but her pair of eyes burnt bright like the morning star. Her eyes looked desperately for the truth missing from the scene and perhaps hiding in another planet.

'What's your name?' asked the police officer.
'Kanak.'
'There's a complaint that you've been raped. Is that true?'
'Yes! It's true!'

'Do you know freedom fighter Digdarshi?'
'Yes!'
'Is he here among us?'
'Yes.'
'Identify him.'

Kanak raised her finger and identified him. Seven eye-witnesses from the village were ready to testify that Digdarshi, the Congress Party worker who claimed to be a follower of Gandhi, had raped her in the ashram. Her large innocent eyes surveyed him. There was no sign of hatred, reproof, sentimentality, hesitation, shame, fear, guilt or vulnerability. Those eyes beamed with the fire of martyrdom and resonated with his consciousness. She looked straight at him without the flicker of her eyes but said nothing despite repeated reminders. One by one, the seven witnesses came forward. Their cold narratives were laden with so much obscene detail that it was hard for a prosecutor to follow them. Dolamani and his zamindar friends interrupted the witnesses with caustic aspersions on rampant immorality among Congress Party workers and their social work.

Once the eyewitness accounts were over, Kanak was asked again to give her statement. She agreed that the horrendous accounts of the molestation were true. She was asked to identify the criminal for the pronouncement of the punishment. Kanak was silent for a while, and the zamindar declared that her silence confirmed her agreement with the witness testimony.

Kanak finally objected, saying that the witnesses were the men who molested her in the punishment chamber. She stated that Digdarshi was a godly person who carried her father's dead body on his shoulder and cremated him like a son would. She urged the judge not to believe the smear campaign against a man having no blemish in his character, and also spare her from being a part of the heinous conspiracy.

The zamindar's manager warned her of the punishment for lying under oath. Kanak replied stoically that no greater harm could be done to her, and after the unspeakable torment, death should be her only choice. She could barely hold herself together, and was dismissed from the room. The magistrate read the recorded statement again, discussed it with the police officer, and came to Digdarshi declaring, 'You're under arrest.'

He wanted to know his crime, and the magistrate declared, 'You've molested Kanak.' Though the victim had denied the allegation, he was arrested based on the accounts of the eyewitnesses. Kanak was declared a woman who had lost her mind after her father's death. If the accused wanted to refute the charge brought against him, he could bring his objections during trial in court. Digdarshi screamed hard in protest and extended his hands in surrender saying, 'I'm aware of the farcical legal procedure of the British.'

The dimming flame in a pyre pushes hard one final time and burns bright before everything dies out. The same thing happened with the people of Harishpur when Digdarshi was arrested and taken in police custody, charged with Kanak's rape. They were stunned initially, but the voice of protest soon became louder. It seemed more like the reaction of someone stunned by the death of a person close to their heart. The aggrieved one mightn't cry immediately, but the awareness of the final departure sinks in after the flames consume the body and wipe out the last remnants of the person's physical presence.

Nobody found Kanak in the village the day after the trial. The zamindar's people came out with countless explanations for her disappearance. But the fire of revolt smouldering among the people flared up in no time. Maithili, Sushila, Sebati, Aziz and Madan reached out to people in the nearby villages and secretly conveyed that the zamindar and his coterie molested Kanak. They cautioned that the same might be the fate of other girls in the zamindar's dominion; the wrongful arrest of Digdarshi might happen with any upright young man in their villages. The masses needed no further proof, and the protest picked up steam. They came in contact with larger national initiatives like the non-cooperation movement, and reform movements of the Congress Party, Harijan Sevak Sangh. The awakening was transformative. The momentum against the zamindar's action continued, and people finally refused to pay the excess taxes imposed on them.

Hari-Govinda-Parshuram, the inseparable friends and conscientious activists, urged the British political agent to come to Harishpur and take stock of the tense situation in the area. He arrived in a few days, examined the situation, and declared that since the area was under pakki mahal or direct taxation by the British government, the local zamindar wasn't authorized to impose or raise taxes on the people at its will. The zamindar was chastened; the popular revolt calmed down, and normalcy returned to the cluster of villages. For the first time, the zamindar watched fearfully that the timid masses were bold and were united in asking for justice. He sensed that the freedom of the country was no longer a remote possibility but rather a reality in the offing, and the line separating the ruler and the ruled would be eliminated soon.

Chapter XI

The news that Digdarshi duped the police and escaped from the jail travelled faster than lightning. People were aware of the brutalities of the zamindar's henchmen and the further amplification of torture by the police inside the lockup. But they couldn't accept the fate of a criminal meted out to Digdarshi, the well-known Congress Party worker in their area. Hari Bishwal and Govinda Das went on an indefinite fast in front of the Balikuda police outpost in protest. Teacher Parshuram visited the police station, discussed the matter with the officers, and obtained permission to meet him in jail. The same night, Digdarshi reportedly broke the iron grill of the jail window and escaped. The government announced a reward money to capture him. Dolamani was furious and claimed that Parshuram was the mastermind behind his jailbreak. But since there was no proof against Parshuram, the dependable school teacher couldn't be arrested.

Parshuram knew that the police shadowed him. It wasn't hard to observe that opposition to the zamindar and the freedom movement gained momentum after Digdarshi disappeared from jail.

Dolamani was adept at smear campaigns and confusing people with alternate stories. He rumoured that Digdarshi and Kanak had a clandestine affair, and once that became public, she sought refuge in his palace but ran away to stay at Parshuram's ashram; her lover escaped the prison and joined her. The couple was in hiding. Some elderly locals verified the facts with Parshuram. He asked them to ignore the baseless rumour. He would gladly have welcomed them if they were lovers, but he was clueless about the missing persons and waiting hopefully to get some information soon. Contrary to Dolamani's goal, the scandal glorified his heroic jailbreak and drew unparalleled sympathy for poor Kanak. The people knew that Parshuram didn't lie but still had unanswered questions about their whereabouts.

The workers from the Congress Party had two different responsibilities: they had to mobilize people for the freedom movement, and bring reform in age-old evil social practices in rural areas. It was often hard for them to accomplish the dual mission. In that critical moment, nature wreaked havoc in people's lives. The Rohia Bachala Dam collapsed in torrential rain, and thousands lost their homes and became destitute. Thus, there was no respite for the workers of the Party dedicated to public service—the rescue and rehab mission for the flood-affected was their immediate priority. Hari Bishwal took the lead, recorded the names of the affected, and devised plans to provide food and temporary shelter to them.

The flood relief committee took up the matter and opened three centres in Balikuda, Borikina and Ghodadian to distribute food and other relief materials. There were countless huddles. The relief workers didn't find enough official support and contacted private organizations like the Marwadi Relief Samaj and Ramakrishna Mission in Calcutta. Parshuram rushed to villages with his team of students who carried bags of rice, dal, puffed rice and old clothes over their heads, and distributed those among the flood-affected. Hari Bishwal managed the

Ghodadian relief centre, and Govinda Das remained in charge of the one in Borikina. Madan Jena, Aziz and others worked sincerely alongside them.

The volunteers missed the good Samaritan, Sama Puhana. He was the daredevil they needed the most, one who would've braved the rising water and saved lives caught in the flood. It was known that the police dumped him unconscious in Chandaka forest, and that tigers might have eaten him in the wilderness. They had no news beyond that. Sebati, his betrothed, never paid attention to the pity that people showed to her hero. In her heart of hearts, she believed that Sama bravely fought the ferocious tigers in the forest, beat up the beasts, and escaped.

'Sama won't die till Mother India wears her crown of freedom over her head. He'll fight with Yama and save the country from the bondage of the English traders; he'll defeat death,' she mulled.

Sebati heard a voice inside urging her to leave for the rescue site of the afflicted. It told her that Sama, the man she loved, might be missing, but she must continue his noble work. Thoughts crashed inside her like billowing waves; the flood water shouted her name. She didn't shed tears for Sama; she knew their marriage was impossible, but she wished to meet him at least once before her death. It was no secret to her that Sama's father was looking for a suitable girl for his son. He hoped that once the country was free, Sama would return to the village and marry, but never to Sebati of Narilo village. The father disapproved of Sebati crossing the forbidden lines for women: she left home, moved around, cleaned the neighbourhoods of the untouchables, didn't cover her head, and worked alongside men. The outgoing, shameless woman brought a bad name for her village and couldn't be their daughter-in-law.

Parshuram believed that Sebati would marry and return home as Sama's bride someday. Govinda Das talked to the father and persuaded him to let Sama settle down with Sebati. He also questioned that if he let his only son leave home, move free, and work for the Harijans, he shouldn't object to Sebati going beyond the threshold and working outside. The old man believed that a woman's world was strictly within the four walls of the home. Like an earthen pitcher, she would lose her sanctity if seen or touched by others and thereafter couldn't be taken inside. A man was like a precious brass pitcher; any blemish could be rubbed off to make him new and shiny.

Sebati overheard the conversation between the men and kept quiet. She didn't share her feelings with Maithili or Sushila. She stayed steadfast in the mission to serve the needy. Service was her call, and it remained inseparable from who she was. She had planned to spend the rest of her life in Ramadevi's Bari ashram. But she had some faith in Sama; he wasn't unreasonable, she often thought.

The flood was terrible. People took refuge with their families over the dam. The downpour was continuous; it paused momentarily and then began lashing hard with renewed vigour. The rush of clouds and rain sometimes blurred the line between the earth and the sky. Those stranded over the dam became sick with cold, fever, cholera and diarrhoea; many young ones died in their mothers' arms; people saw nothing but hunger, hardship and sickness. The volunteers built temporary shelters with palm leaves and bamboo poles, and the displaced squeezed themselves inside. Snakes and frogs roamed around. Nothing scared people; the thing that worried them most was the ceaseless downpour.

The river kept rising frighteningly. The bigger threat for them was the periodic shaking of the dam.

Early in the morning, as darkness hung everywhere, Sebati moved from one shelter to the other with a cover over her head. The flickering lamp in her hand flashed like a thin ray of lightning against the dark sky. She had been relentless in serving the sick and ailing. She went around giving water and a little barley or sago in the mouths of the older patients. She consoled a woman who had lost her child, and rushed to attend to a birthing mother in labour pain. She didn't hesitate to separate the dead body of a child from the arms of a wailing mother and gently release it into the water. The next moment, she held with tender care a crying newborn who came out of the mother's womb covered with blood and fluid, and the placenta tangled along. She assured him of a safe, warm place in the grip of her arms. She rendered selfless service to the people who needed it the most. She lived not for herself but to serve others.

Deadly ebony clouds rushed across the night sky continuously. The harsh croak of the frogs and the wailing of street dogs made the atmosphere more fearsome. The dam at the end of the village was on the verge of collapse. The volunteers were on guard. The currents in the river were fiercely powerful. It swept away humans and livestock; some clung to roofs and some hung from tree branches hoping for someone to rescue them. But it wasn't always possible to save the victims in distress.

Sebati felt someone's heavy steps hasten towards her. He looked like a shadow in the darkness. She assumed that the person might be a volunteer. She raised the lamp beneath her veil; the faint flame flickered in the damp wind. The volunteer turned to her and said, 'Can you please zoom the light on this little one? Let me check if he's alive or not. He was stuck on a thatched roof swept away by the flood. No idea how long he has been soaking in the flood water.'

She calmly held the lamp in her palm. A slim ray of light fell on one side of the man's face, covered with a thick beard. Sebati was startled. She couldn't be sure if that was real or a hallucination. The man beside her was Sama; she couldn't believe her eyes. Overwhelmed with shock, she took a little time to realize that he survived the wild tigers of Chandaka forest, and was there to help the victims inundated in the water. Dreams, at times, seem real; one can even laugh in deep sleep. Likewise, the truth to her was so unbelievably real at that moment that it seemed like a dream. Sebati raised the flame and looked at the face of the man of her dreams. Unwittingly, a word of endearment escaped her lips, 'You?'

The man was checking the semi-conscious kid and was startled to hear the voice. He, too, reacted loudly, 'You! Sebati? What're you doing here?'

'Yes! It's me,' she said, choking with emotion, and added briefly that she joined Mahatma Gandhi's freedom movement with a few other women from her village. She couldn't complete the sentence, nor could she say that she searched for him everywhere, and stopped abruptly.

Sama was a bit astonished. He advised her to return home and ruled out the possibility of his return to the village in the near future. He wanted to see the freedom struggle through and the motherland become a free country. Sebati fumbled for the right words. She didn't know how to convince that quirky fellow to understand that she didn't want him to marry her right then and there. She wanted to say that she was grateful to God for finding him alive, but she choked.

Sama had no sentiments; he chastised her, saying she shouldn't be selfish and think of those women who lost their husbands in the freedom struggle. 'Don't worry about me—follow your call—I'm happy that Gandhi's words inspired you, he'll be happy to know that. If I meet him, I'll tell him about your work.'

Sama took the lamp from her and handed over the child, saying, 'Please take care of him and help him recover.' During the exchange, their hands touched. He had a high fever. Sebati was alarmed.

'Oh my God! You have a high fever, and on top of that, you're thoroughly drenched!' screamed Sebati.

Sama didn't care. He laughed carelessly, saying that he wasn't a special person or a prince; many in the camp were sick with fever and drenched in the heavy downpour. He stood unflustered, looking at the dark sky, and said that Gopabandhu Das had died untimely while serving the flood-affected; he never thought about his wellness. He tried to make Sebati understand that people like them shouldn't care for their ordinary lives or live like cowards; instead, they should save the lives of five other people. He found no higher purpose in living like a slight flea, a mosquito, a bug or a leech. One should live like a man or be dead. She watched him and thought that Sama had completely lost his mind. She failed to understand the man who ran a high fever but still had the energy to brave the swirls of surging water. A whip of wind put out the flame in his hand; the flooding river rose violently, matching the plume of darkness. It was hard to know if the dam collapsed on the other end. In the brief flash of lightning, she saw someone pushing hard to keep himself afloat in the water; his hands rose in a desperate bid asking for help.

Instantly, Sama threw a glance at Sebati and jumped into the river. The rattle of a thunderbolt closed Sebati's eyes, and when they opened, seamless darkness blanketed the river like a black bedspread wrapped over Sama's sick body. The next moment, lightning flashed again. Sebati saw in the swirl of the water two shadowy figures struggling in each other's arms; the dark currents tried to swallow them. Her instinct was to jump into the water, but the child she held close to her bosom cried out desperately. Her legs shook in fear. How could she end her life and make the baby an orphan? What would she tell Sama when she met him after death?

Nobody believed Sebati's encounter with Sama on that stormy night. Some assured her that he would return; he wasn't a quitter to succumb to flood water. Some ignored her talk as pure delusion. Sebati debated that Sama Puhana might be a dream, but the sick orphan she saved from the flood and held in her lap was real. Why should she ignore reality and run after a dream? Ramadevi heard her carefully and agreed. 'Sama Puhana can't die ever—he has no death. He'll come back, if not today, maybe tomorrow. Many more like Sama will be born in Alabola, you needn't worry,' she assured her confidently.

Sebati looked at Ramadevi bewildered, and wondered if Sama wasn't ever going to show up. But she believed her; she was happy that Sama promised to tell Gandhi about all the great work she was doing in the freedom struggle. It wasn't Sebati alone who waited for him. In Alabola village, Sama's parents, family and friends, young and old, trees, groves, meadows, temples, inns, pastures and the cremation ground, all were waiting to welcome him back. And Sama wasn't the type to fail the expectations of so many! Sebati wasn't desperate anymore. She kept that naive hope alive and lived in Bari ashram. She dedicated her entire time to making khadi and waited for Sama's return.

Kharasua and Birupa rivers flooded every year. Sebati went out to work for the disaster-affected and waited calmly for Sama on the sand barricade with a humble kerosene lamp in her hand—like an eternal symbol of wait and indefatigable hope.

In Bari, Ramadevi and her husband Gopabandhu Chaudhury built two rows of humble thatched homes in an empty patch of land close to the burial ground to shelter the freedom fighters. Sebati and other volunteers changed that nondescript land at the end of the village into a beautiful habitat called Sevaghar. Ramadevi called Sebati Seba—the incarnation of service; Sevaghar became the temple of service to humanity.

People of that area were proud to be arrested and kept behind bars as patriots, for their active involvement in the freedom struggle; it was a shame if someone fell victim to the zamindar's conspiracy and was captured and jailed. The generation of that time was keen to value dignity and not willing to submit to the rule of the mighty.

There was no place for guilt and remorse in the life of a rebel like Digdarshi, but he worried that if all the zamindars joined hands with the British and dumped all the young men in prison, then the freedom movement would stall or be delayed. Many joined the struggle covertly. Digdarshi wanted to remain underground but didn't have a safe hiding place. The prize money over his head had gone up too. Dolamani was vigilant like a watchful dog.

Like the mother's warm lap, a very cozy corner of the earth kept inviting Digdarshi; it enticed him to come home and complete the work he left in the middle. He jumped out of the dark cell of Balikuda jail and landed on the ground; his hands folded quickly in supplication to Alka River. The fugitive instantly took to his feet and melded in the darkness in no time. After escaping the jail, he wandered through Balikuda and nearby areas. For a revolutionary like him, any place in any part of India should've been like a place of pilgrimage, but he was more concerned about the wellbeing of the poor peasants of Balikuda. He didn't want to leave his people. Leaders like Haribabu, Parshuram and Govindababu intervened and brought down the peasant revolt temporarily. When a few peasants died, the otherwise calm subjects were ready to revolt.

He remembered Kanak briefly and the tragic episode that changed her life. But worrying about whether she was in hell or heaven, hidden somewhere on the earth or beneath the deep underworld, couldn't be the most important issue to preoccupy his thought. He felt that countless other women like her were victims of lust and abuse by zamindars, kings and powerful men. If a single instance weakens his resolve, and he cringed and withdrew his steps, marching towards freedom to uplift scores of women like Kanak who are in trouble would never be possible.

No sooner did he think of Kanak than the faint memory of Chakori's shadowy face flashed before his eyes. His mind had enclosed forever that middle-aged woman's worn-out, unkempt, abused and powerless face that he saw from the train. He couldn't believe that time had washed away so much from her delicate looks. He wondered how the young woman of yesteryears could be so haggard and charmless in a few years. He recalled her brother Dukhabandhu who, before he was hung to death, pleaded for her emancipation. Chakori became a living, breathing person standing before him.

It was routine for Chakori to put Zamindar Graharaj to sleep and return to the outhouse late every night. He never wanted her to leave, but things in the palace no longer worked according to how he wished. There was a visible shift in command, and invariably, Devaki's order prevailed in every matter. Their sons were grown. Devaki often sided with her sons, and the young men were increasingly discourteous towards their father.

'You're paying for your sins!' she taunted him impassively; the punitive tone was never veiled. Graharaj kept quiet. Dasi Chakori stood by him demurely and served her old master without participating in their conflict. It was nothing unusual; that's what a dasi was supposed to do—she must submit to the master's semblance of authority even when someone else had usurped it. In such instances, he gently leaned on her shoulder. Any other dasi in those vulnerable moments might've asked the master for special favours to secure her future, pleading, 'What'll I do after you're gone? Are you doing me some favour, master? Write some land in my name...'

Chakori was different; she never begged for any favour from him. It was the other way around. One day, Graharaj volunteered with kind gestures, 'I'll mark some land in your name. You needn't worry about your sustenance after I pass away. You needn't worry...'

'Don't utter such fateful words, master! I would rather wish to leave this world before you! That would set my soul free,' Chakori responded emotionally.

Graharaj was selfish as usual. He wanted Chakori to live and care for him in his last days. He knew Devaki and his sons wouldn't turn their eyes towards him even when maggots crawled over his corpse. He knew that his wife eyed his estate and wished to see her sons as the heirs. He confessed that Diganta Kesari, the missing son, was his worthy inheritor, and desired the beloved son to lay him on the pyre. Though he did not admit it, he was remorseful about being a fallen man, lecherous and undignified, and sorry for the turmoil it created and the separation of his son from him. Chakori consoled him, saying that the young zamindar was alive, might have joined the freedom movement, and would probably return home once the country was free. The old zamindar seethed with anger. He never loved Gandhi and the freedom movement, and could not imagine a country where slaves and bastards could talk back to their masters.

'Are you out of your senses, you rotten scrounger? Are you—the one fed by me—wishing my end? Get out and get lost. If ever I hear these lines from you…' He blabbered madly.

Nervous, Chakori looked at the old man's face. It wasn't hard for her to understand that at the fag end of his life he wished for his legacy and the zamindari system to thrive in perpetuity. He still believed in his rebirth into a zamindar's family, and was in denial of the possibility of the freedom of the nation that would wipe away the differences between the ruler and the ruled.

Chakori didn't argue. She realized it wasn't the business of a lowly dasi to bother about Gandhi and freedom. She clung to an impossible belief; a faint shed of hope hung like a thin ray of light in her life of unrelenting misery. She returned every day from the palace, believing that the young zamindar might come one day and seek refuge in her modest outhouse. She had kept that tiny room clean like a place of worship. Spinning the charkha and making threads from cotton remained her regular habit. She never forgot that duty even if she returned late from work; it was like a sacred vow. Her half-brother, Dukhabandhu, had told her that the young zamindar spun thread on the charkha, made his khadi, and travelled across villages to teach the folks to make and use khadi. She was inspired by the example and made khadi-making a part of her life. She thought that the noble act might lessen her share of sin and redeem her.

Dukhabandhu didn't stop at the outhouse anymore, and seldom did any of his friends seek refuge at Chakori's place. If some of them ever came, they avoided talking about Dukhabandhu. If she probed, they said, 'Who knows where he has been? Even the sages and yogis can't say where a man comes from and where he goes!'

Such answers worried Chakori; she feared for Dukhabandhu's life. Both of them came from the same mother's womb. She repeated, 'Is Dukhabhai alive?' The visitors averted their eyes, and said that hundreds of brothers and sisters like him were in jail; many were hung to death for reasons unknown. The truth, thus, was sealed in darkness. She kept alive the tiny flicker of hope of his return. She crouched on the ground and continued spinning her charkha every night.

Someone gently tapped the door one night and softly asked her to let him in. Chakori listened in apprehension; two gentle taps followed. She rose and opened the door carefully, and found a sadhu standing there. His head was covered with tangled hair, and a long unkempt beard obscured his face. His powerful eyes seemed to pierce through the screen of time and know everything about the person standing before him.

'Master, why did you come to the doorstep of a sinner like me?' she said, offering her humble pranam.

'I'm not your master; you're your master. No one here is the master of another person. All are pilgrims on a journey,' said the sadhu calmly.

Chakori couldn't make out his words. She offered him a seat and rushed to arrange food and bed for his rest. The baba folded his legs, sat comfortably on the floor, and asked her not to rush to treat him. He proclaimed that he was there to build an ashram at the end of the village, would stay in her place for two days, and then shift to the village inn. Chakori was awkward in that tricky situation, and humbly confessed that she didn't own the place. As a mere dasi—an ignoble mistress of Zamindar Graharaj Chaudhury—she was obliged to seek his permission if she hosted anybody. Things were beyond her control, and sadhus being know-alls, it was hard on her part to hide anything from him. The old zamindar was suspicious of the followers of Gandhi and had ordered his guards to keep an eye on people coming to the outhouse. She won't be spared by the police for providing a safe haven to a stranger. She sounded very nervous and confessed that though she promised her brother Dukhabandhu to help the freedom fighters, things were tougher now. The baba shook his head calmly like an omniscient yogi, saying that her past, present and future flashed before him like images in a mirror, cryptically declaring that Dukahbandhu was free eternally, and it was better if she assumed he was absconding. He ended the discussion by saying, 'One who's missing will always be missing! Let's get over the topic. Why someone goes missing or vanishes from the earth is unknown to anyone. Wipe him off your mind.'

The multiple arrests and release of the brother, who was on the run from the police, surprised her. Chakori's growing feeling was that for humans, it was difficult to wipe out everything from the mind and make it clean. Certain things leave a permanent mark on the mind and sit there like a faint patch of the purple stain of *jamun* berry on a bleached white cloth, delivered fresh from the *dhobi*. She felt that the grey stain of pain in the innermost corner of her mind would never leave. She went out to arrange the bed for the baba to rest, but thoughts rumbled in her mind. On his part, the baba had been observing her without flipping his eyes, and wondered how fast the comely young girl he knew some twenty years ago had lost her magical charm and greyed into an ordinary-looking older woman.

Chakori's skilled hands went busy cleaning the storage space adjacent to her room. In no time, she made a place for the baba to rest. In one corner of the room sat the yarns of the thread she had been spinning, bundled carefully in a piece of rag. She asked him to sit on the floor, and served dinner. She was apologetic about her poverty, the lack of good food and the usual comfort for someone to rest in her place. She repeated that she was a poor dasi raised by Zamindar Graharaj Chaudhury and owed everything to him. She offered the baba some puffed rice and jaggery that she secretly brought from the palace for the freedom fighters who took shelter in her place. He refused to eat anything late at night, saying, 'The zamindar's wealth and opulence are soaked in the blood of the poor subjects…I'm a vegetarian. I can't have this food. Please take away the plate…' His voice was unforgiving.

She eyed the plate blankly. The puffed rice mixed with jaggery slowly seemed like fresh human blood to her eyes too. Her face went pale in terror. He explained that the sweat of the poor peasants who worked for free was not sweat but blood. He paused and assured that those dark days of mindless exploitation were about to end. Naive Chakori turned her eyes to the east. She felt he was right; the night was about to end, giving way to dawn; patches of darkness still needed a little more time to go. The young zamindar who used to talk of such high-sounding ideas to her was gone in such a transitional moment; it was neither day nor night that day. Her guest that day also wanted to leave her place in a moment of cusp. The difference she saw was that the former was a zamindar's son and the latter was a mendicant. But she was sure it was time for the sunrise.

While Chakori left home for the palace, the baba was in meditation. She was very anxious all day, guilty that he would be without food. She didn't eat, and saved her share of food—four pieces of cake—for the guest. She was elated imagining serving him, washing his feet carefully, and offering him to eat when she returned. She had many unanswered questions to ask the omniscient baba about the missing young zamindar—if he was alive and when he would return. That night, she pressed the old zamindar's feet, laid him to rest, tucked her share of the lunch carefully in a pouch, and came out of the palace for the palanquin to take her to the outhouse.

Crooked Prapancha Mohanty, the spy, checked what she was taking from the zamindar's palace. He saw the food, and blamed that the food was for someone she planned to spend the night with. He claimed she met her lovers in the outhouse and that she kept her place lit at night. When Chakori opposed, he retorted that her mother used to make the same plea and secretly went out to meet her lover. He accused that the dasi community couldn't be content with a single man, and wanted to know who was in her place the previous night, and if he was a Congress Party worker. Chakori denied the accusation with folded hands, saying that he might've seen a ghost or a spirit.

The zamindar rushed there, screaming and threatening to lash her hard. He wanted to know if her visitor was a follower of Gandhi, a terrorist, or someone working for the Socialist Party. Two of the zamindar's strong men thrashed her hard. The torture was unbearable. She couldn't reveal that the baba was hiding in her place. She wasn't sure if he was someone in disguise. She was thrashed till she became unresponsive, and was thrown into the palanquin. The zamindar ordered Prapancha Mohanty to search the outhouse and bring anyone found there to the torture house for trial. He feared that if the police found out from any source that the zamindar had harboured anti-British forces like Gandhi's followers in the outhouse, he would be in big trouble. Chakori regained consciousness inside the cart and prayed that the baba had foreseen the trouble ahead and left. The zamindar's men lifted her off the cart and dumped her on the floor. They checked inside the outhouse and went out with flaming torches screaming for the trespasser. There was nobody. Prapancha Mohanty had heard from the zamindar that he hadn't visited her the previous night. Suddenly, a thought struck him that the shadowy figure he saw might be a real ghost. He was mortally afraid of ghosts and spirits.

Physical abuse, beating and scolding had been like trifling dust on Chakori's thick skin. She ignored pain like stings from flies or mosquitos. But the pain that day was different; it wounded her not on the surface but deep inside her mind.

Despite her ignominy, she still had a special identity as the only known mistress for the people surrounding the zamindar. The zamindar didn't care to look at other dasis; the other women he visited in between were prostitutes. She was proud of her position as the handmaid who held the poles of Devaki's palanquin and entered the zamindar's palace. The master fathered seven children with Devaki, but enjoyed the nights in Chakori's bed in the outhouse. In sadness or joy, sickness and suffering, he never had looked for his wife's company and instead longed for the care and love of the dasi. She stood beside him in moments of crisis more diligently than his wife. Devaki proudly carried the hefty bundle of keys of the palace tied to her sari's end as proof of her absolute authority. The keys to the zamindar's heart were unquestionably deposited in Chakori's humble sari's end.

Devaki wasn't a keen mood-reader of her sulky husband, and used Chakori as a pawn to shield herself from the rage of the zamindar. The zamindar was as old as Chakori's father, but her tender feminine self submitted unconditionally to his ferocious masculinity. The relationship started with a rape, but she accepted the molestation as something ordained by destiny. She willingly never desired to violate that pact either.

Whenever she looked at his dreadful, angry face, she imagined the face of a father she hadn't met in her life. She wasn't sure who fathered her. Strangely, she felt like a beloved daughter while interacting with crude Graharaj and often felt she wasn't destitute. She found the soil beneath his feet to be her safest repose. She surrendered herself completely to the mindless abuses and disgrace wreaked on her. Her surrender to the abuser, like the surrender of tender leaves and branches to the rising wild flames, often softened his cruel heart and insuperable temper.

There were times when the zamindar spared some moments to look at her with tender love. In those flashes, she found a loving, caring friend in him—someone she had dreamed of living with forever. In those rare moments, the zamindar's face resembled closely his son Diganta Keshari. When Devaki and her insolent sons pounced upon the senile, powerless zamindar in anger and hatred, he seemed to her like defenceless Arkhitia, the son she carried in her womb but lost. She was protective of him as a mother. Imagined from any angle, Graharaj shared a deep invisible bond with every page of her life. So, despite his mindless abuse, she clung to him and felt that those brutalities were but her dues. She understood that it was the zamindar's birthright to beat, scold and torture her; she bore it all like a lifeless toy that didn't know how to wince or protest. But the pain she felt that day crossed the limits of her tolerance. Her mind returned to the day the zamindar watched her being beaten mercilessly while pregnant with his child.

The baba wasn't in her home when Chakori entered the outhouse. She needed no further proof that he was all-knowing and was gone before Prapancha Mohanty ordered a thorough search of her home. She breathed a sigh of relief. She didn't care for her ordeals, but witnessing the baba beaten in the zamindar's torture chamber would have been a nightmare. Physical pain no longer mattered to her, but she regretted not asking the baba about the day and time of the young zamindar's return, or the day she would be released from the palace. Those two questions, she thought, would hang over her mind indefinitely like the weight of an enormous load on an animal who drags his steps, counting the ripple of the ocean in front of him with the hope that somewhere, someday, the journey would terminate.

※

In the morning, the Mullah rushed out to check the incantations from the Hindu scriptures, rising at the same time as the daily call to prayer, *Allahu Akbar,* from his mosque. He was surprised to see a young sage with a beaming face in a saffron khadi robe, chanting, seated in a lotus asana. The baba told him politely that the Hindu mantras wouldn't defile the Muslim place of worship.

The Mullah was equally nice. He advised that his mosque had never hosted a Hindu sadhu. It was customary for visiting Hindu sadhus and mendicants to stay in temples and village inns, and enjoy the hospitality of the zamindar, a great patron of Hindu spiritual leaders.

'Neither a Hindu nor a Muslim, I'm a humanist who believes in God. I'm here to spread my guru's message. We've finished the pooja and are ready for the final offering—the havan. I'll collect a handful of alms to observe the event. The temple priests and innkeepers saw my saffron khadi robe and thought I was a follower of Gandhi. Their zamindar has denied entry to those men,' he declared.

Slowly, people thronged the place. His words were magical, and the people in Zamindar Graharaj's area accepted him with open arms. A small ashram emerged beside the mosque in a few days, and the baba named it Karma Mandira. The curious villagers flocked to listen to him, and he urged them to give up ignorance, rise and act, saying, 'The human body is a temple of karma; man is here to act; he would perish without action. For this reason alone, Krishna urged Arjuna to shun inaction, take up arms, and fight. Arjuna was in a dilemma, and was reluctant to take up arms against the evil Kauravas in the great war of the Mahabharata. For peace and justice to prevail, we need the awakening that Krishna urged in his disciple. Fellows, we must rise from indecision and inertia. We need an uprising—revolt and nothing but revolt!'

Chapter XII

Soon Digdarshi came to be known as Digbaba, and he won the unshakable confidence of the naive villagers. The yogi could narrate every past event in their area with absolute accuracy as if he were an eyewitness. He told people's life stories—their genealogy, caste, vocation, events and accidents—as if they flashed before his eyes. He even described the architectural designs inside the zamindar's palace. He stared straight into Prapancha Mohanty's eyes and accurately narrated his secret rendezvous, buried hopes and aspirations. No one needed any further proof to believe in his extraordinary power to read the time—past, present and future. They believed in his prescience in telling what was to come. His face beamed with joy as he read people's palms, forehead, and the horoscope together, reassuring them that all the bad days of their lives would end soon and a new dawn of good days awaited them.

The baba's words filled the hearts of the poor peasants with hopes of a better time. They visited him in small groups the whole day, and carried small givings for the havan he planned to perform. Mired in poverty and suffering, they found a new lease of life, enabling them to walk through difficult days. Women reached the ashram secretly and donated whatever gold and silver they had, hoping that the havan would bring better days for all and bless their children with a good life.

The baba read the events happening around him on a positive note. No one dared to harm him. The police watched his actions without interference. They had nothing against a wandering, penniless mendicant having nothing, not even a hut, in his name. Whatever money he collected was used for the service of the people. So the police believed that he wasn't a freedom fighter in a saffron garb. Still, the police and the zamindar were very watchful. As soon as he sensed that vigilance was tightening over him, he vanished unannounced for a few days and reappeared after the break with the message of revolution. The Karma Mandira was more crowded than the village temple and the mosque. The gods inside the temple were pieces of cold stone; they didn't hear or speak, and were indifferent to the sufferings of the toiling masses. The baba was an exception; he talked and instilled faith in people's hearts like a living God, and stood beside them in times of need.

Like the countless distressed people of the village, Chakori, too, was eager to meet the baba and know about her future. It was hard for her to forget the recent disgrace in the palace over stolen food. A captive to Zamindar Graharaj Chaudhury's whims and caprices, she wondered if a dasi had any claim to dignity. She was pained that she did not have any worth or a voice to oppose. She didn't dare to seek any answers from Graharaj Chaudhury, the man who had, all his life, been the one to squander her love, care, service, kindness, motherhood, womanhood, youth, body and honour, and rewarded her with nothing but senseless torture, unfathomable cruelty and heartless distrust. She thought to herself that the zamindar owned her gross physical entity, not her 'self', the invisible finer being.

Someone she never forgot, understood her well. He felt the presence of a self pulsating inside her and resurrected it, the way Rama Chandra saved Ahalya from the burden of a curse that damned her to remain trapped inside a piece of stone for ages. Ahalya was condemned unjustly for her transgression, which someone else had committed in disguise. She wondered if Digbaba would tell her when her soul would finally be released from the trap of the tired, tortured body to eternal peace and freedom.

She returned from the palace and set out for the Karma Mandir, carrying a small sac under her arm in the dead of night, and gently tapped on the door. A dimly lit lamp burnt inside. She could see the baba engrossed, working at the charkha. He was none other than the sadhu who visited her home asking to spend the night a few days back. He could read the wonder and excitement in her eyes as she entered. He immediately apologized for the trouble his presence created and the torture she endured following the probe. She quickly understood his supernatural power, and believed nothing could be hidden from a seer. She was grateful to have hosted him that night. She blamed the vengeful zamindar for suspecting that anyone visiting the outhouse was a freedom fighter.

As Digbaba wondered why she was in the ashram late at night, Chakori carefully took out some jewellery, a few rupees and some changes from a tiny pouch, and offered everything for the havan. It was her life's savings—the inheritance from her mother. She said that there was no hope for her brother Dukhabandhu to return, and her son Arkhitia died a few years ago. She had none in the world to save for. She then followed with her questions about the missing young zamindar. She wanted to know if he was alive and returning home.

'He is the prince of this land, Diganta Keshari! Twenty years back, he left this place because he was repelled by the conduct of a dasi. He rejected the allure of the zamindari and didn't even look back once. The zamindar performed his last rites and removed his name as heir. Everything happened because of me… He was so compassionate towards a mere dasi! Had he been here, he might not have allowed the old zamindar's servants to beat me hard in public…,' said Chakori.

She wiped her tears with the end of her old sari. Digbaba sat silently, overwhelmed with emotions. Events of the past flashed before his eyes. He was stunned that while Diganta Keshari was no more in the memory of the people of that area, the poor woman still clung to the hope of his return to the village. From her worn-down looks, it was hard to visualize that she would have been a pretty young woman in the past. There was no trace of the magic in her looks, nor the colour, grace and scent that youth might have bestowed upon her body. Twenty years weren't long enough even to wash away the colour of the walls of the temples and mosques; patches of colour here and there reminded of their previous splendour. Looking at her, he was no more in disbelief that the charm of youth in humans was very short-lived. His thoughtful eyes were fixed on her face. She stretched out her hand uneasily for him to read her fate, and asked him to tell her about the day she would die and be free from the chains of a dasi's life. He looked at the withered palm with compassion. Years of hard work, lack of care, and the swollen blue veins matted all over made it look like the cracks on an earthen barn floor left neglected for years. Like the preface to a heart-wrenching tragic epic, her hand remained stretched before his eyes, filling each passing moment in Digbaba's heart with extreme pity. He was overwhelmed with a strange, inexplicable feeling, wondering if there was some connection between them. He gained composure and declared dispassionately that her future looked good to him; she would be free soon. He continued in a matter-of-fact tone that Graharaj disowned his eldest son and was rewarded with the title of Raybahadur. If Diganta Keshari ever returned, he wouldn't be allowed to enter his father's area. If the father doesn't seem to worry about his son's future, she shouldn't worry too much about him.

Chakori hung her head down and sat there. Words failed her even as she wanted to talk about her wait for the zamindar's missing son. The conflict in her mind was that the omniscient baba knew everything, even her unspoken words, by looking at her. She didn't know what to say about her relationship with the missing young zamindar, Diganta Keshari, or her heart's unusual longing for him. Back in the old days, when she was young, a glance at his beaming face brightened her gloomy spirit like the scarlet, ruddy glow of the rising sun at dawn. She had been missing that spritely spirit since the day he left the palace. The elusive feeling seemed like the faint brightness of the sliver of the moon in the sky. But those feelings did not give the poor daughter of a dasi the courage to say that the young man entirely belonged to her. She could say that he inspired a reassuring sense of belongingness in that terrified innocent girl. The zamindar's son, who made her feel special, understood their bond better. Chakori didn't know how to explain the subtle entanglements in her heart to a baba who did not know the ways of the world. Lowering her head, she confessed, 'He is the one to set me free! He's my savior—he's my master!'

'What does that mean?' asked Digbaba, bewildered.

Chakori explained that Krishna was born to Devaki when she was in prison, but he was not the one to set her free. He rather freed the *gopika*s, saved Kubja from the curse, and protected a thousand princesses that were held hostage in evil Narakasura's palace. She claimed that Diganta Keshari was like her son. He vowed to set her free. She paused and continued that he was older than her by age, but she was his father's mistress, therefore they were mother and son. Though the father never gave her the honour of a wife, she had honoured him as her husband. She wanted to confide about something unsettling that happened in the palace twenty years back, but stopped abruptly. Chakori's depth of understanding astonished Digbaba.

∞

Many well-known people slowly became followers of Digbaba; common men donated generously for the havan. He sent whatever was collected to the baba higher in the hierarchy. Sometimes, Govindabhai, Haribhai, Jayaram, Baikuntha and Madan Jena also stopped by the ashram to spend time with him. He didn't discriminate against people based on caste or religion. Even Aziz Khan believed in Digbaba's teachings. He didn't prevent the freedom fighters from staying with him in the ashram and mingling with all. Prayers and worship went on for days together in the ashram; religious discourse continued for hours.

Two female followers of Gandhi, Maithili and Sushila, came and stayed in the ashram for a few days. They were there to work in villages to uplift women who were subjected to bias and abuse. Ramadevi had specifically asked the duo to address issues affecting women's lives in the area. The followers of Digbaba walked across villages, and tried to help people solve their conflicts and disagreements. The female workers had no inhibition in going to any home from any community and rendering their services; they also acted as midwives and assisted women in delivery.

There were moments when Maithili felt she was a mother, and the other feminine attributes didn't remain with her except the blessed state of motherhood. Years back, Maithili, the child widow, had promised Digdarshi to remarry and support Gandhi's mission to remove prejudices against widow remarriage. Accordingly, her marriage was planned, but she changed her mind at the last moment, refusing to marry a man who Digdarshi felt was suitable for her without asking for her consent. She claimed that the qualified, good-looking freedom fighter wasn't the man of her dreams; he then married someone else.

Digbaba faced Maithili in the ashram and asked why she forwent her promise to marry. He agreed that marriage was a personal choice, and he was ready to help her solemnize the relationship if she had found someone. He was in disbelief that the frail, reticent and saintly woman's heart did not pine for somebody's love. He was curious to hear a name. She looked intently at his face covered with beard, delved deep into his eyes, and replied in a calm but firm voice that a woman could have faith in gods made of stone and wood, but she couldn't twine her life with them or build a nest with their support. She asked him not to discuss the topic anymore; the time for marriage for her was over, and it would never come back. She declared that she would stay with him in the ashram and dedicate her life to the cause of freedom. Her love for Digdarshi remained sealed inside her restive heart. She moved away slowly, unsure if he sensed her feelings. His eyes were fixed on the horizon where day and night met, creating that mystic screen of the evening joining earth and the sky.

Meanwhile, Aziz Khan led a huge procession; the crowd, mostly students from Balikuda High School, chanted 'Hindu–Muslim bhai bhai'. It headed towards the Congress ashram beyond the Baragach Squire, near the Bauri Sai. The mosque was close by, and the crowd needed to reach there to start the meeting in time. Headmaster Parshuram pushed through the sloganeering crowd from his school and screamed, 'Stop this march! Stop this farce! Who permitted you to leave the campus and join this show? All of you must get back to your classes.'

Parshuram's behaviour shocked Aziz. He couldn't make out the change in his friend, who had been an ardent supporter of communal harmony between the Hindus and Muslims all his life. By then, people all over the country knew that the Muslim League under Jinnah's leadership opposed having a single independent nation. Jinnah demanded that the British divide India into two separate countries along religious lines. It was one thing that both communities had distinct cultural and religious identities, but statesmen worried that Jinnah's attitude divided the people strictly on the basis of the faith they followed.

'Ishwar and Allah are one, and the blood of the human race is the same. Jinnah's demand can't divide the Indian people,' declared Aziz and continued to chant, 'Hindu–Muslim bhai bhai!'

The young students repeated after him. Parshuram was enraged. He screamed out like sage Durvasa, 'Who gave you the right to influence the minds of these young kids with those words and frighten them? I can easily ask the police to arrest you for infusing anti-nationalist ideas among the students of my school.'

Parshuram's words greatly wounded his childhood Muslim friend Aziz. The two used to eat from the same plate; his conservative Hindu wife didn't hesitate to take out his plate; and his home was Sarvadharma Ashram—a secular sanctuary for all. Aziz felt that the scene reflected the workings of Parshuram's devious mind. It exposed the mean fundamentalist behind the mask of a liberal humanist.

Aziz gnashed his teeth and said in a mocking note, 'Did you lose your senses today? This meeting is essential for the peaceful existence of Hindus and Muslims here. Dolamani Srichandan is presiding over this meeting. Why the hell do you oppose the whole thing? Do you support Jinnah's Muslim League? Have you been hiding your feelings all these years?'

Parshuram's bloodshot eyes looked straight at Aziz. He asked him to stop the march and the planned meeting immediately. The friend warned that he would bar him from visiting his home if he didn't listen. A single scream from the headmaster returned the pupils to the classes. A silly kid still mumbled, 'Hindu–Muslim bhai bhai', irritating Parshuram. The school gate closed. Aziz stood alone on the road, unable to comprehend things. In no time, Dolamani emerged from the crowd in his trademark khaki dress, smiling. Leaning over his fancy horn walking stick, he reached Aziz and whispered, 'Parshuram is a traitor, a rogue, and a fake nationalist. He's a secret agent of the British.' Aziz didn't reply and walked towards the Congress Party office.

It was a puja day at home. Manorama observed many festivals around the year. Parshuram was hardly interested in puja, fasting, priests, Brahmins and temples. Nobody ever saw a sacred dot of sandalwood paste on his forehead, or him sitting in his puja room closing his eyes. He doubted if someone who followed the rituals was necessarily religious; prejudice, not faith, controlled their minds. For Manorama, praying to God wasn't a prejudice. He tried to convince his conservative wife that if someone prayed to God to save her husband or do good to her children, that was not love for God but selfishness. He gave her lengthy discourses on righteous action, saying that if one served the people, used his time to alleviate the miseries of the poor, and didn't side with the morally wrong—that was worship of God. If one committed hundreds of sins and dipped in the waters of the holy Ganga to attain salvation, that's not spiritual action. He asked her if she believed that the wretched zamindars who built ornate temples with the money they collected from the poor were God's greater devotees. Manorama's world was simple; she didn't adorn God with a golden crown, or dip in the Ganga to wash away her sins. Her simplicity moved Parshuram. He looked at her with adoration and said she shouldn't harm her body by observing painful fasts. He knew festivals were her pretexts to invite guests to her home and mingle with people.

During a conversation, Manorama casually enquired about Aziz. She was concerned that he had skipped some celebrations in her place though he was invited. Parshuram declared that he had barred Aziz from coming to their place, so he wouldn't come to his home ever. The words bothered Manorama. She knew about the intimacy between the two men and worried that something might be wrong between them. She had already written a note asking Aziz to come. She expected him to honour her special invitation. Aziz arrived. The two friends washed their hands and sat for dinner without a word. Manorama served in two plates and kept the khiri in one bowl for them.

'Your Hindu husband might lose his caste by sharing food from the same bowl with a Muslim. Please serve me separately,' said Aziz on a serious note. Manorama didn't understand what was going on there. Aziz began to narrate the entire episode to her.

'Parshuram disagreed with the line "Hindu–Muslim bhai bhai". How can I eat from the same plate with him? I'm not his brother but a mere Muslim,' Aziz spoke sadly.

Parshuram smiled, dragged the plate to the middle, and forced his friend's hand into the plate; the argument ended there. He explained that it was redundant to reiterate that Hindus and Muslims were brothers. It would be as ridiculous as someone screaming outside that Parshuram and Manorama were man and wife. He feared that while the big cities were caught in the tension over communal unrest, chanting 'Hindu–Muslim bhai bhai' in a peaceful situation would make people suspicious of each other. They would fear that conflict was brewing in their area, though the two communities lived peacefully. Hindus went to pray at the *dargah*, and the Muslims joined in the Durga puja; there was no need to upset the status quo. He reminded Aziz that the zamindars welcomed religious unrest. They were good at using the politics of divide and rule taught by the sahibs, and implanting distrust and hatred in people's minds.

Aziz listened to his friend and admired his foresight. He found him very sensible, and needed no further clarity. He could join the dots and understand Dolamani's interest in having the procession of school children chanting the line 'Hindu–Muslim bhai bhai'. Parshuram informed him that Dolamani was busy in a smear campaign and created the rumour that he was anti-Muslim and had deliberately destroyed the Muslim neighbourhood and displaced the residents to expand the school. The situation was rife for a violent confrontation between the Hindus and Muslims. Parshuram was unmoved. He knew that the zamindar's family was very upset with him for admitting untouchable and Muslim students to the school. He ignored the conspiracy theory, believing that hot water would never burn down a house.

The three of them sat down for some casual talk. Aziz did not come to Sarvadharma Ashram for some days and wasn't in the loop of many things. He was sorry about Digdarshi going missing from jail. Manorama shared that after the jailbreak he emerged in another area as a sadhu and asked people to donate for some grand havan he had planned. Aziz mumbled that Dolamani was probably right to say that Digdarshi had sent Kanak to that area first, and then appeared in disguise there. Parshuram interrupted, saying that Digdarshi might not even know that Kanak was present there. He warned his friend not to get swayed by those baseless rumours and to focus more on the freedom struggle. He urged that patriots must dedicate themselves to the success of Gandhi's August Movement.

∞

Graharaj Chaudhury, the proud zamindar representing the feudal gentry, wasn't ready to accept a free country. However, the British slowly realized that the flames of the August Revolution that engulfed the entire country couldn't be suppressed. Graharaj still believed that freedom was a hoax created by the Congress Party leaders. Shrewd zamindars like Dolamani and Dakhinray realized that political leaders yielded great power and influence; they didn't want to be irrelevant after independence by supporting overseas merchants who occupied the land and became kingmakers but would under no circumstances take them back to England and assign them the ownership of estates there. The likes of Dolamani attended Congress Party meetings secretly, collected funds for the party and registered their names as freedom fighters.

Graharaj didn't shilly-shally. He opposed the Congress Party from the beginning and stuck to the stance. He didn't take Dakhinray's advice but was worried for his children's future. He couldn't imagine becoming irrelevant after the country became free. The memory of his missing son was still like a fresh wound in his heart and bled with the slightest pricking. He wondered if he missed something about being a great father. Devaki's sons were non-compliant. His wife never understood the zamindar's ardent longing for Diganta Keshari. He held on to his sorrow, but that frustration showed up as his deadly machismo. His anger and frustration got directed towards Chakori as if she were responsible for everything that went wrong. He screamed at her when remembering his sons' misconduct, Devaki's indifference, the sporadic unrest as peasants rose in revolt, the march of the Congress Party, and his culpability in the son leaving home.

Digbaba didn't visit the palace after starting the ashram in the village. The zamindar had heard that the baba was omniscient, and everybody believed his predictions. He was tempted to go and ask the baba about his missing son, ascertain if he was alive, and if he would return home to meet the father before he died. But he was too proud to seek a nameless mendicant's advice.

He was unwilling to show his desperation for a patriotic son who he disowned to prove his loyalty to the British. He didn't care for anybody but wasn't ready to confess his woes to the all-knowing baba or take his pity. The baba moved from door to door seeking donations but never appeared at the palace. The palace sent him invitations several times, but he didn't honour them, saying, 'He who gives with love and a clean heart, his donation is accepted for the havan. If the zamindar wants to contribute, he should reach the ashram uninhibited. Let him come and understand the goal of the havan. We need money, but funds for that righteous cause must be collected correctly.'

The zamindar thought that the baba wasn't an enlightened soul but a common man blinded by pride and indifference. People wondered how looking for the zamindar's help for a noble cause might not be the right path. From time immemorial, the kings and the zamindars had patronized yogis, sages and *sannyasi*s, and the hungry. The baba's decision sounded strange to them.

⚭

Graharaj was sick. The news of the country's freedom made him sicker and even more nostalgic about the memory of his missing son. None of Devaki's capable sons were there to share the misery of his sickness, sin, or old age. The whole world is ready to share the fruits of man's righteous action, but man has to suffer the outcomes of his sins all by himself. Chakori understood Graharaj's agony. She rushed to the baba, asking him to alleviate his pain and help him forget the long-missing son. The baba was silent over Graharaj's fate. Once he told her seriously, 'There's no place for emotion and attachment in the quest for freedom. Digdarshi is a man on the path that leads to freedom. If ever he returns, he will return as a man without fetters. He won't be a zamindar's son at that point in time. A friend of the people can't confine himself as the son of a king. The zamindar should get rid of his excessive attachment to his son. Attachment is the root cause of human misery...'

Chakori didn't convey this message to Graharaj. She knew that the news would upset him terribly.

Chapter XIII

'The situation's critical in Balikuda,' Aziz announced when he reached Digbaba's Karma Mandira. He described that a merchant from Cuttack, who regularly came to procure fish from Machhagaon, was struck by cholera. He added that the man's severe vomiting and diarrhoea didn't stop. His skin shrunk and eyes didn't move due to dehydration, so his friends abandoned him and ran away, fearing that they might get infected by the dreaded disease. In the morning, children from Nalio, Borikina and Dagaon, on their way to school, found the sick man struggling for life in a pool of vomit and faeces. His bicycle rested against the tree as if it watched over the owner. The children rushed to headmaster Parshuram.

The group that the school devoted to social services, followed the headmaster's call, packed some life-saving medicines, and reached the patient abandoned on the road. The villagers prevented Parshuram from approaching the cholera patient and objected to bringing the latter to the village. The outbreak signified the wrath of the goddess for the rural folks. Everyone—not just the Hindus—thought that cholera was a bad omen. The Muslims brought out a procession to ward off the epidemic. Parshuram was in a fix—if he got the critical patient inside the village, he would upset the Muslim community. There already was a simmering antagonism between the Hindus and the

Muslims. On top of that, his school was located in a densely Muslim-populated area in Balikuda.

But he couldn't leave the man to die. Parshuram wasn't governed by dogma and believed that one who neglected another man in need was neither a Hindu nor a Muslim. He lifted the dying man to a bullock cart, brought him inside the school, and cared for him. The man slowly showed signs of recovery. His family in Cuttack was thrilled to know that he was alive, and rushed to take him back. Before leaving, he thanked Parshuram for giving him a second lease of life and wanted to repay the kindness by delivering fish for free to his family for the rest of his life. But Parshuram stated that it wasn't him alone; a group of teachers and students were equally involved in saving his life, and suggested that donating two hundred rupees to the school's humanitarian services fund would be a good gesture. But that money never arrived. Parshuram didn't follow up but sometimes joked that God saved him for not accepting the supply of free fish from that scroungy guy.

Parshuram saved a life, but was soon in hot water over his handling of the cholera case. Zamindar Dolamani alarmed the Muslims that Parshuram was against their faith; the headmaster aimed to discredit 'Hindu–Muslim bhai bhai', the catchphrase for brotherhood between the two communities. Also, because the Muslims believed that cholera was not an epidemic but a manifestation of Allah's anger, the headmaster deliberately brought the patient inside the village to upset them. The Muslims were aggrieved. They united and declared that if there happened to be an outbreak of cholera in Balikuda, Parshuram would be banished from the village.

Parshuram wasn't ruffled. He asked people to judge if the

person who provoked them against him was an honest, sincere and informed person. He said that cholera was a contagious disease and could be removed through proper treatment and hygiene. As a family man with his wife and children living inside the school campus, he wasn't a fool to bring a cholera patient inside and risk their lives. He visited each home and urged people to take preventive measures like vaccination against cholera, and taught them how to disinfect water and get rid of flies.

'Allah was merciful! Cholera never came to Balikuda or broke out in nearby villages. The situation was under control,' narrated Aziz to his friend Digbaba.

Aziz detailed the other nasty conspiracies that Dolamani weaved and dragged Parshuram into. Dolamani wanted to take away Tahibulla Khan's impressive mango orchard next to the high school. Accordingly, when he laid his father to rest in the orchard after death, Dolamani sent a notice stating that Parshuram had petitioned earlier to include the orchard for the expansion of the school so that no burial could take place there. As the local zamindar, he asked Tahibulla to dig out his father's coffin and rebury him in another area. He promised some compensation to the aggrieved. The notice shook the family, who were still mourning the loss of the father. The community felt threatened; exhuming and relocating the body was not just disrespecting the departed soul but was a collective humiliation to the Muslim community. Tahibulla was ready to lay down his life but would not disturb his father's body. While Dolamani engaged his strong men to dig up the casket, many angry Muslim young men confronted them and got wounded. Dolamani watched the fight quietly and urged them with folded hands for peace, saying, 'Brothers! I won't gain anything. I understand your sentiments!

I'm just acting on behalf of the headmaster. Including the mango grove with the school's property would serve a greater public interest.'

Digbaba listened to Aziz carefully. He could see some angry men getting impatient and screaming, 'Where's that headmaster? We'll smash his head.'

Dolamani claimed that Parshuram was a coward hiding in his wife's village, Patapur, but would get him arrested upon arrival for inciting communal violence. The headmaster, however, did not know the developing story.

Aziz's elaborate narration aimed to ask Digbaba to return to Balikuda and pacify the angry mob. He didn't want Parshuram to get arrested upon arrival; the police had already issued an arrest warrant against him. He wanted the drama to end. The chaos didn't seem to worry Digbaba at all. He listened to Aziz carefully, and said calmly that the people of Balikuda respected his guru, headmaster Parshuram, very much. The naive village folks were temporarily incited; they would find out the truth soon, and things would be normal again. He refused to return there, saying that it was risky for him to move around in disguise; people might be tempted to inform the police because of the prize money announced for his capture.

During their lengthy discussion, Aziz asked if he had any information on Kanak. The name brought back some painful memories about her. Digbaba assured him that he would find out about the poor girl if she were nearby. The two friends continued talking till late that night. Aziz confided his decision to marry his Hindu friend Kamala, and believed that their union would bring greater harmony between Hindus and Muslims in the Balikuda area. He found no real disagreement between the two communities, but mean zamindars like Dolamani planted distrust in their minds. He advised Digbaba to marry the woman he loved. Since marriage is a vital part of life, and Gandhi, too, didn't ask those who joined the freedom movement to stop marrying; it was time for Digbaba to enter matrimony. In Aziz's view, couples like Gandhi–Kasturba, Gopabandhu Chaudhury–Ramadevi and Parshuram–Manorama empowered each other.

Digbaba curiously listened to him and asked, 'Who's my beloved?' Aziz had determined that Digbaba's rumoured love for Kanak was baseless; their relationship was as pure as that of a brother and a sister. He felt that Digbaba wasn't forthcoming in saying the name of Maithili, the petite child widow who lived in the ashram and worked with him; and their union would be the most ideal one, as opined by all. Manorama and Ramadevi knew about Maithili's love for Digbaba and sent her to the ashram for the two to be even closer. Aziz told his friend that Maithili rejected the freedom fighter she was supposed to marry because she found her ideal man—the man of her dreams—in Digbaba. Whatever details Aziz gave about the love Maithili harboured for him, didn't impress Digbaba. He solemnly declared that the ashram was a shrine of action, not love. He didn't want to linger over the topic. That night, Aziz wanted to drive home the delicate nuances of love to a friend who seemed completely unmoved by the topic of matters of the heart. He paid no heed to Aziz saying, 'Love doesn't hinder the path of action; rather, real love inspires to achieve the goal.'

Digbaba clarified his mission in life: 'My goal is not marriage. I left home dreaming of freedom. I aim to see womankind free and the dasi tradition completely abolished. The struggle for our country's freedom is heading towards its end, and with that goal in sight, I hope to see all women free—none bound as a dasi. At this point, marriage and home have no meaning for me.'

Aziz didn't give in. His views were also hard to refute. A female's involvement isn't a hindrance for a man to realize his goal; some lack the resolve and blame the woman for their failure. A woman is not a distraction. Man lacks self-control, gets easily distracted by her, falters, and absolves himself of wrongdoings.

'Do you know why even the most pious woman can't persuade an addict from giving up alcohol or visiting the brothel? Because the man here doesn't want to forgo those habits,' Aziz continued.

Digbaba agreed with his friend, and said that resolve comes from within for both men and women. No power on earth can prevent a person with a strong conviction from reaching his goal; a coward only blames his or her failure on others. He declared that he was so preoccupied with reaching the goal of freedom that thoughts of love or marriage created no ripples in his mind. It was almost daybreak; the duo hardly realized they had spent the entire night talking without sleep. The sun seemed ready to rise.

Apart from sharing some of their innermost thoughts on love and marriage, Aziz and Digbaba pondered the fate of the freedom struggle that night. They concluded that their struggle was part of a bigger conflict that the whole world was caught up in at that moment. It was not just England's hegemony over India that worried them; they felt that other nations, too, dangerously swung from their moral boundaries. They felt that the war that was fought to liberate men from the control of a domineering group was a worthy one, but a war where a nation aimed forcefully to control other people and their land was a sin unpardonable.

The signs of trouble had been everywhere. It was 1941. As India had intensified its freedom struggle against the British, Japan attacked the eastern coast of India unprovoked. Prime Minister Churchill sought the absolute cooperation of the Congress Party for the Empire to declare war against Japan. Representative Sir Stafford Cripps discussed the matter with Congress Party leaders. He offered that once the war with Japan was over, Britain would grant greater autonomy to India, devise administrative principles, or might even grant independence. He assured that Britain would provide security to India as long as the war with Japan continued.

The Congress Party rejected the proposal. Gandhi questioned the purpose of the war. No one was satisfied with the explanations the British offered. The Congress Party said, 'India might participate as a free nation that aims to protect its territory, but we can't join the war to facilitate the agenda of the British Empire.'

In response, the Empire didn't hesitate to play its most devious game that aimed to shatter the Hindu–Muslim unity. Governor General Linlithgow announced that at the end of the war, the people of India would be allowed to participate in framing rules for the governance of their own country, except that nothing would be imposed on the minority. He deliberately kept aside the ten crore Muslims on Indian soil who were opposed to the constitution of the Federation of India Administration Rule since 1935. Thus, the British principle of divide and rule that pitted one community against the other gained official sanction. Gandhi opposed the promulgation and started the civil disobedience movement.

Global events were interlinked. The year 1941 was critical in world history. On 7 December that year, Japan's pre-emptive attack on Pearl Harbor—the strategic US naval base—made the placid waters of the Pacific restive. America declared war on Japan, Germany and Italy, and World War II began officially. Japan attacked Singapore, an important British naval base, on 13 January 1942 and upset Britain, the most powerful Empire over which the sun never set. Violent bombardment over Singapore's sky, sea and soil followed relentlessly. Terrified British officials fled to Australia, the British army took a defensive stance, and countless Indian soldiers were pushed to the forefront. They lost their lives in resisting Japan, but their names never got recorded in the list of martyrs of the British army; they were mere slaves fed by the British Empire.

Gandhi didn't support the war. He believed that supporting an unjust war by draining money and human capital was morally wrong. He argued that Japan was Britain's enemy, and if Japan attacked India, that would be due to the British presence on Indian soil. He demanded that the British must quit Indian soil.

The situation in Odisha was more complicated. An interim autonomous government had been looking after the administration of Odisha since 1936. Following Gandhi's call, all the ministers serving in the cabinet resigned and joined the non-violent movement. In that turbulent moment, the Hindu Mahasabha, purportedly protecting the interests of the Hindu religious majority, opened a branch in Odisha. Some groups in the state didn't believe in the non-violent movement. The zamindar of Madhupur supported the British. Dolamani attended his meeting. Not a single person from Balikuda and its adjoining areas joined the Hindu Mahasabha. Parshuram helped people understand the narrow sectarian agenda of the Hindu Mahasabha.

The police warrant against Parshuram in the case over Tahibulla's mango grove was still there, but he went forward with the work to include the mango grove with the school boundary. Colleagues and students followed him readily with diggers and crawlers to begin fencing the new enclosure. Dolamani's plan to appropriate the mango orchard in his name didn't work out. He never expected the headmaster to move forward without asking him to mediate. He couldn't stand imagining the faces of scoundrels from the Congress Party sitting inside the school with Parshuram and chewing nice juicy mangoes. He ordered his followers to disrupt the work. The police prevented the school from extending the boundary, and Dolamani declared that to avoid a face-off between the school and Tahibulla and so that the Hindus and the Muslims remained good neighbours, the mango grove should be in his safekeeping. Tahibulla was promised monetary compensation. The villagers understood the devious tricks of Dolamani, and they hailed Parshuram's goodness. The mango grove remained Dolamani's property forever, and Tahibulla was never compensated. Records showed that Tahibulla's father owed a lot of money to the zamindar from the loan he took from him, and the mango grove went towards loan repayment.

At this juncture, a new approach to the freedom struggle came from Subhas Chandra Bose. He announced over the radio from Berlin, 'This is Subhas speaking—freedom is never given to a nation; we must snatch it. For this cause, people of India—irrespective of their caste, creed or color, must stay united.'

On 10 April 1942, Gandhi officially started the Quit India Movement. Many leaders of the party, including Gandhi, were arrested. In Gandhi's voice, slogans like 'Quit India' and 'Do or die' resonated beyond the air, water, forests, cities and villages, arousing the masses to join the momentum. The nation was awakened, and everyone—young, old, women and children—unanimously supported the August Movement.

At the regional level, all the prominent leaders of Odisha were arrested for joining the Quit India Movement. The enraged students of Ravenshaw College in Cuttack set fire to the college building protesting the massive police brutality against the student leaders. Digdarshi played a major role in that violent resistance. He couldn't sit in peace at Karma Mandira while the country's dignity was at stake. Disillusioned with the non-violent movement, he was ready to join the violent opposition to the British.

However, before leaving to stir the Quit India Movement in the remote areas, Digbaba was destined to face two remarkable women. The more he tried to distance himself from the fetters that bound man to worldly worries, the more they chased him. After Aziz left, he was tempted to ask Maithili about the dream man she wished to marry. He met her while she was spinning cotton at her charkha.

Maithili was caught off guard by his query. Her bare hands, not adorned with bangles, instantly stopped over the spinning wheel; her face turned red in embarrassment; beads of sweat came up over her forehead, and her gaze became unusually sad but stern. Digbaba said that he was leaving Karma Mandira to join the direct struggle, and she should be in charge of the ashram in his absence. The British government was acting with vengeance and didn't care about eliminating countless freedom fighters. He reminded her of the death of the martyrs in Eram, and Lakshmana Nayak's hanging in Berhampur jail. He was not sure if he would meet her again. She was unmoved. Her hands stayed over the charkha. She replied calmly that she knew him as a great human being who understood everything except the matters of the heart; therefore he needn't know. The time was also not right for sharing feelings buried deep inside; a precious secret can't be disclosed anywhere, anytime. She wished for him to join the direct struggle for freedom with a peaceful mind and, like a wise woman, advised him to pay attention to personal safety as well and survive the critical time to watch the end of British rule. She was ready to take care of the ashram in his absence. Digbaba reiterated the question that he had posed earlier. Maithili asked him to stay calm and stop being curious about whom she loved. She hurriedly left the place, went to her room, and closed the door from the inside.

Maithili's behaviour seemed very strange to him; his mind was still processing the course of action ahead. A little later, Sushila appeared and announced that Maithili was crying in her room. Digbaba took a little time to gather himself. He was distracted, thinking over the steps of the impending mission. It was hard for him to withdraw his mind from those thoughts and plunge into the world of tears, sentiments and tender feelings. He rose from his reverie, asking, 'Why is she crying?'

'She is crying because you're leaving,' replied Sushila.

He thought crying for this parting was childish for a mature person like Maithili. For him, it was not the time to cry, and if she created a river of tears and flooded the place, he wouldn't stay back, he announced. Maithili opened the door and appeared. She looked different. She apologized and then said in a stern voice that Sushila didn't understand that the life of a child widow was a stern penance. Rajan's love had distanced Sushila from the reality of others' suffering. Maithili declared that sentimentality had no place in her life because her father had, in the first place, made her realize that emotions had no place in the life of a child widow. Digdarshi too sounded equally detached and reiterated calmly that sentimentality would never obstruct him from his goal of liberating the country. He left informing Maithili that he would return to the ashram in four days.

The parting was meaningful. It made the village people emotional even though they weren't very familiar with the mystic. They knew he was leaving them to end his long penance with a havan, the finale of his sacred vow, and bring good luck to remove all the miseries in their lives. Even the most miserly of them showed up at his ashram with some offerings for the havan. For the simple folks, Digbaba's appeal involved his abrupt disappearance occasionally; they believed he didn't stick to one place lest it should breed worldly attachment. They thronged the mendicant's door, who was in a great hurry to set out on the noble mission. Zamindar Graharaj, too, desired to donate something for the havan. He felt that his sincere offerings for the havan might do some miracle and bring home his missing eldest son, whom he wished to meet before death. But Digbaba was very strict and keen to know about the giver who wished to contribute to his cause. He had particularly refused to accept anything from the zamindar. Graharaj was powerful enough to oust the arrogant mendicant from his area, but he feared upsetting the people who loved the baba dearly.

∽

It was past midnight, silent and eerie. Digbaba sat on the floor and was engrossed in spinning the charkha. It was usual for him to spin in the dead of night to avoid suspicion by the zamindar and the police about him being a follower of Gandhi. That night, he heard the faint voice of a woman urging him to open the door. Digbaba kept his charkha aside and let her in. Her face was hardly visible beneath her veil. She handed him a letter, saying that it was from the zamindar's new courtesan, who had arrived in the village a few days back.

He opened the letter and began reading:

> I dare not come before you. But once I read your leaflets distributed secretly in villages for Gandhi's August Revolution, it wasn't hard to make out the mission of your havan. So far, I wasn't sure if I should give, meet and request you to read my palm, face or horoscope; I knew you wouldn't accept the money I made from sin. I know my destiny. But today, I understood that the collection has been for keeping up the freedom struggle. My question is, 'Can a prostitute with a clean mind donate to your fund?' You might say, 'How can the mind of a prostitute be clean?' Baba, it's my body that has been sacrificed numerous times to satisfy the carnal desires of men, but my mind has always been free. I'm a complete split between body and mind; the two have no connection. Whatever wealth I've made in exchange for my body, I don't wish to submit to the freedom fund. But whatever I earned with a clean mind, I want to leave that at your disposal so that the uneasiness inside me might subside. Waiting for your approval.

The anonymous letter moved Digbaba deeply; each word sounded genuine. The decency and fortitude of the fallen woman emerged from the letter like the sight of a delicate lotus emerging from the mire and soaring over clean water. Her moral judgement dazzled his mind. He wanted to meet her; she was waiting outside in the palanquin. He asked the maid to bring her in. He was ready to accept her donation to the freedom movement. The maid returned accompanied by the woman, whose face was covered. She wore a simple khadi sari. No jewellery adorned her, and she held a bundle close to her heart. The woman bowed, kept the bundle at Digbaba's feet, and retreated awkwardly. Shame and guilt seemed to crush her being. Inside the bundle were stacks of thread she had spun and saved carefully. The baba was astonished to see a prostitute in a plain, coarse khadi sari; he was further surprised that her donation wasn't money or precious jewellery but bundles of thread spun on the charkha. He was very moved and stated seriously, 'I need you by my side.' The woman didn't react and stood immobile. He asked the woman to remove the cover and show her face, and said he wouldn't accept anything from a stranger. The petrified woman stood unmoved. The baba commanded, 'Unveil your face! Where do you belong in Calcutta?'

The woman stirred and moved two steps closer to him and cried out 'I'm Kanak!' as she slowly unveiled her face. She stood cold, unmoved; large drops of tears clung hard to the corner of her eyes, refusing to roll down.

Digbaba hurriedly called Maithili and Sushila from their sleep and asked them to take Kanak inside the ashram. Kanak refused to go inside the inner yard, saying, 'I've lived through ultimate harm! No further damage could be done to me. I don't want to enter the ashram and stain your reputation. If the zamindar's sons know I've been to the ashram, they'll burn it down; the scandal will erode people's trust in you.'

She was ashamed to relate the baseless scandal involving the two of them that changed the course of her destiny. She didn't want to be pushed to the fire again. Freedom of the country remained her priority; she wanted Digbaba to help the country get freedom. His head came down in admiration for her. Whatever impacts of her entry to the ashram she anticipated were highly probable; none of her fears were baseless. The simple information of her presence in his ashram was enough to scandalize him as an immoral pseudo-saint. Maithili rushed in and held Kanak's hand and asked, terrified, 'How could this happen to you?'

She couldn't excuse herself her silly mistake of drawing a rangoli in Bhuja Rout's front yard that led to Kanak's ending up in a brothel; the tragic denouement was wicked and unjustified. Kanak related that when she refused to follow the zamindar's order to testify against Digdarshi as her molester, vengeful Dolamani didn't let her stay in the village. She was taken away to Calcutta to avoid public outcry. He raped her repeatedly, brought her back, and handed her over to Zamindar Graharaj's sons. She realized that the maid by her side might be Dolamani's informer and didn't give any further details. The details of her ordeal moved Digdarshi deeply. He urged Kanak to give up that life and join him in the freedom movement. He said that whatever she lost was purely physical; the external abuses could do no harm to her soul, and she should get out of hell.

Kanak listened carefully and warned him of the fallout of her sudden disappearance. The police would search her everywhere, and even the baba's ashram would be razed. Her evaluation was correct. He realized that no one would ever write down the story of her patriotism or her sacrifice for the motherland anywhere, but her story was never to be erased from his heart. She bid him farewell and left; her palanquin slowly vanished into the darkness. Digbaba's conviction that darkness must give way to light but that it needed a hand to light the lamp, seemed prophetic. He thought that while innumerable hands like Kanak's had come forward to light the lamp of freedom, its flame would shine bright to ward off the darkness.

The Quit India Movement became a litmus test for Gandhian ideals of peace and non-violence. At that point, the reverse logic that non-violence gave rise to violence woefully seemed more and more real. Initially, during mass protests, the participants came out peacefully and shouted 'Long live Mahatma Gandhi' and 'Quit India' in unison; the slogans resonated in the air. The angry British government replied to those cries with guns, bullets, cannons, torture and mindless arrests. So, instead of ensuring freedom, the peaceful opposition created an atmosphere of unrest and hostility that plunged the nation into chaos. Police burnt down the ashrams and homes of some Congress Party workers, beat peaceful marchers mercilessly, and fired at people unprovoked. Gradually, the demonstrators too lost patience and became violent. It was natural for action to generate a reaction, and the clash, like the clank between two pieces of stone, sparked the fire.

Parshuram sat dispassionately and wrote down like Chitragupta—who in the scriptures is the recordkeeper for Yama—each karma of every human. His Ashram in Balikuda was burnt to ashes, and Hari Bishwal, Govinda Das and Madan Jena were sent to the Cellular Jail in Andaman and Nicobar Islands. Digbaba took recourse to violence and secretly helped anti-British organizations in subversive activities. The situation was fluid, and it was hard to keep track of events. The police searched Digbaba's Karma Mandira and arrested Maithili and Sushila, and burned down the place.

Rajan and Sushila were kept in one jail. Aziz led the movement in Bhadrakh, his native place. In the meantime, he married Kamala, his beloved from the Hindu community. He wished to set an example for those who wanted to divide the country on religious lines. Their marriage was solemnized in the Congress Party office. He thought the union would get the support of both communities and strengthen the bond between them, but the result was different. Both the communities considered them their enemies and termed their marriage anti-religious; his wife had no place in his house nor her parental home. The couple felt unsafe coming out and were confined to the Congress Party office. Aziz also wrote in a letter that he wished to leave Kamala at Parshuram's place till the situation became normal. He confided in his friend that their marriage hadn't been consummated, and like the rest of the workers in the Congress office, they were celibates. He was sad that there was no light to admire the flower of love that blossomed in a bleak moment in history, when the country was caught in battle for its freedom. However, his quest for light was relentless, and he hoped that light would permeate and wash away every darkness someday.

Aziz arrived with his wife Kamala and left the same day, leaving her in Parshuram's place. Her husband's ideology completely moulded her. She didn't regret the hardships she endured for marrying a Muslim. She mingled quite well with Parshuram's family. Manorama, too, found a great friend in her. But Dolamani had been uneasy since Aziz's wife began living with the family. He had been planning to incite communal violence but had hardly any takers for his ideas. He had lost credibility among the masses after being found scheming to grab Tahibulla's mango orchard. Parshuram had declared that the marriage between Aziz and Kamala was sacred because of their total dedication to one another. He said that their bond would last not just a single lifetime but endure through many more births; their sacred union couldn't be violated and no bloodshed between Hindus and Muslims would separate them.

Misplaced jealousy and thoughts of vengeance prevent man from being sensible. Unfortunately, Dolamani had been seething with those twin vices against Parshuram all the time. He was so taken over by the idea of harming the poor headmaster that, one night, Dolamani set out in the darkness with two of his faithful followers to set his home on fire, but was accidentally caught by constables while soliciting help for arson. He was arrested for encouraging two naive young men to participate in the crime, promising some land as reward. Land was priceless and a sure bait for being free from working for the zamindar. Dolamani's face wasn't visible in the darkness; he was arrested as a criminal who conspired to destroy Parshuram's home. He didn't show his face during the detention. News dashed fast in the village, and curious villagers thronged the police station in the morning to see the criminal. They couldn't believe Dolamani could be kept behind bars like a regular criminal. The police were embarrassed about the arrest and released him on bail.

Shameless Dolamani justified his action to the police by saying that Parshuram's home was a hideout for anti-government Congress workers, terrorists and socialists, and the government should burn down his home. He said the exact opposite to the

Congress Party workers—the arson would've convinced people that the police were behind the crime and turned them against British rule. Thus, he tried to reap the best of the bargain from both sides. Parshuram knew that the plot aimed to harm him personally.

⁂

By the time the news came that Sama Puhana was alive, Sebati was no more in this world. Her soul had fled to a mysterious land looking for him. She walked slowly along the dam's side and moved towards the vast stretch beyond that area; she didn't turn back. Sama had been missing before the Rohia Bachala Dam collapsed in the monsoon. Some people also said that tigers in the Chandaka forest killed him. But Sebati, at that time, was the only one to say that Sama wasn't dead. Sama wasn't dead in reality. Ramadevi, too, had assured her of his return. The hope got firmly implanted in Sebati and branched out in every possible direction like the spikes of a robust tree. 'He'll return, and return for sure. He has no death,' she used to mumble.

Time moved inexorably. The Second World War consumed the world. The brutalities of the police during the Quit India Movement didn't stop. A powerful flood swept across Bari, and the volunteers got involved in the relief and rescue operations. Sebati worked devotedly for those afflicted and held on to the belief that Sama, swept away by the river's strong currents, was rescued somewhere and would return. She had a high fever but didn't stop working in the rain and storm. Others in the team urged her to return to the shed and rest inside, but she refused. All the while, her eyes were silently on the lookout for Sama. She was determined that if Sama showed up for the relief work, which he did invariably during every deluge, she would urge him to assure her that he was safe somewhere. She also wanted to clarify that she wasn't desperate to marry him, but keeping up with his vanishing tricks was hard for her. The Sama she knew was a quirky fellow; he swore to serve Gandhi and Mother India, and those two were his gods. So, she felt that Sama might not take her urgings seriously and rather slap her hard, saying, 'How dare you swear in the name of Mother India and be my wife? I'm not henpecked!'

Sebati didn't care. She wasn't ready to accept rumours of Sama's death, for after every hue and cry over his final exit, he invariably was found alive. She sat like stone and continued waiting for him on the river dam. She thought if he didn't come back walking on the track stretching beyond the dam, Sama was no more in the world. Her mind swung between hope and hopelessness. He appeared in her dreams and made her cry. Once sure of his death, she would give up the hope of marrying him, be resolute on the journey as a single woman, and devote her entire life to serving others. Sebati was finally inside the tent; her condition was critical. She was delirious. Her temperature fluctuated. Sometimes the medicine worked a miracle; her temperature would go down, and she would rise and sit up in bed. But when it relapsed, her condition became alarming. Strangely, one day it seemed that the medicine did its wonder, and Sebati looked better, but still she was watched carefully.

That night, the weather became worse; dark clouds rose and strong winds swept across the site. On that dreadful night, everybody except Sebati fell asleep as if some spell drove them to deep sleep. She heard someone calling her name and urging her to come to the dam, saying, 'Wow! What a dedicated follower of Gandhi! It's almost daybreak, how could you sleep? I'm hosting the tricolour here, and you don't want to witness it?'

Sebati rose and ran like someone possessed. She didn't care for the storm or the lashing rain. Nobody could guess who gave the frail woman that strength. She was drawn by a shadowy image of Sama, who stood like a brave hero on the embankment. The tricolour in the shade of white, orange and green, and the Gandhi charkha in the centre, fluttered in the wind in one of his hands. She was euphoric that it was the real daybreak.

It undoubtedly was the end of the night. In the morning, the inmates in the ashram found that she was gone from her room, and her cold body lay on the floor of the dam. She had no fever, and there was no sign of struggle in her body. Her soul had left her mortal frame and wandered free in a land where the flag of liberty flapped unhindered.

Following Sebati's last rites, someone informed people that Sama was alive and had a long beard, and curls of matted hair cluttered his head. Clad in rags, he stood in the front line of a demonstration and screamed, 'Long live Mother India' and 'Quit India', raising the tricolour proudly. He swam the currents and reached the riverbank. The police incharge, Nawab Das, caught him and put him behind bars. He served the term in jail, but joined the independence movement when he was released. He invariably appeared from nowhere in such protests, and screamed 'Long live Mother India' and 'Quit India'. In innumerable nameless villages of India, countless spirited workers like Sama Puhana, Jagiri Swain and Madan Jena fought against the Empire, and sacrificed their lives for the country's freedom. Nobody cared to keep a record of their names.

Quit India wasn't a successful movement, but it made the British government aware that the momentum to oust them from Indian soil was absolute. History didn't record the names of countless patriots who succumbed to police shootings or were caught and banished to the dark waters of Kalapani, or languished in the dreaded Cellular Jail in Andaman and Nicobar Islands. It didn't chronicle the names of those who were burnt alive or those whipped to death during the freedom struggle. But their stories have been preserved carefully beneath the soil of India. Even today, if someone scratches her surface, the stench of the blood of martyrs like Bhuja Rout, Lakshmana Nayak, Bhagat Singh and Bagha Jatin soaked in the dust, wafts up and fills the nostrils. There was no time to weigh the pros and cons of the Quit India Movement for those actively engaged in it. They were anxious to seize the surge and the tempo, and amplify the gains of their action.

Headmaster Parshuram, a silent worker in the freedom movement, guarded Balikuda High School like an old banyan tree that had lost its copse of leaves but still refused to wither out. The situation was so chaotic that he couldn't keep track of freedom fighters like Hari Bishwal, Govinda Das, Madan Jena, Baikuntha, Diganta Keshari, Maithili, Sushila or Rajan. He got the news that Sama was alive and Sebati was dead. He was neither excited nor worried, and remained stoically calm. But the murder of Aziz, his dearest friend, brought him down thoroughly. The loss made him so inconsolable that Aziz's wife Kamala bottled up her own miseries and came forward to console him, saying, 'Let's pray that deaths similar to Aziz's may help to retain the unity of the Indian subcontinent.'

Aziz died under very unfortunate circumstances. On 14

July 1942, a meeting was convened to discuss the details of a Muslim religious procession in Bhadrakh. Participating Muslims and Hindu young men in the discussion didn't find common ground for agreeing on the pageant to move into town; the heated exchange of words amongst them took a nasty turn. Aziz volunteered to mediate and pacify the rival groups and bring the situation under control. He urged everyone to say together, 'Hindu–Muslim bhai bhai!' The mob found the call a mockery of their faith. Aziz's marriage to Kamala had deeply hurt the sentiments of both communities. At that moment, the mob considered him to be a traitor and took out its vengeance on him violently. They brought up the legitimacy of his marriage to Kamala, and pounced upon the defenceless man. Aziz was mortally wounded in the attack. The incident flared into a communal riot, and police fired shots to bring the situation under control. Ten people died in the violence, and those dead bodies weren't handed over to their families. The police performed their last rites.

A commission was set up to investigate the matter. Famous lawyers from Punjab and Calcutta came to fight the case on behalf of the Muslims. Mr John Brutes, the English judge from Patna High Court, came to deliver the judgement against the Muslims. Aziz was declared the mastermind of the riot and was held responsible for the death of eight innocent young men. He was hanged. But ironically, Aziz was neither Hindu nor Muslim; he was an untainted human being. Before he was hung to death in Cuttack jail, he expressed his last wish to hug the Hindu executor. When Aziz hugged and held the Hindu hangman tight, tears filled the eyes of the man. He declared, 'Brother, I've no say in the act I'm assigned to do. My hands may be responsible for ending your life, but my heart is filled with love for you.'

'Long live India! Hindu–Muslim bhai bhai!' were the last words that Aziz said when he breathed his last.

Parshuram had no words to console Kamala. Aziz wasn't just a friend, he was also a brother, inseparable like a chunk of his heart. Nobody could fill that vacuum till his death. Parshuram looked at Kamala and understood that the young woman was putting on a brave face despite crumbling to pieces inside. Worried over Kamala's future, Manorama was bedridden.

'Do you want to return to your father?' Parshuram asked Kamala.

'Yes! I don't know what else to do,' she said.

'Will you like to go to Bhadrakh tomorrow?'

'No! I'll go to Bari.'

'Bari?' He asked, surprised.

'Yes! My parents, Gopabandhu Chaudhury and Ramadevi, are in Bari.'

Kamala said that their Sebaghara Ashram was the safest place for her. She had no entry to either her father's place or Aziz's. Both sides had disowned her. She was a sinner in their eyes who brought shame upon them. Aziz also wanted her to go to Sebaghara in case of his death. Parshuram thought that even an untainted woman like Kamala wasn't spared being termed fallen in a highly prejudiced society. He realized there was no safe place besides Ramadevi's ashram to welcome her.

Chapter XIV

Sunrise in the middle of the night is an unprecedented phenomenon. But defying every norm, the sun rose in the middle of the night, which made the impossible possible. It was said that the sun never set over the British Empire, but controverting that saying, the sun went down over the Empire on India's sky, and the sun of freedom rose at midnight at twelve o'clock on 15 August 1947. Rejoicing over the feat, people lit up rows of lamps emulating Diwali in every nook and cranny of India, its towns and nondescript villages. The rhapsody involved blowing conches and bursting firecrackers. Waves of ecstasy and celebration swept across the country, and the people finally realized that their country had become free from foreign rule.

For five long years, the message 'freedom is an absolute reality—freedom is bound to happen' rang in the air for the rural folks like a prophecy, and gave rise to countless hopes and anticipations in their hearts. Especially after the August Movement, they were convinced that freedom was imminent. It seemed that the resolve of the vast populace made the impossible possible. At daybreak, they woke up to find the tricolour soaring over their firmament.

The flag ruffled in the wind inside Balikuda High School. Starting with 'Ramdhun', Gandhi's favourite morning prayer, the celebration melded the school children's proud, passionate singing of the national anthem, *Jana gana mana adhinayaka jaya he...* The melody rippled in the air and wafted beyond the Alka River, fields, forest, valley, sky and mountains. Thousands of curious villagers thronged the celebration in the school to feel and witness first-hand freedom's look, shape and colour.

The villagers had attended many meetings of the local freedom fighters in Parshuram's Sarvadharma Ashram and heard about the great leader Mahatma Gandhi, whom the British called 'a half-naked Indian Fakir'. However, they weren't interested in learning about the man who made the impossible possible. That day, they were overtly watchful that freedom reached their villages and didn't stay confined just to the bounds of the big cities. Each person wanted to witness the momentous happening.

Cries of 'Long live Mahatma Gandhi', 'Long live Mother India', and 'Long live the brotherhood of Hindus and Muslims' echoed everywhere. That day, conspicuous by their absence were freedom fighters Madan Jena and Aziz; also missing from the throng were some known and lesser-known patriots. Parshuram sat dazed inside; he looked sad. It seemed strange that he, who dedicated his life to fighting silently for the freedom of India, remained unmoved in the most jubilant final moment.

Three friends, Hari, Govinda and Parshuram, sat together. The people of Balikuda—Hindus and Muslims—sang the praise of Mother India loudly outside. Jayaram Mahapatra, with his usual sarcasm, cursed the British: 'The crooks rushing for their homes now must be in the middle of the ocean. I wish a powerful thunderbolt would crush and sink their ships! Bloody looters shouldn't ever dare swindle someone else's fortune and occupy their land! They robbed and destroyed our country completely!'

Dolamani Srichandan, clad in a pair of handloom dhoti-kurta, topped with a shawl over his shoulder, arrived at the school and stood before the masses like their saviour. A Vaishnava tilak in sandalwood paste adored his forehead to complete his genial look. He addressed the crowd screaming at the top of his voice, so that Parshuram and his friends sitting inside could hear him: 'The foreigners subjugated us and ruled over our country till date. It's over now! Gone are those days! We have ousted the British, the kings and the zamindars, and brought democracy—the rule by the people. We're our rulers; there's no difference between the master and the subject. Irrespective of caste, creed and colour, all are entitled to live in this country as free citizens.'

Dolamani declared that he had donated huge patches of land for the people and expressed his hope for more people to get an education and rise above poverty. The school happened to be the nucleus of the small village, and he found the audience receptive to his ideas. At that opportune moment, he made public his vow to dedicate his life to the service of the people, and his desire to be the school's secretary. He promised good classrooms, a library, laboratories, equipment, tables and chairs for the learners. But he said that Parshuram didn't want him as the school's secretary. He sought the people's opinion. The euphoric public took his side unabashedly and believed that the magic of freedom had changed the heart of the mean, miserly zamindar overnight. Amid loud cheers, Dolamani announced that he would host a celebratory feast in the village ground and distribute clothes to everyone. He asked people to find Parshuram, and said sarcastically that the British stooge was hiding somewhere like any other English-educated person.

The three friends—Hari, Govinda and Parshuram—were pensive; they didn't know what to tell the jubilant villagers who didn't know about the Hindu–Muslim riots, the senseless bloodshed in Lahore, Calcutta, Noakhali and numerous other places over the country's partition, and the birth of Pakistan. They were ignorant that the pavements were rife with communal violence, and splashes of human blood vied for prominence with the bright rays of the rising sun of freedom. People didn't know that in those places, Hindus and Muslims killed each other, and raped and murdered women, or that trains crossed the India and Pakistan borders loaded with countless dead and wounded bodies. They didn't know that the godly Mahatma Gandhi, instead of remaining in Delhi and rejoicing in the feat of freedom, was lodged in a dingy, decrepit dark home in Belghoria Road in Calcutta in readiness to avert the eruption of violence in the city. Calcutta was on the verge of a communal riot over the partition of Bengal. On the eve of the country's freedom, Gandhi made a sad declaration that while India would be free from British rule from the following day, it would also be divided at midnight. He noted that 15 August would be remembered in Indian history as both a day of jubilation and a day of sadness.

That day, Dolamani, who was opposed to the freedom movement all his life, celebrated the country's freedom with fanfare. Hari Bishwal, Parshuram and Govinda, who were ready to sacrifice their lives for freedom, sat inside in a sombre mood. The gullible villagers didn't know that India was divided while they were asleep the previous night. There never was any communal violence in the history of Balikuda; no conspirators ever succeeded in dividing the people. The three freedom fighters fathomed the national mood of loss and anxiety, but didn't want to dishearten the jubilant crowd. Finally, Parshuram controlled his emotions and rose with folded hands to talk.

'Brothers! The country is free now, but with freedom comes responsibility. The question is, can we handle the bigger responsibility of a free nation? The English did us immense harm, but we can't sit back and blame everything on them. We went to slumber for a long two hundred years. We must now think of what's right or wrong for us.'

He also told people that dedicated workers should come together to think about the development of their area. He compared nation-building to the building of a temple; if he set the foundation, some would build the walls, some the floor, and some the doors and windows. Everybody would do their bit. It would be a collective effort to build Ramrajya—the ideal state imagined by Mahatma Gandhi. The ecstatic crowd was ready to work. They wanted the freedom to be tangible. Parshuram explained that one needed inner vision to see freedom and must know how to preserve it.

'You confuse us. Why don't you speak up clearly? Without seeing it with our own eyes, we don't believe freedom is here,' the people urged.

Parshuram clarified that free people were those without bondage and subjugation, or control by masters. The explanation of freedom made Dolamani uncomfortable. People asked that if the British left, Zamindar Dolamani and countless small and big zamindars should not be masters in a free country. Hari Bishwal assured that the master–subject relationship wouldn't exist in a democracy.

Sama Puhana had routinely seen the sun rising in the east when the British ruled over India. But he sat in rapt attention on the river dam for the special sunrise Nehru talked about on the first day of independence. From sunrise to sunset, he sat on the dam over the Brahmani River, flowing near the Bari Sebashrama. He didn't care to join the revelry over Independence Day. Ramadevi made khiri for celebration. Sama loved khiri very much, but once he left his village and joined the freedom movement, he didn't have craving for food; he ate only a little so that he didn't die. That day, he was free to eat khiri in a huge brass bowl, but he ignored the tempting aroma of the sweet dish and sat over the dam to view the sunrise. Everyone thought that he was melancholic because he missed Sebati. He returned in the evening and asked Ramadevi, 'Did you see any difference in the sunrise? I saw nothing new.'

The kind woman asked him to be patient for change to come. She said freedom from the British was the beginning, and more change would come quickly. He looked at her, confused. He doubted his senses for not seeing the rising sun in the middle of the night. He was relieved that credulous Sebati, his fiancé, was no longer there to hear such unprecedented information. He asked Ramadevi about the pending task for the country and wanted to help. She said the task meant making a king and a pauper equal, providing food, cloth and shelter for all, and making the country an ideal place like Rama's kingdom. One question led to another; Sama wanted to know where Rama was. She explained that both Rama and Ravana—good and evil—resided inside everyone, and one had to awaken the Rama inside them and destroy the Ravana. Sama got irritated. He didn't understand how a man could be both good and evil.

He didn't believe in words; he believed in action.

'Don't confuse me. Assign me some task—that's it,' he said, spreading his arms towards Ramadevi's husband, Gopabandhu Chaudhury.

'Someone who believes in action is Rama. Have you seen someone who doesn't act ever become a Rama?' Chaudhury said.

Sama got the point and mused that a man of action was virtuous; a man acting wrong was vile. If your action follows the right path, you can create a kingdom of Rama. Sama set out on his mission for the right action. The memory of Sebati and his vow to return to his village became inconsequential.

∞

Diganta Keshari, in the guise of Digbaba, was far away from his village on Independence Day. Years ago, he left home with a vow to set free a dasi trapped irrevocably in the system, but he couldn't fulfil that mission. He believed that as long as the dasi system wasn't completely uprooted and the term 'subject' wasn't removed from the lexicon, he still had to go miles to reach his goal. He was undecided, and debated whether to enter his father's territory or stay out. He would be a nowhere-man till the zamindar–subject binary existed.

Devaki's father, Dakhinray, was in Graharaj's palace to celebrate Independence Day. He believed in going with the flow and ensured that he and all his grandsons wore homespun khadi. He was extremely loyal to the British as long as they were in power, but in the changing scenario, he was keen to show his loyalty to the new government formed after independence. But Graharaj's stance was clear; he was adamant that the national flag shouldn't fly over his palace. He opposed India's freedom and argued that since he did nothing to oust the English nor he ever was in trouble during the Raj, freedom of the country didn't excite him in any special way.

Dakhinray tried hard to convince the cynical Graharaj that as a British loyalist, he disowned the eldest son, Diganta Keshari, and received the title Raybahadur. As the father of the freedom fighter, he might be honoured with the title 'Friend of the Country' after freedom. He urged his son-in-law to stop acting like a fool and to stop resisting change. As a zamindar, he appeased the rulers during the Raj and reaped enormous benefits; he needed to stand with the new government and let his sons benefit. The new generation won't aspire to be a small zamindar like him, but join politics and rule over the state. Dakhinray took over the charge to induct his grandsons into the new game of politics.

Graharaj believed that one should stick to their core values and never give those up. Dakhinray cautioned Graharaj not to separate the two: Gandhi's call for the British to quit India and the end of the zamindari system. He explained that the government and the zamindari system were one: 'The title of kings will be replaced with ministers. Change would be superficial. Try to remember that the ruler is the head and the government is the body, and the body can't function without the head. Even in Rama's state, there was a ruler. The status quo will not change. You're the zamindar, your sons will be the government. Don't obstruct the path for your sons to rise!'

Graharaj felt if anyone deserved to be part of the government, it was his eldest son Diganta Keshari, who became a fugitive like Subhas Bose. He still hoped that someday Diganta might appear before him and teasingly remind him that, like the British who were driven away, the kings and zamindars would become redundant soon, and that all would be equal as they used to be at the beginning of time. But hope dwindled, and he fretted that Diganta had decided not to meet or seek reconciliation with him.

Less than one year into the declaration of independence, the assassination of Gandhi—the father of the nation—came as a huge blow, stunning everyone. It was announced over the radio that someone shot and killed the Mahatma in a prayer meeting in New Delhi. Bereaved people looked for the name of the assassin. Dolamani declared in the village that Gandhi's killer was a Muslim. He justified that no Hindu would kill Gandhi, a godly man and a devotee of Rama. He planted anti-Muslim sentiments and asked the angry Hindus to burn down the homes of Tahibulla and other Muslims in the area.

Dolamani that night whipped up violent communal passion in the minds of the gullible Hindus, and incited them to commit acts of violence and arson in the Muslim neighbourhood. He wanted the frenzy to look like it was plotted by his arch-enemy Parshuram and his friends, the loyal followers of Gandhi. He planned to emerge as the leader, the man of the moment pacifying the mob and brokering peace among the warring factions, and the leader who advised Hindus and Muslims to live together. He banked on the popular support to translate into votes during the upcoming general election.

It was a cold January night. Parshuram, Hari and Govinda, the three friends extremely devastated over Gandhi's death, sat silently outside Parshuram's home. They worried about the fate of the young nation without the beacon of hope to guide its people. Manorama didn't cook; she gave the friends tea and puffed rice for dinner. The death of the father of the nation was a bad omen, and they worried that it mightn't be easy to fulfil Gandhi's dream of an ideal nation.

Suddenly, they could hear the wrestle of hurried steps approaching them; the discussion stopped abruptly. To their surprise, they saw the faces of some peasants from the village in the darkness. The mob marched angrily beyond the school wall with flaming torches in their hands.

'Where're you guys rushing with torches in the dead of the night?' questioned the friends.

'We want to avenge Gandhi's murder. We'll kill the Muslims. They killed Gandhi,' replied the mob.

'Stop! Do you know who killed Gandhi?'

'No.'

'You're the killers of Gandhi. Because the perpetrator, Nathuram Godse, was a Hindu. Go and torch your own home,' said Parshuram.

The mob stood in shock. They didn't understand why Dolamani told a lie and incited anger and hatred against the Muslims in them.

The abolition of the zamindari system was almost a reality. The sprawling line of servants, dasis, mistresses, attendants and assistants would no longer be at the beck and call of the rich landowners. The government planned to fix some acres of land per owner and confiscate the rest of their property. Some shrewd ones, like Dolamani, wanted to fool the system; they hurriedly sold out their excess land and bought precious metals like gold and silver. They invested in factories and businesses in the name of their heirs. Dolamani went a few steps further. He sold his excess land but donated some to the school. The gift to the school, he knew, would bring him name, fame and some political mileage as well.

Graharaj didn't panic; he seemed disinterested. Devaki, on her father's advice, forced him to distribute the land among her sons so that the government won't get much to take away. But Graharaj wanted to divide the landed property in Diganta Keshari's presence. He was determined to keep the process on hold till his son stepped in. Devaki reminded him that he was pronounced dead long back and that if he were alive, he might've resurfaced and asked for his share. The zamindar was unmoved. He didn't listen to his wife and sat with the stubbornness of an old aristocrat. His hauteur came from the feeling that he wasn't a nouveau riche like Dolamani, and that his lineage had been inseparable from the power and privilege of zamindari for generations.

Devaki didn't seem to win over the zamindar and took to indefinite fasting. She refused to take food or water till the parcels of land were distributed among her sons. Chakori, the most trusted dasi, thought that the zamindar was right in his decision to wait for his eldest son. Devaki wasn't wrong either; she had been unyielding from the beginning, and as the zamindar grew older, she leaned on her sons for support and gained the upper hand in decision-making. Chakori brokered on her behalf and suggested keeping aside the eldest son's share, and distributing the rest among Devaki's sons. Her calm, genuine voice soothed the zamindar's cold heart. She was single-mindedly devoted to him.

Graharaj knew that Chakori stood beside him when he faltered in sickness and misery. He didn't react to the dasi in indignation. The brutally egoistic man was oddly sublime in the last days of his life. Like the setting sun, he was a tired mass of burning fire that waned into a tender and fading saffron glow in the west sky before it sunk. He was like the winter sun with a brief outlet, never knowing when evening would let the darkness swallow him unannounced. He didn't fear death, but his mind often got embroiled in the grey areas of after-death mysteries. He pondered over questions like, what happens to the body after death? Where does the soul go? Does karmic retribution get carried over to the next birth?

At a ripe age, taking stock of the accrued sins and misdeeds of one's entire life shakes even the bravest of hearts. Unforgiving old age makes the most powerful man look fragile, vulnerable and timid. Sitting alone, Graharaj felt the gradual sinking of his arrogant self before that merciless mighty force. He spent his entire life amassing wealth avariciously and never cared if the means to the wealth he made was just. In the last days of his life, the treasury wasn't in his control anymore. The sons born to him didn't care for him in his old age; they listened to their mother Devaki, and those spoilt brats spent money indiscriminately for idle fun and lechery—mostly on wine and women.

Left to himself, the zamindar found the calmest moments for self-reflection. In his heydays, he was constantly surrounded by self-serving minions. His so-called steadfast followers were nowhere around him in his old age. Knowing that his power had waned dramatically and his days were counted, those creeps deserted him and enclosed his young sons. He was sure that only a little of his vast fortune would be spent on his last rites, and on religious and charitable work. It suddenly struck him that the wealth he made and saved for the next three generations was a futile mission. He looked desperately for atonement. Chakori, his soulmate, watched him curiously, as if she was urging him to take the road to redemption.

A lighted path flashed before the zamindar's eyes momentarily. He remembered the popular saying, if your son is gifted, or if your son is a good-for-nothing, there's no need to save in either case. He decided to spend the money on some greater cause in the village, instead of leaving the fortune for the good-for-nothing young sons. He still hoped that his missing son might come and pardon his transgressions.

He summoned his accountant and lawyer immediately, and kept aside Diganta Keshari's share of wealth for building institutions named after the son. 'Diganta Sebasadan' was dedicated to public service, 'Diganta Vidyalaya' was for education, 'Diganta Matru Magala Kendra' for women's health and wellbeing, and 'Diganta Pathagara' for public library. Devaki and her sons opposed the move initially, but Graharaj was unyielding; his grit prevailed.

Devaki's father Dakhinray wanted to use the benevolent acts as political capital; he quickly turned the tide of change in favour of her grandsons. The young men worked sincerely and ensured that all the charitable initiatives were completed quickly. They said proudly that their father donated his wealth in memory of their elder brother, a great patriot who left home and fought in the freedom struggle. The election was approaching, and Dakhinray had calculated that the gains would be massive for them. He hoped for his grandsons to become ministers in the new administration. He didn't care if the institutions were named after Diganta Keshari. He knew that once the democratic system was in place, Devaki's sons would be in office and replace the name with their own.

Diganta Keshari always dreamed of a classless society, while his father inspired his son to be a brown sahib—get an English education, and adopt Western manners and mores. Needless to say, he renounced the cushioned life of a zamindar's son and left home.

Graharaj never knew if the actions of his youth were sinful, but he knew for sure that the allure to do wrong was irresistible, and the restraint to stay away from sin was very feeble in him. Those opposed to him didn't care to stop him from doing wrong because they wanted him to fall—and fall miserably. There was none to encourage him to do the right. From the beginning, the zamindar was surrounded by many who enabled his sinful actions, but the same enablers opposed his move to change and take the right path later. Man never understands such strange realities of life at a young age and goes on diverging from what is just. This lack of judgement makes one say that to err is human; our limitations make the world what it is: a place where opposites—sin-virtue, happiness-unhappiness—coexist, and don't make the earth a flawless, perfect place like heaven.

The zamindar seemed to inch towards a blissful resolution; if not in life, at least in death, he could see the meaning of being a human. He wanted to donate land to the landless and atone for his sins. He offered Chakori some land, and when she declined and wished to die while he was alive, the old man was upset. He desired the dasi to outlive him and his wife, and serve them till their last days. He didn't trust his sons. Chakori promised him to hold Devaki's feet over her head when the matriarch breathed her last and vowed to remain a dasi even after her death. The zamindar promised her a safe corner in the palace in her old age. She was eternally obliged to him for providing food and shelter all her life.

Chakori had been hardy throughout her life, but at times she couldn't bear the blatantly unfair deals she got from the zamindar. She had no illusions about her position in his life. But the poor dasi had moments of abject denial of the servile position forced upon her. She felt hurt by the bargain that the zamindar made for Devaki to secure her peaceful demise under Chakori's care. She wondered how easily he forgot about the poor dasi who had surrendered her youthful body for his pleasure. Chakori wondered if she wasn't human enough to need care in her old age. She knew the intimacy he shared with her was more gratifying for him than his relationship with Devaki; he had spent more time with her than his wife. Still, she was a dispensable dasi, and Devaki was his honourable wife. The glaring difference was that while all the children Devaki carried in her womb were entitled to live as the zamindar's children, her boy Arkhitia was denied life. She, too, was a mother like Devaki but was never allowed to be one. Arkhitia's innocent face flashed before her hazy old eyes in that painfully angry moment.

Chapter XV

There's a subtle relationship between ruling and serving. Ruling entails service, but when someone gets the right to rule, the attitude to serve becomes less important. Mahatma Gandhi knew this code pretty well. He took the pain to liberate the country but handed over the charge to rule the country to a different set of people. He wanted to remain a servant of the people rather than a ruler. Many freedom fighters followed Gandhi's ideal and stayed away from administration and power; they wanted to fortify the foundation of freedom in the country.

Parshuram was one such man. Many urged him to join politics; he enjoyed undivided popular support. He clarified that he preferred to educate people and create conscious citizens as a teacher rather than joining direct politics to serve the nation. In an ideal world, his argument would be perfect, but in real life it was a hard posture. He didn't know, perhaps, that the ideal method of education that he postulated had to go through the scrutiny of the policymakers. He didn't foresee that education policy someday would directly be embroiled in political rhetoric. He was not interested in direct politics after independence, but politics didn't let him go. Dolamani, whom he didn't approve of as the secretary of his school, joined the election and won. As luck would have it, he became the deputy education minister, assumed office, and became the quintessential replica of a minister in independent India. He wore khadi, donned a Gandhi cap over his head, and a tilak—the pious mark of sandalwood paste—adored his forehead. He learned to walk with ministerial grace. The people who voted in large numbers and helped him win were still in disbelief that their erstwhile illiterate zamindar could morph into a minister so effortlessly! When Hari Bishwal blamed the rural electorate for their bad choice, they asked, 'When did we ask to make him a minister? Why'll we ask our tormentor to serve the country?'

Govinda Das, known for his disarming sarcasm, said that they would only be blamed for the fiasco. The villagers still didn't get him. They reiterated, 'How's it possible that we wrote he'll be a minister? We're illiterate folks. We don't know the alphabet. We didn't attend any school! So how did we do this?'

'All of you stamped on his party's symbol, "twin trumpets", on the ballot paper and dropped that inside the sealed box. Simple! It showed that you agreed to make him a minister. Can you say now that you didn't vote for Dolamani?' Parshuram explained. The discussion went on.

'As long as the masses are illiterate and ignorant, nothing will change. Till everyone is educated, and aware of things happening inside the country and in other parts of the world, and can use their mind while making decisions, we're not going to achieve the freedom that Gandhi imagined for this country,' Parshuram told his friends.

The people fumbled. They swore to have voted for Mahatma Gandhi and didn't understand how those were counted for Dolamani. The majority said, Dolamani's followers came to their doors and gave them money, saying that Gandhi sent the cash for the wage they would miss for not working on election day. The voters didn't believe that illiterate Dolamani could tamper with the ballot box. Hari Bishwal sighed; his voice sank. He made it clear to the villagers that Dolamani was not from Gandhi's party, so they voted for the wrong person from the wrong party—simply because none of them could read the names of the candidates written on the ballot paper.

Hari Biswal's words opened their eyes. They didn't want to remain blind despite having the gift of sight, and vowed to send their children to school. It was decided that under Parshuram's supervision, teachers would travel from village to village, hold classes on people's verandahs, and teach on holidays for free.

On their way back home after the meeting with Parshuram and his friends, the folks were stopped by Dolamani's followers with some very real-world concerns. They warned that going to school wouldn't bring food to their homes. Their children needed to work on daily wages, cut grass and weeds, clean the cowsheds or tend livestock, so their families didn't die from starvation. If Parshuram and his followers knew the books, Dolamani would understand the needs of the hungry. They advised the peasants to send their kids to Dolamani's vegetable garden to clean the weeds and get fifty paisa each towards wages. One of the followers made fun of Parshuram's idea of the open school, saying, 'Teachers are armchair fools; they can't be primary witnesses after teaching for twelve years! Parshuram's three generations had been teachers. He's an impractical fool, his father is a greater fool, and his grandfather is the greatest fool ever. Can he pay any pupil five, ten or fifteen paisa from his pocket? He is a poor teacher with a mere thirty-rupees-salary a month. He runs his home with the tuition fee the students give.'

Dolamani's men didn't seem to exaggerate. The simple folks were torn between two choices. They could not decide whether to toil in the field and curb hunger, or learn to read, write and be aware. They judged that Parshuram knew the books, but Dolamani understood the pangs of hunger. Dolamani was their former zamindar and a minister in the newly formed government. He had enough in his treasury to provide for the poor. The choice was clear. They wanted to ignore the useless literacy classes and agreed unanimously to follow Dolamani, who was back in the village after becoming the education minister. He had sublet his bungalow in the capital to an industrialist relative and stayed back in the village most of the time. He wanted to serve the electorate and didn't want to cut off his relationship with them. If needed, he preferred to stay in the guest house in Bhubaneswar. The capital wasn't his native place; he was a guest there and preferred to stay in the guest house.

During Dolamani's visit to the village, chamchas wanted his views on headmaster Parshuram's proposal to open schools in every village and educate even the poor and untouchable kids. They also wanted to know if he agreed with the headmaster's proposal to use the maidan—the Nagpur open ground—to build a village middle school. Dolamani didn't spoof or dismiss any of Parshuram's proposals. He remained thoughtful like a minister and twisted his mouth with a subtle snobbish smile, without feeling intimidated. He knew his title yielded immense power. He said that being illiterate was a blessing, allowing him to serve as the education minister; it helped him find light in the darkness of ignorance. The argument didn't sound baseless to the folks. They deduced that a minister in charge of the forest department needn't be a wild-forest dweller, a minister of animal husbandry needn't be an animal or a husband, and the minister of health needn't be a bodybuilder. So they deduced that no education was required for the education minister.

Dolamani didn't lose his composure and said that he didn't have the power to advise people on what or what not to do. The Constitution of the land prohibited him from interfering in people's independent thought. But he had his reservations: 'Theoretically, if everyone goes to school, who would be there to till the soil? There'll be food shortages, and I can see famines coming frequently. Second, it doesn't mean that the government is going to provide jobs to everyone who has an education. Your children won't get jobs after completing their studies; ultimately, they'll end up as servants to the children of the rich like us. Third, converting the maidan—the open ground—in Nagpur to a middle school isn't a healthy idea either.'

The folks listened to Dolamani with rapt attention. Elaboration on the maidan, where village women defecated every morning and evening, was an eye-opener for all. He said that the maidan was the only place for women of Nagpur to relieve themselves, and no home had any other provision to accommodate that basic need. Besides, the place helped retain unity in the village and preserve rural culture. He said that those old village grounds were like great 'folk schools'. Young women learned and transmitted skills of rendering doleful parting songs in marriage and songs of merriment in *Kumar Purnima*—the autumn full-moon festival—at the maidan. It was the essential training ground for them to get well-versed in cuss words, riddles, gossip, slander, and the art of home-breaking. The ground fortified women's faith in spirits, goblins, witches, black magic, sorcery and human sacrifice. Women learned chants and mantras to cast spells and control the minds of their husbands, fathers-in-law and brothers-in-law; they shared secrets of terminating sinful pregnancies. Besides, they also shared skills with regard to cooking, making pickles and condiments, stitching, making artful drawings, and so on. They got advice on tricks to control a wily mother-in-law and tame an unyielding husband. The maidan was the most sought-after place for imparting religious knowledge and sex education. It remained the only meeting ground for the village women, who went there twice daily, talked freely, and had fun.

Dolamani further said that if the maidan was taken away, there wouldn't be any place where women could socialize and exchange ideas. Without the exchange of ideas among them, it would be hard to retain unity in the village. He emphasized that women united families or broke homes; men had been just simple dupes dancing to their tunes. It was common knowledge that the maidan was the silent witness to the exchange of letters in many clandestine relationships, and was crucial for solemnizing many marriages. He ended the discourse with a high dose of spoof. He said that while great men, caught up in the mire of woeful worldly worries, struggled for years to calm their minds, the women going there retained their equilibrium effortlessly. They withstood the putrid, revolting stink of rotten faeces in the damp rainy season, and continued talking for hours while they plucked twigs of grass from the ground and picked tooth unabashedly. Such a sight, Dolamani claimed, was hardly seen in any other civilized country. He concluded by saying, 'Gandhi insisted that women should give up their inhibitions and come out into the open. The maidan fulfils that goal. A newly married young woman doesn't care to cover her head while defecating in the ground in public.' He urged the folks to decide if it was a good idea to eliminate the 'folk school' and build a middle school on the free defecation ground in Nagpur.

'The headmaster is telling each family to have a service latrine and to use the excrement as compost. He said that open defecation pollutes the air, and human waste shouldn't be used,' someone pointed out.

Dolamani, this time, lashed out sarcastically, 'Headmaster Parshuram should be the health minister. Isn't it stupid to think that relieving pee and poo inside the home is hygienic? Is it our culture to grow vegetables from compost made from poo? The people who aped the depraved and built latrines inside are sick people. Suppose we cook beef and make a stew, will it be food or beef? Can we Hindus eat that stew? It's the same thing to grow vegetables with poo compost and make stew from beef and eat that as food.'

The masses heard with rapt attention and no more doubted Dolamani's impeccable intelligence. They said, 'We'll not agree with the idea of a middle school in Nagpur. We'll tell Hari Bishwal about the importance of the folk school, and we should have more and more of these folk schools everywhere. These'll preserve our culture.'

Dolamani agreed to provide every possible support for open defecation grounds everywhere. The villagers left the meeting happily. Dolamani wanted to know from his cronies if his delivery was good. They praised him for diligently mugging the entire speech written by his secretary in justifying the 'faeces ground' as a 'folk school', and delivering flawlessly. He chuckled, saying, 'One must know how to appropriate someone else's wealth, name, fame and knowledge to his advantage if he's a politician.'

Sama Puhana whizzed down like a comet in Balikuda that day. Parshuram wondered where he had been all those days and asked him to return to his old parents in the village. Sama was unkempt; dishevelled hair flung wildly, and a measly grown beard covered his face. Sama's eyes were blood-red like a man in revolt. But the headmaster didn't know what angered him so much.

Sama asked, looking into his eyes, 'Where's freedom? Where's Rama's just and benevolent kingdom that Gandhi promised? Nothing has changed. The kings, zamindars, masters and moneylenders are still there; the poor, destitute and hungry enslaved labourers are there too. Still, cholera breaks out in villages and kills hundreds. Earlier, people feared the British police, but now they're mortally afraid of the desi police. Whoever tells the truth, speaks for the poor, or even fights for the rights of the poor, gets punished. He's put behind bars over baseless charges.'

Parshuram listened to him patiently. 'Do you need proof?' Sama asked and then turned around, removing the shawl over his back. Ruthless sharp blows had frayed his wide brown back; grey-blue marks of thick blood stain covered his skin; and bruises made it look like a bloody gutted battlefield. Parshuram winced in horror and wanted to know who had beaten him so inhumanly.

Sama grinned like a madman saying, 'This is no torture! This is the reward I received for raising my voice for the rights of the poor. This is what freedom gave me!' Sama said that he worked with Digbaba, tried hard to stop the peasants from working for free on Dakhinray's land, and asked them to collect and stack the harvest in their barns instead. The move upset the erstwhile zamindar, leading to a war between the peasants and Dakhinray's people. The police arrested and tortured those who refused to abide by the zamindar's order. Sama looked for a peaceful resolution and went to meet Dakhinray, and returned severely beaten and bruised from his palace. He asked the zamindar to stop eyeing more since he didn't have a son to inherit his fortune, and to instead give back the land he took forcefully from the peasants citing false hand notes. Angry Dakhinray got him arrested, and the police beat him, for the alleged crime of threatening to kill a respectable person in the area.

Parshuram, too, was disillusioned with freedom and the Ramrajya it promised. He consoled Sama, saying that so long as everyone was not looking for freedom, self-rule, and the ideal kingdom of Rama, the reign of terror wouldn't stop. He advised him not to lose hope and to return to his village and spread the message of education with the same enthusiasm he had in popularizing Gandhi's message. Sama refused to return to the village; he wanted to remain in the semi-developed Balikuda and experience freedom. Govinda Das asked Sama to go to the bazaar and listen to the education minister Dolamani and social welfare minister Dakhinray, who were there to talk about democracy, freedom and the ideal state to the people who still didn't grasp the new concepts. There was free food at the Patitapabana Temple, to be followed by the play 'Ravana's Kingdom' in the open ground after their speech.

Sama shuffled onto the meeting ground. He found that Dolamani wasn't as haughty and uncouth as he used to be in the days of zamindari. He was patient and calm. Dakhinray, as the minister for social welfare, had a soft, simple and approachable disposition too. Both answered the audience pretty convincingly. Sama sat in the back row and listened attentively.

The people were ready to hear from the two ministers. And thus began the questioning session.

Question: 'What's the difference between freedom and bondage? We village folks don't understand the difference between the two. Can the ministers please help us understand?'

Answer: 'The fundamental difference is that, Independence Day is the only day when the national flag will fly in public places. Schools, colleges and offices will remain closed. The children will hear Gandhi's name only on that particular day. This wasn't possible when the country was under foreign rule. Further, Independence Day will be a day of revelry—many goats will be butchered for mutton for feasts; people will eat heartily and drink to the brim to enjoy the gift of freedom. The police will be free that day to prevent disruption of law and order.'

The masses nodded their head and approved Dolamani's answers collectively. Dakhinray answered the next question.

Question: 'What's the true meaning of freedom?'

Answer: 'Do whatever you want. Nobody has the right to control the actions, speech and will of another. In a home, the father is free, and so is the son! Thieves, criminals, goons and police—all free on the road. Nobody has control over them. The government does whatever it wants to do; the public does whatever it wants to do; and the law, too, does whatever it wants to do. Such freedom was unimaginable during the Raj.'

The public cheered. The audience liked the minister's answer to the question on the meaning of freedom. They felt the line between freedom and lawlessness was blurred and everybody did things as they pleased when the country became free. Fear of authority during the Raj that restrained people was gone from every walk of life. Dolamani answered the next question.

Question: 'What's the meaning of democracy?'

Answer: 'Democracy means winning the election. In a democracy, one can win elections by hook or crook—by any means—say by magic, sorcery or even spell, and grab the mandate to rule over people.'

The audience whispered among themselves that Dolamani held a special puja to appease the stars of his horoscope and sacrificed goats and hens to ward off evil spirits during the election. Dakhinray answered the next question.

Question: 'What's the meaning of the word "minister"?'

Answer: 'He who seduces the audience with his speech, with words sweeter than honey, and casts a mantrik spell over them, is a minister.'

The rhetorical skills of minister Dakhinray astounded the audience. Dolamani answered the next question.

Question: 'What's the meaning of *rajaniti*, or politics, in free India? Why do we call it the king's policy while we've removed the kings from power?'

Answer: 'Rajaniti means the rules framed by the kings. Do you think the kings have lost their power to rule? Only the names are replaced. Those who were your kings yesterday are your beloved ministers now. If we say the rule of the people instead of the king, our neighbours would think we're a weak nation.'

Someone shouted from the back with the following question, and it was Dakhinray's turn to answer.

Question: 'Is the ideal state that Gandhi imagined supposed to be run by the rules made by the kings? Do corruption, theft, looting, lawlessness and disrespecting women fit into the idea of Ramrajya?'

Answer: 'Both king and subjects live in Ramrajya. There're

palaces as well as huts. The demons perpetrated killing, stealing, lawlessness and violence. Ravana abducted queen Sita; old Dasaratha forcefully brought beautiful Kaikeyi to his palace and married her because he was rich and powerful and could afford a fourth wife. Rama abandoned his wife Sita, for no fault of her own. In order to declare themselves king of kings, the rulers held the *Ashwamedha yagna,* where a horse was offered to the sacrificial fire. In present-day politics, human beings are killed. In every age down the recorded time, opposites like rich-poor, king-subject, hedonists-pessimists, and sage-criminal have coexisted in every society. So, there's no real difference between Ramrajya and free India. In every age, God assumes avatars and descends from heaven to lessen the imbalance caused by the rise of evil, lawlessness and absence of virtue. No sage or avatar will manifest here if the earth becomes a place like heaven. Therefore, some elements of evil, pain and misery should be present here. That's for the wellbeing of the planet.'

People pondered appreciatively over Dakhinray's answer. They didn't want their country to become heaven where God wouldn't take an avatar! Dolamani got ready to answer the next question.

Question: 'We came to know from reliable sources that you wear khadi to show people, but your undergarments are all imported, and also that you use quite a lot of things at your place made in other countries. How will you justify such conduct?'

Answer: 'This is called foreign policy. In order to have a stronger foreign policy, we've to use things made in other countries. If we won't import anything from other countries, why'll they export things to us? Foreigners show great interest in our applique works from Pipili, Sambalpuri dress material and sarees, Pattachitra paintings, and statues carved out of stone.

If we don't buy clothes, alcohol or cigarettes from them, we'll look mean and fail in foreign trade. We've to change the trade policy of pre- and post-independent India drastically.'

The answer was quite convincing. They clapped and cheered at the witty reply. The next question was for Dakhinray.

Question: 'Mahatma Gandhi urged people to follow noble practices like self-sacrifice, righteousness, simple living, hard work and self-control during the freedom struggle. Some freedom fighters still follow those principles and live a simple, frugal life, but why do you live in such pomp and luxury?'

Answer: 'This is a very hard question. Hari Bishwal and Govinda Das might've poked you to ask the question. But it's not difficult to answer.'

Dakhinray cleared his throat and said, 'When you want to gain something, you need to think of effective methods to reach your goal, or let's say that someone has forcefully occupied your property or has borrowed money but refuses to leave your home or doesn't pay it back. As the plaintiff, you must convince him that you're in very bad shape; you gather witnesses to strengthen your point. We know that no one is ever moved without tales of pain and misery. The struggle for freedom was a similar situation. Gandhi asked people to adapt to a life of hardship and sacrifice. But now we've got our freedom. So what's the point in leading a life of austerity? Human life's not for pain or misery; we're born to enjoy a happy life. We don't see any hardship ahead of us, there's no point in making our lives miserable.'

The answer that there were no hardships ahead didn't convince some. The next question was a curious one. Dolamani answered it.

Question: 'Are there really no difficulties ahead?'

Answer: 'There's no hardship ahead. We don't have to fight for freedom; we'd rather give freedom. Giving isn't a difficult thing. We might surrender our freedom to someone in the future, but we won't struggle to retain it. So, there's no hard work for us henceforth.'

People were stunned for a while. The idea that 'we don't have to fight for freedom and rather surrender our freedom' didn't get inside their heads. While they pondered over the words, a handful of the minister's chamchas and officials cried out 'true! true!' in unison, and clapped vigorously in support of the statement. The meeting wrapped up peacefully. But soon chaos erupted; the village folks ran around, pushed one another, and thronged into unruly clutches to glimpse the sahibs and memsahibs present there. Very few of the people of that area ever had a chance to meet the sahibs and memsahibs in person when the country was under British rule. So, once it was known that some sahibs and memsahibs had accompanied the ministers from Bhubaneswar, the capital, each of the curious rustic folk pushed the other to have the first glimpse.

The villagers carried very weird ideas in their heads regarding sahibs and their wives. They believed the beard and mustache of the sahibs were made from gold. The memsahibs—their female counterparts—were fairies from heaven with two golden wings instead of arms; their limbs were made from a gold-like metal, and therefore, they didn't feel cold and didn't need to wear sari; they roamed without cover. They also thought the sahibs had no language, and they chirped like birds, and the natives gestured like deaf and dumb when they talked to them. They've also heard that the sahibs, though extremely civilized, didn't know the polite gesture of folding their hands and greeting someone;

they grabbed and shook violently the hands of someone they met and greeted.

While all those thoughts played in their minds, someone asked, 'Why're the sahibs here again?'

'They're on duty here,' answered one ubiquitous Sabjanta.

'Whose duty?'

'Ministerial duty. They accompany visiting ministers and ensure nothing goes haywire during the visit. They're paid for that,' said the all-knowing man Sabjanta.

'Are they working under the ministers?'

'Yes! What else do you think? They're government servants!'

'Wow! All this happened due to Mahatma Gandhi! This is sweet revenge! He turned the tables against the sahibs and made them servants!' said someone.

'But I understood that the sahibs ran away in ships to save their lives? Where from did all these sahibs come then?' asked another.

'Those who didn't get a seat in the ship stayed back. Our government now uses them as its servants,' Sabjanta said.

'That's good! Our government is great!' declared the man.

'But what are these memsahibs doing here?' asked another, lowering his eyes.

Sabjanta smiled once more and said, 'The sahibs are here on official duty; the memsahibs are here for sightseeing. The government bears all the expenses. Call it killing two birds with one shot!'

The commotion over the presence of sahibs and memsahibs originated from the corner, where a bunch of the peons, drivers and attendants who accompanied the officials began talking about them. While the meeting was going on, the idle staff talked about their bosses' good and bad qualities. Passers-by heard a repetition of the terms—sahib and memsahib—and became curious. They asked, 'Who're you talking about?'

'We're talking about our bosses,' they replied.

'Are they here?'

'Who will attend to the ministers if they're not here? Is it for nothing that the government is rearing the expensive white elephants?'

Those two terms—sahib and white elephant—stirred up the frenzy to see them. The unruly crowd didn't care for the police cordon. The police used mild force to control the crowd and bring the raucous situation under control. Once restrained by the police, the crowd became orderly and got glimpses of the sahibs. But people were extremely disappointed seeing them, 'Hey! These sahibs are no different from us! They're dark, Odia-speaking, regular people with hands and feet like us. Why did you unnecessarily create the hype that there're sahibs and memsahibs, and made the situation tense for no reason?' they asked Sabjanta, irritated.

'These are brown sahibs, meaning, they're our desi sahibs. The white sahibs left the country in 1947,' answered Sabjanta.

'How could the desi people be sahibs?' questioned the angry crowd.

'Those who get a sahib's education, visit the sahib's land, get a sahib's job and show the attitudes of a sahib—those became desi sahibs...,' replied Sabjanta.

'Oh! You mean to say that they're someone like our Parija sahib?' queried someone.

Sabjanta had no patience to talk to the village folks. Someone in the crowd mocked, 'we call their wives, *meme* sahibs', with a tongue twist that sounded like the belting of the goat. He struggled to straighten his pronunciation; he punned mem with the 'meme' of a goat as he left the place.

In the meantime, someone came forward and handed over small pouches of prasad—offerings—from the temple to people. Sama was upset that there was no sumptuous feast or even the simple rice and dal for the hungry audience. The party workers who came with the minister from the town said, 'Since the dams Dalei and Barada collapsed in the flood in 1945, there was less food production in the area.'

Someone pacified Sama to take the offering from the temple gracefully and not complain. The crowd left the ground listening to the meaning of democracy and independence. They didn't care to complain over the little food they got to eat that night. Nowhere in the world would someone find such timid people who accepted the dictums of their scriptures; it might be so only in Ramrajya—the ideal state.

The same night, the aroma of mutton pulao from the zamindar's kitchen wafted in the air. The guests from outside were treated very well; otherwise they might have had a bad impression of the place. Dolamani was determined to keep up the good name of his area.

Sama didn't return to Parshuram's place at night. Manorama waited until quite late for him and finally shut the kitchen. Govinda Das joked that Sama got a headache after listening to Dolamani and Dakhinray, was full from the temple food, and slept on the village library verandah. Parshuram hardly paid attention to whatever Govinda Das said about Sama; he was restive. A deep sigh escaped his heart. In retrospect, it seemed good to him that Gandhi didn't survive long after independence to see the chaos the nation descended into quickly. Corruption was quite endemic in the Congress Party, and some malicious crooks like Dolamani and Dakhinray were the ministers. The hope was that the few upright leaders in the Congress Party might contest the election, and things would improve after five years.

Govinda Das hurriedly set out for Alabola to tell the villagers about Sama's patriotism and selfless service during the freedom struggle. He felt that the younger generation needed to remember Sama's inspirational story. Elusive Sama wasn't in Alabola or Balikuda. Someone told him that after the meeting at the ground, Sama set out on a mission with a bamboo pole in his hand and fizzled into the darkness like a shadow.

∽

Zamindar Graharaj was bequeathed the decadent life of the landed aristocracy, and enjoyed its trappings all his life. Decorative titles from the British—Raybahadur and Chaudhury—preceded his name. When zamindari was abolished, zamindars all over the country lost their wealth, power and influence. The carefree young men of the new era in flashy dresses stamped their shoes and walked with umbrellas unfurled over their heads. They refused to work for free and dared to say that they had no time. Fate ordained something different for Graharaj. He wasn't there to witness the miserable days. Opportunely, he left the world in the heydays of zamindari with his imperial titles and power intact. He didn't have to deal with any of the emotional agony and despondency that most zamindars went through. It can't be said how someone like Chaudhury, who built his estate by squelching the poor, passed away so peacefully.

Chakori knew quite well that all the zamindar's noble deeds at the fag end of his life didn't come from the penitence to lessen the sins of a lifetime, or the desire to go to heaven or leave a legacy. She knew his action sprang from a desperate bid to escape the relentlessly haunting guilt and remorse for the sins he committed in Diganta Keshari's eyes. Blinded by filial love, his heart pined only for his missing son, who never returned. Diganta Keshari was the mover for all the noble actions the zamindar did in his old age. As death shadowed him, the desire to unite with Diganta Keshari, his eldest son, became more powerful.

A week before his death, he went inside his son's room which hadn't been opened for years. Dust and soot hung everywhere and enclosed the floor, bed, table and books, like a musty blanket. Time had sealed eternally the scenes of life that once played out in that arena and refused to roll them back. Graharaj's hand plucked the sturdy walking stick tightly as he sauntered across the room. He touched the stack of books, notebooks and the study table. He held Diganta Keshari's dusty photograph, and his fingers moved over it in tender remembrance. The strokes of hand didn't seem to lessen his agony; rather, they made him more miserable. He was reminded of his irreconcilable differences with his son. He atoned for not being a good father to the son who lost his mother at a tender age. He regretted the formidable cruelty and debauchery the young man witnessed in silence. He hadn't been a great father to his sons that Devaki gave birth to; it didn't surprise him that they shaped up to be extremely arrogant and unruly young men.

The old zamindar was left to revisit the saga of his despicable cruelty and moral turpitude, and his arrogance was crushed miserably that day. He couldn't get over his nagging sense of inadequacy. He flared up in his son's room that day; spats of rebuke and swear words gushed out from his mouth. The agitated zamindar threw some moth-eaten books at Chakori, who stood by his side, and screamed, 'Didn't I give you the charge of this house for this? You made this room a graveyard! Get out, all useless people! Get lost!'

He was overtaken by anger, fell on the son's bed and didn't rise. Chakori rushed to hold him; otherwise he might've tripped and fallen on the floor. When he came to his senses, his body was limp; he couldn't get up. The doctor determined that he was paralyzed—his condition was critical and he might not survive long. The zamindar couldn't move, and most of his babble and moaning made no sense. Two days before his death, his condition seemed to improve. He was stable and looked around, and gestured for a pen and paper, and scribbled with his unstable hand that the Raybahadur title shouldn't be used before his name after death.

∞

Diganta Keshari stood at a crossroads; the freedom movement was over. The birth of the free nation rattled an ancient society, but the new unset political order hardly challenged the stratified system. The land he knew was no longer familiar. He felt lost in his own country and looked for direction from his guru Parshuram to remain focused on the right course of action. He travelled across numerous villages in the country. He tried to understand the best ways to free the masses from exploitation, injustice, ignorance, disease, hunger and suffering—a path that would transform them into 'free humans'. Zamindari was abolished, and kings were gone. But the superstructure of master-slave, rich-poor, capitalist-landless, haves-have-nots remained as they had been. He wondered if freedom changed anything for the poorest of the poor.

The panorama of a changing India had caught Diganta's discerning eyes. The presence of the neo-zamindars was ubiquitous—these didn't collect tax directly from the people, didn't take away their land, or owned filthy acres in their names. These were traders and industrialists who manipulated the common man in subtle ways. Prices of essential commodities—food, cloth and medicine—rose steadily. Adulterations in food remained as stark a reality as the surefire alloy of lesser metals in gold ornaments for durability and appeal. The euphoria over freedom from foreign rule was a magic veil over people's eyes, and the rapture didn't let them see reality. They got carried away like the folks in the fairground watching moving images in a bioscope, and didn't realize that whatever they saw on the screen was an illusion. Freedom was nominal, with the exception that while the exploitation earlier was by the British, in independent India, it was by the natives.

Diganta Keshari, the thinker, often looked for the causes of the mass inertia and timidity. Historically, in 1857, almost a hundred years before the independence of India, the country united against the British occupiers. Soldiers from Hindu and Muslim regiments in the British army revolted against the deliberate use of beef and pork tallow as greased covers for the cartridges of the Enfield rifle, to undermine the religious sentiments of both Hindus and Muslims. From the garrison in Meerut, the revolt spread to other parts of the country. Veer Surendra Sai from Odisha played a very important role in that first war of independence. In free India, he wondered if the people were too forgiving and not ready to oppose the morally outrageous, or were completely exhausted after pushing out a stubborn mountain by the name of foreign rule. Sometimes he thought that Gandhi's death marooned all so deep in grief that they couldn't recuperate from the tragedy. He remembered the quote, 'eternal vigilance is the price of liberty', but didn't know the right course of action to keep the people's minds eternally awake.

Parshuram, Diganta's guru, was calm. He never got carried away by emotions. He argued that the situation of a country couldn't change overnight, for human habits seldom change in a lifetime. According to him, the country languished long in the darkness of repressive foreign rule and lost its moorings. The condition gave rise to an inferiority complex in many, while a handful imbibed an aggressive and superior position. The few natives enjoying the patronage of the Britishers felt equally entitled to suppress and dominate the rest. After independence, corrosive power divided into multiple channels and dominated the common man. He predicted that India might take another hundred years to become a true democracy, and advised Diganta Keshari to remember Gandhi's path of non-violence and the never-ending struggle of mankind. He said that the human spirit becomes cold and disenchanted in inertia. Inaction in the mass after independence is like the sleep of the postpartum newborn, who is often poked to drink the mother's milk. He thanked Dolamani and Dakhinray for pinching the sleepy mass and keeping them awake.

'Once the temporary confusion is over, the nation's idleness and flagging energy will be gone. That's one of the fundamental rules of social change. If we don't feel the pangs of hunger, no one will feed us. Without awareness of our rights, social inequality is going nowhere.'

Diganta Keshari was worried that the common man wasn't ready to exercise his rights. The zamindari system was abolished, but still the common man showed fealty to the feudal lords and thought that the zamindar was his master. Parshuram called the attitude 'a thick layer of ignorance blindfolding his eyes', and believed that education was the panacea. Govinda Das sat listening to their conversation and warned that none of his friend's plans for a middle school in Nagpur or opening schools in other villages would materialize. Dolamani, the deputy education minister, stalled the ideas and was keen to introduce the maidan, the common ground, in every village. Balikuda High School might become a government high school, and Parshuram as headmaster would be removed and sent to a school in remote Kalahandi or Koraput in twenty-four hours. That didn't surprise Parshuram. He declared, 'I'm a teacher; send me anywhere, I'll build schools and educate children. A goldsmith knows how to mould gold. I'd rather be proud to go wherever they send me.'

Parshuram was aware of the situation. He planned to send Manorama with the kids to her paternal home in Patapur. She would be with her ageing mother and, as the only child, look after her ancestral property. Parshuram assured his friends not to worry too much about the kids' education at Balikuda High School. They were concerned that the school might not survive in his absence, and the teachers would leave asking for better pay. In the worst-case scenario, he was ready to resign and teach the students for free. He wanted to wait till the government decided over the matter. If it agreed to accept the school's assets and liabilities, he was okay with a government takeover.

Diganta Keshari interrupted, asking his guru what should be his next move as the county was free. Parshuram advised him to return to his village, get married, and settle down with the fortune he inherited. He asked Diganta to care of his father in his old age, work for the people of his locality, and never turn his face away from challenging issues.

Parshuram's advice was timely. It was hard for Diganta Keshari to ignore the role his father played in his life after his mother died, or the brutal fallen zamindar he had been all his life. The zamindar, too, had his own rule of love that had him keep his dark perversity and sexual misconduct from his son. The young man's coming of age was elegiac; he negotiated his tender, undefined feelings for dasi Chakori by putting his father's illicit relationship with her down to him being a slave of his desire. Disillusionment with life in the palace made him determined to leave home and end the dasi system for good. A voice within often asked him to refuse to inherit the paternal fortune tainted with the blood of the poor. He was caught in the dilemma within, but decided to return to his birthplace—not looking for reconciliation with his father but to complete the journey of penitence for the sins his clan had perpetrated for generations. He wanted to come out of the guise of a baba, confront his father, and explain the meaning of democracy and freedom to the haughty zamindar. Before saying goodbye to the guru, he asked about other members of the group, 'Where're the others? What're they up to these days—Rajan, Sushila, Sebati, Madan Jena, Sama Puhana, Kanak and Maithili? I couldn't keep track of them after independence.'

Parshuram had been the proverbial record-keeper Chitragupta—the assistant to Yama, the lord of death—in his group. He said that Madan Jena was martyred before independence; Rajan and Sushila were happily married and ran a cottage industry using local products like palm, date and coconut branches and leaves, and trained many young men to make household goods. Sama Puhana was missing. Maithili had been very active in Bhoodan, the land-donation movement led by Ramadevi and Gopabandhu Chaudhury. People largely believed that Kanak died in the arson that police staged to destroy Karma Mandira, the ashram that Digdarshi started in his village. Sebati was dead. Parshuram, in the end, choked, saying that his dearest friend Aziz died in communal violence.

Govinda Das tried to ease the situation and said, 'We three—Hari, Govinda, Parshuram—still keep rolling, hoping to enjoy the fruits of freedom someday.'

Hari Bishwal joined their conversation. He wore a handwoven dhoti that didn't go beyond his knees, and a khadi shirt that barely covered his torso. A cotton bag hung from his shoulder, and an old walking stick helped him to stand straight. His face beamed with round Gandhi glasses on his eyes, and the neatly parted, short, two-inch-long hair was combed carefully to one side. He looked like Gandhi's younger brother.

Parshuram asked, 'What's up? You're just back from the relief work for the flood-affected. Are you going somewhere?'

'I'll set out to work in the Sarvodaya and Bhoodan movement. Vinoba Bhave can't continue the Bhoodan movement alone. Vinoba is my next guru after Mahatma Gandhi. Gopabandhu Chaudhury is in charge of the Bhoodan movement in Odisha. He needs volunteers. Henceforth, I will beg from door to door.

My wife showed me a *kendera*, a small musical instrument, that I should play while asking for alms. But I don't know how to play it, so I didn't bring it with me. Well, friends, see you soon. I shouldn't get late for my bus,' he said and left. Digdarshi rose too.

'Sooner or later, Swaraj or self-rule that Gandhi dreamed would be ours,' said Parshuram.

Struggle rhymes with the strumming music of human life, and in Parshuram's case, the note rang relentlessly. It didn't end with the struggle for the country's freedom. Rather, one can say that after independence, when Dolamani became the deputy education minister, Parshuram's life became the battlefield of Kurukshetra. On this ground, the Kauravas and Pandavas fought the war in the Mahabharata. Truth prevailed in the Kurukshetra, but who fared well in this battle was yet to be seen. The matter was that educationist Parija sahib had granted funds for the new school building, but that wasn't enough for the project. Parshuram tried hard to get money from other sources to complete the project. He even took the bare minimum of his salary to run his household and gave away the rest towards the ongoing construction work in the school. Inspired by his action, other teachers and students donated to that cause happily. They volunteered to carry bricks to the site from the factory to see that work was completed in time. It went on slowly.

One fine morning, the government withheld the construction fund for Balikuda High School and ordered an immediate inquiry by the Public Accounts Committee, charging Parshuram with misappropriation of funds. Balikuda Bazar was rife with the news. Parshuram was like the seamless sky far above, clean and fearless; he was like the light, and no shadow touched him. The baseless scandal didn't worry him. But without the government grant, the construction work of the institution benefitting the people of Balikuda would stall indefinitely. He worried that the shutdown would deny the gift of education to many.

The president of the Accounts Committee appeared unannounced at nine o'clock one night, walked through the school area, surveyed the construction work, and found nothing wrong. Then came a chief engineer to investigate the quality of the construction work. He scratched the walls and collected soil, concrete, brick and sand for lab testing. He, too, didn't find any misuse of money, and instead got the final proof of Parshuram's clean character. Before he left, Parshuram sought the engineer's help adjusting the spare iron rods for some ten thousand rupees sitting unused in a storeroom.

The engineer understood 'adjustment' and 'regularization'. He mightn't be safe in his job without the knowledge of those two terms. He immediately understood that Parshuram was a wise fool who didn't know how the real world of civil engineering operated. The people the engineer encountered daily in his office mightn't be very educated but were far from innocent; meaning, they were all too conniving. He often wondered why 'manipulation' wasn't there in the engineering lexicon along with 'adjustment' and 'regularization'. Parshuram understood *patha*, education, but didn't understand *satha*, the ability to manipulate things in the real world. Parshuram was knowledgeable; rules of honesty and sincerity were sacrosanct to him, but he never took care to imbibe the attribute of satha. He asked for the chief engineer's approval to use the spare iron rods for the construction work in the school. The chief engineer was in a fix. He had thought that Parshuram asked him to do the 'adjustment' and 'regularization' of the excess stock and wanted to pocket the ten thousand rupees. But he lacked the basic skills of manipulation. The engineer feared that the headmaster had never handled money, or was extremely rich and needed no extra money to run his household.

He asked, 'Aren't you married? Don't you have kids?'

'I'm married and have two sons and five daughters.' Parshuram felt slighted answering.

'Strange!'

'What's the big deal? I don't think fathering is the monopoly of the rich and powerful zamindars and officials. Can't a humble teacher be the father of many kids?' asked Parshuram.

The engineer was in awe. His mechanical mind couldn't process the fact that a humble teacher with a salary of just thirty rupees a month wasn't tempted to pocket the ten thousand rupees from disposing of the unaccounted-for iron rods, and instead drew the attention of investigative authorities. He didn't know how to implicate that man in embezzlement charges and satisfy the minister. He realized that the headmaster might be an impractical fool but can't, under any circumstances, be named corrupt.

Chapter XVI

Bhoodan—the land-gifting movement, an appeal to the rich landowning class to part with their excess parcels for distribution among the landless and dispossessed—started immediately after the country gained independence. Under the leadership of Vinoba Bhave, some freedom fighters who spearheaded the non-violent battle and ousted the British entreated the landowners to volunteer for the noble cause. The Sarvodaya Movement—the call to help everybody rise—also gained momentum. Sloppy and gentle Maithili, who worked for quite some time with Diganta Keshari during the freedom movement, was a leading activist in that movement. She pursued her goal with dedication, grace and humility. Diganta Keshari met her a few years after independence at the Bhoodan office and found that she no more was the shy, faint-hearted young girl of yesteryears; work had helped her flourish as a confident, bright young woman. They talked briefly on the verandah of the office and related the tragic deaths of their friends Bhuja Rout and Kanak. Strangely, neither was curious to know how the other person was doing. He was Maithili's confidante in earlier days; he remembered her promise to share her feelings at the right moment but felt that the time hadn't arrived yet.

After the death of Zamindar Graharaj Chaudhury, Chakori discovered a completely unknown side of Devaki's personality. She knew that people usually were jealous of another person's beauty, fortune and happiness. She didn't know that a total destitute's misery, misfortune and loneliness could make someone like the rich zamindar's wife livid and jealous. After Graharaj's death, Chakori gave off all her adornments—she removed the red dot from the forehead and discarded the colourful saris, bangles, silver bracelets, and the small *haradafalia*[*] necklace and *Mankedi* earrings. Devaki saw the bereaved Chakori in the customary white sari of a widow and was blighted with anger and jealousy. The dasi's very look seemed to belittle her sorrow of losing the zamindar, and slighted her select status as the sole widow of the zamindar.

Devaki's screaming terrified her. 'What do you think of yourself? Are you married to him? Are you his second wife? You're his dasi—you never married him. You spent time with him and kept him happy. You slept with him, I know! You're just one among his hundreds of dasis and mistresses. Who gave you that right to be his widow? How dare you think of yourself so fortunate?'

Until that moment, she didn't know that the right to be an unfortunate widow couldn't be that of a dasi. It became clear to her that she was neither a mistress nor a wife, so she couldn't be a widow, and to be someone's widow was a matter of huge luck. She was pushed to unwind the grieving process and returned to wearing colourful saris, jewellery and the red dot of vermilion on her forehead. Earlier, she thought that Devaki was jealous of her donning of these adornments, but now she realized that it had been derision of her aping the rites of the

---

[*]It's an old-design chain popular among women in rural Odisha. Round gold flakes resembling/shaped like half of a *toor* (*harada* in Odia) grain are strung in a gold chain.

sacrosanct institution of marriage. Devaki mocked that a dasi was disposable, like cheap jewellery and sari. Her adornments were fake—never real gold but made from either brass or some cheap alloy; the dasi wasn't the real wife but a kept woman. She shared the bed but didn't have the right to be a mother. She was fed but denied sharing of the wealth. And ultimately, the dasi didn't even have the right to be the zamindar's widow.

'How cheap is the life of a dasi—how fake it has been! Her happiness is an illusion. Her sorrows can't be genuine. Her sari, *sindur*, love and loyalty to that man are nothing but lies,' Chakori dwelled over the predicament.

She had thought of the zamindar as the only man in her life. She was sad that her entire life was a chase after an illusory relationship that didn't even exist per se. It was no secret to her that Devaki had no love for her deceased husband, and her heart was filled with anger, indignation, jealousy and callousness towards him. But she sat silently in a corner, shed tears for hours, and didn't care to eat much; she became frail and looked older in no time. The unseen devotion for her husband seemed like the delicate binding thread that stayed invisible all those years. She knocked down Chakori and won the race vying for superiority in love for the zamindar. A dasi was bereft of feelings of pride, arrogance, happiness or sorrow. Chakori didn't know if she was subhuman or above the humans, a creepy-crawling insect or a piece of lifeless wood.

In old age, Devaki's abuses became more violent. She randomly threw at Chakori the mortar and pestle used to crush and soften the paan she chewed. At times, the weapons of assault might be her heavy walking stick or the shoes. Devaki flung things and cried deliriously that she took no proper care of her husband, didn't give him medicine in time, and didn't handle him with love even in the last days of his life. She screamed, 'You're my eternal enemy! My nemesis!'

She sometimes offered leftovers from her plate or pushed some coins into her hands in pity. Devaki hurled at her abuses and curses that bruised her body and mind. Chakori was just an object for Devaki to release her pain upon and get over the stubborn sense of loss, grief and hurt sitting inside. None of her children or grandchildren found the death of the zamindar a relatable memory. None came forward to abate her sorrow, and rather said, 'He lived up to a ripe age and was quite mobile till death. No one is immortal. It's good that he aged well and passed away without major issues.'

Chakori stood by her compassionately. Devaki refused to admit that her husband was old and sick. She recalled him having a few strands of grey hair with all his teeth intact, and standing straight. She wasn't happy about Chakori calling him 'manly'. The young brides of her grandsons made fun of the fight between the two women over the late zamindar's manliness.

Devaki, in a few months, became very sick and passed away. She wasn't bedridden or suffered terribly for a long time. Her death wasn't mourned much; it passed quickly like a floating cloud and things became normal in the palace, except for poor Chakori. She became very lonely and worried that no one was there to look after her after the zamindar's wife was gone. She came to the palace as Devaki's handmaid. Devaki owned her, and though she abused her, those hands that hit her also extended to save her. As Devaki's body was taken for cremation early in the evening, she sat motionless in a corner, dazed; no tears came to her eyes. She revisited the day she came to the palace holding the poles of the palanquin with Devaki, the bride; the zamindar's clandestine relationship with her from the very first day; and many more experiences from the bygone days. Like drops of ink blotting over a page, two stars, one big and a smaller one beside it, emerged slowly and twinkled in the evening sky. They reminded her of the zamindar and Devaki.

At times, life seems like an epic that's not yet been written, and you are the one to fill each empty page with whatever you want to write. The next moment, life seems like a book that has already been written, and one has to turn the pages to match the lived experiences. And more so, one isn't free to turn the pages of the book at their own will; the timetable to turn those pages is also predetermined!

∞

Parshuram vowed to set up the ideal progressive school with innovative educational goals and train young minds to be responsible citizens guarding the country's freedom. Ironically, he couldn't raise his voice against injustice in free India, which he did during British rule. In free India, he wasn't alone; whoever supported his move was in trouble. He had to make certain painful compromises to save the rest from trouble.

The authorities couldn't implicate Parshuram in embezzlement of the school's funds. But the file requesting additional funds didn't move. Teachers weren't paid for months, and the construction stopped halfway without grants. The school couldn't function normally. Many teachers joined other schools and some looked for other jobs to survive. Few loyal employees stood with him during those trying moments. Some teachers complained that the headmaster didn't care for his salary because his wife Manorama inherited a lot as the only daughter of the Patapur zamindar, and had a free supply of essential items like rice, dal, ghee and jaggery. The teachers, on the other hand, needed a salary for sustenance. Parshuram heard the discontentment, appeared with a bundle of cash, and handed it to the whining teachers. Office assistant Yudhishthira informed the staff that the headmaster pledged his wife's gold ornament and borrowed money from the cobbler next door. He decided to hand over the school to the government and hoped that when the ministry changed, the person in charge would help the school without bias. The teachers hoped that the government takeover would offer them a regular salary and a pension after retirement.

However, the takeover was denied because education was a non-productive department giving no return to the government on its investment. Investments in agriculture, forest and mining offered tangible returns. Therefore, spending money on a remote rural school in Balikuda was a loss in a crunch situation. Parshuram deplored the fact that while stone, wood, coal, trees and animals were national treasures, and the government was willing to invest in them, it didn't care to invest in education—the department responsible for producing good citizens. He understood that as per the view of the wise and educated people in charge of planning the future of the newly freed nation, 'young humans' weren't national treasures. He also deplored people's attitude to attach some form of divinity to stone and wood and willingness to spend an egregious amount of wealth to build temples and worship the gods.

Balikuda school trained some of the most brilliant minds, like scientist Pranakrushna Parija. The political leaders from

Balikuda were powerful but corrupt. Parshuram was vocal about their wrongdoings; therefore, those people joined hands to oppose the grants to the school. Dolamani in particular wanted to stall the school's takeover process till the retirement of Parshuram. He offered two choices to Hari Bishwal, who went to negotiate for the grants: either Hari join his Sheep Party or stop Parshuram from meddling in the activities of leaders like Dolamani.

Soon Parshuram went through a litmus test. Dolamani lodged a complaint against him for stealing from the local hospital. The police arrived with a search warrant and found the missing hospital manual on Parshuram's table. He rose and offered his hands for the police to arrest him. The angry students stood at the gate with stones and rubbles in their hands to attack the police if they arrested their headmaster. Parshuram strictly warned them to abstain from violence and walked behind the police with a triumphant smile.

The row over the manual started accidentally. Parshuram, Hari Bishwal and Govinda Das, the members of the administrative committee of the local hospital, didn't find Dr Bishwal at work. The patients, including sick children, old men, women and expectant mothers needing immediate care, waited for hours. It was chaotic while the doctor was busy attending to the areas of the erstwhile zamindar. Disappointed, the trio considered action against the negligent doctor. Parshuram borrowed the administrative manual governing the doctor's conduct from the pharmacist, and the three men sat over the log bridge on the canal reading the rules. In the meantime, the doctor, who rushed to work, saw them and asked his pharmacist to complain to the police that Parshuram broke the lock of the hospital almirah with a paperweight from the office, and stole the manual. The police arrived and laughed at the silly allegation, saying only a magician could break open a sturdy brass lock with a fancy glass paperweight. Ashamed of his action, the pharmacist tended his resignation and left the village for good. Dr Bishwal went on a long leave, got a posting in another hospital, and never returned to Balikuda. He was extremely sorry for his action and wrote a letter to Parshuram explaining the difficulties he faced in attending to his patients in the hospital while acting as Dolamani's physician. Parshuram, in his reply, advised him never to cede his self-esteem and values under pressure from the powerful.

Change didn't seem to match people's expectations after independence. Leaders delivered heartwarming messages to keep people eternally hopeful. The grandiose promises created massive euphoria like a fairytale sweeping children's minds. Festive meetings, speeches, songs, music, warm greetings, flowers and garlands were the Independence Day celebration staples. The hungry, the half-clad beggars, illiterate labourers, the homeless who lived on the pavement, the cowherd tending livestock, the tramps who scavenged for food from the trash—an entire lot of the nameless lousy pests were completely dazed by the splendour of the celebration. They thought that freedom was extremely attractive and priceless, but it wasn't within their reach like things precious and beautiful. Freedom for them was a wounded dream—an unreachable dazzling chimera. But they still waited desperately to realize that ethereal reality. Perhaps freedom was locked inside the iron chest of the rich; it was held hostage in the pen of the powerful and their threatening inquisitions. Freedom was stuck in the costly suits and drinks, epitomizing the power and callousness of the movers and shakers. Freedom meant the optimum gratification—a decadent immersion in life's trappings. A few lived life the way they wanted to; it was the exclusive gift of the privileged because fortune favoured those select few only. Those who were unfortunate had neither freedom nor rights.

The common man didn't understand that his rights were sacrosanct in a free country; instead, he blamed fate and God, and tolerated injustice and exploitation. He had no say over the initiatives the leaders proposed to improve his lot. Always outside the barricade, he walked the silent pageant of the hopeless. Poverty crushed him hard, and he often forgot his child's birth date and didn't remember the number of independence days the country had observed. The politician in crisp white khadi kept count of the years, rose to the dais as naturally as actors to the stage, and addressed the people routinely, inspiring optimism year after year.

Over the years, the tiny log bridge connecting the road beyond the inspection bungalow with Balikuda market became old. Many classrooms in the high school, made from clay and sand, crumbled as the wind blew away the thatched rooftop. Without government grant, concrete walls couldn't rise over the foundation for new classrooms. But still, a large number of students graduated from the school and joined college in the town. Parshuram grew old and was not as sprightly as in the earlier days. An incorrigible optimist, he opened a wonderful science lab and spent most of his time exploring new ideas and experiments there. He returned home in the evening and tutored a group of poor students for free till late at night. Manorama didn't like such hard work, but she smiled and stood by him in every difficult situation. He was emotionally invested in his school, taught every subject, and never let classes go unsupervised. There's a saying in Odia that a piece of jute stick might break but it never bends, and he was that unbending frail man. He never gave up his values and didn't submit to the will of the political machine.

At long last, days before Parshuram's retirement, the government took over Balikuda High School. He held his son's marriage in his home and on campus some days later. One night while he was asleep, miscreants torched down and reduced the office building and laboratory that he dedicated his entire life to build, to a handful of ashes. His enemies started the smear campaign to taint his clean image, saying that Parshuram started the fire to burn down the record of the funds he swindled before his retirement. But as luck would have it, he had saved every record, bank book, receipt and voucher in his house. Once more, the conspirators failed, but he was hurt that the destruction did greater harm to the people of Balikuda than him.

Parshuram's character was as dazzlingly clean as gold; gold doesn't rust like iron. But he remained sad and hurt till the end. The government overtook the school one year after his retirement, so he wasn't eligible for a pension. He was denied his savings in the provident fund, and his younger brother refused to share the paternal home and land in his native village. He didn't care for the wealth his wife inherited. Finally, after retirement, he relocated to Cuttack with his family and all his belongings, and lived with his eldest son. Govinda Das, old and sick, lived with a Bengali family in Banka Bazar, Cuttack. Parshuram walked from Petnisai to Banka Bazar to meet him every day. He sat by his bed till noon, revisiting countless episodes of their lives.

Parshuram said that poverty was a sickness of the mind and believed one could have a good life with some simple meals and a few simple clothes. A humble teacher, he derived great pleasure in teaching and never cared to know the caste, class, colour or creed of the students he taught in Cuttack.

Jayaram Mahapatra, known as Tungamamu, came to Cuttack to collect his pension as freedom fighter. He was sorry for the financial hardship Parshuram—the brightest boy in his class, who left a well-paying corporate job and worked as a dedicated headmaster—faced. He never understood why Parshuram didn't enlist his name as a freedom fighter, though he galvanized the freedom movement. Tungamamu coaxed him to apply for a pension for freedom fighters who didn't go to jail but worked outside.

Parshuram sighed that his children blamed him for lacking foresight and said that there was a constant push and pull between life and death, and that a mysterious urge propelled man to chase life. Govinda Das said that generations coming after them found fault with the actions of Rama, Krishna, Jesus, Nanak, Buddha and Muhammad. Gandhi would be criticized in free India. Great men like Gandhi are born in countries languishing in servitude; they fight for the people, win the struggle against mighty opponents, and are worshipped universally as saviours. But these great men cannot thrive in a free country; they would be pulled down, smeared, crushed, blamed, disapproved and assassinated. For this reason, some said that Gandhi should have had the foresight that death hung over his head, asked for heavy security, or used a bulletproof jacket.

Parshuram's friend Hari Bishwal was fit and running. He spun thread over a charkha that looked even older than him.

His thick white hair ruffled in the wind, and his wobbly face drooped over his chest. No one in the village wore khadi, but he hadn't given up spinning, and taught the art to some poor kids at home. He also ran classes for women and older adults in the same school. His children and grandchildren wore khadi and also taught there. Hari loved gardening, sang the Ramdhun prayer, and played with kids. He made time to discuss religion, culture and current affairs with adults. His clean, beautiful home looked like the patch of clean water in a dirty pond with the tangle of weeds removed.

∞

Diganta Keshari, the wearied traveller with a long white beard and a calm face, stopped at Hari Bishwal's place after his long journey through villages big and small. Bishwal recognized him immediately and greeted him graciously.

Digdarshi offered his regards with folded hands and enquired about his guru Parshuram, Govind Das and Sama Puhana. He said that Parshuram and Govinda were like the pair of singers in the folk show *Pala*. Parshuram, the lead, and Govinda, the one to follow his tune, were no more. Manorama died less than six months after her husband's death eight years ago. Diganta Keshari folded his hands in memory of his guru Parshuram, his wife Manorama, and Govinda Das.

Biswal said that Sama was very active in Zamindar Dakhinray's area, urging him to donate his excess land to the landless. He sat in front of his palace on an indefinite fast and vowed to die there. People claimed that they found a seriously bruised, bloodied body lying outside the zamindar's boundary for four to five days, and then he rose and walked away. Nobody was sure if he was Sama Puhana. His parents died shortly after that, but till her death, Sama's mother vowed in the names of all the gods and goddesses of the village—Kausuni, Gopaljiu, Kunjabihari—claiming that her son was alive, and that he would return to his village one day and recognize the ruins of his home.

'Time has slowly washed away Sama's name from the memory of the younger generation. But the elderly in the village say that Sama isn't dead because his last rites were never performed; the lore of Sama can't vanish into thin air,' reiterated Hari Biswal.

The death of some dear people like Parshuram and Govinda reminded Diganta Keshari about the fleeting nature of life; he felt the sudden urge to go to his village. Bishwal didn't let him go that night. The two friends spent quite some time remembering people and events they met during the freedom struggle. Diganta Keshari recalled Maithili—the frail, shy child widow who, in Ramadevi's care, rose as a devoted worker. Images of his first meeting and their growing familiarity flashed momentarily before his eyes. He said that his recent meeting with her at the Sarva Seva Sangha in Banaras was fortuitous; she was the assistant director there. Age had washed away much of the charm from her looks; her hair had thinned down and there were gaps between her once-beautiful teeth. She leaned against her walking stick and ambled around. She also couldn't recognize him. Long back, during the Quit India Movement, the ruthless police rode over the protesters, and the stampede permanently impaired her spine. Diganta Keshari and Maithili had no regrets or grudges; service to humanity was their goal, and no worldly shackles bound the two enlightened souls. He was happy to notice that Maithili worked tirelessly for the sick, hungry and abandoned;

people called her mother Maithili. She also praised the changes in Diganta Keshari, the son of a rich zamindar who masqueraded as a mendicant and became the real sadhu Digbaba.

Digdarshi thought they had evolved during the journey, and change came gradually. They understood the pitfalls of the physical phase, and learned the need to get rid of the instincts that pulled them down and transcend the narrow boundary of the self in the third and final phase. Emotions didn't sweep him, and he no longer felt pleasure or pain like an ordinary man. Maithili, he reflected, had transcended the narrowness of 'I' to become the larger 'we'. He sensed that the meeting in Banaras was their last meeting, but he didn't regret leaving a dear friend behind.

∞

Diganta Keshari started for his village at daybreak. He went through the Ichhapur market to Parahata village, visited the Bhagabati Devi Temple, and then went to Nagapur. He made a detour to Balikuda High School, which his guru Parshuram had built. He collected some flowers from the neighbour's garden to offer at the feet of guru Parshuram's statue. It was still a little dark. A veil of mist hung over the campus and fading shadows of trees danced in the thin light. He was confused by the image he saw. It seemed like somebody else; he thought the artist wasn't good enough to carve the real Parshuram. He read the name and date of birth written on the marble at the base. Digbaba was stunned that it wasn't Parshuram but Dolamani Srichandan. He was anguished that a petty politician stood in the place of his revered guru. Disoriented, he felt it was a complete misrepresentation of the history of Balikuda. He kept the flowers aside and came out with a heavy heart, thinking that the death of a person didn't mean the death of the ideals and values he stood for. He believed that the foundation of the school his guru laid was very strong and that even though there were cracks in the walls, it would stand the test of time.

Glimpses of change in his village following independence caught Diganta Keshari's eyes. He realized that the sky, sun and moon remained the same, but temporal things—the roads, lanes and homes—seemed to have changed. Trees and creepers were overgrown. The narrow village road was wider, soiled with muggy rainwater and dirt; it resembled the wide, uneven parting of an elderly woman speckled with vermilion over a thinning hair cover. A new road linked the village to the heart of the bazaar; the lanes inside were pebbled. A few concrete homes replaced mud houses, and the number of homes with cement front verandahs, porches and painted walls had increased. But tiny ramshackle homes seemed crumbly, and morose vacant lots rose in places where homes stood earlier. A few passenger buses waited at the village bus stand. The market, too, had gotten a facelift. Shops sold fancy items in the village store at a higher price. A cinema hall, a tailor shop that made fashionable modern dresses for young women, and a store selling lipstick, bangles and artificial jewellery, had also come up. A college stood at the corner of the road leading to the raucous bazaar. The gramophones blared out popular movie songs as college-going young men and women moved around. A desi liquor store behind the college seemed to negate Gandhi's ideal of prohibition completely. Nothing was orderly; development in the village was patchy. Its ugliness showed like the holes in a vest beneath the veneer of a fine terylene shirt someone wore.

Three new buildings—a school, a hospital and a library named after Diganta Keshari, in the heart of the village—caught his eyes instantly. He was confused; his name was anathema to his father Zamindar Graharaj. He quickly assumed that the zamindar's charitable endeavours aimed to gain political mileage, win the election, and become a minister like Dolamani. But he later understood that Graharaj Chaudhury donated a larger portion of his property towards building institutions serving the common man before his death. He also instructed those to be named after his missing son Diganta Keshari.

∞

Villagers thronged the Masjid's verandah and talked to Digbaba in detail. They said that the zamindar looked for his missing son on his deathbed. Some said he changed, became a very kind man and donated much of his fortune to build the school, the hospital and a library to benefit the poor. They maintained that the old man was selfless and didn't name anything after himself; he was a patriot but didn't want to publicize himself, and named the institutions after his missing son.

Digbaba controlled his emotions. All the dead are good! Some very ordinary qualities of a person are glorified after death. His father's legacy stirred him momentarily, but he was incisive and quickly realized that the givings stood for penitence, not humanism. Base and fallen, the zamindar couldn't exculpate himself from the goading sense of guilt and remorse for causing his son to leave home. He repented the debauchery and sin the young man saw in an unguarded moment. Digbaba was sorry that, ironically, the innocent subjects thought of his father as a great soul. Zamindar Graharaj was actually a self-seeking manipulator filled with every imaginable vice and moral shortcoming. Mean and selfish, he was mired in greed and lust, and the so-called good things he did were to appease himself and get fame after death. A tiny wave of compassion ran through his mind as he pitied the insufferable zamindar who was out and out a miserable person.

Digbaba learned about his stepmother Devaki's death, her three sons living in the city, and her second son who had become a powerful political leader. The palace, once his home and a busy place, was deserted and had lost its glory after the abolition of zamindari. He was curious to know if Chakori was free. He learned that the zamindar provided her with some subsistence before his death and allowed her to stay in one of the rooms meant for the dasis. She was worn out; her body curved like the inverted English alphabet L. Her small land and money might've helped the poor woman live a hassle-free life, but getting out of the palace never struck her. She was like the old burnt brick that refused to crumble despite the peeling off of the coats of concrete and the colour covering it. A few days after Digbaba reached the village, her condition deteriorated. She breathed like a shrunken old bitch in one corner of the palace, her soul obstinately stuck to a useless haggard body. Ironically, when she longed hard to live, chilling eyes of death stared at her, and when she desperately prayed for death, life grudgingly clung to her. She had heard that Digbaba had returned to the village, but she was immobile, and her limbs became limp. She couldn't go to meet him. Before she breathed her last, Chakori declared that whatever little she had in her name belonged to the young zamindar, and if he didn't return, that should be used to benefit the poor.

Digbaba stood calmly on the road, not far from the cremation ground, watching fire slowly consume Chakori's mortal body. He was relieved that death finally led her to freedom.

'If suffering cleanses the human soul, she must attain nirvana. She was the last dasi. Let there be no Chakori anymore in the world. The land's free. There are no kings, zamindars, dasis and slaves now. Everyone here will be born free and live a free life. No one will bear the seals of caste, creed, class or colour. The path of awakening welcomes mankind and reassures love and acceptance everywhere he goes, as if the whole world is his place,' Digbaba prayed, closing his eyes.

As he rose from his reverie, Digbaba saw four men carrying a palanquin in a sombre mood; he wondered if a dead body was inside. Old Madana Behera, who walked beside the carriage, rushed to him. He fell at his feet and wailed painfully. Distraught, Madan said he was nervous and didn't know what to do with his unwed pregnant granddaughter sitting inside. The old man had sent the young girl with the local representative, the former zamindar as old as her father, to the town, after he assured her of a job. He kept her in the town, saying that there were many rounds of written tests and interviews for a job. She became sick and returned, but the local doctor determined that she wasn't sick, and that her pregnancy was at an advanced stage and couldn't be terminated. The doctor suggested that Madana take the girl to the town, let her deliver the baby at some hospital, and give away the newborn for adoption at an orphanage, or leave the baby unclaimed on the roadside.

Digbaba didn't interrupt the old man and listened patiently. Madan banged his chest and sobbed, saying that he might poison himself and the granddaughter, and die to save the family from disgrace. Digbaba walked to the palanquin and opened the door. A young, innocent, pale-yellow face, tender like a rustic flower that hadn't been stung by vices, looked at him. The radiant innocence of the girl stunned him.

'What's your name?' he asked.

'Ketaki,' she said.

Confounded, the baba erupted, 'Chakori's dead. She attained nirvana. How can there be another Chakori?'

'I'm Ketaki,' repeated the girl.

'I'm Chakori! Chakori! Chakori!' Digbaba heard her repeating.

Digbaba was old. He couldn't hear or see well. Ketaki looked exactly like the comely Chakori he met in the distant past. He felt that Ketaki was another avatar of Chakori, and like the kings and zamindars who reappeared as ministers and public servants, the dasi, too, had assumed a different form.

Years back, Diganta Keshari, the renegade, refused to inherit the sinful legacy of the zamindari system, and left home, avowedly following the radical call to end the dasi tradition and redeem Chakori from the shackles of the mordant practice for good. After long years, he returned to his village; the country was free, but the mission wasn't accomplished. There was no room for complacency; he felt the struggle needed to be kept alive. Digbaba stretched his mellowed hand for the girl to grab and get down.

'Let's go,' he said stolidly.

'I'm as good as dead. What's the meaning of such a life?' asked Ketaki.

Digbaba pronounced that a person might die, not a nation. He asked her not to confuse ignorance with death, and to avoid inaction. He urged the girl to accompany him to awaken the nation from slumber and assert that human life was invaluable. Ketaki wanted to know the village's name and how far they would walk to reach there. Digbaba assured that life would be blissful in that village; no one carried hatred or distrust for another person there.

'It's neither far nor near. We will walk there without misgivings, with complete awareness and our awakened minds,' he promised as he looked at the dying flames at Chakori's pyre. He realized that while freedom, like the sun, rose on the nation's sky after the long night of servitude, its rays were still not powerful enough to wash away the lingering darkness from the nooks and crannies.

'Once the sun rises above the sky, its brightness will wash away the darkness. We can't ignore the sunrise though there are patches of darkness here and there,' he reflected. The bright light of sunrise reflected like the indivisible union of the blessed lines of Swastika on the grey mirror of Digbaba's eyes.

'I don't care if we've to walk miles to reach the far-off promised village. I'll follow you...Take me away from here,' Ketaki said, offering her hand to him.

The magical touch of the young hand shook away the momentary dejection in Digbaba's ageing spirit. Like the vibration coming from the incantation of the sacred Om, the morning stirred the earth with primordial energy, and made the vision of the lighted path—the road to freedom—clear before his eyes. He had traversed the path to metanoia, and illusion or fear no more clouded his mind. The choice before him was clear. He vowed that the country should never revert to the darkness of ignorance and servitude. He wasn't disillusioned with the imperviousness of the maladies in the free land and decided that resistance to the negative forces must be ceaseless. The steps of the pathfinder rose in readiness for the mission ahead. The incorrigible optimist in him said to Ketaki, 'Look up to the sky, young girl! The nascent sunlight dawns over us like the blessings from the Swastika. It aims to give us the power to be humans who hold their heads high—enlightened, creative and inspirational. It's urging us to work for peace, prosperity and unity! This chosen moment eliminates the gap between the mundane and the eternal.'

Lines from the Bhagavad Gita came to his mind spontaneously—when a man harbours no ill feelings for anyone and wishes the best for all around him indiscriminately, his presence spills happiness in every direction.